NEMESIS

Also by Gregg Hurwitz

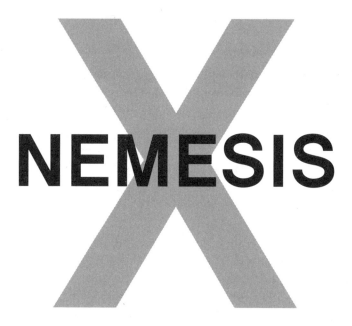

NEMESIS

Gregg Hurwitz

MINOTAUR
BOOKS
NEW YORK

First published in the United States by Minotaur Books, an imprint of St. Martin's Publishing Group

NEMESIS. Copyright © 2025 by Gregg Hurwitz. All rights reserved. Printed in the United States of America. For information, address St. Martin's Publishing Group, 120 Broadway, New York, NY 10271.

www.minotaurbooks.com

Library of Congress Cataloging-in-Publication Data

Names: Hurwitz, Gregg, author.
Title: Nemesis / Gregg Hurwitz.
Description: First edition. | New York : Minotaur Books, 2025. |
    Series: Orphan X ; 10
Identifiers: LCCN 2024025617 | ISBN 9781250871749
    (hardcover) | ISBN 9781250389961 (international, sold outside
    the U.S., subject to rights availability) | ISBN 9781250871756
    (ebook)
Subjects: LCGFT: Novels.
Classification: LCC PS3558.U695 N46 2025 | DDC 813/.54—
    dc23/eng/20240617
LC record available at https://lccn.loc.gov/2024025617

Our books may be purchased in bulk for promotional, educational, or business use. Please contact your local bookseller or the Macmillan Corporate and Premium Sales Department at 1-800-221-7945, extension 5442, or by email at MacmillanSpecialMarkets@macmillan.com.

First U.S. Edition: 2025
First International Edition: 2025

10 9 8 7 6 5 4 3 2 1

For my readers,
all of whom conjure a unique story in their mind's eye
from the words on the page.
Patrons and collaborators both.

To be alive is to be in trouble.

—Jordan Peterson

It is horrible to be a human being.

—Marshall Herskovitz

A friend's a person who's right
when they tell you you're wrong.

—Tommy Stojack

NEMESIS

PROLOGUE
Meet-Cute

Fifteen Years Ago

Tommy Stojack.

The guy's name is everywhere, a hushed referral at an ammo trade stall, a proper noun rising above the buzz at the Green Beret Foundation booth, a fleck of sea-foam shot from the swirls and eddies of the churning crowd on the convention floor. It is a secret handshake, a dropped name to prove bona fides, a password to a private club.

Depending on which snippet of conversation is trustworthy, Stojack either gunsmithed at the local police range, *or* he ran the veterans' parade, *or* he demilitarized obsolete and surplus munitions at the Hawthorne Army Depot, *or* he'd bare-assed the Ward 5 councilman at last year's city meeting for cutting survivor benefits for the spouses of firefighters. The valets joke about Stojack's filthy rig, and the bartenders compare notes on his generous tips.

Evan does not know the man nor has he come here looking for him, but his situational awareness demands that he take notice.

NEMESIS

He's been trained to read the street wherever he goes, to assemble unofficial dominance hierarchies in his mind—which warlord oversees which zone of rubbled mountainside, which bureaucrat requires a palmed-off wad of yuan in a well-appointed consulate office, which oligarch demands more elbow room in which forgotten corner of Eastern Europe.

Muscle memory pounded into his cells from the age of twelve, when Evan had been taken from a foster home and ensconced in the dark arts of the Orphan Program, a full black operation buried so far beneath the DoD that its protocols never glimpsed the light of day.

A throwaway child brought to the water's edge of his American promise, a promise that receded from him when he bent to it, a promise that is his to uphold, if not for himself then for others.

Like the other products of the Program, Evan had been a clean asset with no familial or community entanglements. Any record of his brief pitiful existence had been wiped from the databases. His face was unknown, his biometrics uncaptured. As the twenty-fourth recruit, he'd been assigned the matching letter of the alphabet for his operational alias.

X.

It was stamped on him, his alias, the cruel power of his own nothingness. Two bloody strokes against oblivion, the awesome, awful power to obliterate.

They'd turned him into an expendable human weapon deployed around the globe to complete missions unsanctioned under U.S. or international law. If caught, tortured, or killed, he would be neither claimed nor missed.

His mind is a treasure map of buried bodies, verboten knowledge sufficiently radioactive to overthrow administrations and unleash wars. Which makes him all the more dangerous to the Powers That Be since he'd fled the Program, slipped off the radar, and rebooted himself on the left coast under a new alias as an importer of industrial cleaning supplies. A great number of powerful men would sleep more soundly in a great number of soft beds could they ensure that Evan joined the legion of corpses he'd put six feet under.

Meet-Cute

They'd already executed Jack Johns, the handler and father figure who'd raised Evan from the age of twelve, training him in isolation aside from myriad subject-matter experts brought in to augment his instruction. Jack had been the first person to treat Evan as if he had inherent worth, a dizzying concept that even now as a young man Evan struggles to embrace.

Early on, Jack had told him that the hard part wouldn't be making him a killer. The hard part would be keeping him human.

Turned out the *hardest* part was to contain both warring directives inside one person.

Recently Evan had chosen to disappear from his countless enemies by hiding in plain sight, tucking into a penthouse lair in a residential tower on Los Angeles's Wilshire Corridor. Step by step he'd been surreptitiously hardening his sanctuary—replacing the windowpanes and sliding glass doors with bullet-resistant Lexan, upgrading the Sheetrock to five and eight-tenths commercial grade, hiding a steel fire core in his front door beneath wooden laminate matching the other residences. Wanting further protection from snipers, explosives, and prying eyes, he'd been seeking some sort of discreet-armor shades for his windows and glass sliders. That's what had brought him here to the SHOT Show, the world's biggest trade exhibit for firearm manufacturers and aficionados of tactical products.

The second floor of the Las Vegas Sands Expo and Convention Center is where most of the action is. Partitioned into conference rooms, exhibit spaces, and booths, it features cutting-edge law-enforcement and military gear alongside the most ridiculous shit on earth.

Spray-on thermal camouflage. A brassiere holster designed to nestle an inverted pistol between the breasts. Kevlar inserts for school backpacks. Exoskeleton therapy machines. Sniper cartridges machined into bottle openers. Concealed-carry leggings for women. Challenge coins of every unit and branch of service. Mylar-coated tents. Key chains and bumper stickers and beverage coasters.

Not a beer coozie lacked a logo.

Evan moves anonymously among the sixty thousand attendees.

Surveillance cameras, Las Vegas Metro, and other eagle eyes are on the lookout for Chinese spies, Turkish peddlers of subpar ordnance, and entrepreneurs willing to bend FARA regs past the breaking point.

To thwart facial recognition he'd mashed dental wax around his molars, which gives him a movie-star jaw that makes him—amusingly—better-looking than he is and pleases him in an odd way he finds mildly confusing. He is easily overlooked, average size, average build, not too handsome, and he is dressed to blend in further. Worn blue jeans, olive-drab jacket, desert-tan combat boots. He'd infused a sloppy smoker's stench into his outfit with the ceremonious wagging of a cigarette. John Deere cap slung low, the white netting yellowed by last night's application of olive oil, several spins in the microwave, and a dusting of sand taken from outside this morning's breakfast-burrito joint, a crooked shanty that had likely since collapsed.

Testosterone hangs musk-heavy in the air. There are cargo shorts and Oakley Blades, drugstore perfume and décolletages aplenty. The big draws are Marine Gunnery Sergeant R. Lee Ermey at the Glock booth; Duane Dwyer talking chisel pike blades, karambit knives, and Zen Buddhism; and celebrity booth babes over at Dillon Aero autographing calendars featuring twelve months of provocative poses and pistol clutching.

Grabbing a bottled water from a vending machine, Evan pauses near an overladen table to take a few sips. His elbow knocks over a sturdy police boot of suede leather and nylon. He picks up the boot, gives it a flex. Stitched heel and toe, rustproof hardware, nonmarking rubber. He notes the name.

Original S.W.A.T.

Continuing on to various vendor booths, Evan makes inquiries about discreet-armor window shades, but the pickings are slim. He receives a special invitation to a conference room on the third floor, but the only offerings there are knockoff habergeon silliness out of Bangalore and aluminum idiocy better suited to Renaissance cosplay than mil-grade defense.

As he withdraws, he hears a two-pack-a-day voice floating out of an adjacent conference room: "—swear to Christ amen, you lot are rock-chewing stupid. Who in the good Lord's name puts a Pic rail foregrip on a cut-down Kalashnikov twelve-gauge? It'll cheese-grate the flesh right off yer dickskinners."

Passing the doorway, Evan slows to peer inside. He catches a glimpse of a hefty man in a beat-to-shit red trucker cap facing away, cocked back in a chair at the head of the conference table, boots of aforenoted Original S.W.A.T. make propped up on the surface. The man's quarter profile shows a sun-beaten cheek pouched with chewing tobacco and a downstroke of what looks like a biker's mustache. Arrayed around the table, a half dozen suits from a gun manufacturer stare at the man with submissive chagrin. The decaled espresso demitasses before them look all the more delicate contrasted with the thirty-two-ounce paper cup with coffee bleeding through at the seams set beside those sturdy Original S.W.A.T.s.

Before Evan can hear more, someone heels the door shut.

That name again.

Tommy Stojack.

Evan hears it this evening as the punch line of a bar story told through a smoker's laugh. And not three minutes later on the lips of a middle-aged woman wearing swaths of too-broad aquamarine eye mascara, whispering in a manner that suggests carnal knowledge. The guy is low-profile, hard to spot, just like Evan. But unlike Evan, he is woven into the fabric of a community in a way that Evan finds perplexing and intriguing.

Evan sips an insufficiently shaken Grey Goose martini at the cocktail lounge of the newly constructed Palazzo next door to the convention center. The couple beside him are having a meet-cute over a spilled Amaretto sour, a beverage sufficiently cloying in its liqueur-and-simple-syrup stickiness to double as a tool for enhanced interrogation.

The marzipan smell is making his nasal passages throb, so he leaves his barely touched drink and a hundred-dollar bill on the bar and takes a long, circuitous route toward his room. The Third Commandment, pounded into his head by Jack: *Master your surroundings.* He notes the location of the cameras overhead and

5

searches out alternate means of egress—a swinging door to a restaurant kitchen, a service elevator, a side door between the Grand Canal Shoppes that lets out onto an alley.

As he starts to withdraw from his quick check of the alley, a commotion near the loading docks at the far end catches his attention. A man wearing a chef apron drags a little girl toward a parked car in which a woman in a housekeeping uniform waits angrily. He is shouting at the woman in Spanish as he approaches, gesticulating angrily, and she is shouting right back at him. From what Evan can hear, he gleans it is a custody handoff. The father tugs his daughter like a rolling piece of luggage; she stumbles alongside him blankly in her Frida Kahlo crown braids, stained Disney princess gown, and scuffed sandals.

She clutches a stuffed-animal elephant, ragged gray with a striped blue shirt and red bow tie—a business-casual pachyderm.

When the father jerks the girl up to shove her into the car seat, the stuffed elephant falls into a puddle. He and the mother are too busy screaming at each other to take note.

Though the girl can't be older than three, she secures her own chest buckle and then stares longingly through the half-rolled-down window at the fallen elephant beyond. Soaking up water on the asphalt, it looks woefully postapocalyptic.

In the threshold of the doorway, Evan hesitates a moment longer, watching.

The parents keep bickering but he senses the argument contains more bitter exhaustion than threat.

The girl doesn't cry and her expression remains blank but she reaches her hand out the window toward her stuffed elephant, fingers splayed.

A movement by the loading dock draws Evan's focus. A broad guy emerges from the shadows. He is spry on his legs but his gait shows hints of damage in the knees and hips, a waiting arthritic future.

Unseen, he ambles over and picks up the stuffed elephant. Evan can't make him out clearly, not from this distance, but he can see a biker's mustache and catches a glimpse of hound-dog eyes beneath the ragged brim of a trucker's cap.

The man hands the stuffed elephant to the girl through the rear window, musses her hair, and withdraws into the darkness from which he'd emerged.

Locked in their feud, the parents don't even notice.

The next morning is range day, where Evan hopes to suss out a new supplier of custom 1911s. He doesn't get five strides in when he spots a guy with media credentials firing a full-auto 5.56 with one hand while filming himself with a selfie stick in the other.

He exfils immediately.

Back at the convention center, he resumes his search for discreet window armoring. Threading up the broad central aisle of the Sands Expo ballroom, he takes in the sundry tactical offerings.

A guy decked out in an army Fifth Group beret-flash T-shirt sits in a large exhibitor booth. A snazzy presentation video on a suspended flat-screen behind him shows a computer-rendered simulation of the seemingly impossible—a .50-cal sniper round with embedded reconnaissance capabilities. Fire a shot over a target and the round itself records telemetry, land contours, temperature, wind speed, and air density, and then feeds them back to an encrypted militarized tablet.

"Think of the private-sector applications," the guy is saying. He has late-stage Elvis's gut with none of the latent grace. "We're open to series-A-round investments now, slugs of twenty-five kay." He wears a sheathed Yarborough combat field knife adhered to his belt and a name tag identifying him as ROBBIE OLSON. "The tech's only a few years out. We're talking a ten-, twenty-ex ROI *at least.*"

As would-be investors crowd in, Evan eases away across the aisle. Before a smaller group, a grizzled vet in an Eighty-Second Airborne shadow cap is showing off a lightweight collared long-sleeved shirt. The shirt has show buttons atop hidden magnetic ones that part without hesitation when you go for your holster, allowing you to draw straight through your shirt. He has the move down well, part frontier gunslinger, part carnival barker. Tucked into the side of the stall, Evan watches a few times, running mental calculations. The magnetic buttons would be useful, giving him an extra eighth of a second on the draw. In his world, an extra eighth of a second means he gets to keep more of his blood inside his body. He notes the shirt's make and designer, vowing to return when the line dies down.

An eruption back at the big exhibitor booth draws his focus. A military-aged woman wearing a black headscarf with a red flower is jabbing a finger at the screen and shouting in heavily accented English at Olson, the portly guy from Fifth Special Forces. "This was mine," she says. "This was *my* idea."

"I told you yesterday, I'm doing business here," Olson says. "This is how capitalism works in the civilized world."

"I understand how capitalism works. *And* engineering—better than you do."

"Yeah? Where's someone like you learn engineering?"

"I studied at Erbil Polytechnic—"

"Erbil Polytechnic?" A braying laugh. "You're a regular Bill Gates then, huh? Look, consider your sweet ass *lucky* to be here on a special immigrant visa instead of cowering beneath a heap of rubble back in Buttfuckistan. SIVs are a privilege. They can be revoked. One phone call." He snaps his fingers. "Don't poke a sleeping eagle, little girl."

"You stole from me. The telemetry algorithms. The whole idea."

"How'm I gonna steal anything from you? I barely remember you." Olson makes eyes at the crowd. "Some third-rate translator."

"Not just a translator." Her eyes are on fire, her cheeks flushed, and finally Evan places the accent as Kurdish. "A warrior." She turns to the onlookers. "I fought by his side."

Enduring in the battle zone between Turkey, Syria, Iran, and Iraq, the Kurds are as tough as any people Evan has encountered. American foreign-policy jackals had been spurring them to conflict against whichever neighbor they deemed inconvenient, arming them in proxy wars and pledging alliances they never backed up when the time came to honor them. The Kurds had been betrayed by America at nearly every turn—seven times in the past hundred years. Not by the quiet professionals in BDUs but by orders initiating from the five-sided building in Arlington. There was an old Kurdish proverb Evan related to all too well: *No friends but the mountains.*

Meet-Cute

He had seen the rot in the military-industrial complex from the inside, up close enough to know the Kurds were still being used every bit as roughly as he and his fellow Orphans had been. He feels the sting of his own complicity as a cog in the wheel of empire, of the blind adamance of his own youth, of the blood he's spilled in the name of causes he does not understand. Still he musters hope that the best and the brightest will do right by the Kurds whenever the time comes for the United States to withdraw from Iraq and Afghanistan.

The conflagration at the exhibit booth rages, the woman now talking to the crowd as well: "When ISIS was stealing stolen oil from the fields of northern Iraq? *We* were the ones shooting armor-piercing incendiary rounds from .50-cal Barretts to light up their tankers." She gestures at Olson. "While these *sagbab*s were back in the green zone soaking their pedicures."

Olson is on his feet, leaning over the table, jabbing a finger at her. "You'd best get the hell out of my sight. You don't question a Green Beret's honor on his own land."

A ripple of hostility moves through the throng, a few men nodding in agreement. A familiar red trucker's hat pokes up into view at the back of the group, but an instant later it is gone.

The woman's face is set with calm fury, her gaze locked on the man. She refuses to step back. Evan eases close enough to hear her say, *"Hezar heval jî hindik in. Yek dijmin pir e."*

She turns and walks away, her expression holding strong, but Evan catches a glimpse of the shaken young woman beneath the surface. In a rare flash of empathy, he can see that she feels demeaned. Treated like an expendable thing. That flicker behind her face finds resonance with a part of him long- and deep-buried, a part he's walled off under muscle and callus because he is too weak to have done otherwise.

The crowd parts for her, giving her a wide berth, several folks still glaring.

"The hell's that gibberish she's babbling?" Olson says.

As Evan floats past the table searching for that trucker's cap, he translates in a low voice: "'A thousand friends are too few. One enemy is too many.'"

"A threat?" Olson says. "That bitch threatened me."

"Oh, calm yourself, Robbie," someone says as Evan moves away.

"Fuck you, calm down. She comes in here lying about me, showing me up in front of my clientele."

Olson is still ranting when Evan turns the corner and gazes across the breadth of the second floor, still trying to spot the man in the trucker cap.

Currents of people sweep past him in both directions. The floor is packed; footfall and voices and laughter echo off the tall ceiling, the convention center seething with life and movement, a carbonated fizz.

A sharp voice cuts through the commotion behind him—"*warned you not to stir the pot*"—and he whirls in time to see Olson slam into the Kurdish woman from the side, banging her into the crash bar of a metal door and propelling her into a back hallway.

It is no more than a blip, the passersby still passing by.

Evan walked the rear halls yesterday. He knows them to have spotty surveillance cameras. And he knows that's why Olson had pressed her into that corridor, removing her from view.

Evan is hustling, moving fast enough to catch the door before it swings shut.

He slips silently into a wide corridor crowded with shipping cartons, empty weapon containers, a few haphazardly parked forklifts.

The conflict has moved about fifteen meters down the hall, Olson and the woman partially in view squaring off between two pallets stacked high with crated gun racks. Olson grips the woman by the wrist, flinging her against the wall. As she wrenches her arm free, he cuffs her with an open palm.

A grown-man slap with grown-man weight behind it snaps her head to one side, knocking the headscarf askew. As Evan runs toward them, the woman drives into Olson with a knee in the crotch, slamming him into a pallet. Several of the heavy crates spill, crashing thunderously to the floor. As the gun racks topple, they reveal another man beyond, approaching quickly from the opposite end of the hallway. Just a silhouette, but Evan recognizes the gait and the red trucker cap at once.

Olson howls, shoving himself off the crumbled tower of crates and ripping from his sheath the combat knife, which he holds in an expert forward grip.

Evan is still eight and a half strides away from the fight, the man in the trucker cap farther than that on the other side and moving slower.

Olson lunges at the woman's throat, a skilled thrust that leaves little but the blade to grasp.

Five strides out, Evan braces himself for bloodletting, and then the woman's hands move in a skilled parry and then the knife is out of Olson's hand and spinning around and then it is embedded at an upward tilt between his ribs at the dead center of his torso and he is standing stock-still and shocked and already dead though his brain doesn't know it yet.

He slides diagonally to the floor, legs limp, torso flopping, head smacking tile.

No movement.

Evan comes to a halt behind the woman.

The man in the trucker cap stops behind Robbie Olson's corpse.

They stare at each other.

The first clear look Evan gets of the man. Sagging eyes held in textured pouches. Biker's mustache touched with gray. T-shirt featuring a bald eagle clutching Old Glory in its talons. Left forefinger blown off at the first knuckle. A combat veteran's face, a face that has seen things not easy to see but has come through still capable of holding emotion.

The woman is breathing hard. She looks at her hands as if they've betrayed her. Her pleading eyes go to the other man, standing protectively over Robbie Olson's body, and then they find Evan. "You saw. You saw he tried to kill me."

The hallway is tinged with Lysol, axle grease, sweat turned acrid by panic, and exposed organ meat.

It is a serious smell.

It is a serious situation.

"What's your name?" Evan says.

"Deijly. I am here on a visa. For my service. I am not American. They will not believe me. No one will believe me." She fights down a tremor in her voice. "Will you help me?"

Before Evan can respond the door bangs open behind him and two uniforms from Vegas Metro trot over. In the lead is a young kid with a blond starter mustache.

"The hell was that crash? Sounded like someone touched off a Bouncing Betty in here. You'd better—"

He comes around the fallen crates, spots the body, and freezes.

His partner takes his side, thumbs hooked through his belt loops. He has a seen-it-all face aged up with crow's-feet and graying sideburns. His name tag reads CARR.

"The *hell*," the younger cop, ID'd as MCCLOSKEY, says. "The hell went down here?"

Deijly makes a small noise at the back of her throat. The air conditioner hums overhead. Sounds from the convention floor wash through the walls at them.

They all look at one another, a Mexican standoff without the benefit of any Mexicans.

Evan breaks the relative silence: "Guy was showing off his flashy edged-weapon moves with a Yarborough combat knife. Tripped on the edge of the pallet there, went down with the crates, and impaled himself."

A long silence. McCloskey sucks his teeth. Carr blinks and blinks again. Both cops' gazes shift simultaneously to the man in the trucker hat.

Evan follows their stare. Deijly keeps her eyes lowered, afraid to look up, her heartbeat showing as a faint flutter at the hollow of her throat.

The man's eyes are unreadable. He looks down at the corpse, rolls his lips, making that mustache dance. He smells of tobacco, coffee, and cigarette smoke.

The silence lasts maybe five full seconds but feels a great deal longer than that.

Then the man sighs. "I go back with Robbie Olson forever and a day, but we all know that boy's corn bread ain't done in the middle."

McCloskey clears his throat. "You're telling me that he tripped and fell exactly so? I mean, forensically, that angle of entry indicates—"

"'Forensically'? 'Angle of entry'? Son, you're talking chicken to Colonel Sanders. How many knife fights you been in?"

"Uh, I'm not saying—"

The man points at McCloskey with the stub of the finger severed at the knuckle. "I ain't big on stupid, McCloskey. I knew your old man back before he knew how to field-strip a .45. So let's not start dick jousting, not when you're bringing a pencil to a bazooka fight. Robbie Olson played *Enter the Dragon* to impress the young lady here and Darwin had something to say about it."

Carr covers his smile with a fist, gives a faint cough. Deijly doesn't move, doesn't lift her gaze, but Evan hears the soft hiss of an exhalation through her teeth.

"Now let Carr here teach you how to handle an accidental death," the man says. "Same as I taught him when he was fresh outta the academy."

McCloskey looks at Carr.

Carr gives an amiable shrug. "You heard the man."

"Okay," McCloskey says. "I'll need to take statements from everyone present for—"

"They don't need to give statements. I just did. You want a character reference from your captain?" The man pulls a barely intact flip phone from his pocket and wags it. It looks like it might disintegrate. "He's at his boy's high-school graduation today but if he don't answer, I'm happy to call the missus to pull him out by the ear."

McCloskey looks down at his polished boots. "No, sir. That won't be necessary. Of course I trust your word and your . . . your experience. I didn't mean to imply—"

"Don't bother with all that," the man says. "I'm immune to charisma." He squats beside Olson's sprawled form and rests a hand on the corpse with surprising gentleness. Evan is caught off guard seeing his baby-blue eyes mist. "Goddamn it, Robbie, you fool," he says, quietly. "It was your own damn fault. Your own damn fault." He bridges his eyes with his thumb and that stub of a forefinger for a moment and when he lowers his hand, his eyes are deep with grief. "How the hell am I gonna break this to June Lynn?" He looks up at Carr, gives a snap of his head. "You know where to find me when you need me."

Carr taps his forehead with two fingers, an affectionate salute.

The man in the trucker cap turns to the woman. "Ms. Deijly," he says, with perfect pronunciation, "I'm sorry you had to witness that." He proffers an elbow, and she takes his arm with a trembling hand. At her side, he escorts her out like a gentleman.

Evan nods at the officers and follows.

They move past a few more pallets and forklifts and step through an outer door into an empty alley wide enough to be a street. The sun lays itself across their shoulders, locking their shadows underfoot.

"Thank you," Deijly says, her voice hoarse. "Thank you both."

The man nods. "What kinda fool picks a fight with a Kurd?"

She smiles but it is fleeting. She rubs the back of her neck.

"You okay?" Evan asks.

"Fine. What do you say? 'Dinged my bell'?"

"Close enough," Tommy says.

"And I hit my hip pretty hard." She rubs her thigh, pauses at the feel of something, then reaches into her pocket.

She pulls out a challenge coin broken in two from the force of her hip striking the wall. The halves glitter in her palm.

The top half reads: NO GREATER FRIEND.

The bottom: NO WORSE ENEMY.

Two raised ledges had once intersected at ninety degrees, dividing the coin into quadrants, but the metal disk has snapped horizontally, leaving a V to embrace the upper words and a caret angled down like a lampshade across the lower phrase.

"From my time in the fight." She peers down at the pieces thoughtfully. "I want you two to have it."

She hands a half-moon to each of them, the pewter interior showing at the rough edge.

Gifting a token from her elite military unit is a show of great respect, and Evan and the man in the trucker hat receive the gesture as such.

She hugs the other man quickly and then gives Evan a peck on the cheek. "Sometimes help is where you least expect it."

She walks away.

Evan and the man watch her go. She does not look back. Reaching the end of the alley, she turns out of sight.

The man shifts chewing tobacco around in his cheek and spits a brown stream through the gap in his front teeth. "I had McCloskey's asshole knitting a sweater back there." When he grins, his eyes gleam. "He's an okay kid. He'll be all right." He produces a card from a cargo pocket, offers it to Evan. "Never know when you might need a friend."

The jagged piece of metal is heavy in Evan's hand: NO WORSE ENEMY.

"I don't have friends," Evan says.

"Well, lookee here. The first true lone wolf ever to walk God's green earth." He shoves his card into the pocket of Evan's jacket. "Why don't you keep it for when you're stuck and need to make bail. What's your name, young man?"

"Evan."

"Evan what?"

"Just Evan."

"Ain't you fancy. One name, like Madonna and Elmo." A wink. "Heard you were having some trouble locating armored shades worth a damn thing."

"How'd you hear that?"

Those hound-dog eyes twinkle again. "Never know who's who in the zoo." He starts up the alley and Evan holds pace at his side. "The chain mail here at SHOT Show's about as useful as tits on a bull. I got a vendor outta Scandinavia, weaves sheets of it, tiny interlocking rings of unobtainium. Hell, you can even order it in harvest gold or avocado green."

Evan's nose wrinkles at the thought.

"Or periwinkle. We'll get you hooked up, son." The man slings his arm across Evan's shoulders, an easy, affable gesture. No one has done anything like that to Evan since his foster-home days and even then rarely. Evan suppresses his instinct to underhook the arm, gable the shoulder, take the man to the ground. "Bet we could square you away on some hardware, too. You look like a 1911 man, that right?"

Evan feels . . . What is it he feels?

Warmth?

He pulls away, turns to face the man. He tells himself to proffer his open palm and then he does.

The man shakes with his intact hand. "Tommy Stojack."

His palm is as callused as Evan expected.

Side by side, they keep on up the alley, a wide stripe of sunlight illuminating the way.

"Like the gunrunner said, 'I think this is the beginning of a beautiful . . .'" Tommy pauses, spits another stream of brown juice. "Well, whatever the hell you wanna call it is just fine by me."

1

What Tommy Had Done

Fifteen Years Later

Tommy Stojack had supplied weapons to a psychopathic female assassin called the Wolf.

That's what Tommy had done.

The Wolf had been at the center of Evan's last mission. The Wolf had attempted to kill Evan with a .357 Magnum revolver and a Savage 110 sniper rifle and an SUV with an unyielding front bumper. She had shot a father in the head in his own home and had tried and tried again to put a sniper round through the critical mass of his orphaned seventeen-year-old daughter after failing to garrote her with a zip tie. Through all of that and more, the Wolf had been armed by Tommy.

That's what Tommy had done.

The man who'd coaxed into Evan's stone-hardened heart the first faint heartbeat of trust since Jack Johns had plucked him from that desolate rest stop on the side of the highway in Evan's twelfth year.

The man who'd shone a ray of friendship into Evan's shadow-eclipsed soul.

The man with whom Evan had walked the past decade and a half at some distance but together, who'd manufactured his guns and field-tested his weapons and provided crotchety remote backup on his missions.

A dead father. An orphaned seventeen-year-old. A betrayal of what Evan had thought was a shared code.

That's what Tommy had fucking done.

Since Evan had deserted the Orphan Program, he had operated as the Nowhere Man, a pro bono assassin devoted to helping the powerless and terrorized. There'd been precisely one person he'd been able to count on for the entirety of that time.

Not anymore.

At the moment it was less than helpful for these thoughts to be cycling through Evan's head with white-hot OCD compulsion. Not when he was nestled into bushes outside a heavily armed Hancock Park house nearly big enough to be called a mansion, his face darkened from a loam paint stick, superglue glazing his fingertips to obscure prints, suppressed matte-black ARES 1911 in hand.

This was not the time to be musing about Tommy. Or the weapons he'd supplied to the Wolf. Or the purpling face of Jayla Hill, the seventeen-year-old Evan had held in his arms as she'd gasped for breath. Or the slit through Jayla's trachea, the splatter of blood across her face. Or the fact that his own supposed friend had indirectly broken the Eighth Commandment: *Never kill a kid,* and directly violated the Tenth: *Never let an innocent die.*

Evan had already scaled the spiked wrought-iron gate and waited now, tucked into the shrubbery, twenty-four meters off the front of the unlit house-mansion, twenty-three if the Angeleno darkness was screwing with his internal range finder. Night blooming jasmine perfumed the air and as anyone familiar with night-blooming jasmine understood, "perfumed" wasn't too fancy a word for it.

A crunch of movement issued from the blackness of the wraparound front porch. Evan thumbed off the ambidextrous safety, but he couldn't make out the source and couldn't risk reaching for his night-vision headset. Three hours ago, as dusk had filtered into nightfall, he'd surveilled the property from atop a telephone pole one long block over. He noted the movements of each of the four hired guns—which one walked with a shuffle of the left foot, which one took smoke breaks every quarter hour, which one scratched at his dandruff, which one was close protection. For obvious reasons, Stavros's house-mansion was under extra-heavy security tonight.

Evan's brain clicked back to Tommy. Certainly Evan had other associates with shady intentions and deadly intent. But they'd never crossed his missions. People had been murdered on Evan's watch with Tommy's weapons. Was he supposed to just forget that? Was he supposed to make this the only time in his life he didn't trace a threat to its source and uproot it? If he allowed a crack in his code, he had no idea what else might leak through, widen the gap, and surge into a torrent.

The snick of a match on the porch.

Evan waited.

The flame flared and rose.

A glimpse of a downbent face, the crackle of a cigarette breathed to life.

Then just the cherry floating in total darkness five feet and eleven inches off the ground.

Evan lined the high-profile tritium Straight Eight sights ten inches below—*pfft pfft*—and the cigarette twirled away in a streak of sparks, and then came the pleasing sound of crumpling meat and laundry hitting wooden planks.

He rolled from cover, tucking up against one of the porch columns, a fluted Ionic monstrosity befitting the home of a shipping magnate with deep syndicate connections and delusions of Old Country grandeur. A slight lean gave Evan a decent vantage of the bowed balcony rails directly above.

On the last mission, Evan had saved Jayla Hill despite Tommy's best hardware and the Wolf's best efforts. Every time he finished a mission, he asked the person he'd just helped to find someone else in dire straits and to pass on the number to his encrypted phone: 1–855–2-NOWHERE.

That helped his clients transform from victim to rescuer.

In less than two weeks, Jayla had identified his next Nowhere

Man mission. On a follow-up visit to her otolaryngologist at Cedars, she'd come across a distraught woman, Neva Alonso, surrounded by police officers in the lobby of the pediatric ward. Neva had been hysterical, barely able to render a report.

Jayla had waited, followed the woman home, earned her trust, and passed on the secret phone number.

So here he was.

Fully operational, in the red-hot center of a mission, and yet his mind remained stubbornly fixated on Tommy. These past weeks, Evan had forgone comms with his former friend and ally, performing his own weapon checks, oiling his Strider knife, cleaning his pistols, running bore brushes down his shotgun barrels. Though he field-tested his magazines regularly, it was time for a fresh batch, but he'd put off heading to Tommy's armorer den in Las Vegas to pick them up.

He'd been avoiding Tommy's face, knowing the unspoken conflict between them would ignite when they next squared off. Evan had countless skills for countless varieties of conflict and clashes, but with—what was it? intimacy?—in the mix, he was unsure.

Or afraid?

Afraid of what?

Of how he might *feel*?

How ridiculous was that?

From above came a creak of decking and then the *scritch-scritch* of the dandruffed guard. A shadow moved into view, the guard resting his hands on the railing, and Evan leaned out farther from the preposterous Greek column and fired upward.

Against the faint backlighting of the stars, he saw a spray leap toward heaven. A grunt, a topple, and then the guard piledrived into the hydrangeas by Evan's feet.

At some stage of the last mission, Tommy had known that his hardware was putting Evan's clients at risk, that his specialized weapons had even been used in multiple attempts to kill Evan.

And he hadn't spoken up.

That was a declaration of war by omission, wasn't it?

Evan was inside the house-mansion now, having used a diamond pick to make the spool pins of the front-door lock dance into alignment. Instead of a foyer, there was a gallery lined with resin sculptures of Greek gods, Poseidon featured most prominently as befitted the owner's profession and ego.

Evan had just drifted inside; he hadn't checked corners.

He did so now, a full two seconds too late.

This level of distraction was untenable. It put the current mission in jeopardy of failing.

Dark of face, firm of grip, he drifted through the gallery, the gods flanking his progress from either side.

Stavros would be awake and waiting.

Tonight was his big night.

Two guards remained, one tall and slender, the other tall and as wide as a deep freezer.

Evan heard footfall in the adjoining hall, the padding of boots. Radio silence of the first two guards must have drawn notice. The steps were inconsistent, one crisp, one shushing across the Thassos marble in a slight limp. The slender guard, then.

If Tommy had in fact declared war by omission, that had to be answered, didn't it? Evan had to confront him no matter what emotional complications that might produce.

In the middle of the gallery, he struck a flawless isosceles stance, raised his ARES, and waited for the lanky guard to limp into his sights. A few more steps and he surged into view, his head framed beautifully by Hades' two-pronged staff. Evan took a micromoment to appreciate the Jungian synchronicity of dispatching a man by shooting him through the bident of the god of the underworld. Then he exhaled smoothly and pressed the trigger—*pfft*.

Moving swiftly now, Evan swept past the guard as he was still falling, dumping another two rounds into his chest—*pfft pfft*—for good measure.

Six rounds burned. The ARES held eight in the mag and one in the chamber. Evan had Stavros and the deep-freezer guard left. Stavros would be easy given his state, but the big man's muscle mass would eat up rounds. While the 1911 had decent stopping power, Evan couldn't let his luck ride on three bullets.

His Original S.W.A.T.s skimmed silently across the marble. Hustling up the next hall, he extracted a full backup mag from the concealed pocket at his right hip, lifted it adjacent to the still-loaded partial mag, and ejected the partial into his waiting palm.

It snagged on the lip of the well.

A slight hitch on the drop, which from feel and habit he guessed was caused by a tiny burr lifted from the top right corner of the magazine tube between the catch notch and the opening.

A half-second delay.

A half-second was the difference between this side of the dirt and the other. One of Jack's Unofficial Rules stood Voltaire on his head: *Good is the enemy of the great.*

Feet blurring, breath low and steady, Evan stripped the mag free and instinctively added the repair to a mental task list: *Replenish mags from Tommy.*

The thought escaped him before awareness could catch up but when it did, it came like a gut punch.

His weaponry was a part of him, and that meant Tommy was a part of him, too. And now he'd have to lop that part off and trust someone else to supply and service his weapons. For Evan, trust was not easy.

Three-fourths of a second had passed now. He was unsettled but could not spare a moment to reset himself.

Head down, swapping the clean mag, shoving it north.

His momentum carried him around the turn toward the back hall of the house, and his gaze rose from the union of his fists around the Micarta checkered grips and aluminum receiver, noting only now, too late, the massive form before him aiming a double-barreled sawed-off shotgun directly at his forehead.

Evan froze, pistol still aimed ineptly, unforgivably, somewhere at the junction of the ceiling and the wall at his ten o'clock.

Evan said, "Oops."

The big bores of the twelve-gauge gaped at Evan. The deep freezer grinned, gave a quick jerk of the barrel. "Why don't you step into Stavros's office? He's waiting for you."

Stavros looked like hell.

Baggy jaundiced skin, a prodigious gut that bulged outward to sit heavily across his thighs, ankles swollen to bell-bottom proportion. He sat stuffed into a distressed leather armchair, wearing it like a carapace. He was shirtless, his hairy torso mottled with blots and bruises, too-small athletic shorts showing the marbled wreckage of his legs. Dry flaky skin, bright yellow sclera, white paste gumming at the corners of his mouth.

The office smelled of stool, sweat, and urine. Photographs in dark wooden frames wallpapering the room showed Stavros in younger days and slighter form beside various leaders and celebrities, the one constant his openmouthed "this guy" finger-point at his companions. Medical supplies were scattered everywhere—snapped-off latex gloves, bedpans, vials and orange pill bottles scattered across the leather desk blotter at his side. Syringes overflowed a red sharps container. IV in his arm, oxygen feeding his nostrils, rattling breath finding resonance in the bulging prow of his chest.

Across from Stavros, Evan sat in a much smaller chair. The guard loomed at his back, from time to time tapping the nape of his neck with the shotgun muzzle, no doubt concerned he'd be forgotten. He was standing so close Evan could make out the tip of his size-sixteen boot.

Stavros's voice came as a great-cat purr. "Who are you?"

Evan shrugged.

The guard prodded the back of Evan's head with the shotgun.

Evan said, "No one."

"And yet you know me."

Again Evan did not answer. Again he was prompted by steel.

"Yes," he said.

Stavros's amused rumble of a laugh deteriorated into a coughing fit. "You come here in judgment." A wave of his monstrous hand to Evan's 1911, which the guard had placed on the desk at Stavros's side. "With your little gun."

"It's not *that* little," Evan said.

"I am to assume you know about tonight's proceedings?"

The Strider knife in Evan's front left pocket pressed into the top of his thigh. The deep freezer had been overconfident in his girth, shotgun, and frisking abilities. "I do."

"And you find it"—Stavros's tongue poked out, tasting the air—"distasteful."

23

"'Distasteful' is too meek a word for what I think."

"Hardly worth making a fuss," Stavros said. "Nice room upstairs, well cared for, won't know a thing. I'm not a savage."

"No?"

"You hold that I am not within my rights?" A wheezing breath. "My name, it is derived from *stauros,* the Christian cross on which Jesus Christ was crucified."

Evan said, "Impressive."

Stavros crossed himself Orthodox-style, right to left, thumb joined with the first two fingers, the others close to the palm. "That means I am worthy of making sacrifices."

"Ah," Evan said. "An allegorical justification."

The retort brought another tap of the double-barreled shotgun from behind. Evan let it tilt his head more than necessary so he could steal a backward glance. The tang-mounted safety was still engaged.

Stavros flared sausage fingers. "I am also immensely significant in my own right."

Evan said, "Huh."

Stavros tried to lean forward but his gut would not allow it and he settled back, winded. "Do you have any idea how powerful I am?"

"Yes, I do," Evan said. "You're the third-most-powerful person in this room."

He waited for the shove of the muzzle into the back of his head.

There it was, right on cue.

He seized the barrels with his right hand, jerking the shotgun aside as he rolled off the chair, left hand already grabbing for the Strider, hooking the shark fin atop the blade on the corner of his pocket to snap the knife open.

The guard stumbled forward, his substantial weight tugging him into a fall, and Evan cleared the chair away with a kick and stabbed him three times up the right side through the rib cage— *tap tap tap*—hitting a trifecta of key organs.

The guard hit the floorboards hard, leading with his chin, which knocked him out cold, a stroke of compassion since it would have taken his brain at least a few excruciating minutes to figure out what had happened.

Evan stood facing Stavros. "Now you're the second."

Stavros gasped and tilted forward, trying for the 1911 on the desk.

Evan watched him.

Stavros's catcher's-mitt hand knocked the pistol farther away and he tumbled from the chair onto the beautifully woven kilim. His face mashed into the earth-toned wool, the fulcrum of his enormous distended belly tilting him forward onto his chest. He made muffled noises into the carpet.

He lay there, suffocating, his chest unable to expand beneath his own crushing weight.

Evan reclaimed his ARES. Crouched near Stavros's head. He'd managed to tilt his face slightly so one straining eye peered pleadingly at Evan.

He wheezed into the carpet.

That yellow eye stared at Evan.

Evan stared back at it.

It blinked and blinked, tears clinging to the lashes.

A subconjunctival hemorrhage leaked through the sclera, red bleeding through yellow.

Stavros was trying to speak but his lips remained mashed to the floor. He made a sputtering noise and then was still.

Evan rose from his crouch.

He walked out of the study and through the quiet hallways to the base of the cherrywood stairs.

The doorbell rang—the Westminster Chime melody. Classy.

Evan walked back through the gallery of tacky statuary and opened the door.

A nervous man in blue scrubs stood on the porch. Late-middle-aged, round glasses, old-fashioned doctor's bag. At his side stood a burly nurse a decade younger with a septum pierce and buzz-cut hair died in orange and purple swirls. Behind them a mobile medical Sprinter van idled.

To the side of the porch, barely visible in the darkness, the leg of the fallen guard poked up barely into view among the hydrangeas. This amused Evan darkly.

"Listen," the sweaty little doctor said, "get the others. We have a lot of unloading to do and we still have to prep and sterilize the theater."

Evan shot him in the face—*pfft*—swung his arm a foot and a half to the right, and shot the nurse through his gaping mouth—*pfft*—and chest for good measure—*pfft*.

Leaving the door ajar, he withdraw once again to the stairs.

At the base, he drew in a deep breath. He reloaded the 1911 with a fresh magazine and then gingerly unscrewed the still-warm suppressor and secured it in a thigh cargo pocket. With one fluid motion, he swept aside his shirt with the baseplate of the ARES magazine, seating the pistol into the appendix carry holster and securing the shirt's magnetic buttons *click, click, click* as he had thousands of repetitions before.

He ascended to the second floor.

Walked quietly along the corridor.

The third door on the left was locked. From the *outside.*

He hesitated, unsure what he might find within.

Steady breath in, steady breath out.

He unbolted the door and swung it open.

The room was jarringly bright and nicely decorated. A queen bed with a princess canopy and a yellow-and-blue quilt. A cheery circular rag rug. Dolls of all shapes and sizes, a rocking horse, and a plastic kitchen with play pots and pans.

A girl sat in the middle of the rug, playing with Lincoln Logs.

Querida Alonso, eight years old, universal blood type negative, healthy two-pound liver just big enough to harvest.

Neva's daughter.

"Querida?"

She looked alarmed.

"Oh," Evan said. "My face. That's just makeup. Like baseball players wear."

Querida nodded. Smooth skin, big brown eyes, her hair taken up high in a ponytail spout. She was wearing a yellow dress two sizes too big for her.

"May I come in?"

She nodded again.

Evan took a few slow steps forward. The girl did not flinch.

He nodded at the Lincoln Logs. He kept his voice soft, so soft. "What are you building?"

"My house," she said.

Evan took another step toward her and lowered himself onto his knees, making himself smaller. "Are you okay?"

The girl shrugged. "I miss Mamá. They said I had to come here. Like for camp. They said this is what she wanted. But I don't understand why she didn't just say so herself."

"I don't think this is what she wanted," Evan said. "I think it was a misunderstanding."

The girl added some green split logs to the roof.

"Did anyone hurt you?"

She shook her head. "But they won't let me leave. Or call Mamá."

She had matching dimples in her cheeks and her lashes were long and curled. He pictured the man lying downstairs on the woven carpet, a man who'd been ready to absorb this child, to slice her open, part her out, and discard what was left so as to leave no evidence.

Evan's distraction had nearly left her to that fate.

His focus, judgment, and gear had been compromised by his rift with Tommy.

If he'd wound up with his gray matter spattered on Stavros's office wall, that was one thing. But what his failure would have cost Querida and Neva was unacceptable.

Observing the girl's delicate wrists, the way she chewed her bottom lip with focus as she lowered another plastic log into place, he replayed the closeness of the miss. On his knees before her, he felt penitent. This child deserved perfection from him.

That was it, then.

He'd deliver this child to her mother. He'd ask Neva to find someone else to pass his number on to, someone else in need of the kind of help that only he could provide.

And then?

He'd deal with it.

He'd deal with Tommy.

"Your *mamá* sent me to get you," Evan said. "Would you like to leave?"

A vehement nod.

"I'm gonna ask you one favor, okay? I want you to keep your eyes closed until we are out on the street."

"How'm I supposed to know where to go?"

"I could hold your hand. Or I could carry you."

She scrunched up her face, thinking. Then she shot her arms up, straight at the elbows.

Something twisted inside Evan's chest, drawing pain.

He scooped her up.

She closed her eyes and nuzzled into his side, legs clamped above his hip, arms around his shoulders, forehead at his neck. He kept his forearm beneath her bottom. Her breath came feather-soft against his oft-broken collarbone.

He moved smoothly down the stairs.

Eased around the fallen guard in the hall of statues.

The front door remained open as he'd left it.

Holding Querida tight, he knuckled the keypad button mounted by the sidelight window. Out in the darkness, the wrought-iron gate started to rattle open.

He stepped over the body of the doctor, toed the nurse's arm out of the way, and carried the girl to safety.

2

A Ph.D. Who Could Win a Bar Fight

Evan awoke floating three feet above the floor, flat on his back, arms crossed pharaonically at the chest.

The slab of his bed hovered in a weightless push-pull, hoisted by neodymium rare-earth magnets and tethered with cables. He felt the thrum of the healing magnetic field in his bones, or at least that's what he liked to tell himself. When it came to his battle-torn muscle and tendon, even placebo effects were welcome.

He felt different.

He'd woken up a different man.

He *was* a different man.

He knew unequivocally that his sole enduring friendship had ended, that the bright red line that Tommy Stojack had crossed finally had to be answered for, which meant that this morning confronted Evan with a fundamentally different world than the one that had greeted him yesterday.

Casting back the thin sheet, he swiveled to the mattress's edge and set down his feet on the poured-concrete floor.

The anger was right there waiting for him, augmented with a burn of betrayal.

And . . . something else.

He could barely pin it down beneath the wash of fury and righteousness. Emotions roiled, shrouding his center. He felt adrift.

Intentional stillness and movement. That's what he needed. To hammer his mind and body back into a state fit to carry him into whatever this new day would hold.

He was an autodidact in matters of steel and strategy, buoyed by the tools Jack had bequeathed him. From the age of twelve, he'd received a gutter-and-alley liberal arts education. Jack liked to quote a dictate of the CIA's WWII-era predecessor, reminding young Evan that the Office of Strategic Services' ideal recruit was "a Ph.D. who could win a bar fight."

For a twelve-year-old foster kid from East Baltimore, the latter part of the stipulation seemed achievable. The former sounded like science fiction.

Moving into the great room composing the lion's share of his seven-thousand-square-foot penthouse, he started with a twenty-minute meditation before the lowered periwinkle sunshades. Cross-legged, eyes veiled, trying to quiet a mind that refused to be quieted.

Then heavy bag, speed bag, water bag, pounding until his wrists ached.

And then he removed his samurai sword from its mount on the wall of the brief hallway leading to the master suite, stood in the dead center of the plain of training mats, and practiced his iaijutsu cuts.

Clumsy.

It had been awhile.

He worked himself into a lather performing kenjutsu movements with the seventeenth-century sword. The Japanese tradition of *kaizen*, the art of perfection, had been inculcated in him by two different sensei under Jack's watchful eye. It was the basis of the Second Commandment: *How you do anything is how you do everything.* Jack had pounded into him a deep-rooted respect for the wisdom of other cultures, demanding he learn as much from a tea ceremony as a session on the sniper range.

A Ph.D. Who Could Win a Bar Fight

At the workout's end, Evan dropped to a knee in a *kasumi* defensive posture, protecting against an overhead strike. His sword held in an unquavering horizontal before him, tipped slightly downward so the imaginary blow would slide away.

He caught a glimpse of himself in the blade's reflection, the band of his eyes and bridge of his nose.

His expression was calm, resolute.

He was average size, average build.

He was an ordinary guy, not too handsome.

He was the most feared assassin of a generation.

He was Orphan X.

When he replaced the sword on the wall, his breathing was steady.

Mens sana in corpore sano.

The doorbell rang.

Josephine Morales, a Program washout and world-class hacker, was a bundle of caffeinated energy and a torrent of competence. Evan had collided with her on a past mission and they'd been stuck with each other ever since. She was sort of his charge, sort of his niece, sort of his colleague, sort of his backup.

In his world as the Nowhere Man, everything had its place and category. In his life outside, nothing did.

He created order from the insane but encountered chaos in the mundane.

He answered the door and Joey breezed in, a hundred-ten-pound Rhodesian ridgeback trotting at her side. The dog's name was Dog, thusly named by Joey so she wouldn't grow attached to him. Like most manipulative language play, the ruse had failed utterly.

Spotting Evan, Dog the dog lunged forward, tail spinning like a helo rotor. He buried his face in Evan's crotch, rammed tight so his nose stuck out the back of Evan's thighs, a perverse impaling. Evan crouched and Dog lavished his workout-sweaty face with slurps as if it were a salt lick.

A shower would be forthcoming.

He pushed Dog aside and rose, Joey fixing him with her affectionately irritable emerald gaze, arms crossed. "I brought him to elevate your self-esteem. When's the last time *anyone* was that happy to see you?"

"When they were about to press the trigger," he said.

She smiled. It was radiant, transforming her entire face. He'd yet to see another smile that compared. "I can relate."

She trudged in and dumped her rucksack on the kitchen island, surfaced with poured concrete that had neither an item nor speck on it. Her black-brown hair was pulled back in a high ponytail—*rare*—fastened by a scrunchie polka-dotted with tiny skulls and crossbones—*on brand*—showing off a freshly shaved undercut on both sides rather than just the right—*new*. A red splotch the shape of France marred her chin.

He gestured at the splotch. "What happened to your face?"

She smirked. "What happened to *your* face?"

"What are you, eight?"

"You know when you take a bite of pizza and all the cheese just slides off and thwaps against your chin? And it's burning hot?"

"Why not wait until it's *not* burning hot?"

"'Cuz pizza."

"You're an id with limbs."

Smirking, she slid her laptop from the rucksack and booted it up. "I have that intel dump for you."

"You're seven and a half minutes late."

"I stopped in the lobby to let your old-people neighbors pet Dog. It was an act of social responsibility worthy of commending."

A bunch of memes popped up to tile her laptop screen but she closed the windows before he could get a good look.

"What's all that?" he asked.

"Just a new project I'm, like, super excited about. I met this girl in Intro to Western Civ named Cassidy Ann—that's seriously her name. When white people get rich enough they hit that double-first-name zone same as if they get broke enough. It's just the ones in the middle who have boring names like Tom and Bob. Or Evan."

Though she was only seventeen, Joey attended UCLA. After rescuing her from a strike team of assassins, Evan had set her up with her own place in Westwood and demanded she enroll in college, a hapless attempt to keep her out of trouble. Since Joey knew more about computer science, programming, and computational systems than the entire combined faculties, she'd taken to sampling other courses beyond her wide realm of expertise.

She'd failed to become an Orphan for good reason, but nonetheless the failure gnawed at her. Like Evan, she was stranded at a threshold between two identities. He hoped going to college would help push her through to a more anchored sense of herself.

As Dog heaved himself down by Joey's barstool with a harrumph, her hands purred across the keyboard, retrieving files. "Anyways, Cassie Ann is super smart and worldly and she invited me to dinner at her house in Pasadena, which is, like, a crazy Norman Rockwell town."

"I've been to Pasadena."

"Well, ain't you posh. Anyways, we ate fowl, like guinea hen in apricot sludge and the legs, they have, like, them tinfoil Shakespeare collars, and hell, X, those folks eat weird! Anyways, then it was all polite conversation but someone brought up the Loch Ness monster and some girl at the table mentioned a recent theory that the Loch Ness monster was really a whale penis." Though her head didn't move, Joey let her eyes flick over to him. "Spoiler alert: It's me. *I* am the girl in this story."

"You brought up whale penises at a dinner with a family who named their daughter Cassidy Ann?"

"It's true. There was an article on said penises. Google it."

Evan did.

His revulsion at the visuals must have shown on his face, because Joey said, "I know, right? You miss the person you were five seconds ago."

"Isn't Loch Ness freshwater?"

"That's not the point!"

"*Is* there a point, Joey?"

"Yes! So her grandma, who's, like, old enough to be a Daughter of the Confederacy, looks it up on her phone just like you. And she laughed, X! And then everyone at the fancy-ass table was laughing. 'Cuz I made a joke about whale dicks. It was epic. Anyways, afterwards Cassie Ann invited me to join her club for, dunno, women's empowerment or something. That's what they're all about, these college girls. Empowerment."

"Understandable," Evan said. "Just last week I mistook Bruin Plaza for a Kolkata slum."

"X! Don't get all chauvinisty. Rich college girls have feelings, too. Anyways, that's not the point. The point is I'm in my first club! With a bunch of girls who are cool enough to laugh at whale penises."

"As one should."

"Zactly. Okay. Here's the goods." She slid her laptop along the slick concrete slab and Evan caught it before it could zip by.

It showed a digital compendium of various ordnance that had passed through Tommy Stojack's hands recently. Given Tommy's predilection for confidentiality—the precise reason Evan had engaged him for fourteen-plus years—piecing together any of the transfers required a Holmesian reconstruction of shipping receipts, bank wires, and occasionally surviving serial numbers.

Evan's satisfaction that his own cash-only acquisitions were nowhere to be seen didn't last a second before he zeroed in on a Manurhin MR73 Gendarmerie, a Phoenix-S thermal sight, and a Dragunov SVD he knew to have been used by the Wolf to put people in the ground.

The connection between Tommy and the Wolf had been made initially by Evan's documents-and-counterfeit expert, but Joey had picked up the trail as only Joey could.

He clicked through the intel she'd compiled, feeling the heat of her gaze on the side of his face. Any undercurrent of humor had vanished.

It was awful to see it all laid bare in black-and-white.

The First Commandment dictated: *Assume nothing.* But it was hard to conceive of an exonerating interpretation of Tommy's putting lethal weapons in the hands of a killer of innocents. He owed Tommy a final chance to explain himself. And he owed himself— and those he helped—answers and clarity.

Joey had met Tommy through Evan. She was fond of him and Tommy was fond of her. The sense of betrayal cast a long shadow that darkened her face.

A Ph.D. Who Could Win a Bar Fight

Evan looked at her, noticed a faint moistening of her eyes. Not tears welling but outrage pressed to the surface. Joey had met the young woman the Wolf had orphaned and then tried to murder just to cover her tracks. A seventeen-year-old girl, just like her.

"I can't," he told her. "I can't ignore it any longer."

"What are you gonna do, X?" Joey's voice held a slight quaver.

Evan rubbed his face. "Go talk to him."

"Talk. *Talk?* That's not very Nowhere Man–like."

"This isn't a mission," he said. "This is a . . ."

"What?"

"He's my friend."

"What's that mean?"

"It means this is a mission I'm trying to avert."

"Avert?" She blinked twice rapidly. "First time?"

"Yes."

"Why?"

Evan felt a twist in the place beneath his ribs. "Because he's worth it."

3

A Greater Darkness

Las Vegas floated past Evan's passenger window, the skyline muted by dusk. The lights and glitz were amped high in anticipation of nightfall, but without a greater darkness it all looked naked and cheap. So the city hovered purgatorially between drab day and glam night, waiting to transform from a collection of neon and LED bulbs into a state of mind.

Dodging a snarl of mounting traffic, Evan veered his F-150 into the parking lot of a fancy steakhouse at the periphery of the Strip. It wasn't until he'd gone inside and pulled up a distressed leather stool at the dimly lit bar that he realized why he'd decided to pit-stop.

He needed to gather himself for the encounter with Tommy.

The restaurant was quiet and sparsely occupied, only a few patrons speckled throughout the old-school booths. A promising space for him to order his thoughts.

The Fourth Commandment repeated in the back of his mind: *Never make it personal.* He'd run aground of the Fourth before on missions but he'd never started a mission knowing in advance that it would be impossible to uphold.

A Greater Darkness

The minute he left this barstool to head for Tommy's shop, he'd be on uncharted ground, a new topography unswept for land mines, impossible to recon or anticipate. Maybe that's why he'd put off the confrontation.

The bread basket arrived, a bouquet of gluten with an Oreo-size disk of flake-salted butter. He indulged, gazing at the vodka section rising before him, a bulwark of purity.

He'd chosen his seat strategically.

The bartender swept by once more, and once more Evan waved him off politely, wanting more time for his selection. He let his eyes pick across the glass vessels. Tucked behind slender twin towers of Elit was a squat mouth-blown bottle capped with white wax.

When the bartender cycled past once more, Evan pointed. "Tell me about that one."

The bartender warmed his hands against an invisible chill. "This," he said, "is a very special handcrafted vodka." There was a rehearsed cadence to the words—memorized, not understood. His hipster facial hair glistened with styling wax. "Smooth mouthfeel gives way to a constellation of sensation. First? A creamy blend of black pepper and toffee with citrus undertones. Then a hint of vanilla and caramel on the aftertaste. The double-distillation process is overseen by an *actual witch*, who rests it under a full moon during May's lunar eclipse."

Evan said, "Why?"

A few rapid blinks. "It, erhm, cleanses the spirit and imbues it with otherworldly energy. Here, let me show you."

He ducked beneath the bar and came up with an engraved wooden box. Nestled in hay around the impression of the missing bottle were mystical accoutrements expounded upon in a pamphlet. Evan eyed the parapsychological accessories—ritual candles and oils, a rosemary smudge stick, tarot cards, and a trio of crystals designed to manifest abundance and prosperity.

At the moment, Evan craved neither lunar energy nor manifested abundance, but he was game to try a new 88-proof, so he ordered two fingers on a spherical ice cube in a lowball glass.

In seconds the bartender had it before him centered on a coaster, as any good bartender should.

Evan left it sitting before him, letting the fumes reach his nose. A high hard yellow note from the organic-corn base, not entirely pleasant.

The couple in the booth behind him was quarreling, the husband's voice rising above the generalized murmur. Evan held a partial view of them in the mirror backing the bar shelves.

The wife wore a sleeveless blouse. Thin freckled arms, too-red lipstick, flat hair worn plainly down around her shoulders. "It's a lot easier to be the fun one all the time," she replied quietly. "You don't think *I* want that? Just to hang out with him, play video games, eat pizza? But he's starting third grade. He needs more than that."

Evan took a sip. The bites of buttered bread had softened his palate so the vodka hit strong out of the gate.

"—get the hell off my ass." The husband's words cut through like a sword, silencing her. "I wish I'd married someone who was either more ambitious or more content doing whatever the hell you do all day. But to not do shit *and* be miserable not doing it? Uh-uh. No. Don't put that on me."

Evan thought about Tommy's sagging eyes, filled with mischief and affection. And then about the time Tommy had figured out how to literally curve the trajectories of sniper rounds to cover Evan's six o'clock during a shoot-out in a razed block of downtown Los Angeles. Tommy had saved Evan's life that day. Joey's, too.

No greater friend.

He thought about a Manurhin MR73 Gendarmerie and a Phoenix-S thermal sight, a father lying face down on the floor of his town house with an entry hole in the top of his skull and his seventeen-year-old daughter's gaping mouth as she nearly choked out at the hands of the Wolf.

What the hell was he supposed to do with that?

"I don't have the choice to be lazy like you," the husband was saying, his voice pushed low and menacing through clenched teeth. "I have to be a *warrior*, understand? It's not just mortgage sales. No. It's an economic battlefield. I go out into the fight every day to put clothes on your back and keep a roof over your head while all you have to do is clean up after yourself and a seven-year-old and put food on the table a few times a day."

Evan noticed he'd retrieved the broken challenge-coin piece from his cargo pocket and balanced it across the back of his hand like brass knuckles. The stamped phrase peered up at him.

NO WORSE ENEMY.

Slipping the jagged metal back into his pocket, he took a second sip, seeking out the citrus. No, he couldn't taste it, or much of anything else.

He set the glass aside.

The bartender had kept at a respectful remove, tapping at his phone and smoothing his ducktail beard. Now he made his way back and tipped his head at the vodka. "Well?"

Evan said, "Tastes like marketing."

More rapid blinking. "Can I get you something else?"

"No."

A passive-aggressive smile and the bartender retreated once more.

In the reflection Evan watched the wife, slumped back in the booth, slender arms crossed at her stomach, crying silently. Resting on the table next to a pint of beer, the man's bulging wallet sported a decal that read DEATH BEFORE DISHONOR. The husband picked at his molars with a toothpick and then dry-spit a fleck of something onto the carpet.

"You got anything to say?" the man asked his wife.

She shook her head.

"Just gonna sit there and look miserable like always?"

Evan rested a few bills beside his glass and pushed back from the bar. He walked over to the booth. The man watched him approach, his glare intensifying.

Evan stood over him.

"Stand up."

"What?" The guy snickered, made eyes at his wife.

"Stand. Up."

The man did.

He was a few inches taller than Evan, significantly wider through the waist and thighs.

Evan stared right into him. "Hit me."

"What?"

39

"Hit me."

The man had sweated through his shirt in splotches, the tang of his deodorant biting the air. He met Evan's stare, working himself up to something, but it was clear as day that he couldn't work himself up into something big enough to confront what he saw behind Evan's eyes.

Evan didn't move. Didn't blink.

Another freighted moment passed and then the man loosened his posture, gave a dismissive laugh.

"Sit back down," Evan said.

The man sat and folded his hands on the table next to his death-before-dishonor wallet.

Evan said, "Don't talk to your wife that way."

The man studied his thumbs.

Evan started to leave when the woman said, "You know the difference between a bully and a bigger bully?"

Her voice was thin, tremulous.

Evan said, "No, ma'am."

She said, "Neither do I."

Heat came up beneath Evan's face.

He walked out.

Since he'd entered the restaurant, night had come on swift and dark, transforming the skyline into a fire of neon. Hoisting himself up into his rig, he turned over the engine and pulled back onto the freeway, leaving the Strip behind.

His face was still burning.

He hadn't stopped at the bar merely to gather himself to confront Tommy. He'd come to screw up his courage.

But he'd hidden his true aim from himself. So instead he'd worked himself up to play a cheap hero and rightly had a strip torn off for it.

The headlights cut swaths through the night, pointing the way to Tommy's place.

Never make it personal.

Good luck.

4

Pig-Ignorant Sortie

Basked in a chiaroscuro glow from a workbench-mounted swing light, Tommy cast his own bullets while smoking a Camel Wide, a calculated risk he took because he was a goddamned professional in his own goddamned armorer's den and he'd been doing this as long and as well as a Ming dynasty gunsmith.

He tapped a finger of ash into the rusting porthole he used as an ashtray and assessed the tools of his trade. The mold blocks were things of beauty—cast iron, double cavity. A trio of jars housed tallow, beeswax, and lubricant, fringed with goopy excess like honey pots. His two thumbs and seven and a half fingers, ridged with calluses and scar tissue, moved with surprising grace as he finished prepping the cases. Before gunpowder made its entrance in the charging process, he dropped his cigarette into a red Solo cup a quarter full of tobacco spit.

He tapped out allotments of powder from the hopper, weighed them on an old-school balance scale, and fed them through a tiny aluminum funnel into each case. Then over to the press, where he cycled the handle, the ram thrusting up to seat each bullet smoothly into a case mouth, round pegs in round holes just as God intended.

Aside from the orb of illumination casting Tommy and his workbench in a golden, medieval light and the faint gray glow thrown from a bank of wall-mounted security monitors, the lair stretched into seemingly endless darkness. Machines and weapon crates hid in shadow all around, and somewhere at the periphery there were walls.

Tommy didn't need to see anything beyond the bench. None of it even had to exist. Right now there was only the work.

When his phone rang, he started.

Being a gunman meant having his eyes open all the time. Always waiting to see who'd bang on his door in the middle of the night or trail him in his rig or pull up next to him at a stoplight to flash a smile and a shotgun in his direction. He never knew whose brother or son or father was out there waiting to take delivery on a lifetime of resentment. Which meant he couldn't ever let death recede too far in the rearview. No, he had to keep an eye on that nasty bastard morning, day, and night with teeth-gritting resolve.

It was wearying.

And now he had Evan to worry about, too. His own damn friend. Evan had found out that Tommy had supplied weapons to the Wolf. Nothing had been made overt; they'd just picked at the edges of the conversation, but Tommy knew Evan had keyed in, and Evan knew Tommy knew, and Tommy knew he knew he knew, so it was only a matter of time before they'd have to square up.

Tommy grabbed the phone, clicked to answer: "Pawpaw's Pre-Masticated Meals Fer Seniors, would you like to look at one of our nutrition plans?"

"Uh . . . Mr. Stojack?" A hoarse voice of a young man, maybe early twenties.

"Last I checked."

"This is Delmont Hickenlooper, Jr., sir."

Tommy shoved back a few feet on his rolling chair, hoisted his battle-weary legs up, and set his heels on the bench. "Hick's boy?"

After the Arab Spring, Tommy had done some off-the-books cleanup work in Yemen with Delmont Senior. An irascible sonuvabitch who'd bled out in Tommy's arms in the grain shed of a shit village to the north of Raqah. Abdominal mortar wounds, the cruelest way to go, two and a half hours of agonizingly slow exsanguination. Not once had Hick whimpered or cried, not with the Houthis sweeping the roads and rubble outside. He hadn't even let fear into his eyes. He'd just lain in Tommy's lap, his blood-crusted hand gripping Tommy's elbow, telling Tommy to choke him out if he started convulsing or making noise.

Tommy was grateful he hadn't had to. He didn't need another ghost floating around inside his head.

Hick had been as mean as he was tough. The only glimmer of humanity to break through in those final hours was the promise he'd extracted from Tommy to look after his boys if they ever needed backup or bail money.

Well, here it was.

"That's right," the boy said. "You can call me Hick, too. Hick Junior if you want, but with the old man gone, you don't really gotta specify."

"Okay, Junior. Why you ringing me?"

"I need . . . I need your help."

"Goddamn it," Tommy said. "I got enough problems of my own."

"The old man said to—"

"Yeah, I know. Don't you have brothers?"

"Did."

"Did?"

"Fentanyl."

"Both of them?"

"Richie and Dale both, yeah."

Tommy blocked the phone against his neck, cocked back in his chair, and blew a breath up toward the ceiling. Another two notches for the opioid scytheman.

Phone back up, his mustache brooming the screen. "What happened?"

"I told you. They overdosed."

"Not to them, stupid. To you."

"What? Oh." A long pause. "Some Mexicans got killed."

43

The passive construction pissed Tommy off. "What, they were running with scissors and tripped in unison?"

"Huh?"

"Went down in a hail of Acme safes?"

"Sorry, sir. I don't—"

"Jesus Christ. How'd they get killed, Junior?"

"They was run over. So I'm lying low."

"I'm failing to make the connection here, boy. Or you are. Are you to blame?"

A long silence. "Yeah."

Tommy's legs had fallen asleep. He used his hands to pull them down off the workbench, one after another. Pins, needles, flares, shooting pains, and more whathaveyou. Like the goddamned Fourth of July in his femurs. "Where ya at?"

"Town of Calvary, sir."

"Plenty of Calvarys, Junior. I assume it's pinned down on a map and not a floating empire?"

Hick named the state.

It'd be a drive.

"You got any other people?"

"No. Friends, sort of."

Sort of.

"You got church?"

A long pause. "Not really, no."

Tommy's joints ached. He'd need some time to pack and organize his gear. And before heading off on some pig-ignorant sortie, he'd have to load up with go pills.

"Text me the address," Tommy said.

"It's secret," Hick said. "I'm hiding."

"How'm I supposed to help your running-folks-over ass if I don't know where you are?"

"You coming?"

"I'll see what I can do."

An alert on the security monitors caught Tommy's focus.

A Ford F-150 sweeping up the dirt drive. Its headlights coaxed horror-movie shadows from the engine blocks and rusting car husks he kept out front as props to augment the auto-repair-shop façade he hid his operation behind.

He recognized the truck.

He should.

He'd built it.

"You'll hear from me," he told Hick, and hung up.

His knees and ankles creaked when he rose to amble to the sturdy metal front door. His boots knocked against the oil-spotted concrete, echoing in the darkness.

He paused.

Leaning to his side on a creaky hip, he snatched up a Benelli combat shotgun resting against one of the lathes.

Then he headed out to face Evan.

5

A Streak of Bad

As Evan eased his pickup forward along the loosely packed dirt drive, his heart jerked in his chest.

Atypical.

The rusted auto-repair sign over the reinforced metal door was lit, as if Tommy were expecting him. The long-necked security cameras on the low-slung roof swiveled to track his arrival, an unsettling humanoid effect. Tommy always shut them off before Evan arrived, but he knew the deal wouldn't hold. Not this time.

He was glad he'd worn one of his tactical shirts, not just because of the magnetic buttons that would quicken his reach for his holster, but because of the adversarial pattern woven into the design. The pattern, the least ugly and most muted available, thwarted the artificial neural networks used for object recognition, rendering him undetectable to artificial-intelligence deep-learning systems. It did so by adding a storm of pixel noise to fuzz the thresholds and criteria by which AI could determine whether something was an object or not—or a person. For all surveillance intents and purposes, Evan was not here.

A Streak of Bad

The Nowhere Man.

He parked the F-150 and climbed out. Gusts of dirt plumed up behind the wheel wells and then drifted toward him like an armada of sluggish ghosts, enveloping him and putting grit in his lungs. When the air cleared once more, he felt calm.

Operational calm.

That's what this was now, he reminded himself. An operation.

He moved cautiously toward the front door. The neon sign crackled and hummed. He checked the rooftop, windows, eyed sight lines from the surrounding sand dunes. Felt the comforting weight of his ARES 1911 in the appendix carry holster. Every sense went to high alert—the taste of the desert wind, sweat drying on the small of his back, the jangle of a loose piece of cladding lifted sporadically by the breeze.

Before he could raise a hand to knock, the clank of a lifted security bar announced Tommy's presence behind the door. A pair of dead bolts retracted into their holes, vibrating the air, and then the façade gaped open on squealing hinges and Tommy stood backlit in the darkness, a silhouette of a man, shotgun at his side pointed at the floor. A few bristles from his biker mustache stood out, limned gold from a single light source somewhere back in the belly of the shop.

Evan said, "I'm guessing you know why I'm here."

His voice was steady, calm as ever.

Tommy stood still. Then his head shifted up, down. He was wearing a battered trucker cap just as he'd been when Evan had met him, and all there was of his eyes was twinning glints beneath the brim. "We fightin' or talkin'?"

"Talking," Evan said. "For now."

Tommy leaned to prop the gun in the corner just out of sight.

He said, "Fire pit."

The imposing door winged shut, wafting a breeze across Evan's cheeks.

It was not lost on him that Tommy was making him walk around the outside of the building rather than inviting him through. The shop had a larger footprint than it seemed from the inside, giving Evan time, his thoughts punctuated by the crunch of his footsteps.

When he reached the back, Tommy was already sitting in a crooked lawn chair. Another rested on its side across from a roaring cedar fire.

Evan set the second chair up on its legs and lowered himself into it. He remembered the two of them sitting here one night taking potshots at empty bottles of Jack Daniel's with a refurbished Borchardt C-93 from the late nineteenth century. They'd shattered the bottles one after another. Well, Tommy had. Evan had mostly missed, the antique gun with its iron sights too idiosyncratic for his precision training. That night felt like yesterday. It also felt like a decade ago.

The wind was at the fire now, shoving it to and fro, sparks lifting up to die in the night chill.

Tommy didn't have a bottle with him and he hadn't offered one to Evan. They'd never sat out here to contemplate the universe without lubrication before, but it was clear they required sober clarity for the conversation ahead.

"You know how this goes," Tommy said. "I work for other people, too. People with a streak of bad like you. Maybe some got even wider streaks than you."

Evan looked at him through the flames. Tommy's eyes were dark. He couldn't see into them very much and it wasn't just because of the nighttime.

Tommy met his stare for maybe a full minute; then his eyes darted away, discomfort breaching as anger. "You never worked with fucking bastards?"

Evan held his gaze steady.

"When I was in the wavy navy, we used to talk about Churchill bombing the French fleet at Mers el-Kébir. One thousand, two hundred ninety-seven Frenchmen died. All of them allies not seven days prior. That man took their souls, sunk a battleship, and winged five others just to keep that fleet from falling into Nazi hands. Big men make big choices, Evan. Life's messy. There's collateral. What matters is our brothers. Loyalty above all else."

"Except honor," Evan said.

"I don't gotta answer to you. Whatever choices I've made, I've squared it with my God."

"Convenient."

"Convenient? Fuck you, strong letter to follow. Asking forgiveness ain't a lap around the dog park. You gotta figure out all the shit you did wrong first. All of it, link by link. Then you hit your knees and turn it over. Either that or you carry it the rest of your life and then what good're you to anyone else? I figured it out. Between me and upstairs." Tommy pointed to the stars. "Who the hell are you to come into it now?"

Tommy's hands twitched, as if eager for a flask or a Camel Wide. No alcohol, no cigarettes, no chewing tobacco, no coffee. Just a man in the elements looking at another man across a pit of fire.

"The worm has turned, man," Tommy said. "People don't give a shit no more. They wanted to tear it all apart. Well, here we are. Cities and towns, the whole damn country torn apart. Everything's a fucking hustle now. All of it is."

"There have to be lines," Evan said.

"Lines? You mean like good guys and bad guys? Cowboys and Indians? Nah. Everyone's got feet of clay. Everyone's not enough. Everyone breaks. Life breaks everyone. What are you holding on for? For what? The grand fucking narrative? It's all a farce. All of it. Except the brothers at your side. Me . . ." Tommy's voice caught a wobble and for one terrible moment Evan thought it might crack. "Me and you."

Through flame and darkness, Evan stared at him.

"That has to matter more," Tommy said. "Than anything else."

"It doesn't. There has to be more."

"There isn't, young man. There isn't."

"There has to be."

"Why? Because without your code you're just a murderer?" Tommy's gaze skewered him. "Well, without mine the world's not worth living in."

"What's your code, Tommy?"

"The world consists of those who have your back. And everyone else. That's my fucking code."

Evan stared at him, dead-eyed.

Tommy's mouth shifted and shifted again and then pressed tight into a line, the thinned lips of anger. "You don't want to come for me, son. You've gotten soft in ways you don't understand."

"Soft?"

"Living in that city with your fancyboy cocktails and kombucha enemas."

Evan recalled with some chagrin the two sips of moonlight-imbued vodka he'd imbibed not an hour ago.

"Flyin' around on planes, having your gear delivered with a bow, playing daddy to sugarbritches."

"Don't pretend you don't have a streak of affection for Joey," Evan said.

"Course I do. I would go to war for her. But not *with* her. You've forgotten the difference. Soft. Makes sense you don't know what's what. You don't get the human side of things. Never have. You view everything like a . . . like some kinda math equation. Reality don't fit into that."

Beneath his rib cage, Evan felt an unraveling, the sensation of his insides coming unspooled. His deepest doubts shoved to the surface, a shiv of bone through the skin, naked in the cold night.

He swallowed.

The broken half of the challenge coin had made its way out of his pocket once more. He was shuttling it across his knuckles, a nervous tell, so he set it on the arm of the lawn chair, where it teetered but held balance.

"No one gets outta this rodeo alive," Tommy said. "But now and again we get to pick our poison. If I go down, it'll be in a pile of brass. And it'll be for something worth going down for. You want to go down over this?"

"You gonna kill me, Tommy?"

The fire kicked high so now there was just a gravelly voice coming through the flame: "I can't blow that bridge up till I get to it." When the wind settled, Tommy was right there, a dark reflection of Evan across the pit. "You coming for me? Is that what this is?"

Evan looked at him.

The brim of Tommy's cap rose and fell not an inch and then did it again, the effect sinister.

"Good people died because of the steel you put in their hands," Evan said. "I saw it with my own eyes. The Wolf knew she was killing innocents. And you knew she would use what you gave her to kill them." Evan couldn't bring himself to phrase it as a question but the last word ticked up at the end and Tommy answered by not answering. "I can't let that go. The last piece. I don't know where to put it."

"Ignore it. It ain't yours."

"No. The mission. When you gave that woman the tools she required, you made yourself part of my mission. And I have to finish the mission."

"The mission ended when she did."

"No," Evan said. "That's how it starts. The smallest compromise. But it doesn't stop there. There'll be another. And another."

"That's the problem with you, Evan. You see the universe as . . . dunno. Moral."

"No," Evan said. "I just see it."

"You got enough money to burn a wet mule. Go find another armorer. Another . . ." Tommy's voice hitched. "Another friend. We part ways. Don't come back here."

"I can't promise that."

"You try'n lay hands on me, there's gonna be slow singing and flower bringing."

Evan stood. Despite the night chill, he'd sweated through his shirt.

Tommy rose as well. It took a good bit longer.

They stared at each other.

Tommy beckoned with three and a half fingers. "C'mere."

Evan approached warily and they stood before each other and there was more information in Tommy's eyes than Evan could process in two lifetimes.

"Brother," Tommy said. "I'm gonna miss you."

"Right back at you, brother."

Tommy hooked his neck, pulled him in for an embrace.

He smelled of cigarette smoke and long-cut tobacco and a faint note of sandalwood cologne on his shirt from a previous outing.

Tommy gave Evan's back two avuncular taps and then pushed him away firmly but not too hard and fixed him with a flat stare. Nothing that had been in his eyes before remained. "Now get off my property."

Evan's legs held steady but they felt dead beneath him as he walked away. He sensed Tommy behind him every step of the way. It felt like an eternity until he turned the corner of the building.

Out of sight, he walked across stone and sand toward the dirt drive where he'd left his truck. A fingernail moon was slung crooked and low in the sky like someone had thrown it there. It watched his progress, unimpressed.

He pulled himself up into his rig, the rig Tommy had built to spec for him. The driver's seat held the shape of his body sure as his holster fit his 1911. The holster was from Tommy. The pistol, too.

Evan's breathing felt irregular, like he had to remember to do it. His clothes clung to him, the sweat-clammy fabric choking him, a claustrophobic second skin.

His engine roared to life. The noise shattered the fragile equilibrium in his mind, relegating what had just gone down to the past. He was driving away from a whole version of himself.

It wasn't until he'd reached the frontage road that he remembered he'd left his half of the challenge coin resting on the arm of Tommy's lawn chair.

6

The Weakest Link

The front door to Evan's condo looked like every other front door in the Castle Heights Residential Tower. Raised panels, engineered cross-grain patterns, thin wood laminate of a dated honey-colored hue. But underneath, the steel interior housed a water core designed to impede a battering ram.

When Evan threw the lock, a labyrinth of hidden security bolts withdrew their tentacled clutch from the doorframe. A nearly imperceptible sloshing sound accompanied the door's swinging inward. He crossed the threshold, heeled the door shut, and exhaled.

The encounter with Tommy simmered inside him. He could still taste the cedar fire, the grit in his mouth. Snapshots of his friend popped like camera flashes in his mind's eye, that grizzled face through the dancing wall of flame, the depth in those sagging eyes and then that flatness.

You don't want to come for me, son.

Glass walls provided stellar views of Century City to the south and showcased the downtown nightscape in the not-too-distant east. A freestanding fireplace rose like a tree trunk in the center of the great room, offset by a sinistral staircase thrusting up to the reading room. The wiped-clean surfaces of the spotless kitchen with its stainless-steel fixtures gleamed. An earthy scent wafted from herbs and nightshades sprouting from a drip-fed vertical garden, a wall of nature that breathed his opposite, carbon dioxide to his oxygen that nourished him on top of that.

You've gotten soft in ways you don't understand.

A bizarre sensation struck him. He was rich. It was a rich man's penthouse. Of course it was, but he saw it now as such for the first time.

He didn't like it.

His hands twitched.

He texted Joey: Need backup.

The dot-dot-dots blinked, heralding her response, which came not two seconds later: c u in 1 hr.

Instead of lounging around like an affluent asshole, he changed into workout gear. His thoughts were a storm, so he took stock of his body. Aching shoulders, tight hamstrings, a sharp complaint on the left side of his neck shooting down into his trapezius.

Grabbing a fresh bottle of Advil from his bathroom, he popped the lid, punched a thumb through the tamper-resistant seal, and peeled it off. He palmed three pills into his mouth, swallowed them dry. A stubborn strip of foil clung to the mouth of the plastic bottle. He dug at it with his thumb, trying to lift it, but his nail wasn't long enough and the seam of foil was crammed tightly around the lip. It was driving him crazy, making his brain itch.

Ignore it.

He couldn't.

He couldn't let it go with Tommy.

He had no idea how.

His repeated efforts frayed his thumbnail. He was already reaching for the tweezers to pry up the foil by the time he realized that his OCD had run away with him. With considerable effort he stopped himself, screwed the lid back on over the perfidious strip of safety foil, and shoved the Advil out of sight in the medicine cabinet.

The Weakest Link

He sensed it there even as he walked out of the master suite and down the brief hall to sit cross-legged on the training mat.

He did some circular breathing, blocking one nostril and then the other, cycling the breath in one direction and then the next to connect the hemispheres of his brain. When he'd first been taught the technique, he'd thought it was a bunch of guru body-hack bullshit.

Until he didn't.

Don't come back here.

His tight hamstrings usually sourced to his lower back, so he planned the angle of attack. He couldn't find the right position, so he grabbed the elaborate remote control and coaxed the flat-screen up from its slot in the floor. He called up a recording of a yin yoga instructor and let her voice wash over him. She was a fit practitioner of her trade, young and feminine, and she guided him deeper into his body.

The Second Commandment: *How you do anything is how you do everything.*

Every stretch ran through his left groin. The weakest link. It had sustained the kind of damage he could only treat and contain, never heal. So he did everything he could to keep the muscle healthy, nourishing it for the inevitable next tear. Equipment maintenance, same as with any weapon.

You try'n lay hands on me, there's gonna be slow singing and flower bringing.

He needed to feel greater pain and so he rose from the mat to beat it into himself on the heavy bag, blow by burning blow. It raged in his biceps and forearms and shoulders and it was intolerable but he tolerated it and then tolerated it a little bit more until he collapsed against the bag, clinging to it, his arms barely strong enough to hold him vertical.

Now get off my property.

He was opened up now, could feel the oxygenated blood flow into the nooks and crannies of his damaged but enduring body.

He had to go back to Las Vegas.

He had to confront Tommy again and see if he could break through.

He had to make it right.

And if he couldn't, he had to make Tommy answer for what he had done.

Whatever that meant.

Across the great room, he heard the scratch of Joey's key at the lock. Then the metallic cacophony of shifting bars and hidden gears. Rucksack on, laptop in hand, Dog in her wake, she breezed in and plopped on the black leather couch.

Evan sat on his heels with his legs bent under him, a screaming toe-crunch asana that compressed his knees and stretched the arches of the feet. It ached but he didn't want to come out of the shape to greet her. His mood felt thick and dark, and when Dog came over to wet-nose him, he pushed the boy's big head aside.

Joey scowled at him. "Dogs are easy. They don't ask for much. All they want is your undivided adoration. People are that way, too. Hint hint, nudge nudge."

He was irritated, Tommy's words still working on him. He wondered how much of a fruity Californian he'd become, collecting ridiculous vodkas and doing yin fucking yoga.

Joey said, "You okay?"

"Yes."

He felt cold and withdrawn, uncharacteristically angry with her. It made no sense.

"How'd it go with Tommy?"

He told her.

Dog had curled up at her feet. Through the course of the story, Joey hunched more and more forward, digging her nails into his scruff. His head jogged languidly as she scratched, his eyes closed with contentment. Her emerald gaze was large and focused and she looked just shy of alarmed.

"What are you gonna do?"

"Go after him."

"Go after him or *go after* him?"

"That's up to him."

"He said not to come back."

"People say lots of things."

"Yeah. But it's *Tommy*."

"I need you to monitor his future transactions. I need to know if he's still running guns for assassins."

"Assassins who aren't you?"

He hit her with a glare and she recoiled a bit.

She reset herself. "Okay, look. It feels weird 'cuz it's Tommy but I'm watching his bank accounts." She slid off the couch, sat beside Evan, and flipped open her laptop. A series of memes were still up on the screen and he caught sight of the top one before she closed the tab. "I've been monitoring wire transactions—"

"Hang on a second. What was that?"

"What?"

"That image. The top one. Pull it back up."

She did.

It showed a cartoon of an Arab man with a long beard and dark eyes stomping a jackboot down on the shoulder blades of a woman in a hijab sprawled prone on the ground before him. The man was dressed in stereotypical clothes—wool *pakol* hat, *perahan tunban* with a cotton scarf. The meme read: INJUSTICE AGAINST WOMEN ANYWHERE IS A THREAT TO JUSTICE EVERYWHERE.

Evan said calmly, "What is that, Joey?"

"It's just one of the memes Cassidy Ann made. You know, the club I told you about."

"You're making propaganda?"

"What are you talking about? It's a paraphrased Martin Luther King quote."

At her tone, Dog lifted his head and eyed her and then Evan warily.

"I can have an opinion about women being mistreated. And besides, I'm just helping the club propagate it. I didn't *make* it."

He stayed quiet, letting her argument eat itself.

She slammed her laptop closed and shot to her feet. "I'm not asking for a lesson, X. I came here to help *you*. And women are being subjugated—"

He left the pose creakily, the joints of his legs burning. "How much time have you spent in the Arab world, Joey?"

"I don't have to in order to know—"

"Ever put your life in the hands of a female 'terp? Bartered weapons with a Tajik *mujahidat*? Negotiated safe passage with a female militia in Raqqa?"

Joey's face reddened. She was breathing hard, nostrils flaring. "Okay. So you know everything and I don't."

"No. I killed a lot of bad people in that part of the world—Hamas, al-Qaeda, Boko Haram. And I survived with the help of good, brave people there. If you can't tell the difference, don't step onto the battlefield."

"I didn't! It's just a meme!"

He said, "Did you acquire *any* ground truth on the population you and Cassidy Ann of Pasadena are speaking for?"

"You have no right to question me for standing up for women."

"Save outrage for higher stakes."

"Don't tell me how to feel."

"I'm not telling you how to feel. I'm telling you what's strategic."

"You don't get to decide what's strategic."

"Jack hammered *years* of cross-cultural competence training into me so I wouldn't step on my own dick the minute I deployed. The real world is complicated. More complicated than a meme."

"I'm not *deploying*."

"You're propagating psyops on the internet."

"What the hell, X!" She flung her laptop onto the couch. "*Everything* is on the internet. What am I supposed to do? How am I supposed to have friends? I get it—I'm not an Orphan. But you don't want me to *just* be a normal college kid either. I can't live up to all the standards all the time. How am I supposed to be in the world?"

He pointed at the laptop. "There is nothing in *that* world worth being."

"That's not the answer. That *can't* be the answer." She started packing up furiously, ramming her laptop into her rucksack. The toe of her Doc Marten nudged Dog's ribs and he flew up as if he'd been zapped with a cattle prod. Slinging her rucksack around a shoulder, she stomped to the door, Dog trotting at her side.

The front door slammed.

This time he heard the sloshing water more clearly.

The Weakest Link

Whatever measure of calm he'd instilled in himself had evaporated.

Tommy's words chewed on his brain stem. Was Evan really using a college girl as his backup on the most treacherous mission of his life? Why was he wasting his time edifying a seventeen-year-old about online war games? *Had* he gotten soft in ways he didn't understand?

Cracking his neck, he strode to the kitchen to grab a spherical ice cube before heading back to his bathroom. The shower handle hummed slightly when he gripped it, hidden sensors reading the vein pattern in his palm. A secret door clicked open, its outline concealed in the tiled wall.

He stepped through into the Vault, a roughly furnished four-hundred-square-foot cubby of space beneath the public stairs to the roof. Weapon lockers. L-shaped sheet-metal desk housing hardware. OLED screens tiling three of the walls.

Vera III spun lethargically in a state of levitation, her tiny white pod floating above its magnetic base. A fist-size aloe vera plant, she required scant enough maintenance that even Evan could manage to keep her alive. She needed only a cluster of rainbow-colored glass pebbles for her roots and the occasional ice cube nestled in the artichoke splay of her leaves to water her.

She received the ice cube with silent gratitude. He was pleased to see she was faring better than her two predecessors, who'd died, respectively, from neglect and a fireball.

His mind was made up. He'd drive back to Tommy's shop in the morning, talk under the sun of a new day. Less shadow, fewer hiding places. They'd see each other's faces more clearly. Maybe that would help.

If not, there'd be clear lines of sight for whatever kind of exchange would follow.

Every single last thing would have to be perfect.

Swinging open the door to one of the weapon lockers, Evan pulled out a matte-black Benelli M1 combat shotgun, a perfect match of the one Tommy had wielded at the door. Of course it was; Tommy had acquired it for him.

Evan fed it seven solid slugs, slotted one more in the chamber, and ghost-loaded a ninth on the lifter. They were door-openers and hinge-destroyers, necessary in case Tommy didn't answer when he knocked and he needed to force the conversation. Once he was in, verbal engagement, even heated, would be preferable, since neither of them would be eager to throw lead in an armorer's shop loaded with Chinese stick grenades and spools of det cord.

Next he field-tested his Strider knife. No residual flecks of blood from Stavros's house, no corrosion on the blade, no give on the screws, no lint hiding out in the slot of the handle. One drop of lubrication at the hinge, one over the locking mechanism. He polished the hooked nodule atop the blade designed to catch the pocket edge on the draw. He dropped the folding knife into the front left pocket of his workout shorts and pulled it a few times, snapping it open. The action was smooth as ever.

Last he double-checked the ammo for his 1911. He unloaded and reloaded the magazine, examining all eight rounds before thumbing them back in and gauging the tension of the spring. He slotted the mag into his ARES, quick-dropped it from the well. No hitch.

Then he validated the next magazine.

And then another.

He could take care of his own goddamned gear just like he had before Tommy.

Tomorrow.

Tomorrow was a day that would change everything.

Evan took a blistering-hot shower to burn his looping thoughts into submission, but they paid little heed. He couldn't sleep, so he went back out to the leather couch. A scattering of dog hair remained in the shape of a crescent on the floor, an echo of Dog.

He swept it up with wet paper towels and then sprayed cleaning solution and wiped that up as well before taking a seat. The flatscreen TV remained above-floor, the obsidian rectangle throwing back his reflection. He felt small sitting alone in the yawning chasm of the great room.

His chest felt heavy. And his face.

Sadness.

That's what sadness felt like.

The Weakest Link

With his remote, he powered on the rogue GSM base station he'd recently popped up on his east-facing balcony and then clicked the TV to life and accessed YouTube. Surfing the offerings, he let the algorithms nibble at his preferences for a few minutes before they led him to a montage of oddly satisfying videos of soap cutting, paint mixing, ice cutting, hydraulic pressing, fruit cutting, slime shoving through colanders, pressure washers stripping paint.

Tiny clips of symmetry and repetition that massaged his brain.

The heaviness in his chest and face did not dissipate, but he grew tired.

He let the algorithms soothe him until he could no longer keep his eyes open.

7

Waiting to Go Boom

Even in December the desert sun was blinding, heat wobbling the asphalt at the horizon. Every reflective road marker, every passing windshield, every steel billboard outrigger felt like a scalpel to the eye. When Evan exited the freeway, the surrounding hills were no less vivid. Sand and scrub and brush blazing at him in golds and yellows.

Despite the air conditioner cranked up high, he still felt waves of warmth rolling off the baking dashboard.

The shotgun rested in the footwell of the passenger seat, barrel to the floor mat. His Strider was snugged in his left front pocket, his loaded pistol in the appendix holster, and he had two spare mags tucked in the streamlined inner pockets of his tactical-discreet cargo pants.

As he neared the turn to Tommy's place, he felt his temperature rising and told himself it was the Vegas heat. His pickup bounced along the road for a time and then the dirt drive came up and before he could lose nerve he goosed the gas and pointed for the armorer's shop.

Waiting to Go Boom

Confronting his friend again required a blatant approach—nothing sneaky, nothing untoward. He parked on the sand not ten feet from the big steel front door, a here-I-am arrival, and stepped out of the cab, bringing the shotgun but holding it loosely at his side as he pocketed his keys.

He figured he'd at least have a chance to raise the question of why he'd—

His right foot blew out from under him. He was already airborne, leg flung wide from impact, by the time he heard the supersonic crack of the sniper round.

Facedown in the dirt, grit caking his teeth, he looked at his tingling right foot, expecting a morass of red. His leg was still intact but a chunk of tread the size of a deck of cards had been blown off the front of his boot, the toe torn open to expose his miraculously intact foot inside a bright white sock.

He stifled a cough, chin grinding into the earth, already looking to the surrounding dunes. At his one o'clock atop a sandy rise three hundred meters to the north, a scope glinted.

Before the rifle could be cycled, he rolled back toward his pickup, clanging an elbow against the running board. Tucked in behind the truck, he unlaced his shredded boot and checked his toes. Intact if numb from when the thermoplastic toe box had torqued open. A steel cup likely would've severed the top of his foot.

Tommy was the finest marksman he'd come across anywhere in the world.

He wouldn't miss a shot like this.

He hadn't been shooting to kill, not yet, but he'd been willing to take off Evan's foot.

But Tommy also would never fire on anyone he wasn't willing to kill.

Sweat beaded at Evan's hairline. When he wiped his forehead, dirt sandpapered his skin. He had no time for disbelief. His friend had set up on the hill, lying in wait.

Inching toward the bumper of the truck, he held the loose Original S.W.A.T. before him, poking it out into view.

Another round took the boot clean out of his hand, hammering it against the wall of the building.

He rolled back to cover.

Two-second inhale. Four-second exhale.

He cycled his breathing once more.

That was about all he had time for.

He knew better than to engage here and now. Not with Tommy on higher ground behind a long gun. He was grateful he'd kept his limbs intact. He had to retreat and reengage later. The Unofficial Eleventh Commandment: *Don't fall in love with Plan A.*

Withdrawing farther behind the truck, he tapped his cargo pocket, checking for his car keys.

Not in there.

He'd just been pocketing them when he'd been knocked off his boots.

He glanced around, caught a glint at the base of Tommy's big steel door.

Wide-open ground, zero cover.

Shit.

Retrieving the keys would require he leave cover, putting him in the crosshairs for at least three seconds.

Three seconds was two and a half seconds longer than Tommy would need.

Evan debated crawling into the truck and hot-wiring it, but at his own instruction Tommy had built in countermeasures against tampering. It would be a twenty-minute project, him sitting in a metal box with a built-in tank of fuel waiting to go boom.

He eyed the beckoning keys once more. He might have time to grab them if he could do so with slowing momentum to reverse direction. Which meant continuing through the metal front door, regrouping, then making a run for the truck once he had the keys in hand.

Plucking the Benelli from the sand, he put his shoulders against the truck, took aim at the spot where the metal door's lower hinge would be, and fired. The solid lead slug punched a hole through the metal façade. Through the jagged tunnel he could see the reinforced hinge twisted up from the jamb, still holding on.

Boom.

He took a second bite out, the hinge flying away to jangle across the armory floor.

Boom boom boom.

Middle hinge gone.

Door still standing strong, a formidable rise.

He grouped three more shots around the top hinge but the door didn't fall. From his lower vantage he couldn't see through the breach to know which part of the hinge was still intact.

Down to the ninth and final shell, he aimed at the lower end of the twisted metal maw and let fly.

The door absorbed the blast, wobbling in the frame.

He waited for it to fall.

It didn't.

Was the door merely held in place by inertia or was the top hinge still partially intact? If so, was it barely holding on by a screw? He could pepper the door with his ARES, but .45s didn't have nearly the same energy as shotgun slugs, and besides, he didn't want to push his luck firing into a building brimming with ordnance.

At the base of the door, his keys gleamed like treasure in the sand.

He couldn't wait longer for Tommy to reposition on the sand dune and open up a better angle on him.

He had to get off the X.

He pulled off his other boot and sat a moment clutching it to his chest, organizing his thoughts. Removing both socks, he cast them aside. He hated fighting barefoot but he couldn't risk slipping on the concrete floor if he got inside.

Then he crawled to the rear tire and set the boot tread down just behind it. Back to the middle of the truck, rising up onto his haunches, legs beneath him ready to explode.

Picking up the shotgun, he slid it along the sand until the muzzle nudged up against the heel of the boot.

Two-second inhale. Four-second exhale.

He pressed the shotgun evenly against the boot so it slid upright along the dirt a few inches, nudged into sight.

He braced.

An instant later, a sniper round whined in, struck the boot, and sent it spinning up in the air like a top.

He bolted.

Running at the metal door, ducked low, hand sweeping to snatch the keys up, metal against his palm, sand spilling through the loose clutch of his fist. He hurtled sideways into the door, leading with his shoulder.

Each instant stretched out with operational clarity, bare foot driving into the earth, his deltoid striking metal. A shudder of resistance sent a spike of fear through his spinal cord that he was gonna ping-pong right off the door and sprawl flat before the reticle. Pressure rising to full impact, his momentum slowing, a creak, a groan, and then the mighty door tumbled inward.

He landed atop it inside and rolled gracelessly up and across his face, the heat of the sun-beaten door scorching his cheek. A pop in his neck, his spine screaming from the inadvertent scorpion stretch, and then he barrel-rolled onto his bare feet.

He barely had time to rise from his awkward crouch before a burly figure differentiated itself from the sudden dimness of the armory, lunging. A tanto knife flashed in the spill of outside light as it whipped toward Evan's throat.

8

The Angel-Devil Push-Pull

There was no time for information to travel from Evan's eyes to his prefrontal cortex for processing. The threat of the incoming blade bounced straight off his brain stem, igniting muscle memory.

Limboing back, twisting into a reverse turning kick, shoulders torqueing first, leg whipping to follow. He aimed for his attacker's knee, hammering it with his full spinning momentum. Shuddering impact.

Only when he finished the spin did he register who he'd struck.

The man was a hair over six feet, two-thirty of prison muscle. Black high-tops, baggy cargo shorts, a T-shirt with a very low V-neck showing off a wide tattoo at the sternum—a cross-shaped keyhole with Jesus peering through.

The kick had knocked his kneecap out of place and up the thigh, impeding the outer fang of the quad muscle. The whole leg was locked, immobilized, patella and sinew and muscle frozen in knotty confusion.

The man screamed.

It was gut-turning.

Still he clenched the big knife, but his knuckles were pinked up, a fresh looseness to the fist. Before he could reacquire a grip or his composure, Evan shuffle-stepped into a shotokan front thrust kick, chambering his leg, and drove his bare heel forward into the seized-up junction of the limb.

A demolition sound, splintering and tearing and crackling, a terrible symphony of permanent wreckage. The man's mouth was wide and quavering, the sweat-glistening line of his incipient mustache bent tragically, a parenthesis knocked horizontal.

Evan's Strider snapped open as he drew it from his front left pocket. The blade described a fluid arc as he flicked it at the man's throat, liberating the Prince of Peace from the inked crown of thorns.

No time for the guy to make a noise, just the suck of the lungs through the new aperture as he fell away, landing thunderously atop the metal door and sending a cymbal-clash in percussive waves off the hard surfaces.

The vibration barely had time to still before Evan became aware of rustling movement from various spots deep in the lair. He dove from the doorway's shaft of light, racking himself up against a rusting lathe in the shadows.

He was still clutching his keys in his right hand. Having learned his lesson, he zipped them into a cargo pocket. Then he quieted his breath and focused his ear on shaping the noises from the interior into a head count.

Four, five, a half dozen.

And—likely—Tommy still outside behind a sniper rifle.

Tommy had planned the ambush well. There'd been no vehicles outside, no tire tracks. The numbers were bad, Evan's position worse.

He had come prepared for a painful confrontation, but now he was in the teeth of a far worse situation. Footfall and breathing coalesced around him, hard to differentiate in the enclosed darkness.

He felt a rising fear, holstered it.

The good news was that he knew this space intimately, better than any tattoo-intensive thugs Tommy had brought in. And Tommy had taken higher ground outside, ceding home-field advantage.

Evan turned on the lathe, slapping the spindle speed to high. As the whine of machinery rose to a scream, he darted between a cold saw and an Electro Arc disintegrator, powering them up as he passed. An industrial chorus at full volume.

There was some shouting now, a welcome confusion.

As he crawled up a narrow aisle between machines, his palms turned sticky and the knees of his cargo pants grew soggy with oil. He peered beneath a belt sander, discerned partial forms in the semidarkness. Three of the men spread at fifteen-meter intervals, knives flashing in hands.

A voice from the back was loud and firm but oddly calm: "Don't shoot. Do not shoot. There's explosive shit everywhere."

A silhouette came clear between workbenches, easing forward in front of a line of carbon-steel ammo cans. Drawing his ARES, Evan jack-in-the-boxed up from his hidden crouch. He aimed directly for the heart so the bullet would careen around inside the rib cage rather than escape through an exit wound and light off the several hundred pounds of .50-cal BMG rounds forming the backdrop.

At least that was the hope.

He squeezed off a single shot. The man's outline jerked as it caught lead, the face twisted into the dim rising light of a power strip's glow—one acned cheek and long curled eyelashes. Evan ducked back out of sight before the body could tumble. He braced but no secondary explosion came; the man's torso had held up its end of the bargain. A split second later came the sound of dead weight hitting the deck.

Five to go.

That same voice, still shy of a shout: "Don't return fire. Do. Not. We're in a tinderbox. Knives and fists. When we pin him down, we can take our time with him."

As the men regrouped, Evan scrambled on all fours up another lane, smacking buttons to bring more machinery to life. Gantry mill, benchtop grinder, drill press, and table saw causing an inharmonious commotion in the darkness. The erratic movement was helpful, too—rotating bands, spinning blades, and roaring bits drawing the eye this way and that.

Footfall quickened one aisle over, closing in. Evan shot to his feet once more, bare soles gripping the cold floor, and trained his sights on the assailant hurtling toward him. Chrome knuckles squared off the man's right hand, their menacing glint echoed by a spike of light reflecting off a medallion necklace. Just as Evan took slack out of the trigger, his brain deciphered the Cyrillic lettering on the crates all around them—antipersonnel land mines. His finger decided against putting a 230-grain +P JHP into the pile of Semtex charges in the vicinity.

He holstered his 1911 just before the guy lunged for him, a big sloppy haymaker punctuated in chrome. Ducking the swing, Evan swept the front leg and drove a shoulder into the guy's ribs, knocking him askew as he swept past. The man pinwheeled up the aisle, tangled in his own feet, and fell supine onto the roaring circular blade of the table saw.

Evan dove to the side of the table as the scream migrated from mechanical to organic.

Four left.

Blood snaked down the sturdy steel legs. The medallion necklace, speckled in crimson, tumbled free, bouncing on the concrete floor not two inches from Evan's face. It popped open, a hinged pendant, and rattled to a stop. A roughly cut photo was jammed in either side—a thin-boned wife wearing a dour smile and a boy with giant brown eyes in an ill-fitting confirmation suit.

The sudden intrusion of humanity threw static across Evan's tactical filters and sent a bitter taste along the sides of his tongue. He shoved sentiment down deep, slammed the lid, pounded nails into the coffin to seal it tight. No time for any of that.

Scampering beneath a soldering bench, he put distance between himself and the impaled body.

"Shit, oh shit!" one of the men shouted, flashing into view as he headed for his friend on the table saw. A tattoo of a sturdy matriarch stood out across his Adam's apple, a banderole scroll beneath announcing dates of birth and death. "No. Oh, no. Oh, God." He dipped out of sight near the power cord and then the circular saw stopped revving, grinding to a moist halt. "Janus, you have eyes on him? Where is this motherfucker?"

"Ssh ssh sssh, Telly." The voice from before—Janus?—much calmer than the others and yet still loud enough to be heard over the machinery from afar.

Silently Evan rolled out from under the soldering bench, beneath two folding tables laden with ball bearings, and came to a stop beside a sturdy polypropylene case a touch smaller than a deep freezer. Halting, he controlled his breathing.

He'd moved deeper into the building toward Tommy's favorite workbench, the one by the bathroom. The new vantage gave him a slanted view across the workshop, Janus strobing into view between various rises of ordnance, largely lost to shadow.

The entire side of the man's face was scarred.

No—covered with a strawberry birthmark.

No—tattooed.

Janus eased past a crate of frag grenades announced in stenciled Mandarin, a fall of light hitting the side of his face. The tattoo was oddly positioned across his entire left cheek and neck. From below, an inked devil whispered into Janus's ear canal behind a cupped hand with pointy dark claws. And fanning onto the temple above, a sweet-faced cherub gripped the top of the ear, tiny digits curled around the cartilage of the helix, leaning down to offer loftier counsel. Two visages drawn atop Janus's own.

Even from this distance, the artistry looked vivid, three-dimensionalizing the angel-devil push-pull, the dynamic exploding off his skin. The movement of his facial muscles and the play of light and dark animated the tableau into living parts, the effect unsettling.

A deep, booming voice issued startlingly close to Evan's hiding position: "Boss, clear out. It's not worth risking you in here."

Across the lair, Janus stopped. His tongue poked out, wet the corners of his lips. For a moment, Evan thought about drawing his pistol once more, but his line of fire was impinged upon in more ways than he could count by objects engineered to blow up.

Janus lifted his nose slightly as if to sniff the air, his bare skull glinting. "Okay, Demetri." He bared his teeth when he spoke. "Make him a stain on the floor."

His shoulders rippled and suddenly he disappeared from view. An instant later came a jarring sound—the deep-throated, syncopated roar of a Harley inside the building.

Clever. Hiding the bikes in here prevented telegraphing the ambush.

The motorcycle screeched into invisible motion. The only movement Evan could track was the top half of Janus's shaved head skimming above the machines and cabinets. The Harley whipped toward the entrance, stuttered across the fallen door, broke into daylight, and then it was down to Evan and three men in the darkness.

Three men he could hold in his peripheral awareness. But it would be useful to have something besides a Strider knife for close-quarters flexibility. Before the sound of the bike faded away, Evan pivoted to snap open the chunky case behind him. Inside: a Javelin portable anti-tank missile launcher nested in a bed of convoluted foam.

Not useful unless he hoped to spark off Armageddon or a land war in Europe.

Knives and fists, then.

As he eased the lid silently back down, he remembered Tommy's ashtray of choice, a rusting porthole always kept within reach. Crawling toward Tommy's rolling chair, he reached up to grope across the surface of the favorite workbench. Solo cup, mold blocks—there.

He slid it off, let the cold ash spill across his knuckles, felt the reassuring heft in his hand.

Knives and fists—and a naval-strength ashtray.

A pair of well-worn slippers rested on the floor beside the rolling chair, stretched into the shape of Tommy's feet. A thought intruded: Tommy in the evening puttering around in those slippers and his Santa Claus spectacles, tidying up the shop.

Another thought consigned to the nailed coffin.

Evan sensed Telly inching around the table saw, and Demetri, the deep-voiced man, closer than he would have liked behind him. The third man was farthest away, a good twenty-five meters across the building, nosing around bullet traps and clearing stations along the west wall. He was squat and powerful-looking, a grappler.

Evan hated grapplers.

The hum of the machines worked against Evan now. He could only read shadows and register bigger movements. Tucking in tighter to Tommy's workbench, he could no longer see anyone or track the sounds of breathing. If Demetri held his previous course, he was due to close in on Evan's hiding spot in the next three or four seconds.

Coiling his legs, tightening his grip on the ashtray.

Four . . . three . . . two . . .

Evan sprang up, drawing back the ashtray. Demetri was two steps out of reach, facing partially away. A burly guy with a smashed-flat nose, he was dressed jarringly well in khakis and a sky-blue golf shirt, as if he'd been called in on short notice from a social event. The country-club look was at odds with his face and the fixed combat knife in his right hand. As he spun toward Evan, Evan let fly with the ashtray, swinging it like a hammer.

Demetri reared back but the porthole clipped his long-suffering nose, knocking it further askew. Dark eyes flaring, Demetri countered with a wild thrust of the knife. Evan seized his forearm, shattered the locked elbow with a hammer punch, caught the combat knife as it tumbled free, and buried it to the hilt in Demetri's side just below the floating rib.

Though the machinery drowned out the sounds of any approach, Evan knew Telly would be coming from behind. Digging the knife farther into Demetri, he spun the big man, steering him with a twist of the sunken blade and sliding his free arm around Demetri's neck from behind.

Demetri coughed out a choked roar, wet and rumbling. Evan swung them both into a one-eighty just in time for Demetri's stomach to catch the stabbing knife flying in from behind them.

Telly looked down at his fist gripping the knife embedded in his friend's stomach, then up to catch Evan's eyes over Demetri's shoulder. His glare hardened with rage.

NEMESIS

Telly ripped the knife free and jabbed it again at Evan but Evan tugged Demetri a step over so his torso caught the blade again. Demetri grunted in agony, the air leaving his lungs in a sea-lion bark. Evan skipped back, bringing the big man with him, a shield of meat. Telly's face twisted with fury, a flush creeping up beneath the tattoo of his mother's face on his throat. He'd kept the knife, his fist and blade slick with Demetri's blood.

Evan's grip on the prong sunk into Demetri's kidney and his one-arm choke hold meant he could keep holding the big man on his feet to steer him. He shuffled back into an opening between workspaces, noting the line of motorcycles parked beyond the bathroom. The lair smelled of gunpowder and spilled coffee, copper and human waste.

Demetri wheezed raggedly in Evan's arms, his words little more than a rush of air: "Nico. Nico."

Trying to alert the third man—the grappler—still across the armory. Miraculously the guy had his back turned, oblivious to the death match being fought behind him.

Evan was losing his grip around Demetri's neck, their flesh slick with sweat. Demetri jerked his head free and Evan used the opportunity to snatch the Strider from his own pocket and bury it between Demetri's ribs high on the opposite side from the combat knife.

Air hissed free over his knuckles. Demetri gurgled. Evan had him skewered from both sides, a life-size puppet.

Telly remained focused on Evan, upper lip peeling up from bleached white teeth. The bloody knife trembled in his hand, nerves fired from adrenaline.

He charged and struck with prison-honed speed, a series of quick thrusts.

Evan bared Demetri's chest to each attack, swinging his body this way and that. Telly jabbed and cursed and cried with horror as each blow sank not into Evan but his own partner. Demetri's legs finally gave out completely, and Evan let the big man spill to the floor.

Telly emitted a sob that caught the third man's attention at last. Nico turned, caught sight of them across the armory, and started running toward them. Telly stood stooped, gathering himself for another charge, but he was done already—the cortisol dump and bursts of exertion leaving him depleted. The puffy skin around his eyes looked bruised, his lips chapped.

His next thrust of the knife was halfhearted, slow enough for Evan to trap the wrist and take the arm. He rode Telly's momentum down, landing on top of him, nose-to-nose, the combat knife in their shared grip. The point hovered above Telly's throat, pointed down at the Adam's apple and the face of the tattooed matriarch memorialized across it. Now Evan could read the name above the inked dates—an inevitable MARIA—and a disloyal part of his brain recoiled from discovering in these final moments the name of the mother of a man he was about to end.

In his side vision, Evan sensed Nico hurtling toward them, leaping over duffel bags and dodging machines. He'd get to them before Evan would have time to force the blade down into Telly. Telly's eyes bulged with renewed confidence—he'd made the same calculation.

But then: a crash.

The jangle of metal against concrete.

Evan didn't know what had happened until a scattering of frag grenades rolled past them with yellow markings in Mandarin.

Nico had gone down, tripping over the crate of Chinese ordnance.

A few more grenades skittered out beneath the workbenches and machines like a wave of rodents. They pinballed off Tommy's rolling chair and Demetri's still-wheezing body.

Telly's knife remained trapped in a lock between his face and Evan's. Evan's hair fell forward, sweat burning his eyes, all four of their hands locked around the handle of the knife. Evan readjusted his right hand, covering the butt with his palm and setting the weight of his chest atop it. The blade lowered, descending a millimeter at a time toward Telly's Adam's apple.

Telly's eyes bulged even wider, the sclera pronounced, showing off thread-thin fissures of broken blood vessels. "Wait," he hissed. *"Wait, wait, wait."*

The point of the blade dimpled his skin. His hands quivered, holding Evan at bay with every remaining ounce of strength. One more millimeter broke surface tension, raising a bead of blood beneath the tattooed mother's chin.

About ten paces away, Evan heard Nico rise, the clanking of spilled grenades against the floor.

Water streamed from Telly's eyes, his breath a sour rush across Evan's cheeks. "Please no. Please no. Please don't kill me. Please don't kill me."

Another millimeter. One more.

Nico's footsteps pounding concrete, growing quicker.

Telly's mouth gaped. "Please," he said. "Please, please just—"

Evan headbutted the union of his hands, once, twice, hammering the blade down. Then he summoned a last burst of power and heaved himself downward. The butt of the blade dug into his palm, his knuckles into his sternum. He lowered his gaze from Telly to Maria's inked eyes and then the resistance gave and he shoved the blade through her neck and his, a multigenerational skewering.

He barely had time to exhale when a flying shadow darkened the floor around him and then Nico crashed down onto his back.

9

A High-Risk Variation of a Roll-of-Quarters Whack

Nico's weight pinned Evan down. Evan read the ripple of movement across his back, sensed that Nico was drawing back one arm. Before the knife could fall, Evan flipped himself over, throwing both hands up in an eponymous X to trap the plunging forearm as the blade fell.

Nico readjusted his grip and Evan solidified his, the quavering knife between them but pointed at Evan's nose, an unpropitious reversal of the grappling position he'd held with Telly.

Not good.

Strength waning, muscles burning, teeth gritted, the back of his head grinding concrete, bare heels scrabbling against the oil-slick floor.

Nico's face was flushed, trembling, sweat popping from his pores in distinct drops. He was grappler-strong, which meant he was as strong as a man could be. His wide grimace shaped upward in joyful anticipation of what would come next.

Evan's arms wouldn't hold out much longer.

The blade sank lower, kissed the tip of Evan's nose.

He turned his head to buy another inch.

Telly was right there on the floor next to him, his dead stare waiting to meet Evan's eyes. His mouth ajar, purple tongue slugged up against the lower lip, combat blade still embedded in his throat like the sword in the stone.

Nico took up ground immediately, the knife tip tracing taunting circles on Evan's temple. Were it not for a few pounds of applied pressure from his frontal lobe, it might have tickled.

Mustering his last bit of strength, Evan bucked into a sloppy bridge, arcing onto his heels and shoulders to create space and flinging Nico's hands away. The blade recoiled slightly from Evan's face, giving him perhaps two-thirds of a second before the momentum shift would bring it down with even greater force.

Evan flung out a hand, ripped the blade from Telly's throat, and slashed blindly at Nico's face.

Flesh tugged against the cutting edge. Nico reared back, the blade flying from his hand. He punched blindly at Evan but Evan had tucked his chin in anticipation so the blows rained down on the top curve of his forehead, the thickest part of the skull. He heard a knuckle break—*good, good*—and then they were rolling across the floor, crashing into the workbench, Tommy's chair toppling over them. They banged off the bathroom door and it wobbled open at them, exhaling the scent of cheap air freshener.

Evan had lost the combat knife. It spun listlessly on its side a few feet away by the fallen chair.

The game of musical knives had become exhausting.

His muscles had little left.

He tried to crawl toward the knife but Nico tangled his legs, grabbing holds, locking him up. Evan's bootless feet left him vulnerable. Nico dug a thumb into the side of his Achilles tendon, issuing a scream of pain up his leg.

Nico advanced farther up Evan's body, a snakelike devouring. His forearm pressed across Evan's calf, sliding up to create leverage as he forced the leg into a bend. The knee closing around the forearm forced the joint to expand in a fashion unsuited to human anatomy.

A High-Risk Variation of a Roll-of-Quarters Whack

Evan heard an animal grunt, realized it had ejected from his own mouth.

The pain was Inquisitional. He'd been subjected to more fighting techniques than he could recount, but the pressure on his knee was a fresh hell of blinding intensity. He had a single instant of anthropological wonder at the limitless horrors the human body could absorb before his vision started to haze, the sparkly tunnel beckoning.

Too much pain. He was going out.

He'd have one more shot at it.

Spinning onto his hip, he jabbed his free heel back into Nico's face, aiming for the fragile edge of the eye socket. He clipped the thicker rim muscle—*damn it*—but then felt the blowout of the thin base of the socket, an indirect fracture.

He rolled free. The pressure had released from his knee but not the pain, which seeped further into the leg with every movement.

Evan lunged for the knife.

Nico grabbed his foot, dragged him back, Evan's fingertips grazing the handle just enough to push the knife farther away.

Evan kicked for Nico's face again, clawing at the floor, the fallen chair, anything to find purchase. The chair spun from his grip, knocking a frag grenade. Evan snatched it up as Nico gathered him in.

Evan pulled the pin, held the spoon in his loose-clenched fist, a high-risk variation of a roll-of-quarters whack. Spinning around, he bludgeoned Nico's caved eye socket with his unyielding knuckles.

Nico bellowed, rearing up onto his knees, clutching at his face.

Evan stuffed the frag grenade down Nico's shirt.

Then he rolled back and jackhammered the bottoms of both feet into Nico's chest. Nico flew into the bathroom, smashing into the far wall, denting the drywall and knocking the towel rack askew.

One terrified intact eye and a smear of pupil floating in tented flesh lifted to Evan. Fluttering stupidly, Nico's hands patted his shirt, groping for the grenade.

Evan swept around the pivot of his hip, kicked the door shut, and flung himself behind a rise of cardboard boxes. The red lettering on the nearest box jumped out at him—C-4 BLOCK, DEMOLITION—and he just had time to say "Jesus, Tommy" before the frag grenade in the bathroom blew.

Eyes clenched, fetal-curled, Evan waited to see if a secondary demolition would convey him to the soupy thereafter. But despite the fact that he'd hidden behind a wall of plastic explosives, he seemed to be intact.

He exhaled.

Then peeked.

The bathroom door was askew in the frame, rocked on its hinges and aerated with ball bearings.

The interior of the room was painted with Nico's insides. A severed leg from the knee down had landed just across the threshold. The boot had been knocked clear off the limb, revealing a Velcro ankle brace. Just beyond the liberated boot, an orthotic insole with considerable contouring rested on the floor.

Evan took a moment to breathe, heard himself groaning with each exhalation.

Tommy was likely still outside atop that sand dune, geared up with sniper rounds and a night scope in case he had to wait Evan out. It would be no easy stroll to the pickup to drive away.

He knew one thing: He had to keep moving or his muscles would lock up.

His knee still hadn't let go, so he crossed the shop in a Frankensteinian Igor stagger, his legs grudgingly obeying him.

He passed Tommy's favored workbench. The porthole on the floor, cracked and speckled with blood. Demetri and Telly stared up at nothing, mouths agape.

Evan's Strider remained sunken high into Demetri's right side. Crouching, he pulled it free, wiped the blade back and forth on the dead man's shirt, and deposited it back in his pocket.

He lowered his head, closed his eyes, took a deep breath. Tobacco, plastic explosive, gun oil, coffee—the smell of this place, of Tommy.

He opened his eyes, turned his head.

That chunky case was just to his side. Beckoning.

He went to it, popped the lid, stared at the shoulder-fired munition inside. The laws of nature and narrative held: You don't open a Pelican case containing a Javelin missile unless you plan to use it.

He lifted the massive unit from the convoluted foam, snapped it into readiness. He'd fired a Javelin precisely five times in his life—twice for training and three times to make an impression.

It was as unwieldy as he remembered.

He lugged it past the corpse on the table saw, up a narrow corridor between machines still joggling with movement.

The big metal front door lay in the fall of light, the body like a paperweight pinning it down.

Evan stayed back in the shadows.

His Ford F-150 remained a few strides from the threshold, parked on a patch of sand. Fifteen degrees to the left of the front bumper was the spot where he'd caught the flash of the sniper scope. If he could see that spot it meant that anyone on that spot could see *him*, so he sidled a half step back to consider his next move.

Tommy could have switched to a new hide in anticipation of Evan's next move, but Evan thought it more likely that he was still set up at the first location. The line of sight was unimprovable and Tommy would have no reason to believe that Evan had identified his position earlier.

The Javelin's thermal sight wouldn't be much use, since Tommy had countless variants of mesh treated with active IR camouflage. And Evan couldn't peruse the scene without catching a sniper round in the face.

Cat and mouse, mongoose and cobra, sniper and gunner.

The Javelin was relatively simple: Aim and click, fire and forget.

He could send it at Tommy's prior location and blast the top off the entire sand dune, his highest odds for a kill shot. Or he could direct the missile at the base of the dune to release a massive sand cloud, giving himself cover to escape.

He weighed the options for another moment.

Then he sat down with his legs in front of him, eased forward, and hoisted the command launch unit atop his shoulder. Taking a deep breath and exhaling evenly, he peered at the display, placed the cursor, aimed just to the left of his truck, and let fly.

Fire belched out the back of the launcher as the eighty-thousand-dollar missile took flight, rocked slightly as it hit its second-stage ignition, and rocketed toward its target.

The smoothness of the launch surprised him as it always did, the absorber at his shoulder muffling the shock, the face shield guarding his head.

The missile buried itself in the dune safely below Tommy's likely perch. Sand erupted, more typhoon than mushroom cloud, obscuring the field of vision and muting the sun. Evan was back on his feet, keys in hand, waiting impatiently for the blast radius to expand so he'd have greater protection from Tommy's scope.

Evan had fired at the base of the dune strictly because it was the smartest tactical move. Not because he wasn't willing to kill Tommy.

That's what he told himself.

Then he told it to himself again.

Gusted by the desert wind, airborne grit billowed back toward Tommy's building, shrouding the line of fire and layering Evan's truck like volcanic ash.

Evan ran for the pickup, hopped in, torqued the key, stomped the gas.

The tires spun in place.

Stuck in the sand.

The mist from the blast had layered the existing sand just enough to force the tires to dig their own ruts.

No plan survives first contact, and all that.

Praying for traction, he stomped the gas once more and the mighty truck rocked forward, straining, straining—and then fell back into the ruts. The air was already clearing, the grit settling, his window of escape closing.

Orphan X had survived this long only to be killed by sand.

It was more embarrassing than anything else.

Cursing, he glanced around—rusting car bodies, engine blocks, cacti, the floor mat beneath his bare soles. Nothing suitable.

His eye snagged on the fallen metal front door and the dead body atop it.

Leaping from the driver's seat, he ran back inside, grabbed the body by the boots, and dragged it out behind him. Dead arms splayed up, head bobbling across the earth.

No time for respect.

The air was clearer yet, the dune starting to ripple back into place visually, a tossed sheet settling across a mattress.

Evan hurled the body beneath the rear left tire, wedging the legs in tight beneath the tread.

Back behind the wheel, punching the gas, the truck revving and spinning and canting, the left rear tread fighting for traction on the corpse.

Evan goosed the accelerator once more and at last the truck lurched onto solid ground. He cranked the wheel, fishtailing wildly, and tore away from the building.

Arming sweat from his eyes, he shot a glance at the rearview and caught a wink of glass through the subsiding cloud—Tommy in the same spot as before.

The higher shot would have killed him.

Careening out from the packed dirt, Evan hit the frontage street on a sideways skid, blasting for the freeway.

He was out of sniper range but couldn't bring himself to let up on the gas just yet.

When he looped around onto the freeway, his heart was still pounding, his mouth dry.

Seven men.

Tommy had set himself up for the kill shot and brought in seven heavies to take Evan out if he missed.

That was it, then.

That was it.

They were enemies now.

10

Chest-Tightening Claustrophobia

For much of the five-hour ride, Evan reminded himself to relax his grip on the steering wheel. The grappling had tightened up his intercostals enough to put pressure on his scalenes, curling his shoulders inward. Aside from a few bites of bread at the steakhouse last night, he hadn't eaten anything in forty-eight hours, a rare lapse in operational readiness. His stomach was a pot of acid, his brain starved for glucose, his muscles fatigued. Lack of calories upgraded the post-fight adrenaline and cortisol charging through his bloodstream. There'd been no need to introduce hunger semivolitionally into the operational equation.

So why had he allowed emotion to suppress his appetite this time?

His mind flitted uncomfortably around the question. He set a promise not to overweight anything he thought until he could get to protein.

An acceptable restaurant with dim lighting and clean food was tucked away on Wilshire's Museum Row, not five miles from Castle Heights. It specialized in catch-all Continental cuisine, so he'd be able to find something to fuel up with despite his lack of appetite.

He'd cleaned up at a truck stop—shower, change of clothes and fresh boots from a vault in the bed of his pickup, antiseptic wipes for the fighting cuts and grazes. A fit of unease had seized him as he'd gassed up his Tommy-customized Ford F-150. Pulling behind a dumpster, he'd swept the truck with a wireless signal detector wand and examined the undercarriage with a telescoping mirror despite the fact that he'd done the same check this morning before setting out for Las Vegas. A sensation of chest-tightening claustrophobia came on, the familiar visitor tightening its clutches, squeezing his nervous system.

Evan weighed other vulnerabilities, rewinding his memory to the last time Tommy had private access to any substance or nourishment Evan had put in his body. Sometime just past 1700 hours on Friday, November 15, Evan had partaken of a vintage vodka from a bottle he kept stashed in Tommy's cupboard. He contemplated ingestible digital trackers and slow-acting toxins and where he could get a tactical workup. Before he could close in on a course of action, his thoughts locked on concerns about his alias. To Evan's knowledge, Tommy had no awareness of the existence of Castle Heights or Evan's penthouse. But on the off chance that his cover *had* been compromised, should he blow off his L.A. legend and relocate operations elsewhere?

Paranoia flicked its forked tongue at him, eager to wind him into its grasp. He stared it back into its corner.

Here.

He would draw the line here.

He took a booth with an unobstructed sight line to the entrance, ordered a large bottle of still water, pan-seared halibut with lemon caper sauce, and a side of steamed spinach. Waiting for his food, he unfurled the silverware from the napkin, set fork and knife in parallel on either side of the charger plate, used his thumb to nudge them perpendicular with the table's edge. The tea-light candle was edged out of its groove in the bottom of the mercury-glass holder, so he tapped the holder twice until it slotted into its proper place.

He'd banged his elbow somewhere along the way badly enough

that even at rest it gave off an imposingly deep throb. His head ached but not as badly as his Achilles tendon or the bottoms of his feet, which were a welcome distraction from his knee.

A pleasant conversational hum layered him into obscurity. He closed his eyes and listened to the various exchanges.

"You're very kind, Charlie. And how're the wife and kids?"

"—scratch golfer but only on second-tier courses—"

"—transferred to a boarding school up in Los Olivos to get away from that L.A. private school bullshit—"

The food arrived.

It was not good.

The line chefs had turned up the salt to cover worsening food quality. He wondered if the deterioration was caused by profit squeeze or supply-chain breakdown or the energy crises from Europe or simple ignorance of the craft. So many vast imperfect systems spinning overhead and underground all the time, screwing up one's ability to get a decent bite of fish.

In a larger booth across the restaurant, a family of six joked and bantered, the parents youthful and hale. Matching mops of sandy blond on three brothers and a sister. She was the youngest; they'd tried and tried and finally gotten their girl. Sodas and steaks and paper wrappers shooting off straws. They looked like one of the families whose photos came prepackaged in picture frames.

Evan got down a third of the fish and then caught a mouthful of gristle, which he discharged politely into a folded napkin. He picked at the sodium-intensive spinach and then set his fork down parallel to the knife once more and sipped his water.

Six men.

He'd killed six men this day.

The operational replay flew through his mind, images catching in the net of his memory.

That cross with Jesus peering through, a reverently designed piece of body art coaxed to life by a thousand pricks of a needle.

Long curled eyelashes and facial acne, a romantic asset and a physical liability no doubt confusedly navigated since the age of puberty.

Khakis and sky-blue golf shirt. What event had Demetri been

beckoned from? A birthday party? A barbecue? With whom had he spent his prior hours?

A mom tattoo lovingly rendered, dates bookending Maria's time on earth.

An ankle brace, and custom orthotic insoles that had been sought after and prescribed to alleviate chronic discomfort.

And the locket.

The locket was the one that did it.

Why the hell did it have to pop open?

The waiter had materialized at Evan's elbow. "You're all finished here?"

"Yes."

She looked down a Roman nose at the mostly full plate. "Everything okay?"

"Yes."

A rattle of porcelain and flatware and then Evan was alone again with the memory of a boy in an oversize confirmation suit, staring from the locket with rich brown eyes.

The boy Evan had orphaned.

What was wrong with him? It was indulgent to think this way. To pay attention to all these parts, the messy personal, the chaotically intimate. His training kept him out of that, above the fray. He could not operate instinctually and dredge deep waters at the same time.

They'd been trying to kill him. Every last one of them. He'd acted in self-defense. His conscience was clear.

He let it go.

He let it go but he still felt raw. Raw behind his face, in his chest, from his breath scraping the walls of his throat.

An older couple shuffled out from behind a two-top. They paused at the big booth across, the elderly man giving the parents a graceful nod. "You have a beautiful family."

Five smiles beamed back and five thank-yous.

"Suzie," the mother urged.

Suzie brushed the curly blond bangs out of her eyes with a hand gripping a broken crayon, and intoned, sans eye contact, "Thank you."

These odd little engagements that filled people's days. So much contact for no strategic end. And yet his mind slipped around the sentiment into new ones—long curled eyelashes and a sky-blue golf shirt and big brown eyes. He thought about an inked devil hissing from below and a cherub whispering from above. And wondered which might give the right advice at the right time.

What was the point of getting hung up over any of this?

If he decided to filter life through sentimentality, then everything changed. He wouldn't be going home from here to a fortress of solitude with strategic sight lines and hardened walls to repel breaches, a place to ready body and mind for future missions. Instead what waited for him was an empty condo leached of color and warmth, cabinets stocked sparsely for one, and no one to talk to but an aloe vera plant.

He dropped a few bills on the table and walked out, leaving the soothing din of conversations behind.

In the farthest spot in the parking lot, his truck waited. Wheel wells dusted with sand, a film of grit across the windshield. Settling into the driver's seat, he took a moment in the quiet. The dome light faded off, allowing him the lovely anonymity of sitting in an unlit vehicle in an unlit parking lot.

He cleared his throat. "You have a beautiful family," he told the darkness.

It sounded dumb.

He tried again: "You have a beautiful family."

The words felt foolish in his mouth, tangibly clunky. They didn't belong there.

A glow surrounded the restaurant's windows, and through the wooden blinds he could see people toasting and gabbing and a woman with her head thrown back in laughter, earrings sparkling in the candlelight.

The view was Edward Hopper desolate.

Evan turned the engine over and eased onto Wilshire Boulevard, heading toward one version or another of home.

11

The Way of the Orphan

Even from across the lobby, Evan could smell the sickly-sweet violet perfume.

Ida Rosenbaum of 6G.

Eighty-eight years old, diminutive of stature, wizened of skin, fierce of tongue—Evan's most daunting challenger of the day.

At the moment, Ida was near invisible—a head stuck up above a full-body feathering of Loehmann's shopping bags.

Evan had gone prey-still a few steps into the building. To his side, sliced cucumbers and mint sprigs floated in an inverted water dispenser, the net result of a nearly ninety-minute deliberation at the last Homeowners Association meeting. Aluminum sipping cups were stacked beside it on a bamboo mat, the strays on a breakfast tray labeled by a petite, artsy chalkboard: *RECENTLY USED.* The softening adjective annoyed him.

He'd just decided on a silent retreat when Ida spotted him. "Well, don't just stand there. The elevator's almost arrived."

Releasing a breath, Evan resumed his path forward, gripping a small foil-lined bag containing his soiled clothes. "Yes, ma'am."

"Again with the 'ma'am' nonsense."

He entered the dispersion field of her perfume and stood next to her, trying not to blink against the fumes. Of course he should offer to carry her bags, but that would mean he'd have to accompany her back to her condo, which in turn meant more Ida Rosenbaum time. Mere hours after his friend tried to kill him, he felt ill-equipped for this kind of bullshit.

Behind the security desk, Joaquin was stuck between a few phone lines and could offer Evan little more than an empathetic shrug. Evan turned his attention aggressively to the floor-indicator lights. The elevator crept downward.

With a pained groan, Ida repositioned various bags around her person. "Pardon me," she said. "My arthritis."

An ache in Evan's molars; he was clenching. The elevator made a stop on the fourth floor, prolonged enough to grant egress to a midsize orchestra.

"Degenerative," she added.

The burn of accumulated carbon dioxide in his lungs reminded him to exhale.

He turned to her miserably. "May I carry those for you, ma'am?"

"If it's not too inconvenient," she said, already sliding armload after armload onto him.

He received them as best he could, wondering how her frail frame had endured under the tonnage. She transferred every last bag to him except a tiny snap purse, which she clutched to her stomach with both hands. Evan waited at her side, exhibiting coatrack stolidity.

Her focus gravitated to his face. "That's not *your* big truck leaking oil all over the garage, is it?"

"No, ma'am." The bags' weight was heavy enough to strain his breathing but he didn't want to give her the satisfaction.

"You know someone has to clean all that up, don't you?"

"Yes, ma'am."

Mrs. Rosenbaum kept on, relentless. "I don't imagine anyone likes getting oil on their shoes."

"No, ma'am."

Six floors and a hallway. He could make it up six floors and a hallway with Ida Rosenbaum. At least he only had her to deal with.

Ida's eyeglasses were slightly fogged on the bottom of the lenses. "We're stopping at Lorilee's place."

Lorilee Smithson, the thrice-divorced, plastic surgery–preserved resident of 3F.

Nothing could be worse than stopping at 3F.

"Where she's having a Fabi party," Ida added, proving him wrong.

Ding!

The elevator doors parted.

Evan swallowed audibly.

They stepped on. The car groaned upward.

He mustered the inquiry: "Fabi?"

"It's a newfangled way of selling clothes," Ida said. "Like Tupperware parties."

Everything with Lorilee Smithson, Evan had learned at great expense, was like a Tupperware party.

"That's why I got all my old clothes out of the storage unit," Ida said. "So I can see what I have and what I need."

Only now did he register the wear and tear on the Loehmann's shopping bags; she'd stored them for reuse.

Human beings were indecipherable.

In a daze, he followed her off the elevator and into Lorilee's apartment, where the party was in full wine-soaked swing, allowing him to unload Ida's bags covertly on the thick white carpet in the corner. His usual allies in the societal churn, Mia Hall of 12B and her ten-year-old son, Peter, were still on a prolonged holiday trip to the East Coast, so there was no safe quarter. Evan tried to exfil quickly but Ida kept demanding he reorder her items by her feet in accordance with some inscrutable reasoning. In the process, his own foil-lined bag popped open. He caught a flash of blood-saturated fabric and caught a whiff of copper before he snapped it back shut.

He was sweating. His bruised elbow ached and the back of his skull was tender from when it had been ground into the concrete of Tommy's floor. Voices and faces pressed in at him like fun

91

house–mirror distortions. Before he could shake the sensation, a wash of mental images arrested him—his friend's sniper-scope glint on a sand dune, air from a punctured lung hissing across his knuckles, a cracked-open locket.

His reverie was broken by Lorilee's rearing up from a rosé-induced slump on a throw pillow, the ribbed pattern imprinted on her Botoxed left cheek. She wore an I'M WITH MY HOA CO-PREZ T-shirt with an arrow pointing at Hugh Walters, 20C, who beamed at her side, ensconced in a mirroring shirt.

"Ev!" she shrieked. "I *hoped* you'd swing by! Hang on, hang on, I got something just for you."

As she stumbled toward the kitchen, another version of Lorilee stepped out from behind a Japanese screen delineating the changing area. Disoriented, Evan took a moment to identify her as Desiree, Lorilee's favorite cousin. Their features hadn't actually been similar to begin with, but a steady progression of fillers, nips, and tucks had moved them into a Venn-diagram overlap of felinity. Wearing too-tight jeans and a shoulderless blouse held aloft by a silicone-enhanced bosom, Desiree flung her arms overhead, hands flipped wide, one knee bent inward. "Ta-*da*!" The button fly on the jeans strained visibly.

"Looks *fabulous*, Desiree!" Sherry Clutterbuck, 17A, grinned. "The jeans can also go with that bougie sweater you set aside!"

Evan drew in a breath to reset himself. The usual nonsense was evident all around. Johnny Middleton, 8E, sitting with his knees spread wide as he slurped red wine from a Dixie cup. Fred Clutterbuck bellyaching that there was nowhere to park cash at a decent interest rate anymore. The Honorable Pat Johnson of 12F double-dipping a glistening stick of celery into a bowl of ranch. Generally Evan endured these encounters with bemused forbearance. But in the aftermath of the ambush at Tommy's lair, he felt emotion brimming everywhere. Buried in Fred Clutterbuck's guffaw, he sensed the lament of an overweight kid who never quite fit in. Justice Johnson scanning the room as he chewed his crudité, a twitch of social anxiety tightening the corner of his right eye. Widowed Hugh Walters watching insecurely for Lorilee's return, fingers drumming the knee of his pleated Dockers.

The Way of the Orphan

Lorilee clapped rapidly in front of her chest, a windup monkey with cymbals. Then Desiree reappeared from behind the changing screen, modeling a floral shirtdress with an assertive knee slit.

As the voices of 3F rose in approbation, Evan set down the cup and slipped out.

12

Alone

Evan ate at the kitchen island. A sleeve of water crackers, a dish of Castelvetrano olives, and a tomato from the living wall, which he cut into uniform slices.

He cleaned and dried the plates and knife and put them away.

He wiped up the crumbs.

He brought an ice cube back to Vera. Spinning sleepily in her pod, she did not register her gratitude.

He undressed.

He burned his clothes from the mission and his replacement outfit, too, for good measure.

He showered.

He got into his floating bed.

He rewound the day, searching out flaws and missteps. He should have run a surveillance route on Tommy's place before approaching. He should have parked the truck farther from the entrance in a position of cover. He should have risked the shot at Janus when he had the chance. He shouldn't have left his Strider buried in Demetri's side with Telly and Nico still threatening. He shouldn't have lunged for the combat knife and let Nico lock up his legs. He should have fired the Jav at Tommy's position instead of below it. He shouldn't have lost himself to self-indulgent pensiveness outside the restaurant. He should have left Ida's bags at the door to 3F rather than entering. He should have figured out something not foolish to say when Lorilee had presented him with the glowing vodka. He should have cut the tomato more precisely so the end piece hadn't come out slightly crumpled.

It would have been pleasant not to run the end-of-day list that the Second Commandment demanded. But after this many years, it was wired into him to do so.

A slight rise wrinkled the bottom sheet beneath his left heel. His head felt slightly off center on the pillow. Had he captured all the crumbs at the kitchen counter or had some escaped?

OCD needling in at him, little jolts to the brain, mental glitches to keep the nervous system from relaxing too much, from slowing down and toggling him off high alert.

He found his breath.

He hadn't had it since the engagement at Tommy's lair.

He breathed.

And then he breathed again.

The hum of traffic was faint through the polycarbonate-thermoplastic-resin windowpanes. Ambient city light seeped around the edges of those hard-to-obtain discreet-armor shades, designed by a vendor out of Scandinavia.

All that life out there and him safe in here.

Safe.

And alone.

Staring at the ceiling, he hoped for sleep.

13

Right on the Verge

Jack Johns is sitting in the farmhouse study with the mallard-green walls and the cedar logs burning, a finger of pale yellow scotch swirling in a cut-glass tumbler. He's telling something to young Evan, something very important.

Evan is fifteen years old and just getting husky. He's having a hard time listening through the ringing in his head from when Jack cuffed him a half dozen times earlier in the evening. A trickle of blood leaks from a cut on Evan's temple, a tiny stinging tear in the flesh where Jack ground his face into the floor.

Behind Jack rise the well-ordered bookshelves, the spines aligned so perfectly they might as well be a painted façade. He is wearing his flannel-insulated utility jacket, the one that soaks up all the peat and smoke, its waxed canvas the color of dark barley.

For Evan, the jacket holds as much mythical power as the man himself. One time coming upon it hanging in the coat closet, Evan had been seized with an impulse to bury his face in it to breathe in the scents, but he'd understood that would represent an intrusion into the kind of space that

Jack didn't want him to occupy. Restraining himself, he'd put his boots away and closed the door.

Sitting on the couch now, Evan is still angry. And wounded in confusing ways that thrum through him with each pulse of his headache.

A flush tinges Jack's cheeks. When he is one and two-thirds drinks in, Jack is his fullest self, vulnerable to offering rare bits of illicit knowledge from beyond the steel parameters that bind the handler-Orphan relationship. Evan senses that now, senses a tiny fissure in the armor protecting them both, senses that Jack is right on the verge of giving him something he needs to know.

Evan woke up with the dream slipping through his fingers. He caught a snatch of it, the rest out of reach.

Sitting upright on the floating bed now, it struck him that this was not a dream but a memory.

In the morning light, it proved just as elusive.

After Evan tended to his injuries and worked out, he checked the encrypted RoamZone. He told himself that he was looking to see if a new client had called in from the depths of an insurmountable crisis, despite the fact that it was way too early for Neva Alonso to have identified the next Nowhere Man mission.

He was really checking to see if Joey had texted.

She had not.

Joey lived less than two miles away in the Westwood Village student apartment building where Evan had placed her once he'd determined she was no longer being hunted by a deep-black kill squad. Despite her failure to graduate the Orphan Program and earn a letter alias of her own, she had been trained by two exceedingly capable handlers in Jack Johns and in Evan's nemesis Charles Van Sciver, the late Orphan Y. That training made her a dangerous asset.

Though Evan had wiped her trail clean, he remained diligent about her safety. That meant extending the circumference of his real-estate portfolio beyond the usual safe houses held inside the impenetrable warren of shell corporations and offshore holding companies he invisibly controlled. He'd purchased her apartment building without her knowledge so he could effect a number of security upgrades. Joey had figured out his surreptitious owner-ship in no time at all because Joey figured everything out, and she chafed under the arrangement.

He stood before the three-story building now, admiring the shatter-resistant windows, the anti-climb spikes atop the balcony rails, the crowbar-defying guard plate on the front door.

He buzzed her apartment on the sturdy call box and waited be-fore the unblinking pupil of the surveillance lens. His face was turned, shoulder blocking the camera, but she'd know it was him.

Her voice barked out amid a spew of static: "What?"

"Let me in."

"Why?"

"I want to talk to you."

An elderly couple shuffled up the sidewalk. A jogger with her dog on a waist leash. A homeless guy pushing a shopping cart. Evan didn't like standing here exposed.

"Well, I don't. Want to talk to you."

He checked the homeless guy's shoes, well-worn with the soles flapping. A black Tesla drifted past and he compared its license plate to that of the matching Tesla that had been behind him at the traffic light at Wilshire and Gayley.

His aggravation rose. "Buzz me in."

"Why should I?"

"Because I own the building."

He regretted it the minute it slipped out.

"Got it." Hard stabbing words from the metal mesh speaker. "You control me because you have more money. It's like that, then."

He set his jaw, risked a peek at the security camera. It offered nothing back.

He exhaled through clenched teeth.

A standoff.

Despite the guard plate, he could get through the front door in thirty seconds. He could throw a carpet roll over the balcony spikes and ascend. He had a master key to the building.

And yet.

He cleared his throat. Pressed the button once more. "Okay," he said. "I retract it."

"'Retract it.'"

She sounded unimpressed with the offering.

A long pause.

He bit the inside of his lower lip, rolled it between his teeth. "I apologize."

He waited, watching the slow traffic, alert to pedestrian repeats. Ten seconds passed. Twenty.

The door buzzed.

He entered. Took the stairs to the second floor.

Her door was slightly ajar in anticipation of his arrival, all three dead bolts retracted.

He pushed inside.

She wasn't in the big front room with her circular desk crammed with computer hardware and mounted monitors. She was back in her bedroom, moving around, making a minor commotion.

Dog the dog sat on his fancy disk of a bed and looked at Evan, forehead wrinkled in canine empathy. He didn't get what was going on either.

Evan shut the door behind him, took four steps in, and halted. Joey was visible now in her bedroom through the doorway. Duffel bag out, throwing clothes into it haphazardly.

"I let you in," she said. "Now I will get out of your building to some place where I'm not considered 'owned.'"

In the truck I bought you, Evan thought. But he didn't say it.

Progress.

Even in her foolishness, Joey was correct. He'd grown too reliant on her in the narrative of his life and she on him. This latest confrontation felt like a breaking point. A certain time—of her, of them—had passed. She was older and that would require different rules, a new way.

Another loss Evan felt in the pit of his gut.

From where he was standing, he could see most of her monitors. Her work for her new college club was still up on her screens, myriad empowerment posters including the one Evan had taken issue with. She'd kept them on display, a declaration. He would not pretend not to notice but he would not comment either; Jack had drilled into him a strong aversion to rewarding passive aggression.

In the bedroom Joey kept on with the angry packing. She was wearing her red T-shirt sporting Hello Kitty with an AK-47, which inadvertently undercut her mood. She'd ripped the sleeves off to reveal the muscles of her arms, feminine and well sculpted, capable of throwing jabs and crosses.

"Joey."

She ignored him, kept packing.

"Joey," he said again, a touch more firmly.

He gauged her movements for theatricality. She was deeply upset, he could read it in her face. This is what she did when shame wrapped itself around her. She ran. She ran like the wild child she was, as far as she could until it caught up to her. Then she curled up in a motel in some other state and let it cocoon around her until it melted her down and she cracked open anew. Stronger.

She ran. But she wasn't a runner. Because she knew it would catch her and knew she'd face it then. And only then could they see together what that would mean for their strange and unlikely relationship.

It struck him that in all the times he had been here, he had never entered her bedroom. He would not do so now.

Over on the foam bed, Dog shifted his weight on his front paws and gave a faint whine. His attention stayed locked on them, ears perked at the unsettling energy.

Impatience rose in Evan at being made to wait on a seventeen-year-old's mood. He felt it at the back of his tongue, honing his words. He saw the chinks in her armor, the angles in, the brutal verbal shortcuts to getting the information he required.

Two-second inhale. Four-second exhale.

He cast his mind back to the first days when Joey had been under his protection. She'd dozed off once in his car and when he'd moved to shake her, she'd jolted awake swinging at him and then flinching away, a foster girl's hypervigilance erupting from just beneath the surface.

He told himself: *Gentle.*

He thought about the time she'd mistakenly thought he'd abandoned her in a motel in Virginia, how she'd come apart with fury and fear and could scarcely be consoled.

He told himself: *Gentle.*

Joey had shared tales of her monster of a foster mom whom they called Nemma, how she'd kept the house stocked with girls, an added enticement for the male visitors she sought.

He told himself: *Gentle.*

Joey was still at it in the bedroom, throwing fistfuls of toiletries into the duffel.

His voice this time was very quiet. "Joey, please come out here."

She walked over and stood in the doorway, arms crossed. "You can't control me." Her eyes darted to the memes on her monitors but he did not follow her gaze. "No one can tell me what to do. Or what to think."

She was young. So young.

Her gaze caught on him, noticing him for the first time. She hesitated.

In the wake of his severance with Tommy, he must have looked different than he had before. He certainly felt different.

"Did you . . . Did you kill Tommy?"

Evan shook his head.

She didn't exhale so much as let a breath rattle out of her.

"You're going to leave," he said. "Okay. Still. I need your help."

"Tracking Tommy?" She hardened herself once more, coming over and entering the circular desk through the slice-of-pie opening. "Looking at his bank accounts? You can do all that." She slapped a few times at her mouse, and the club memes evanesced. "You can do this yourself."

"It'll take me longer," Evan said. "I can't afford that right now."

"So I'm just here to save you some time?"

"Yes. I'm going up against my friend who just tried to kill me." His voice caught the faintest quake and he blew past it but knew on one of the many back burners of his mind that she'd clocked it. "All the shit between you and me? We will square away later. This is the mission. This is your job on that mission. And you will put on your big-girl pants and cover my six because I need you to do so."

Her eyes were glassy. She tilted her head back to hold the tears in place. They did not spill. She'd willed them away.

"Why do *you* get to demand anything?"

"Joey," he said quietly.

She was swiveling on her gamer chair with agitation, knees bouncing. "You can't just expect me to be there whenever *you* want."

"Josephine."

"I'm not your lackey." Her lower lip quavered and her eyes were so, so angry and she was barely holding on.

He looked at her.

"J," he said.

She halted, partially turned to the nearest screens. Her whole face changed. Something washed through it, made it luminescent and soft. A window straight into her purest self, the part of her that could access her vulnerabilities and hopes and the needs she kept hidden even from herself.

She turned her head and looked at him. "Okay," she said. "But I'm not talking to you. Except about the mission."

"Okay."

"We'll deal with what we need to deal with later. On terms *I'm* comfortable with."

"Okay."

"Pinkie-swear on that shit."

They consummated the deal.

"Fine," Joey said. "What do you want?"

"I was ambushed by seven men."

"Where?"

"At Tommy's place."

She blinked twice, lost a half second. "Okay. And you need me to track them down."

"Just one."

"What about the other six?"

"Just the one."

Her eyebrows elevated no more than two millimeters. She cleared her throat. "Okay."

"White male, name or alias 'Janus,'" Evan said. "Mid- to late thirties, angel-devil tattoo on the side of his face, shaved head, owns a Harley."

"Fine. I'll start with the Bureau's Tattoo Recognition Database and NIST's Tatt-E biometric project, go from there. I'll send an update from the road. *Next.*"

It was hard for him to ask because, he realized, he feared the answer: "What did you find on Tommy?"

She spun in a one-eighty, typing before her gaming chair even stopped. A bunch of windows flew upward, birds flushed from the bush. "His bank account," she said. "All kinds of unusual wires flying in and out."

The news came in like a battering ram to the chest, but Evan took it on his feet without a grimace. Joey did a double take at his face. Again, he must've revealed more than he'd wanted to.

He cleared his throat. Took a moment to reset. "What kind of unusual?"

"Weird offshore accounts. Impossible to track. Denominations just shy of ten K, right beneath the bank reporting threshold."

"How many wires?"

"A few dozen."

He forced down a swallow.

"And then what?"

She pointed but he was having trouble focusing on the spreadsheet. "He routes them out. Immediately. Nothing stays parked there longer than twenty-four hours."

"Where's it go?"

"Ping-ponged through Skopje. For obvious reasons, I lose the trail from there."

North Macedonia was a non-AEOI country, not subject to financial compliance or cooperation with most of the international community, which made it a haven for tax evasion.

Evan had several accounts parked in the same city.

A thin line of perspiration had broken out at his hairline, and he felt heat coming up beneath his skin.

Whatever Tommy was into looked worse by the minute.

Never know who's who in the zoo.

And yet Evan thought he had known.

Joey's gaze snagged on his face, and he thought he detected a hint of sympathy deep behind her emerald eyes, but this was not the time or place for that for either of them.

"Send me real-time GPS on his location," Evan said. "I want to know who he's with and what he's doing. I'll drive back out to Vegas and surveil at a distance."

"There's no point in that," Joey said.

"Why not?"

"Because . . ." She toggled the mouse, gave a click. The IMEI of Tommy's cell phone appeared, pinned down by advanced forward link trilateration. "He's not there anymore."

Evan stared at the GPS location. A town named Calvary. There it was on the map, blinking dead center inside the virtual state lines.

And now Tommy had gone on the run. Evan palmed his mouth, tugged his cheeks down, gave an exhalation.

Joey used the cursor to trace a circle around the state. "Them's some backward folks from what I hear. You going after him?"

"Yes."

"Not exactly a dream destination."

Tommy had supplied weapons to a murderer of innocents. He'd tried to kill Evan. He'd trafficked in illicit funds from shady sources. He'd gone on the run.

He had become a menace to others, to the world of men and women and children.

Evan would not turn away. He would stare the unchecked threat in the teeth no matter its face. He would take it seriously even in this world that rewarded everything but seriousness.

"His main phone is turned off but he called me one time from his backup so I had the number," Joey said. "I figured given what you'd told me . . ." She let the thought trail off.

Evan's face felt wooden. He forced words through it. "Thank you."

Joey chewed a wisp of hair that had caught in the corner of her mouth. She gave a slight nod.

He left without patting Dog on the head.

14

Judge, Jury, and Assassin

Aside from Tommy, Evan had one person he could technically call a friend. Aragón Urrea, an unconventional businessman, had vast resources on both sides of the law, including several private jets that allowed Evan to get where he needed to go without contending with airport security, TSA, or travel records. Evan had once solved for him an unsolvable situation involving his daughter, Anjelina. In doing so, he'd won Aragón's gratitude for life.

Sitting on the winding stairs to the reading loft, Evan called him now.

He called his only remaining friend.

"Amigo de borrachera!" Aragón roared. "You're alive."

"Barely."

"When Belicia and I don't hear from you, we assume you are buried alive somewhere. Or hanging from a meat hook being—how do you say it?—'interrogated with enhancement.'"

"Close enough," Evan said, remembering that it was a line he'd borrowed from Tommy. So many ways they were wound together.

What a mess intimacy was. He changed topics quickly. "How is Belicia?" Aragón's wife.

"She is all the light the world can contain. And sometimes more."

"And Anjelina?"

"She bedevils me. She and Reymundo, they have moved to Austin. They will not let us see that baby often enough. Only twice a month."

"I'm surprised you can manage the grief."

"No amount of time is enough," Aragón said. "You will see someday. When you have a grandchild."

No, Evan thought. *I never will.*

"She says the travel, it is too hard for the baby. An air-conditioned ride in a car across well-maintained highways with no bandits." Aragón sighed. "Women. You can't reason with them. Men are too pigheaded to reason with, but women, they should know better." A faint groan and then the wheeze of a couch cushion compressing. "Why are you bothering me at lunchtime on a Sunday? Belicia and La Tía are making *albóndigas.*"

Evan couldn't generate the reason he'd called, not right away. In the silence he could hear the force of Aragón's listening.

"Um." Evan had never said "um," not once that he could remember. "Moving forward, I need a new weapons supplier. Specialty, customized, untraceable."

That was not why he'd called. But those were the words that came.

"I will take care of it," Aragón said. "But what of your friend who does this for you? Tommy?"

Evan had discussed Tommy with Aragón only twice—given name, broad details, points of operational overlap. But Aragón, as perceptive as anyone Evan had ever met, could weave together uncanny awareness from a few threads.

"He and I," Evan said, "are having a problem."

An exhalation blew across the receiver. "How bad?"

Evan said, "Bad."

"Ah," Aragón said. "I am very sorry." A graveled voice from a barrel chest, somber and weighty. Evan could sense his powerful mind churning. "You are at odds?"

"Yes."

"You have spoken?"

"Yes."

"You will speak again?"

"He went on the run. To . . . engage with him, I have to chase him down."

"So you are going," Aragón said, "to fight a friend."

"Yes."

"Old vets like Tommy," Aragón said. "Sometimes they get . . . not right in the head. Too long in the spin cycle—bullets, injuries, the loss of friends. They confuse war games with life, paranoia with honor. They obsess over tools of destruction, playing with ordnance all day long like ten-year-olds waiting for their dicks to come in."

"Dicks to come in?"

A rustle over the line, no doubt Aragón waving a hand. "An illustrative phrase."

"No." Evan dug a thumb into the tightened muscle along his chest plate, much more tender than he'd anticipated. "Not Tommy. That isn't Tommy. He was a patriot before anyone screwed up the meaning of it."

"Then why are you fighting him?"

"He put—will put—innocents at risk."

"So it is moral, yes?"

"Strategic."

"Same thing," Aragón said. "If you pay close enough attention they both come out in the same place."

"Yes," Evan said. "But morality takes longer to figure out."

The moral and the strategic. Over various drinks and conversations, he and Aragón had discussed how the two aligned if approached properly, how they could lay one on top of the other until they became indistinguishable.

At the moment Evan had little clarity on either.

"So," Aragón said. "Going forward, you must pay close attention."

"Right."

"And do not lie to yourself."

"Right."

"Where is he now?" Aragón asked. "Tommy?"

Evan told him.

Aragón whistled. "That *pinche* part of the country? I do not envy you."

Evan squeezed the bridge of his nose against an incipient head-ache. Dozens of wires. North Macedonia. And Tommy bolting halfway across the country to go to ground.

Aragón had asked something.

Evan rewound a few seconds.

"Fine," he answered. "I'm fine."

"Should I come to see you?"

"Why?"

"Because of how you sound. I can hear it in your voice."

Evan, incredulous: "You're offering to fly here because you hear something in my voice?"

"Yes," Aragón said.

The sensation inside Evan felt overwhelming and confusing.

This, he thought. *Maybe this is what I called for.*

He cleared his throat. "That won't be necessary."

Aragón said, "If it does become necessary, you will tell me."

Not a question.

Thank you, Evan thought.

"It's a long drive," he said instead. "I have to go."

"Yes. Me as well. *Albóndigas* beckon."

Aragón disconnected the line.

Evan pressed the hard edge of the phone against his lips.

It was time.

He would pay close attention. He would not hide the truth from himself. He would prepare.

Before every mission, he had to ready himself to extinguish human life. To expose the fullness of his true and terrible being, flesh and blood willing to destroy flesh and blood, prepared to end life for the good of the pack. He would become that thing, singular and awful, a man who was himself a killer of other men.

He would not apparel himself in the armor of something greater than he was—neither flag nor country nor the teachings of his bet-ters. There'd be no masquerade of empire or ideology. No succor of red, white, and blue. No salvation from a God he hadn't the courage or goodness to know properly. He would seek none of that.

Nor would he shy from the task at hand.

He would stand. He would stand in the face of lies and betrayal, stand with the gentleness required for the weak and kind, and stand with the terrible intent required for those who had none. Stand sheltering a last ember in his oft-bitten palm, the best and only hope to stave off the babbling fears of night and the greater terrors to come from barbarians ever sharpening their tools in the age-old darkness beyond the gates.

And if morning dawned again, it would dawn on the vast, great, true, resonant promise of a future that was anyone's to forge, a world where strong protected vulnerable, where every beating heart held an equal right to thrive or fall short of its own accord. Where his own place and purpose might be known once more.

That was all he had.

His own two feet and an ember against the words of man's greatest hope and hypocrisy etched on stone and parchment, warning, *Break this contract at your peril.* And he would. He would break it. And he would bear the consequences of that trespass on his shoulders.

He would become judge, jury, and assassin.

He would become X.

15

A Mood Unsuited to Civility

Tommy was in a shitty mood.

He'd been driving around the town half the night searching for the address Hick had texted him. He'd called the young man a dozen times but gotten dumped straight into voicemail. There were creeks and dirt roads that twisted through brambles and a shut-down coal mine and a shut-down mill and a trailer park and prefab houses stuck randomly on lots and hills with woodpiles in the front yards and fallen fencing and rotting porches and a few proud interwar homes painted white with flags snapping from poles in the front yards. There were long runs of potholed county roads and plenty of trees and patches of desolation and working ranches and working farms and horses and cattle and no shortage of barns in various stages of dilapidation. There were signs up to vote for this sheriff and that proposition and there were no signs saying to vote any other way. There were pickups with shotgun racks and big-ass tires for mud-womping and couches on browning lawns and junkyard dogs aplenty. There were horse stables and grain silos and water towers. There was a billboard for a Wild

A Mood Unsuited to Civility

West ghost town one county over with *PERMANENTLY CLOSED* spray-painted across it in diagonal. There was a three-block down-town with a pair of beautiful churches and the inevitable diner and a defunct movie house with THE DARK NIGHT on the sun-yellowed marquee because the second "K" had fallen off. There was a gas station and a boarded-up bowling alley and a bar that was open because what else was there to do.

Tommy felt at home.

This was his country.

He loved these folks.

They were his people.

But for obvious reasons he couldn't pull over and ask them where the Hick boy might be holed up hiding from the law, so it was just him and his guttering cell-phone signal in a county town so sprawling and run-down that half the street signs were missing or buckshot or rusted beyond legibility.

He pulled off to take a piss by the side of a splintering wood bridge, and the chiggers chewed up his ankles above the boot line beneath his goddamned pants. Even in December it was warm and humid, all that goddamned heat from the polar bears melting on the North Pole or whatever the hell was happening up there.

Forty-five more minutes of ass-backward road crawling till Tommy figured Hick's boy might've swapped around two of the house numbers and prolly meant Mill Road instead of Mill Street. Reversing course, he crawled his rig through a game path worn and widened by pickups past, American elms cascading darkly past his windows. A spell later he spit out onto a roadway popu-lated at this hour by long-haul truckers and not a damn thing else.

His GPS delivered him to a gate set ten yards back from the roadway, embedded into the wall of the forest like a hobbit door. Vegetation vined the tall run of surrounding chain-link. It was topped by barbed wire and littered with TRESPASSERS WILL BE SHOT signs and surveillance cameras that predated the death of Gene Autry. Three beat-to-fuck plastic trash cans tilted this way and that like drunk sailors, next to a crooked mailbox sporting faded sticky numbers for the rearranged address Tommy hoped was correct.

Despite all the chest-beating security theater, the padlock on the front gate was unhooked, so he threw his dually into park and slid from the driver's seat, releasing a minor avalanche of truck mulch—paper coffee cups and chewing-tobacco tins and a few shell cases for good measure. He straightened out his aching knees and hips and lower back, ambled over, and unthreaded the chain-link.

He drove through.

In the pale yellow glow of a gibbous moon, there were feed buckets in the tall weeds and sodden armchairs with coils poking out and veins of trash in the dirt and fallen logs glittering with the glass of shot bottles.

And finally there was a ramshackle two-story house rising at a tilt with a pair of empty rocking chairs on the extant porch and shuttered windows and a torn-up roof and splinter-intensive cladding and swallow nests that hung from the eaves and striped the peeling paint beneath with stalactites of bird shit. Someone had put money into a proper freestanding flagpole in the dead center of where a front lawn would go, a faded American flag at rest above.

Tommy got out again, shouldered his rucksack, and mounted the steps to the porch. A young guy in a stained undershirt slumped on a torn couch by the front door, mouth ajar, snoring cartoonishly. He had sallow skin and a paunch at the waistline and whiskers to hide a runny chin. An ancient Mossberg shotgun rested beneath his knees, one of the early steel over-unders—the International Silver Reserve II with the old ported barrel and the heavy trigger.

Tommy kicked the guy's boot and he jerked awake.

"Delmont Hickenlooper, Jr. live here?"

The guy scrambled up, grabbed the shotgun, his grip slipping. The barrel hit the planks but the Mossberg didn't discharge into his weak chin and then the guy moved back two steps and raised the shotgun so it pointed at Tommy's substantial belly. He was nervous, one cheek trembling, and though he couldn't have been twenty-five years old he stood slumped like a middle-aged man defeated by a lifetime of commuting.

"This is private property," he said. "You can't be here. I will shoot to kill."

A Mood Unsuited to Civility

It was half past one and Tommy was in a mood unsuited for civility. "What's your name, son?"

"Trent."

"Trent, you best not point that weapon my way 'less you want a double-barreled suppository."

Trent swallowed hard enough to bob his Adam's apple. "I'm the night sentry, sir. This is my job." Though he was well out of the clutches of puberty, his voice cracked when he spoke.

"Night sentries stay awake, son. It's right there in the job description. If I wanted to cut your throat and yank your tongue through the slit, I'da done it while you were busy snorgasming." Slowly Tommy extended his hand, placed a single finger on the muzzle, and steered the barrel down. "Now do something useful and go lock that front gate."

Trent swallowed once more, gave a few quick jerking nods, and scrambled off the porch. Tommy watched him lope away until he disappeared into the darkness.

The front screen was battered and shredded enough that Tommy could rap on the door right through it.

Sounds of sluggish movement, then quickening steps, the *shuck-shuck* of shotguns being pumped, and hushed, urgent voices conferring.

The door winged open.

A big burly kid with a shiny red face and a sneer armed the tattered screen aside and filled the doorway, pistol in hand. It was a Smith & Wesson 29, the *Dirty Harry* revolver chambered in .44 Magnum, and the boy held it like he'd practiced plenty in front of a mirror. Unlike the Mossberg, the revolver was well cared for, oiled and clean, ready for its close-up. The young man's shoulders were pinned back, finger on the trigger, that big dick barrel aimed at Tommy's left knee. His teeth gleamed with confidence, his face glowing with the unearned power of holding a weapon better than he was.

Four cohorts fanned out behind him, all wielding guns, perspiration touching their cheeks, eyes scared or a bit wild. Early to mid-twenties, the whole lot of them, their brains still growing in.

"Where's Trent?" the burly kid said. "The fuck are you?"

Tommy looked past him and spotted Delmont Hickenlooper, Jr., a slighter version of his old man. Same cant to the shoulders, those narrow eyes, good head of hair with an Elvis poof floating above a tall nervous forehead. His left earlobe had been burned into a gnarled smear, scar tissue welded to his cheek. He lacked his daddy's menace, that coiled grown-man intensity that you hoped would get aimed the other way when the time came to strike. The boy had a sweet, open face he tried to cover over with scruffle but still you could picture him playing Little League outfield and chewing bubble gum.

Hick cleared his throat. "I asked him here, Red. I told you about him."

Red.

Of course. He had that skin condition made a person always look sunburned. Boys like this were tough and funny. They could dish it and take it, too.

"*Told* me, yeah," Red said. "But we didn't conversate about that and clear it with the militia."

Conversate, Tommy thought. *Militia. Sweet baby Jesus help us all.*

His eyes found a tattered banner nailed up over one of the couches with a crude logo of two crossed shotguns and dripping spray-painted words reading *CALVARY LIBERTY GUARD*.

"I ran it by Burt," Hick said. "And Lucas."

Burt and Lucas nodded at their names, brothers or cousins given the resemblance, and ambled forward brandishing shotguns. They looked all kinds of mean, with squinty eyes and lupine gaits, like they'd spent their lives picking through trash and sniffing out wounded prey. Lean builds, all hard angles and sinewy muscle and shadows catching in the hollows of their faces.

"I didn't give my final approval," Red said. "And it's my house."

He was a dumb, fat, ugly kid with a big warm heart way down beneath all the damage accrued over a lifetime of being dumb, fat, and ugly.

"It's your dad's house," Hick said.

"Well, he ain't around, is he? And your sorry asses are crashing here. So that makes it mine. Any other fucking questions?"

There were not.

Red again: "Elijah, what do you think about this?"

Elijah shrugged. A small kid, skinny enough to slip through cracks. He was doing his best to make the most of the five foot four he'd been dealt—shoulders pinned back, standing up tall enough to put a slight tilt on his belly. His torn-up jeans looked like doll pants. He wore an untucked shirt stretched at the collar with a dappling of holes around the hem. The tragically sparse mustache dividing his boyish wan face did not accomplish whatever he hoped it would.

Not bothering to look at Tommy, Red gave the revolver a loose-wristed wave at his face, the gun bobbing. "What if this motherfucker's outta-town PD? Ever think about that, Hick?" A glower at the others. Red had a down-slashed mouth, thin lips. "Bullshit you're not thinkin' it, too. If so, what're we gonna do with him now? What if he rats us out?"

Tommy's shoulders ached from the long drive. That was okay. Broad shoulders ached.

He cleared his throat. "Let me tell you what I told that mook you call a night sentry, the one looks like his daddy finished him off with piss. Don't you ever, ever wave a gun at me. 'Specially with your booger hook on the bang switch."

There were those teeth again, the whiteness pronounced in that red face. "You gonna tell that to my Smith & Wesson Model 29? 'Cuz last I checked, I'm the one with the say in this here—"

Tommy slapped Red's hand, a quick whack to the wrist. Red's arm slammed into the doorjamb and the revolver flew out of his grip and skittered across the porch.

The others blinked at Tommy. None of them made a move to raise their weapons but he could see the no-good brother-cousins thinking about it.

"First up, dipshit, I'm not ammosexual so you ain't gonna impress me with your fancy gun talk," Tommy said. "Second, you dumb fetishizing fuck, your weapon's a tool, not some *objet d'empowerment*. You want the latter, buy a goddamned Ayn Rand novel."

Red rubbed his wrist, his face even more flushed than before.

His cheeks bulged, jaws pinched down tight, as he tried to figure out how to puff himself up again. "Ayn who?"

"Christ on a Popsicle stick," Tommy said. "Go get yer god-damned gun off the porch so it don't rust."

Red jerked his head as if to crack his neck but nothing cracked and then he sidled out past Tommy, blading his body carefully so as not to bump into him.

Tommy stayed put.

Once he'd retrieved his gun, Red eased past Tommy with extreme caution once more to take up his post again in the doorway. Now he stood back a few steps with the gun lowered and the others in a semicircle around him.

Back to starting places.

Tommy cleared his throat, looked at Hick. "I promised your old man I'd look out for you if the time came. Well, the time came. That don't mean I want to be here. Hell, I didn't even like the sonuvabitch that much. But I gave my word." He eyed each of the other young men in turn. "So don't piss me off and don't kick off an affair of honor 'cause you don't want to find out how well I sling lead. I didn't drive umpteen hours to dig six fucking holes. So let me the hell in 'cause there's no need for y'all to wind up dead when we can just hash out what's what over bourbon later."

A long silence punctuated by the shrilling of cicadas and the murmur of the night breeze through the leaves.

Red heeled back a few steps and the others did as well.

"May I enter?" Tommy asked.

Red said, "Why not."

Tommy sauntered inside. A wide bare room with a warped plank floor and an amoeba-shaped chunk of carpet for a rug, one end chewed by a dog or a raccoon or a meth-head with strong choppers. Rust-colored couches heaped with blankets and bed pillows, water stain on one wall that looked like Florida or that port-wine splotch on Gorbachev's forehead, depending on which way you squinted. A newish window sat wedged in a roughly window-shaped hole in the wall, a draft blowing straight through the exposed gaps around the frame. Raw wood stairs with sun-bleach lines where a runner used to be, the occasional nail poking up its head. Empty beer bottles abounded, Pabst Blue Ribbon, as well as Coors cans, the old-fashioned Yellow Jackets. Cell phones rested everywhere, glowing from cushions and chairs, set down mid-business when Tommy had arrived.

A venerable tube TV wired elaborately to a cable box sat on a no-shit apple crate, tuned to one of the cable news channels with bright primary colors, beauty-queen anchors, and them breaking news graphics that zoomed in every ten seconds like ADHD Superman. It was turned down low, so Tommy just caught the tone, salacious gossip conveyed in high dudgeon. He knew agitprop when he saw it, had drank it in plenty while trekking through other theaters of instability around the globe. He preferred this line of propaganda to the other channels' lines of propaganda: at least these folks praised America and the ladies were fetching. But still, it was just another goddamned cat factory mewling claws-out in the face of America.

Stacks of lawn signs leaned in the corner: PROTECT OUR COMMUNITIES. VOTE YES ON PROPOSITION S. KEEP CALVARY SAFE: RE-ELECT GRADY JOY FOR SHERIFF.

Throw in a few spinsters and some floral centerpieces and you'd have a regular Ladies of Charity clubhouse.

Wheezing and footfall issued from the porch and then Trent busted in through the door, mouth-breathing. "You got him? You got him pinned down?"

Red glared at him. "No thanks to you. Where the hell'd you go?"

"He told me to lock the gate."

"The gate was unlocked? And you followed *his* orders?"

Tommy held up a four-and-a-half-fingered hand to make the dipshit banter stop and—blissfully—it did. He drew in a deep breath. "Here's the rules," he said. "I'll even talk slow and make it army-proof. Handle your guns like you know a goddamned thing about guns. I'm here as a favor so act like it. I might drink too much sometimes but I won't get mean. Don't get mean around me. You'll regret it." He paused, then added, "That's it. That's the rules."

Hick started to talk but his voice was dry so he had to start over. "Okay."

"I've been driving forever and a day and I'm old as shit and need to rack out."

Everyone stared at him some more.

"Here's where you reply," Tommy said.

"Beds and couches are taken," Hick said. "And we don't got another mattress."

"Fine," Tommy said. "Whoever's bed I take snuggle up with someone else." He hiked his rucksack up on his shoulder and headed for the stairs. "We'll deal with the rest in the morning."

16

The One Everyone Answered To

Janus lay on the padded massage table, his right cheek pressed against the plastic cushioning. The power needle punched in and out of the tender skin around his left earhole, inflicting a pleasurable sting each time the surface tension broke. Sir Rubin worked with black latex gloves and knew not to talk. The hum was soothing, soporific.

Today they were reworking the blushing cheeks of the whispering cherub. Pinkish red ovals textured into three-dimensionality. Linear perspective, Sir Rubin called it. Creating the illusion of depth. Janus struggled to do the same inside himself. He didn't feel the world the way other people seemed to.

After just three years, the color touch-up was unnecessary, but he needed the focus that pain brought. Everything narrowed to one sensation that demanded he be right here inside his own flesh, demanded that he experience what he was feeling rather than lose himself to the toxic swirl of thoughts that blew like mist across the landscape of his strange and myriad responsibilities.

He could vanquish them, his thoughts. He did so every day. It took discipline to set each potential terror in its own little box, to hold down the lid, to decide when, how, or if to release it. It was like being a symphony conductor in Purgatory.

So for Janus, the pain—the steady, predictable drumbeat of the tattoo—was helpful.

It freed him by containing him.

It gave him relief.

"That's it." Sir Rubin dabbed at Janus's cheek once more with a nonwoven cotton-fiber towel, silk after barbed wire, and sat back on his rotating stool. He had a round shiny face with stud pierces rimming his lower lip and eyebrows and a spiderweb tattooed across his bald head.

"And the devil?" Janus asked. "Does he require anything?"

"He's holding strong," Sir Rubin said. "We shouldn't overwork the color, man. Don't want to risk a blowout with ink that perfect."

He applied a smear of Vaseline and got busy sterilizing the works.

"We're done then," Janus said.

Sir Rubin caught his meaning, gathered his gear, and left.

Janus sat up, told himself not to scratch. The itch was there just beneath the surface, threatening to claw its way out. A deeper ache, too, a throb that promised swelling and perhaps a nice bruise. It took a lot of work to hold the angel and devil in their places.

Janus didn't like leaving his compound. That's why he brought the world here—his own bowling alley, home theater, presidential kitchen, and a basement containing a tattoo studio, a shooting gallery, and a prized collection of weapons of antiquity. The more powerful he got, the more dangerous it was outside his walls. Not that he feared leaving, but when he drove through the automated gates, whether on a Harley, in a Bentley, or ensconced in his armored Mercedes, he had to stay alert for anyone who might want to kill him. He had eyes in the back of his head. He'd always wanted to live in the world that way, to travel in currents of menace and danger, to have enemies powerful and far-reaching. It was exciting, a perennial cocaine high.

But here inside his impenetrable compound he could rest. And plan.

The One Everyone Answered To

His cell phone rested on the counter, a half dozen updates on conservations in Threema, his preferred encrypted-comms app.

These days his business empire sprawled octopus-like, squirming and ever changing. This was how he managed it, through the portal of his screen. He had more groups at the ready in *chat* than he could count, working groups suited to different jobs. Some were better at cooking and lab work. Some at conveying chattel. Some had motorcycles and intrusion expertise. All had a willingness to engage in what he sought to engage them for if the arrangement was right.

The arrangement had been right for the trap laid at Tommy Stojack's shop. Tommy was important to him—a world-class armorer and unmatched procurer of weaponry rare and unsanctioned. That's why Janus had gone there personally to oversee the job.

The outcome had been unfortunate.

With high-priority executions, Janus had established an automated process so the contract would be handed off from working group to working group in succession until the job was completed. This was an insurance policy to ensure no reprieve for anyone who sought to strike the head from the snake. Few would dare try to kill Janus, but this was an added deterrent. Everyone knew that even if they took him out through a miracle of God, the hits would keep on coming.

He was the one.

The one everyone answered to.

The software program was due to initiate contact with the Horsemen after a three-day delay. Since Janus already knew the outcome of the Stojack job, there was no need to wait.

He wanted the job finished immediately and properly. Which meant calling them forth.

The Four Horsemen.

There they were in the Threema *chats*, way down at the bottom.

He hadn't used the Horsemen, not in some time. They were more expensive than the other working groups, more expensive by double.

Three men and a woman, matching in skill and lethality. He'd never laid eyes on them. The rumors were plentiful. They were the victors of childhood death matches fought on an underground gambling circuit. They were raised in the favelas of Rio or the slums of Tirana. They did not speak. They were cousins in a giant family operation, every Horseman from the same lineage. The chosen quartet was modular, a new member sliding into place every time one expired. They traveled to each job in a discreet-armored black SUV. They wore old-school leather dusters and dark sunglasses. They communicated telepathically.

The ache around Janus's ear intensified, angel and devil purring at him, their words indistinct. But he could hear their murmurs, one as pure as a tuning fork struck on a star, the other a stereophonic growl.

He tapped on his phone with his thumbs.

I require you.

He waited. Threema showed no ellipses to indicate a response.

But in the exceedingly few times he'd made use of the Horsemen, they'd responded immediately. They were like an all-powerful oracle requiring a visitor to be made real.

Sure enough, two words pinged back almost immediately.

We listen.

Patting at the leakage of blood and ink from his cheeks, Janus told them what he needed.

17

Broken Things

At stupid o'clock, Tommy woke up goddamned sore.

Hick's room was shitty and the bed was shitty and the mattress would've been an insult to a hophead in a Third World drunk tank. A menagerie of stuffed animals clustered at the footboard—a pig in overalls, the see-no- , hear-no- , speak-no-evil monkeys, and a well-loved teddy bear with a missing ear and stuffing blown out through a busted leg seam. He'd left them undisturbed because squatters deserved some measure of rights.

There were no blinds or curtains, the early-morning light gray and dreary but sufficient to wake up his cranky prostate.

He heaved himself up to sit with his feet on the plank flooring. Angina crackled in his chest, a nasty fingernailed clench. He'd slept in socks because it took more effort to bend down and take them off than he'd had in him after yesterday's drive. He peeled them off now, his lower back and hip flexors screaming at him. Thirteen years ago, a VA surgeon had yanked Tommy's legs outta the sockets and put 'em back into new hips. No matter how much mental toughness he'd brought to bear in the aftermath, his body had learned something that couldn't be unlearned—that it could be violated in a way that it could make no evolutionary sense of. It knew it was vulnerable in a different manner, and that meant he had to know it, too. Now he was on the losing side of a war of attrition, his body breaking down in ways he couldn't fix anymore, a permanent state of triage. The pressure he'd been facing, this business with Evan, and the long-ass drive hadn't helped, not one bit.

He tugged on a fresh pair of Gold Toes and sat winded in his underwear and socks like a paramour caught out in a British sitcom. The room was bare, cracked walls and junk on the floor—clothes, half-unpacked moving boxes with Hick's name on them, a cheap Dell laptop, a rickety bureau, an old lamp missing a shade. A poorly framed early color Polaroid showed a woman smiling, hip cocked to accommodate a baby clamped to her side—probably Hick Junior and his momma. An ancient tube TV like the one downstairs rested atop a VCR on the floor, layered with a solid millimeter of dust. To its side lay a toppled-dominoes spill of VHS recording cassettes, labeled in a cramped hand.

Tommy dug in his rucksack, came up with his little rectangular eyeglasses, and squinted at his orange prescription bottles, the tiny print illegible unless you happened to be a Swiss watchmaker with a loupe. His readers were out in the truck and he wasn't eager to take on the stairs just yet. From shape and color he figured out the pills as best he could and got them down his gullet.

He dressed, took an unsatisfyingly feeble leak, and made his way out. A neighboring door was open, the master bedroom from the size of it, Red laid out fully dressed on a queen bed with a Jack Daniel's bottle on the floor by his dangling arm. Red's room had proper furniture, a worn rug on the floor, and tacked-up Budweiser posters featuring voluptuous bikini broads. Tommy paused in the next doorway on his way to the stairs. Burt and Lucas, the Brother-Cousins Grimm, slumbered in fart sacks on the floor, a scattering of empty PBR bottles positioned around the sleeping bags like candles from some redneck Satanic ritual. The room smelled of fumes, and by the closet there were two spray-paint cans lying on their sides.

The third door in the hall was closed but Tommy could sense

a person in there, a sixth-sense vibe creeping out from the slit beneath the door.

He wheezed his way downstairs, caught sight of Elijah sleeping cocked back in an armchair and Trent and Hick sprawled on the couch face-to-feet, another twelve-pack's worth of bottles distributed across an uneven coffee table and a bookshelf that held no books. They, too, smelled of propane-butane fumes, and Hick's thumb and forefinger looked gangrenous with patches of black.

More militia-flag spray-painting, no doubt.

The shotguns were tilted in the corners and one of these idiots had left a compact Glock on the sill behind the couch where any passing ne'er-do-well could smash the window and grab it. Tommy would teach them gun discipline, too, in due time but Rome wasn't built in a day and if anyone shot their nose off before then that was between them and God.

The floor planks creaked beneath his boots like he was standing on a rickety bridge. A house with the foundation barely holding, the metaphor right there in case the reality wasn't obvious enough.

He found a tin of stale instant coffee in the bare cupboards along with a mummified mouse, and located a dirty mug on the counter. He cleaned the mug out as best he could, zapped some tap water in a microwave missing the turntable tray, and stirred in a clump of Maxwell House. It tasted like dirt and dried tobacco. But still: coffee.

A red Solo cup floated atop the crest of an overfilled trash can. He filled it halfway with water, ambled back out to the living room, and dumped it on Hick's head.

Hick bolted up with a yelp, swiping at his face. "The *hell?*"

Trent squeezed at his wet socks, collateral damage. Across the room Elijah was on his feet, five foot four of confusion, tufts of hair standing on end at the back of his head like a Pawnee feather headdress. He wore a too-big sweatshirt that hung dress-like to midthigh, one of the sleeves ripped open; the boy seemed not to have any clothes that weren't flea-bitten.

Hick smeared dripping bangs out of his face, squinted at the window. "What? It's, like, six in the morning."

"You wanna be a man in the evening, you gotta be a man in the morning," Tommy said. "Now get yer ass up and wake the others. I'm going outside to enjoy my hot cup of shut-the-fuck-up. I want everyone assembled in twenty."

Tommy went outside before Hick could get in any whining.

No one was standing sentry—evidently danger didn't threaten here in the early hours—and Tommy walked down off the porch to breathe in the scent of bark and dirt and to taste the forever sweetness of country dew. He took a turn around the house just to get his bearings, poked his head into the garage, which fulfilled every expectation of every damp old garage—tools and cobwebs, rust and wreckage, hard-shelled insect husks and broken things saved for a fixing that would never come. To one side slumbered an old-school Dodge Ram with no plates, a dented bumper, one intact rectangular headlight, and a caved-in front panel. Back to the front yard, the house looming slanted and splintery. Edgar Allan Poe woulda had a field day with the place.

Atop its proud white pole, the flag stirred.

Tommy loved that flag.

Loved it deeper and truer than just about anything else.

Never once had he looked at it as a fantasy in which to lose himself. It was a responsibility, not a birthright, a glorious promise forever falling short, the best impossible dream man had ever dreamed. And yet she was worshipped by a million and ten false patriots who'd lost touch with the fact that Miss Ross hadn't apocryphally stitched that tattered rectangle together star by star, stripe by bloody stripe to be worshipped, not ever, but to be a symbol of an idea in all its bloody real-world glory. That flag would endure despite every lie thrown at her and every corruption set forth in her name. Her covenant was greater than that, a promise to heal and gather in the face of every last thing every last tin-pot despot, vainly cloaked emperor, or crybully mob could throw at her. Spite and sin would not cling to her. She'd wash free of them again and again and still fly trembling and tattered with all her battle-scarred and hard-won faith intact and proclaim to the world: *This. This is better than anything else. These wide-open spaces and these rugged individuals bound in shared freedom. This imperfect creaking democracy. These time-worthy proclamations bled into parchment and watered with the blood of freedmen and patriots. This is better than the barbarism and incivility of ages past. This is the best vestment of faith, the greatest hope to knit man together, to yoke him in the goodness of every god's promise.*

And in the hard cold morning of a hard cold country town, Tommy gave the same silent pledge he'd offered up since the moment he'd walked into a recruiting office in a town not unlike this one, a pledge to try'n steer a true course to red, blue, and white like all the honorable and great men who'd strived before him to do the same against equally quixotic odds.

He finished the sludge in his mug and headed back inside.

The motley crew was assembled in the front room and someone had dragged in another few chairs from God knew where. The brother-cousins sat side by side on the dry couch, Lucas reading a local paper, one of those alt monthlies filled with design-challenged local ads and columns about pie-eating contests. Phones were out at their sides or resting on their thighs like digital lapdogs, and Red had the giant revolver shoved into his jeans next to his belt buckle, primed to shoot off his left nut.

Everyone looked tired and resentful but maybe that's how they always looked.

There was one bedroom still unaccounted for, that closed door upstairs, and Tommy wondered why whoever was lurking up there hadn't revealed himself.

Before he could say anything, Red cleared his throat: "Just so there's no uncomfortability, let's get a few things clear."

Tommy rubbed his eyes. "'Uncomfortability'?"

Red blinked twice. "Don't come at me with elitist bullshit. You hardly talk fancy yourself."

"I butcher the English language with elegance, dipshit," Tommy said. "You know the kinda brains that takes?"

Red reset himself: "You wanna stay at the Hilderanch, you gotta obey *our* rules."

"Hilderanch?"

"That's what we call it," Red said.

Tommy stared at him.

"'Cuz my last name, Hildebrandt. So: the Hilde*ranch.* Get it?"

"You come up with that your own self?"

Red glowered at him. "Don't run the microwave when the kitchen lights're on," he said. "It'll blow a fuse."

"Noted," Tommy said.

Hick scratched at that snarl of scar tissue on his ear with a finger dark with paint. His hair had dried some but not in a style that made it look any better. He was blinking slow, still finding his morning gear.

"My pop won't pay for no more new fuses," Red said. "And don't run the water long when you shower. Minute and a half max. You don't want to run a heavy bill or my pop'll take it outta you."

"Where is this notorious patriarch?" Tommy asked.

"Works the Ford factory over in Bowie. Three-and-a-half-hour drive. He crashes with my cousin out there, only makes it back here once in a blue moon."

"Where do y'all work?"

"There're no jobs," Red said. "That's why Pop's in Bowie."

"Then why aren't you?" Tommy said. "In Bowie?"

"'Cuz who the fuck wants to live in Bowie?"

Lucas riffled the newspaper page. "'Maria Estes, thirty-four, of Hayesville, passed away December sixteen, after a lifelong battle with type 1 diabetes,'" he read flatly.

Tommy paused to see if anyone was gonna pick up the non sequitur but no one did and he figured Lucas maybe just read shit out loud in a creepy tone now and again to add to the ambience.

"So," Tommy said, and waited for Hick to look up. "Let's get it out on the table."

Hick's eyes darted away. He started to say something, but Red cut in: "We got a situation."

"A situation," Tommy said. "I see."

"We got problems with Mexicans here."

Tommy looked over at Hick. The boy looked uncomfortable, squeezing his bladed hands between his knees, looking down tight at the front of his chest.

Tommy said, "Okay."

"They come in from Hayesville," Red said. "It's a shithole over there. Crime and graffiti and them living like animals."

"Son, you got a goddamned colander for a sink basin in the garage with a bucket under it. What kind of Palace of Versailles you think y'all live in?"

"'Maria was preceded in death by her mother, Elena, and is survived by her two children, Valeria, sixteen, and Miguel, thirteen,'" Lucas said from behind the paper.

Another moment of silence at the bizarre intrusion and then Burt found his voice there beneath the shoddy militia banner: "Yeah, well, Mexicans, they're different."

"Yeah?" Tommy said. "How many Mexicans you know?"

"Don't play that with us," Red said, looking at the other boys. "You remember just last week those fucking gangbangers blew through here and stopped at the gas station and harassed Mike at the counter and stole a bunch of shit."

"How many were there?" Tommy said.

"Three."

"Okay, those three Mexicans sound like assholes."

"It ain't just three," Burt said. "Frank Mandel's sister said some others raped a white girl over in Jefferson. Half of 'em aren't even here legally. They don't give a fuck about the law or family and they don't respect shit."

Tommy's shoulder throbbed but he didn't want to dig at it any more. He was craving a twenty-ounce black coffee and a lipful of Skoal Long Cut Wintergreen and a hundred cigarettes to smoke at once like a carny doing an act. But right now he had boys to deal with, boys who wanted to be men and had no goddamned idea how.

He'd keep poking and prodding to get a lay of the power dynamics. Red was the nominal head of operations—his house, his rules, his mouth running nonstop to prove it. Lucas and Burt came next. Tommy had seen plenty of Lucases and Burts, who derived their authority from a cold meanness they were unafraid to wear on their sleeve, a willingness to say and do the worst.

Tommy pawed at his mouth, smoothed down the biker's mustache. "You ever sat and had a meal with a Mexican family?"

"No," Burt said, proudly.

"Ever gone to church, prayed with 'em?"

Trent and Elijah shook their heads but didn't speak.

They were the followers, then.

Burt said, "Not interested in their—"

"Ever gone to war with a Mexican? By which I mean a Mexican-American? Side by side, taking incoming?"

A longer pause. Red said, coldly, "No. We haven't."

"Ever been shot in the leg and shoulder and needed said Mex-American soldier to drag your stupid shot ass outta the fight over three and a half klicks of hard terrain taking fire?"

No one answered.

"Okay then," Tommy said, his voice a growl. *"Three Mexicans.* Them three Mexicans were assholes."

They all looked pissed off by that aside from Lucas, who kept his face buried in the newspaper. And Hick, who scratched some more at that knot of scar tissue at the base of his left ear. Tommy could see a thought had taken hold somewhere in Hick's skull and Hick didn't like what it felt like.

He was the one, then. The foothold.

Lucas broke the silence: "'The family requests that colorful flowers and notes are sent to Elaine Mariposa 12012 blah blah blah Wetback Lane in Wetback Hayesv—'"

Tommy froze him with a stare.

Lucas cut the words off, replaced them with a cold smirk. Tommy ignored him because that was the last thing Lucas was looking for.

There was a noise at the stairs and then a young woman appeared, no older than twenty, arms cast overhead in a morning stretch. Copper-colored hair in a tightly drawn ponytail that shot out in a badger-tail frizzle. She wore a red plaid-print long-sleeved snap Western shirt, jeans, cowboy boots, and an aura of confidence.

That explained who was behind bedroom door number three.

The house was a goddamned clown car.

She paused on the stairs. "What the hell are you idiots getting up to now?"

"Get gone, *Les*," Lucas said.

Red said, "You know the deal, not to come through here when the militia's meeting."

"The militia," she said, with an eye roll of a tone.

She came around the newel-post, and Tommy saw she was wearing a name tag from Calvary Tack & Feed: LESLIE HILDEBRANDT. Her Wranglers were straight-legged, baggier than most cowgirls liked, and her Justin ropers were low-heeled.

Red's sister.

"We're discussing private matters," Burt said.

Little Man Elijah piped in: "With serious stakes."

"How to preserve ethno-Christianity from the couch whilst unemployed?" Leslie said. Her gaze was sharp, focused; she looked to have higher wattage than anyone in the room, Tommy included.

It took some discipline for him not to smirk at her crack.

"Nothing a perv like you'd understand, *Les*," Red said.

He said her name like a slur. Then Tommy realized it was intended as such.

"Shut the hell up about perversion, Red," Leslie said. "I seen your search history. Interracial this and ebony that. You may be a racist dipshit but yer dick sure ain't."

"That's not true," Red said. Then intensely to Tommy: "It's not true."

But Tommy was still beholding Leslie, how she'd blown into the room like a fresh breeze that cut straight through you.

"The hell you lookin' at?" Leslie said.

Tommy said, "Not one thing, ma'am."

Leslie ambled through their little knitting circle, heading for the front door. "I'll leave y'all to your 'private matters with serious stakes,'" she said. "I'll be at work earning a common living."

And she was gone.

Lucas's focus bore down on Red. "You'd better not be whacking to interracial shit," he said.

"I'm not," Red said. "I swear it."

Tommy grimaced. He found a not-too-smashed pack of Camel Wides in a cargo pocket and tapped it down. "We gonna get to 'the situation' any time soon? The one that dragged my tired ass out here?"

"I don't know, Red," Burt said, his eyes small and mean. "I still don't trust him."

"While you're all hen-cackling amongst yourselves and rank-ordering self-pleasure techniques," Tommy said, "someone get me an ashtray already."

No one moved so he skewered Trent with a stare and sure enough Trent hopped to and brought over a Solo cup with a thin layer of tobacco spit at the bottom. It'd do. He stood there slouched and uncomfortable until Tommy dismissed him with a flick of his eyes.

Tommy snicked up a flame from his Zippo, mumbling around the stick in the corner of his mouth: "Anyone give a shit if I light up in here?"

"You smoke wherever you want in this house," Red said, with pride.

Tommy brought fire to his lungs, shot a smoke stream to the side, and lowered himself heavily into one of the chairs that had materialized while he was waxing poetic over Old Glory in the front yard.

"Before we get to the situation," Red said, "you gotta understand context."

Tommy rubbed his eyes. They were sore from the night's restlessness or just because sore was what they were now. "Context," he repeated, wearily.

"We got American values under attack here," Red said. "Christian values."

"I ain't met a ton of Hindu Mexicans, son," Tommy said. "So you wanna connect the dots for me about how these Mexicans you said got run over were attacking Christianity?"

"I told you," Burt said. "I told you we couldn't trust him."

"Our border security's a joke," Hick blurted.

That's where Hick was then, nibbling around the edges. His voice was strained, like he'd had to push himself to join in.

"Amen to that," Tommy said. "First sensible thing's come outta any of your mouths since I got here."

Trent piped up, "And those dipshits in D.C. are letting anyone spill in illegally and get naturalized so they can take over America."

"First the Germans and the Irish," Tommy said. "Now this."

"Huh?"

Red said, "This country'd be better off if someone came in and dropped a A-bomb on the Capitol. Bullshit you're not thinkin' it, too."

Tommy heaved a sigh. The last thing he wanted to do was defend aforementioned desk drivers in D.C. with their tin-brained agendas and framed degrees on their walls and yet here he was, caught in a vise of quickening idiocy from every which way. He stared at the TV. An anchor with shiny white teeth was screaming down a guest in a monkey suit, a congressman from the Pacific Northwest who looked like a ferret who'd stepped in a bear trap.

"It is amazing," Tommy said, "that politics can make a state of affairs this dire feel so goddamned boring."

"Boring," Red said. "What're you talking about?"

"The country's on fire," Burt said. "How's that boring?"

On the TV, the anchor railed on. The volume was low but the disgust on his face was loud as ever.

"Pay closer attention," Tommy said. "Day after day they're tossing you the same shit widgets and y'all've learned to perform seal tricks for 'em."

"No, sir," Elijah said. "Nuh-uh. We don't need all the lingo like the crazies. We see it clear."

The line felt rehearsed; Tommy figured Little Man was repeating a sentiment the big boys threw around.

Tommy said, "Do you now."

"That's why we started the Liberty Guard," Red said, gesturing at the sloppy banner in case Tommy required a visual. "Because things are getting outta hand. And we're not gonna sit here and play by the rules when they're bleeding America dry with globalism and threatening the Constitution."

"Threatening the Constitution." Through the large gauge, Tommy sucked in another hit of Turkish and American tobacco. "I served under Tricky Dick, Jerry Ford, and that wet-lipped sissy Carter before Reagan rolled in, unfucked the ROEs, and treated us like men. All that time no matter if I was takin' orders from a crook or a peacenik, I never broke my vow to support and defend the Constitution. Not once. There ain't no threat to the Constitution except the one coming from ignorant assholes on both sides putting you up to tear it apart. You boys are in the bloom of youth. You shouldn't be holed up here playing La-Z-Boy pundits. You should be out picking up girls not bright enough to realize they shouldn't sleep with y'all."

"Maybe you're too old," Burt said. "You don't see what's going on."

"I'm definitely too old," Tommy said, finally giving in and rubbing the ligaments of his rotator cuff, frayed around the scar tissue of that ancient bullet wound, "to see what you're seeing."

Now Lucas again, reading with that psychopath drawl: "'The viewing will be at nine o'clock on Monday, followed by a brief funeral service at Our Lady of Guadalupe Cathedral, followed by a joyful celebration of life at noon.'" He grinned and it wasn't a pretty grin. "Why, that's today."

"This country needs us to defend it," Red said, as if Lucas had never cut in. "We're gonna get Prop S passed and keep going from there."

"What's Prop S gonna get done?" Tommy asked.

"It's a key piece of legislation that protects the rights of law-abiding gun owners." Red spoke in a practiced cadence indicating he'd recited the line a time or two before. "Like stand-your-ground."

"Well, I'm all for smoking a dickwad coming in with ill intentions," Tommy said. "How's it help with this current 'situation' we keep prancing around?"

Burt: "Means we can shoot Mexicans when they're on our turf."

Tommy said, "I'm pretty sure that's not how it's written."

"No," Burt said. "But that's what it's for."

"Sheriff Joy's gonna take this town back, keep it from turning into Hayesville," Red said.

Lucas again: "'Please wear happy colors. The family requests that no one wear black.'"

"If we get S passed," Red said, ominously, "means we don't have to take other measures no more."

Tommy stood up. It took a minute for him to get his joints to obey, but once he was on his boots he felt broad and strong and he knew from the boys' faces he looked it, too. He skewered Hick with a look and pinned him wriggling to the couch. "Other measures like running folks over?"

Hick shrank from him.

"Here's where I get answers instead of canned newspeak," Tommy said, his words pushed through a veil of smoke. "Or I pull chocks and get on my way. So, children. What's it gonna be?"

18

What Hick Did

They're coasting toward a fight, Hick and Red, the night crackling with danger.

They've caught word that Mexicans had taken up again in Calvary Park, the one at the edge of town near Hayesville. But it isn't across the county border, it is, it is on their side of the line and that meant they had a right to protect it. Lately there'd been graffiti on what was left of the jungle gym and needles in the public bathrooms and civilized folks had stopped going and that wasn't right, wasn't right at all.

Hick's driving the heavy-duty pickup and feeling high like he always does when he's behind the wheel. His old man's '89 Ram, a W250 with the 5.9-liter straight-six turbodiesel Cummins dropped in. The 160 horsepower might sound low but it got 400 pounds of torque at only 1,700 rpm, which meant it ripped up hills and across rivers to put a Wrangler to shame. Navy-blue walls and powder-blue trim, beefy five-speed stick, turbocharged with an H1C Holset that had been replaced three times in three decades to keep the roar in its throat.

When his old man came back from the sandbox in a crate, the truck passed to Richie, and when Richie went into the family plot next to Mom and Dad it went to Dale, and when Dale joined the rest of them it finally became Delmont's. Unlike most of Hick's clothes, handed down in tatters, the Dodge has been pristinely preserved, and even though he can rarely scrounge up gas money he feels a responsibility to venerate it as his only inheritance aside from his name, which skipped the first two sons and landed on him along with the full weight of his father's disappointment.

Three months after Hick was born, his mom ran off to Oregon with another man. It had been her ticket out, the boys sacrificed to her fate. When Hick was five years old she came back for three blissful weeks he still sees in images seared into his brain like the old Kodachrome slides they had before the basement flooded. The flutter of her hair when she blow-dried it. The long denim skirt that smelled of patchouli. The crack of her knees when she crouched to feed him a spoonful of strawberry ice cream.

She came back again for another two weeks when he was eight. At the end of the fourteen days she suffocated herself in the closet, fastening a garbage bag around her head with a blue polka-dot cotton scarf, wearing a church hat with a wide brim to keep the Glad bag from sucking against her mouth. He was told it hadn't been painful but still he imagined those last minutes with oxygen out of reach, one millimeter of plastic away. Sometimes he practiced holding his breath as long as he could just to know what it felt like. Just to be close to her. Years later he found out that the man she'd taken up with had been killed before her brief return but he never learned the connection and never would.

Red's swigging Jack out of the bottle now and the bottle's getting low, his face redder. Hick's had a few sips, which could be trouble, open container and all that, but so long as they weren't soused Sheriff Joy'd take care of them if anything came of it. Red's got his wheelgun on the bench seat between them, along with an old Remington pump-action and a long-armed set of bolt cutters resting in the footwell by his leg. He notices Hick's left knee jackhammering up and down.

"Don't worry, Hick." He smiles. "We're just gonna scare 'em some."

Hick kills the headlights and coasts past Calvary Park. It's fenced off except for the front with its turnstile entrances by what used to be the snack shack. The sturdy chain-link's easy enough to see through. The packs of gangbangers ain't there, no sign of the hombres with mustaches, gold cross pendants, and Tecates smoking and kicking around a soccer ball. No, there are just families spread out on the browning lawn past the crumbling handball court. They got picnic blankets and coolers and grocery-store bags filled with food. They got a big pop-up tent over a folding table heaped with bags of sliced mango, grilled meat, and those weird wagon wheel chips they eat with lime juice and chili. There are bright dresses and the men wear cheap suits except the ones in jeans and cowboy hats. The whole scene lit from the floodlights by the bathroom, stretching shadows out like Halloween, the festivities doubled in dark reflections across the sparse grass.

Good, *Hick thinks with more relief than he wants to admit to.* It's just a buncha families out doing nuthin' much.

He keeps on past the park and turns for home but Red says, "Hey. Where're you going?"

"They're just families," *Hick says.*

"Families can be taught lessons, too."

Hick feels heat coming up in his chest, the base of his throat. "I dunno, Red."

"Things are getting outta hand around here," *Red says.* "We gotta do something."

The Ram floats atop big-ass forties. Hick's old man had lifted the truck, added some length to the rear control arms, and extended the driveshaft to accommodate the bigger tires. Six months before Richie froze to death in the Piggly Wiggly parking lot by the interstate with his hand curled around a fentanyl vial, he'd dumped three paychecks into Super Swampers with 27/32 tread depth. Buprenorphine, propoxyphene, tramadol—every last shithead in town is a regular pharmacist these days, knows all the meds for the right fix or from a cautionary tale, but none of that matters when Hick's got these tires running beneath him. The pickup's got the power to take him across the span of this great nation, to every last edge of the continent, even if he's never found the nerve to leave the county.

He feels the force of generations humming beneath him now. It feels like driving his own city.

"What are you doing?" *Red asks.*

"Headin' home."

"No," *Red says.* "No. We got work to do yet tonight."

Hick pulls over. His palms are sweating, so he wipes 'em on his jeans, not wanting Red to see. "What're you thinking?"

What Hick Did

Red hops out, pulls something from his pocket. A Phillips-head. He disappears around the back of the rig.

Hick comes around the truck and there Red is on one knee, unscrewing the license plate. There's only the one; the old man hated front plates, thought them an affront to the face of a truck.

Red tosses the plate in the bed, where it lands with a rattle. An age-old instinct rears up in Hick that they'd better get that plate back on before his old man sees but then he remembers the old man's been dead and gone since Hick was twelve years old.

They climb back in.

Red twirls a finger in the air, meaning: Turn around.

Hick does, the heel of his sweaty hand circling the wheel like he's driving a big rig. They crawl back to the far edge of the park. The music comes audible again, that wailing mariachi crap where the singers sound like someone kicked 'em in the nuts. The window's cranked down and Hick breathes in the diesel tinge lacing the fresh country air, the smell of his old man.

Past the chain-link there's a long slope of grass heading down to the picnic area. The slope's about as wide as a football field but too slanted to be of much use for playing anything. Just above the crumbling curb sits a double gate, cinched up with a chain held by a padlock.

Now Hick understands what the bolt cutters are for.

Red offers them across. "Go on, now."

"We're not taking this truck down there," he says. "No, sir. Not my daddy's truck."

"Blood of patriots," Red says. "That's what it takes."

Hick feels the fear quickening but it's not about the truck. It's because of the way Red's mouth gleams in his flushed face, a predator's grimace.

"Don't be a fuckin' pussy," Red says, wiggling the bolt cutters. "Are we real or are we playing games?"

Hick takes the bolt cutters and climbs out. Way down below, the party is going on, folks dancing and hooting, and picnic blankets dotting the lawn. The floodlights hit the scene sharply from one side, everything at the edge of the celebration lost to darkness, and between the whooping and the music there's no way they hear Hick as he clank-clanks through a metal link.

The chain snakes through the poles and falls away and the gates yawn open from gravity, parting before the shiny, well-loved grille of the Dodge Ram.

That's what Hick did.

He opened the jaws of Hell.

When he comes back around, Red's sitting in the driver's seat.

"Uh-uh," Hick says. "No way."

Red revs the engine.

And he smiles.

"It was a accident," Red said.

Tommy had sat back down in the chair to hear the jumbled front end of the tale. The other boys sat reverently still, watching Tommy and one another carefully. You could've cut the air with a butter knife.

"We was just gonna do three-sixties over their picnic blankets and stuff," Red said. "And we did. We did doughnuts across their party like we meant to. And then when we was tryin' to get outta there the back wheel got stuck on a picnic blanket. It was a accident."

Red was breathing harder than before and he'd pulled his head back to shore himself up, a ginned-up show of cockiness. His tone stayed dismissive, unanchored from anything real, but his cheeks were flushed a color that human cheeks weren't meant to be. No matter how hard the boy tried to poker-face his way through, his skin was like a goddamned mood ring.

Tommy stared at him. There was more to tell but he wasn't about to start pulling teeth, not with where things stood at the moment.

Red's eyes darted away. "You know how trucks skid out?"

Tommy did. They all did. The question was rhetorical and he didn't have the stomach for wordplay right now.

"So it swung around sharp," Red said. "And hit some folks."

Tommy thought about the pickup hidden in the damp garage, that bent front fender, the shattered headlight, the caved-in front panel. He thought about flesh and bone meeting metal hard enough that the metal's what gave way.

He said, "Hit some folks?"

"Three of 'em. And a . . . and a boy."

"That's what happened," Burt said.

Trent said, "That's the story." He was standing in that dumb-ass sagged position, hips forward and spine curved, and Tommy wanted to poke him in the ribs just to scare him upright.

"They ran over some spics," Lucas said. And then he shrugged.

Tommy almost told Lucas to hide his face behind the newspaper again to lessen his temptation to punch it, but things were moving around the room he didn't yet understand well enough to take charge of.

Hick looked down at his hands and Elijah sat stone-still in the armchair.

Red cleared his throat. "We were drunk some. It was a accident."

"Yeah." Tommy kept his gaze level. "You said that."

"Well, we didn't mean it to happen," Red said. "Not like that."

"I'm no attorney," Tommy said, "but I watch a lotta *Law & Order* and I think you might need something more than that."

"No shit, Sherlock." Burt's words were hammered flat, no intonation.

"That's why we're hiding out," Lucas said, and Tommy noticed now that the brother-cousins' inflections were indistinguishable, that they spoke in one voice.

"Protecting the brotherhood," Elijah piped up. "Keepin' it pure."

When he spoke, he leered, his face shiny, possessed by some secret lust.

"You look fucking weird when you talk that way," Tommy told him. "No one with that face is headed for anything good."

Elijah blanched, a sea change. His eyes ticced nervously but stayed on Tommy's as if magnetized. Tommy pinned him with his stare, looked down into him, and he saw the moment it clicked, that Elijah saw something inside himself that he'd kept hidden, that he hadn't wanted to see.

Elijah's throat lurched and his hands took on a tremble and Tommy saw that he'd stripped the boy down enough to let him sit and stew with what he'd found inside.

Tommy turned his focus back to the others. "Who was driving?"

Silence.

He waited it out.

Red drew himself up in his chair, tilting back, crossing his burly forearms. Sweat stains at his pits and chest made him look like a jogger on a TV show. "Well, we're leaving aside the vagaries of who was behind the wheel to protect us both," he said.

Tommy thought: *Vagaries.*

Red sucked something out from between his front teeth. "Ain't that right, Hick."

Hick said, "Yeah."

Tommy got up again. It took time. He dragged his chair across the floor planks toward Red. It screeched some.

He set it down with a thunk in front of the young man.

Sat back down with a groan.

Their faces two feet apart.

He had Red's attention now, his whole attention. He looked right through the boy and the boy was defenseless to stop it.

"Don't you dare," Tommy said. "Don't you make someone else wear your fuckup. If y'all want to talk strategy about what to do when the shit flies in to roost, that's fine, but don't you put another man between your actions and the consequences. You own them. Your honor as a man demands it."

Red's lips were quivering, so he pinched them tight, the color draining from them.

There was almost no peripheral vision to be had, but from the corner of his eye Tommy saw Lucas shift upright, his arm making a casual move for the Glock on the windowsill, and Tommy had his SIG P226 out of a hip holster they didn't even know he was wearing and the SIGLITE sights were aimed dead between the boy's eyes and he never even broke the stare-off with Red.

Tommy's voice was as soft as a whisper but it wasn't a whisper, not even close. "You're three and a half pounds from eternity, Lucas. You reach one inch further, I'll turn you into sticky red soup right there on the couch. Don't think I won't."

It was the first time he'd shown a weapon and it was the right time and way to do it. The room was frozen. Even the floor planks stopped creaking.

Lucas eased back down and away.

Tommy returned his pistol to the holster but kept his shirt tucked behind the grip so everyone could admire the carbon-steel sheen.

Red pouched his lips forward now, walnuting his chin, his expression seesawing through all sorts of emotion. Tommy figured it could go either way.

"It's okay." Hick stood up from the couch. "We went in as brothers, we'll go down as brothers."

"Junior," Tommy said, "I knew about you before you was born. I was with your old man when he got the phone call at base that your momma was pregnant again. I know some shit about which way the world spins. Now sit down. This is between Red and his own self."

Hick sat.

Red was glaring at Tommy still, anger flashing behind the eyes, trying to win out over the rest of what was going on.

"Cowardice is contagious," Tommy told him. "So's honor."

Red's face tightened into a sneer. And then loosened. "Okay, fuck," he said. "I was driving. *I* was, okay?"

Tommy nodded slowly once, twice. "Okay," he said.

He stood up and started for the door.

"Wait," Red said. "Where you going?"

"All's you got in the cupboard is a dead mouse so I'm gonna go fetch some gedunk in town. I'll be back. Try'n not kill anyone with your stupidity in the meantime."

"You wanted to know." Red had lurched up to his feet. "So now what? What are we gonna do? About all this?"

"I don't know yet," Tommy said, and he left.

He was piling his tired bones into the truck when Hick came running after him. The boy had put on a mesh cap worn low to hide his face. "Wait," he said. "Can I come?"

Tommy stared at him through the rolled-down driver's window. "I thought you was hiding out like Billy the Kid."

"Yeah, well," Hick said. "The diner's safe."

Tommy grimaced. "Airtight operation your militia's running here, Junior," he said. "Airtight."

Hick picked at that smear of scar tissue on his earlobe. "It's just . . . I'm, uh . . ."

"What?" Tommy said.

Hick blinked a few times and looked at his shoes. And then Tommy recognized it in his face.

The boy was hungry.

Tommy leaned over and unlocked the passenger door.

19

We Go

There were four of them, slender and strong.

They wore leather dusters, balaclava masks, and wraparound shades to hide their eyes.

One of them knelt on the chest of a man. She was the Female One. She gripped a pair of spring-loaded pruning shears with bypass blades, which gave the cleanest cut.

The man's wrists were staked to the floorboards with six-inch galvanized barn nails and his fingers were missing down to the second knuckles and his tongue was missing. Blackness welled there at his chapped lips, wobbling in the overhead light.

She stared down into his maw with interest, her head cocked. When the wobbling ceased, she could make out her reflection on the liquid surface.

The man had already given up the names their employer demanded, names of co-conspirators. It had taken considerable persuasion. The tongue came out after the names, another demand of their employer. She would have it delivered in a sealed

NEMESIS

Styrofoam box on a nest of dry ice, the loose tongue that had shared corporate secrets with the Chinese.

The man was not yet dead but might as well be. Little noises gurgled through the liquid, freeing bubbles. His nostrils quivered ever so slightly.

He was in too much pain to be sentient.

They had seen that many times. That wavering middle ground between agony and expiry, where nothing but misery remained in this life and yet there existed no quick means to exit it.

The One Who Was Her Half Brother squatted in the corner, looking at his phone. "We have l-l-l-location," he said.

The next job with Janus.

For that they had to pursue a man who did not want to be found. That was okay. They had reach so far and wide that to the prey they swooped down upon, the Four Horsemen felt omniscient.

"We finish here first," she said.

The One Who Was Her Second Cousin stood in the middle of the loft apartment, his duster fluttering by well-oiled boots of black leather. "We have the names," he said. "Three names, all in town."

They used the language native to whatever region they were working in. Their English was rough but at least as good as their other languages. Their focused upbringing had not prioritized verbal acuity.

The One Who Was Her Nephew crouched on the tufted twill cushion of the bay window, keeping lookout over the street two stories below. "We move fast. Today, tomorrow. One, two, three. We clean tracks. And then we go."

Forty-eight more hours in Seattle's South Lake Union neighborhood to finish this job and move to Janus's. Janus didn't just pay well. He paid the best.

She was eager to wrap up this project and embark on the next.

"Where do we g-go?" asked the One Who Was Her Half Brother.

The One Who Was Her Second Cousin smiled. "We go to Calvary," he said, gesturing to the man staked to the floor. "The site of another crucifixion."

The One Who Was Her Second Cousin once studied at the seminary in Shkodër for several months until an unfortunate incident

148

with a youth pastor and a corkscrew terminated his time there. He was pretentious with his learning.

Beneath her kneecaps she felt the creak of the man's ribs.

His lips were cracked and bloody from when she'd forced them apart. She took no pleasure in inflicting pain. None of them did.

It was, however, an underutilized motivator.

The man was expiring.

They had the names.

It was time to speed matters along.

She thumbed up the partially serrated blade from her folding knife. "We release him now."

She dimpled the skin at the side of his neck two inches down from the hinge of his jaw where the carotid bifurcated.

And pressed.

He gave a little moan.

His head lolled to the left. Dark sludge spilled from the corner of his mouth.

She rose.

"We are ready," she said. "One, two, three more."

The One Who Was Her Second Cousin grinned, his teeth a scythe in the black wool. "And then we go to Calvary."

20

Uncommon Sense

The diner had booths as any diner worth its name should.

It was set up for December with a wreath on the front door and Christmas holly along the counter, adding cheer to the fifties-style red-cushioned booths with silver fixings.

Tommy and Hick set up in the corner with Tommy facing the entrance. They'd said hello to every last person on the way in.

The waitress was a big ole gal with a wide caboose and dimples and a smile so kind it about broke you. Her name tag said JUDY and her gait said she was dealing with corns or plantar fasciitis. But still she kept her feet and her cheer, plucking a yellow No. 2 from behind her ear and tapping it on the pad.

"Delmont Hickenlooper, Jr.," she said. "Haven't seen you about in forever and a day."

His gaze darted down. "Yeah, I been busy."

She looked at Tommy. "How you doin', darlin'?"

"Twenty percent better since you came busting into my morning like a ray of sunlight."

"Only twenty percent?"

"Twenty percent's a lot for me."

"Oh, is it now." She fussed with some hair that had escaped her bun, tucking it out of her face. "What'll I get you, hon?"

Tommy slid his drugstore readers back on and double-checked the menu. "Number-four scramble."

"Know what? I'm gonna throw an extra side of well-done bacon in there on the house since that's what the number four needs."

"Look at you, lookin' out for me."

"That's what we do here."

"Any chance I could get breakfast sausage instead of bacon?"

She tsk-tsk-tsked, made a correction on her pad. "I'll pray for you."

"Bacon's that good?"

"With the number four? Bacon's the only way to go."

"Then that's the way I'll go," Tommy said. "Oh, and coffee."

"Course we know coffee already with a number four, don't we?"

"Indeed we do. Apologies for the redundancy."

"How 'bout you, Delmont Junior?"

Hick scratched at his scar, shot a glance at Tommy.

"He'll have what I'm having," Tommy said. "And Judy? I'm Tommy."

"Pleasure to meet you, Tommy." Judy scribbled on her pad, underlined something twice for punctuation, and sidled away. "I'll return with sustenance."

The coffee showed up seconds later and Tommy drank it black and took in the patrons. Folks were dressed nice, crisp jeans and Western yoke shirts, and the music was country, real goddamn music that told a story about something. There were YES ON PROP s ads on the corkboard by the hostess stand and a few pictures of missing dogs and an older flyer, yellowed crisp from sun exposure, of a missing young woman with bruised eyes and stringy hair and a tip line with an area code from a different county. It fluttered there like a dead leaf, that last flyer, all the color and hope bleached out of it but everyone too tenderhearted to take it down.

A TV mounted in the corner showed a commercial with a darlin' overweight girl pitching antidepressants and a simplified prescription process. She was smiling and being her full self when the admen sent up a written scroll of side effects. Weight gain, suicidality, the whole shebang. If they included dropping your lady parts like a busted transmission, those poor girls'd still be gobbling 'em up, looking for help.

The murmur of conversations around them touched on real-world problems a few shades more disheartening than the nonsense Tommy had to wade through from time to time in Las Vegas. Broken tractor axles out of warranty and a fifty-five-mile drive to social services to re-up food stamps for the baby and a fourteen-month wait to get the damn state inspector out to perc the soil for a septic tank.

At the neighboring booth, an old couple held hands across the table, knobby knuckles poking up every which way. She wore a proper dress, and his navy-blue shirt was freshly starched. It was lovely, had the glow of routine to it, him with his folded newspaper to the side, her rubbing her thumb across the back of his wedding ring.

"Nice place," Tommy said. "And nice gal, the waitress."

"Yeah," Hick said. "Big Booty Judy, she's all right. She got a mom at home with old-timer's. Can't remember Judy's name, who the president is, nothing."

"Well," Tommy said, "I wish I could forget politicians myself these days."

Hick caught his meaning and his mouth ticked back at one corner, a smile he was afraid to let loose. He tugged at his burnt earlobe some more.

"What happened there?" Tommy asked.

"Old man got mad one night," Hick said, and he laughed.

Tommy smirked along with him. He'd seen Delmont Senior mad plenty of times and not one of them had ended well for the object of his ire.

Tommy sipped his coffee, took in the smell of cooking bacon. "Know how much DNA we share with chimpanzees?"

"Why'd I know a thing like that?"

"About ninety-eight point eight percent."

"Nuh-uh."

"And we don't freak the fuck out when they fling shit or rub their monkey parts whenever they damn please."

Hick looked at him, confused.

"But when we get to sharing ninety-nine point nine percent of DNA with human folks?" Tommy shook his head, gave a low whistle. "Then we fall all over ourselves fighting about every last difference."

The bemusement left Hick's eyes and something deeper came into focus for a moment and his throat clicked up and down in a swallow and he didn't say one word.

The old-fashioned chime ding-dinged atop the glass front door and a handsome man strode through. Too handsome. Curated two-day stubble, chin cleft, thick tumble of black hair that fell just so above light eyes. He was in his mid-forties, a peak power age for bureaucrats who thought they weren't, and he wore black boots with a broad square toe and fancy feather stitching and a straight heel with a ledge for jean stacking. A chorus of "Morning, Grady" greetings met him and he basked in the glow without returning them individually. As his head swiveled to take in the room, he locked on Hick and Hick shrank a little in his seat.

Grady walked over, his boots clapping on the tile, and slid in next to Hick across from Tommy. He folded his hands on the table, stared at the side of Hick's face.

"What'd we say about you being in town?"

Hick said, "Not to."

"So why are you?"

Tommy said, "I invited him."

Grady's gaze moved leisurely across to Tommy. His teeth gave an actual gleam when he grinned but there was no human warmth beneath the smile. It was a shit-eating dominance display. "Who are you?"

"Tommy Stojack. Friend of Delmont Senior."

"Old Delmont didn't have any friends."

"That's right," Tommy said. "But there's not a better word for what we were."

Grady nodded, wrinkles gathering at the corners of his eyes. His face was a pleasant mask that nothing could put a ding into.

The number-four scrambles arrived, Judy setting them down. "Get you anything, Sheriff?"

"Just the usual delivered to the station."

"Number-four scramble, side of well-done bacon for you, spinach 'n' egg whites for the missus?"

"That's the one."

"I'm starting to pity scrambles one through three," Tommy said.

"As you should," Judy said, as she withdrew. "They ain't much to speak of."

Hick took his cap off, set it on his knee, crossed himself, and said a silent grace. Then he stared down at his food but made no move for it. Steam rose off the plate in little wisps. It was like he was waiting for permission. With his humble posture and his pug nose, he was the picture of diffidence.

"We talked about this, Hick," Grady said. "It's for your own good."

He slid out of the booth and waited, staring down at Hick.

Hick looked at Sheriff Joy and then at Tommy and down at the steaming plate and then back at the sheriff.

He got out, leaving his food behind.

Tommy handed over his keys.

Hick took them and vanished.

Through the window, Tommy watched him sulk along the pavement. Two deputies had materialized to lurk around Tommy's rig, a territorial display. The one who looked to be around thirty had jug ears and a pronounced Adam's apple. He had a kind face and a solid build, gym fit. The other was a big tough bull a touch shorter than the first and a decade his senior. Prominent forehead with a heavy brow ledge, massive biceps made massiver when he crossed his arms. Leaning against Tommy's rig, he shot him a glare through the diner window.

As Hick approached, the younger deputy gave him a nod but the bull just glared at him, took his time shoving himself off Tommy's rig to let Hick get in.

Tommy sighed, refocused on his coffee.

The sheriff still hovered over him, wanting to make sure he'd watched the little scene play out. Grady made no move to sit again. Instead he looked down at Tommy. Tommy didn't want to give him the satisfaction of craning his neck so he stared dead ahead and sipped from his mug.

"That boy's gotta keep his face out of sight for a while," Grady said. "For his own good."

"Why's that?"

"Let some stuff blow over."

There it was, then.

Tommy thought he'd had a rough handle on the task before him. That he needed to figure out how to steer Hick and Red in to the law in a manner where the law could deliver them any consequences worth having. But he realized now that none of that was likely to come from Sheriff Grady Joy or the Calvary Sheriff's Station.

Tommy took another sip. There was no coffee like diner coffee.

"I'd imagine a nonfriend of old Delmont might blow through town bent on delivering some answers," Grady said. "But folks living here have a better sense of how to keep living here. Without unnecessary . . . friction. It's just common sense."

"Should be called *uncommon* sense since most folks don't have it."

Grady gave that matinee smile again, jaw flexing out, squaring his face. That stubble was manicured all right; Tommy could see the precise line on each cheek where he'd cleaned up with a razor.

"Glad we're on the same page, Tommy Stojack."

Tommy said, "Sheriff."

He applied salt and pepper liberally, leaned over his plate, and dug in. He sensed the shadow lift and then those boots tapped away and the front door chimed. The deputies evanesced in their boss's wake, leaving Hick sitting in the passenger seat alone, looking hungry.

The number-four scramble was indeed what to eat and it indeed required well-done bacon.

The instant Tommy had chewed his last bite, Judy was back with a top-off on his coffee. "Happy?"

"As a dead pig in the sunshine."

"Pie?"

"It'd be uncivilized to refuse."

"Rhubarb à la mode's what to get."

"You've steered the ship right so far."

She lifted the empty plate halfway, stopped. "Wanna keep your fork?"

He took it off the plate, slid it into his mouth, put it through the washer cycle.

She was back in a heartbeat with the pie heated and the ice cream just starting to melt.

"Thank you, darlin'."

"My pleasure, young man."

"Sheriff Pretty Ricky's a confident man."

Judy shifted on her feet, bit back a grimace. "Lemme sit. My ankles are killing me."

He tapped the table twice to welcome her. "Now you're talking my love language."

She heaved herself down.

Big Booty Judy. Ah, the badinage of youth.

"He's got good reason for confidence," she said. "Comes from money, won his last race with over eighty percent of the vote, 'll win the next one by about the same, married the actual prom queen."

"Spinach and egg whites," Tommy said.

"Gotta keep a prom-queen figure," Judy said. "And she does. Elise's all right. Brains, too, the whole package. She's his most trusted adviser. It's good when a woman's in on the mind of a man in charge."

"Can be," Tommy said.

"Town's been through it."

"Whole country has," Tommy said.

"Yeah, well, I can't tell if the world's getting shabbier or my eyesight's getting tireder."

"I wondered that for a while myself."

"What'd you decide?"

"It's both."

There was that smile again, lighting up her face.

"What's the scuttlebutt on Junior and his crew?" Tommy said. "You can treat me like I'm someone trying to help."

Judy sighed. "Nothing good ever came from a Buckley. Burt and Lucas. Them boys are wrong in the head. Grew up out by the creek, practically raised themselves. Problems with animals and stuff when they was younger. You can ask Sheriff about that."

"Animals?"

"Puppies. Kittens. Duct tape. Firecrackers. Them kind of problems."

Tommy said, "Roger."

"And Red, Red's a hot mess. You met his father yet?"

"I have not."

"When you do, Red'll make sense. After his momma passed his freshman year . . ." She shook her head. "That boy didn't stand a chance. Shame, too. He coulda been something different. Played power forward, had a real jump shot back before the high-school team lost funding. The others? Elijah and Trent, they're okay deep down. And Hick, too. They're like all the boys these days. But more so."

"Meaning?"

"Plugged into screens day and night. Wander into town pecking at them phones like zombie chickens. I had a slew of kids from the high school in here last night. Know what they was worked up about? Europe."

"Anything specific or the whole landmass?"

"More'n anyone'd care to keep up with. Go look around town some. And then: *Europe? Really?*"

"Same as everywhere else. That's what they're doing now. Shoutin' in the wind."

"And Hick and his crew," she said. "They're at the age."

"What age is that?"

"When they need something to do or someone to be mad at." Perspiration had come up on her neck. She dabbed at it with a paper napkin, fanned at her flushed face.

"Any idea what happened," Tommy said carefully, "to them folks killed at the park?"

"Calvary Park?" Her bright blue eyes found his, the intelligence burning bright. He could see her making connections she didn't want to make. "That poor family. Mother and father gone, adult son, too, home from the marines. And a eight-year-old nephew. *Eight years old.* They had a picture of him in the paper dressed as a cowboy for Halloween. Silver-tassel fringes, the whole thing. Eight years old is too young."

"Way too young."

"Whole community's sick about it, praying for them in church."

"What happened?"

"Who knows what happened," Judy said. "There's been problems both directions between us and Hayesville for years but there's no sense jumping to conclusions. Sheriff's tamping down that whole mess, gettin' it settled. A few folks said it mighta been a drug thing or something from their side."

"Like a hit?"

"Yeah. They got problems with that stuff in Hayesville. We do, too, but ours are more the prescribed variety. Nice, clean, and legal from doctors at the clinic who know best." Her tone held more weariness than bite. "So no, I don't know what happened. I don't know who was behind it. I just hope it goes away without turning into something worse." She pulled herself out of the booth and onto her feet. "We've had enough of worse." She cast a look heavenward. "Just kiddin', Big Man. I know, I know, we got plenty to be grateful for."

Tommy'd been searching for adults in town and was glad to have found one.

"That sheriff," he said, "the one with good reason to be confident. Does he speak for the town?"

Judy said, "How often does a sheriff speak for the whole town?"

"Not a once. But out of respect I thought I'd ask in case this sheriff and this town was different."

She grinned her bright grin, smile lines fanning endearingly from the edges of her eyes. "Top you off?"

Tommy set down some bills, enough to make for a hefty tip. "Thank you, sweetheart."

"You're most welcome."

Judy stared at the full plate resting at Hick's setting. "Box it up?"

"Yes, please."

"I'll put in some extra biscuits," she said. "He looks hungry."

"Yes, ma'am," Tommy said, "he sure does."

21

Rightfuckingnow

Hick devoured every last bite before they got back to the Hilde-ranch. Slouchy as ever, Trent met Tommy and Hick on the porch with the Mossberg, action open, slung over his shoulder the wrong way, the barrel wagging behind him stiffly.

Trent eyed the empty to-go box greedily. "Hey, Hick, what'd you get?"

"Number four," Hick said. "And bacon."

As Trent turned to watch Hick pass, Tommy could see two shells loaded in the chrome-lined chambers. The Mossberg's safety wasn't automatic, so it hadn't engaged even though the gun was open and swinging around like a stripper on a pole.

Tommy snatched the shotgun off the boy's shoulder, closed the action, flicked the safety on, and repositioned it over Trent's fore-arm in an elbow carry, the muzzle angled forty-five degrees to the porch roof. He grabbed Trent's shoulders, squared the boy up, and looked him in the eye.

Tommy said: *"Or."*

He took the shotgun back and put it again in Trent's control in a two-handed ready carry with the barrel pointing up. He uncurled Trent's finger from where it had settled on the trigger and flattened it outside the guard along the silver-scrolled receiver.

Trent had melted into his slump again, pelvis forward, back curled. He looked like a question mark. Tommy hauled him upright once more, patted him roughly on both shoulders, and left him on the porch in a proper sentry position.

Inside Elijah and Red sat on the floor in front of the TV playing video games. For once Red had taken the Smith & Wesson 29 out of his pants and set it on the coffee table. On the couch, the Buckley boys sorted through a few cardboard filing boxes filled with junk, handing items back and forth—a pair of feminine sunglasses, an old iPhone, a pocketknife.

Elijah fired away on the joystick, leaning to and fro in the chair like it made a damn bit of difference. There were all sorts of Hollywood explosions and blood spatter, everything up close and personal but sleek and antiseptic at the same time.

Red risked a quick glance away from the game. "What'd you eat?"

"Scramble," Hick said. "Bacon."

Tommy stepped across the gaming heroes' field of vision and unplugged the PlayStation from the TV, weathering groans and complaints. "We're gonna discuss next steps."

"What next steps?" Red said.

"About how we're gonna handle what happened at that park."

"We don't handle anything," Red said. "We sit here nice and quiet till everyone forgets about it."

"I'm guessing that eight-year-old boy's mom and pop ain't gonna let the memory slip with alacrity," Tommy said.

"That's not our problem right now," Red said.

"No? You think y'all can kill four people and not have it be your problem?"

Hick took a few heavy steps and sank onto the couch. His face looked raw, cheeks pronounced, hollows under the eyes.

Beside him, the Buckley brothers stayed in a kind of shared reverie, assessing items from the boxes silently and setting them aside. A pint glass with a Guinness logo, costume jewelry, an alarm clock.

The old iPhone rested on the couch by Burt's thigh, the case bedazzled with rhinestones. A personalized cursive script cut through the glitter vertically: VALERIA.

The name flicked a chord somewhere in Tommy's brain.

Burt said, "Any war . . ."

". . . comes with casualties," Lucas finished.

"War," Tommy said. "So that's what Red and Junior did? Declared war on a *quinceañera*?"

"Maybe so," Red said. "Maybe we had to."

"It was an accident, though," Tommy said. "Or so you keep telling me. You went there to scare them. So which is it? An accident? Or premeditated murder?"

"Who cares?" Red said.

"The electric chair might have an opinion on it."

Red's mouth jerked. He got off the floor and plopped in a chair. Sweat sparkled in his buzz cut. He rubbed his face and scratched at his neck, raising welts. "A accident. Like we said."

"Then it was a profound mission failure, boy. Call it what it is. Don't try'n frost it with glory and sell it as a cupcake."

Over on the couch, Burt lifted a tarnished silver picture frame from the box. He opened the back, scraped out a family photo, crumpled it up, and tossed it aside.

Tommy looked at that iPhone next to Burt's leg.

VALERIA.

It came back to him now, Lucas reading the obit in that dead monotone: *Maria was preceded in death by her mother, Elena, and is survived by her two children, Valeria, sixteen, and Miguel, thirteen.*

Tommy was surprised that even at his ripe old age he could still muster pure disbelief. He stepped forward, looming over the Buckley brothers. "Did you two reprobates rob the house of that dead woman while her family was at her funeral?"

Lucas and Burt looked up at him in unison with pale gray eyes.

"What do you care?" Lucas said.

Burt: "Aren't you busy hand-wringing over them other dead Mexicans?"

Tommy was breathing hard. "Boy, I'm here now under this roof. Which means you're on *my* watch. This shit won't fly. It stops rightfuckingnow if you want one ounce of my guidance to fix the mess y'all made before I showed up."

"We don't," Burt said.

Lucas: "Want your guidance."

Tommy looked over at Red. "That true?"

Red had his hands on his wide kneecaps and his legs were bouncing. It was like he was trying to hold them down. He jerked his head in a tiny nod.

Little Man Elijah nodded, too, but no one seemed to care.

Then Tommy looked over at Hick.

The boy was hunched over on the couch, elbows on his thighs. He kept his gaze lowered but Tommy knew he could sense Tommy looking at him. Hick's eyes finally flicked over to Tommy, flicked back down, then up again.

He opened his mouth, closed it again.

All eyes on Hick. His mouth made mumbly shapes but no answer came out.

Tommy said, "Well?"

Hick started to speak when Tommy's phone rang.

He yanked it from his pocket, checked caller ID.

Felt the blood leave his face.

"*No one* talk," Tommy said, his voice Master Chief firm. "Not a squeak."

He pressed to answer, lifted the phone to his cheek.

"What the fuck, over?" he growled. "I told you to stay gone."

The boys read Tommy's body language.

They weren't just still.

They were spellbound.

The line was scratchy, no doubt from that crazy phone bouncing the call through Whoknewwhereistan and eleventeen other countries.

"We have unfinished business." The voice came across the line with infuriating calmness, wrenched dry of emotion. "Now more than ever."

Tommy had heard him talk plenty but he'd never heard him sound like that—not aimed at him, at least. It prickled the hair on the back of his neck, put a charge up his spinal cord.

"I warned you," Tommy said. "I warned you what'd happen if you came after me."

"Warnings," the voice said, "are for other people."

Tommy set the phone against the top of his chest and breathed a moment. The young men stayed frozen in their seats, hanging on his every word.

It was scary what was coming, yeah, but he also felt a profound sadness.

That it had come to this.

Back to the phone. "Okay." The word had a heft to it Tommy felt in his chest. "I'm outta town on some business. And we ain't gonna chase each other around tracing cell-phone signals and whatnot. I'm too old for that shit and I'm busy with a"—quick glance to Hick and Red—"'situation.' No. If we're gonna kill each other it can wait till I'm back. We'll do it like men, sit down face-to-face and then decide what's to follow. I'll call you when I'm back. We'll figure out the where and when."

Evan said, "No."

The line cut.

Sweat cooled on Tommy's back, beneath his arms.

He lowered the phone slowly from his cheek.

Hick said, "What was—"

Tommy threw up a stop sign with his hand, palm out, and Hick cut off midsentence.

It was quiet. But it was not peaceful. The wind kicked up through the gaps around the windows, making a shushing sound.

Tommy's mouth was filled-with-sand dry.

A tree branch bobbed, throwing a shadow through the patchy shutter over the front window.

And then a creak.

The third porch step. Tommy had noted the sound each time he'd mounted those stairs.

More silence. More shushing.

A faint thump. Almost gentle.

A zippering sound, serrated plastic teeth ticking through a pawl.

Then the same again.

Rightfuckingnow

Tommy felt sweat trickling down his left temple, clinging to the edge of his jaw. The young men were keyed to him, no one daring to move.

Tommy's focus was locked on the front door. He spoke in a barely audible whisper, not even daring to unclench his teeth: "No one move. Understand?"

Without turning his head he sensed five heads bobbing in concert.

Outside on the porch came a knock of a boot against the wooden slats.

And then another.

And another.

And then nothing.

There'd been no shadow through the slatted shutters, no sign of life. The Nowhere Man gave nothing up. Until he did.

Tommy blinked against the dryness of his eyes.

The old house strained in the wind and a draft sluiced across Tommy's damp shirt and he felt the cold down deep in his old-ass bones. He heard the boys breathing, all five of them distinctly.

He stared at the hammered-brass doorknob, waiting for a twitch.

The door ripped open, the dead bolt freeing a chunk of the side jamb, and a form flew in horizontally through a spray of splinters and goddamn it if Tommy didn't gasp like a choirboy who'd dropped the censer.

Trent landed a good four feet across the threshold zip-tied like a roped calf. His sallow face was smashed to the floor, shoving his cheek into a fat-boy pooch, eyes bulging. His wrists and ankles were cinched tight, the cable ties biting through skin and denim. Trent's mouth was open and quavering but no sound came out.

The boys around Tommy were scared upright in their seats, faces washed of color.

The front door was wobbling closed again after striking the inside wall. It blinked shut, drawing a curtain against the light of day, and then creaked back open once more and when it did Evan was standing in the threshold backlit darkly from the midday sun.

22

High Noon

Evan's face was full shadow—no eyes, no features, nothing but an edge of jawline that caught a hint of sunlight. He had an ARES 1911 in his left hand pointed down at the floor and a Benelli M1 combat shotgun slung diagonally across his back.

Tommy knew the weapons well. He'd procured them.

Twinning bulges in Evan's thigh cargo pocket on the right side gave away the Steiner tactical binoculars inside. Tommy wondered how long Evan had been watching them, and the wondering woke up a fresh crop of fears.

Trent's head lurched against the plank floorboards and then he found his breath and coughed twice and started to cry.

Evan's outline said, "*Sssh.*"

And Trent did.

The others eased back down into their seats. Tommy could feel Lucas and Burt thinking about it.

"Stand down," Tommy said, in that same low whisper.

"The fuck are you talking about," Lucas said.

Burt: "There's *seven* of us."

"Stand *down*." There was a wobble in Tommy's voice this time. Fear. Not for himself.

The young men must've heard it, too, because no one said anything else and no one moved.

Tommy's and Evan's outlines stared at each other for maybe thirty seconds.

Thirty seconds was a very, very long time.

Tommy couldn't tell where Evan was looking but he sensed the stupid militia flag hanging on the wall behind him and the Glock on the windowsill and the shotgun leaning in the corner by the couch like an umbrella.

Anger bloomed inside him, burning away the fear. "I was asked into this house," Tommy said. "Which makes it my turf. You don't come into my house. You don't fucking dare."

There was no response and for an instant it seemed the form in the doorway was nothing more than that, a shape devoid of humanity.

And then it said, "I've kicked in doors to a lot of houses. I've heard a lot of stories about what makes each one different."

"This one *is* different," Tommy said. "Because I'm standing in it."

"There's one motel in town. So you all know where I'm staying, too. You're welcome to come kick in my door anytime."

He said it like a dare, and from the way the boys' eyes widened Tommy knew they'd registered it as such. The outline of Evan's head shifted just slightly and though they could not see his eyes, it was clear he was giving each one of them his focus in turn.

"If you do, if any one of you comes for me, I will end you," Evan said. "Do you understand me?"

Lucas found his voice first. "Fuck you. You don't come in here and tell us shit."

"No one threatens us," Burt said. "We do the threatening."

"I'm not asking you to agree," the form said quietly. "I'm asking if you understand what I've just told you."

A moment of perfect stillness.

Lucas lunged for the Glock on the windowsill behind the couch and Tommy yelled *"No!"* and Evan's gun hand didn't move—it was just already there in position—and a shot ripped through the air and Tommy cringed, shoulders rising.

His gut roiled with acid. He had to tell himself to turn his head to see the damage and then he did.

Lucas was stock-still on the couch, mid-lunge, arm still reaching though the Glock remained a good two feet away. In the couch back cushion not a half inch from his nose, smoke wisped up from a hole with singed edges.

With excruciating slowness, Lucas retracted his arm, pulled his head away, and turned his face to the hole there by the tip of his nose. The room smelled of gunpowder and burnt fabric.

All eyes moved again to the form filling the doorway.

"Yeah." Hick's voice, cracked with dryness. "We understand."

The silhouette of the gun spun once and disappeared into the shadow of the body somewhere around where an appendix holster would sit. The arm swung back down to the side, hand empty, all five digits defined.

"You run off and join a militia, Tommy?"

Tommy said, "Don't bring these boys into it."

"You brought them into it when you fled here."

"'Fled'? I didn't flee shit."

"You just happened to split town after ambushing me at your shop?"

"What the red hell are you talkin' about? I don't need to ambush your ass. I'd set up a thousand yards out, give you one last chance to wave a white flag, then take your head off your shoulders."

"You tried."

"Best not keep speaking in riddles, Evan. I'm plenty of things you may not like but I'm no more a liar than you are."

The first hesitation in that dark shape of a person. No movement, no sound, but Tommy could sense uncertainty coming off the silhouette like a pulse wave.

"You didn't set up seven men in your shop to kill me? You didn't snipe at me from the sand dune behind your place?"

"You really think I'd kill you with no warning?"

"You warned me already. And I don't know what you'd do, Tommy. Not anymore."

"Well, I didn't," Tommy said. "I didn't."

The wind came up again, blowing through the gaps and cracks of the house and tunneling out the front door, setting the boys' hair aflutter. Not Evan's though. That form stayed immobile, immune from the laws of nature and physics.

Then it heeled back a half step beneath the overhang and the light caught the face from the side now, three-dimensionalizing him, turning him real.

Over in his chair, Red sucked in a sharp intake of breath. On the floor Trent gave a pained exhalation and then another. Sounded like a broke rib.

"What about your surveillance feeds?" Evan said.

"I been away," Tommy said. "And I can't get the damn app to work."

"Jesus Christ, Tommy."

"I know." Tommy rubbed his face. "So you're telling me I got a bunch of dead assholes at my shop and I don't even know about it?"

"Yes."

"But my security alarm." Tommy's backup phone was still in his hand and he wiggled it. "I didn't hear shit from my alarm."

"Who's your alarm go to?"

"Who'd'ya think? Me. Who else knows what scenario calls for what and who?"

"Lemme see your phone," Evan said.

Tommy looked at the screen of his phone. He could see his reflection in it, the bristle of his horseshoe mustache, his tired eyes. That goddamned shoulder ached. His neck ached. His teeth ached, too. He wanted an injection of tobacco and caffeine directly into his arteries.

Evan held out his hand.

Tommy glared at him. Then tossed his phone across to him.

Evan caught it on the fly. He thumbed at it a minute.

"Your notifications are off," Evan said.

He flipped the phone back.

Tommy caught it, checked out the notification screen. Sure enough, there the security alarm setting was, toggled off. Stupid-ass thing must've made up its own damn mind during the last software update.

He hated phones.

He punched at the toggle, moving it to green.

An instant of silence.

And then.

Ding. Ding.

Ding ding ding.

Ding.

A four-alarm emergency. From two days ago.

Tommy pinched the bridge of his nose. If he had any sense, he'd be embarrassed, but he was too busy being angry in hopes of staving off the dread.

He knew what it meant. A raid like this set up at his place.

He calculated which three calls to make to clean up this particular mess but he knew that after this mess there would be another and another until the job got done.

"Want to tell me what that's about?" Evan said.

"It's none of your fucking"—*ding*—"business is what it's about," Tommy said.

"Hit team gets sent to your place to kill me," Evan said. "Seems like it might be."

Ding ding.

Ding ding ding.

Tommy fussed at the phone and finally got it silenced so it'd stop undermining him like a vaudeville prop.

Evan wasn't smiling and his expression hadn't changed but Tommy swore something had shifted beneath the skin to convey amusement.

"Set it aside," Tommy said, wagging the phone. "They won't find you again." He gestured at the shabby furniture, the shabby boys, the stupid fucking militia banner. "Set this aside, too. What's between us is between us."

Evan didn't shake his head. He didn't nod either.

High Noon

"There's a ghost town one county over," Tommy said. "I'll meet you there."

"High noon on the morrow?" No smile.

"Sundown tonight," Tommy said.

"Can I wear a Stetson and shiny silver star?"

"You can wear assless chaps and Drakkar Noir for all I give a shit. Just get off my porch."

"Me and you only. If you bring anyone for backup, make sure they're assholes."

"Why?"

"Because I'll kill them."

Evan brought the toe of his Original S.W.A.T. forward and nudged the door. It hinged open, bounced off the drywall, and swung shut.

The dead bolt banged against what was left of the jamb and when the door creaked open once more, Evan was gone.

23

Decent Folks

The Emerald Bay Motel was neither emerald nor within commuter-flight distance of a bay. The proprietor, a stout woman with bristling gray hair swept up in a bun, worked on her needlepoint behind a sign declaiming the place's five-star rating, attributed in tiny print to a single Yelp review.

Evan said, "I need a room."

"Pick one." She conducted business without looking up.

"They're all empty?"

"This look like a hot tourist draw to you?"

"First floor," he said, "corner."

Two walls with windows opened up more vantages and options for egress.

"I'd like to rent the connecting room behind, too."

"For what?"

"Stretch my legs."

Still no glance up from the needlepoint, an incipient throw-pillow cover that read NEVER POSTPONE JOY. She was embellishing one edge with yellow daisies.

"No funny business. Girls, whores, drugs."

Evan said, "No, ma'am."

"How long?"

"Not sure."

"Want me to write that in the book?"

Evan set down a rubber-banded fold of twenty hundreds. "You can write whatever you want."

The marguerite daisies were coming in nicely. "We're decent folks here," she said. "Don't think because you throw around cash you can get away with anything."

He had no idea how she'd noted the bills on the counter without looking.

"No, ma'am."

"Room 117," she said. "The Kinkade Suite."

He stood there. Her knobby fingers were going hard at a run of half-cross stitching.

"Do I need a key?"

"Right there on the wall behind me," she said. "You got legs."

He circled the desk and lifted the key off the pegboard.

"Room 132 connects from behind."

"The Dogs Playing Poker Deluxe Twin?"

"Nope," she said. "Just room 132."

"I won't require housekeeping."

"Tomorrow?"

"Ever."

He started out.

"Ice machine's broken. Extra towels and pillows in the closet. Toilet paper under the sink. I'm here till five P.M. Anything you need after that you get for your own self."

"Never postpone joy."

At last she looked up. Twinkling eyes behind translucent maroon readers. "Not when we can find it," she said.

He nodded.

"Thank you for choosing Emerald Bay. Not that you got a bevy of options but still. Appreciate your business. My name's Dot or Dottie. Not Dorothy."

Evan paused in the doorway. "Nice to meet you, Dot."

"You got a name yourself?"

"Evan."

"Welcome, Evan."

"Thank you," he said.

And he meant it.

The Kinkade Suite was like any other motel room but with a print on the wall featuring a red barn and a pond with ducks and a few sugary-sweet cottages with stone walls and thatched roofs, every last one lit from within by a fireplace glow. A wicker basket atop an empty mini-fridge held two packets of instant coffee and, inexplicably, a generic-brand granola bar that had expired nineteen months ago. The full bed was directly under the front window, and each room had a slipper chair and a humble round table with two folding chairs.

Evan had stayed in places so sleek and efficient it had taken him nine minutes to figure out how to turn on the nightstand lamp. This motel was fine. He was glad for it.

He'd already ventured to the unassumingly named room 132 to unlock the connecting door from the other side. Assessing the layout of the rooms, he called Joey.

She picked up right away. "What?"

Still upset, then. But efficiency was fine, even preferable.

As he cleared the slipper chairs to open up a wide lane through both rooms, he heard Dog making a low roo-roo-roo in the background, wanting attention. "Where are you?"

"Westwood."

He noted she didn't say "home."

Using a roll of Polyken 231 he'd brought from the truck, he taped down the latch bolts of the connecting doors so they couldn't click shut. "You decided to stay?"

"For now."

"Why?"

"I put my big-girl pants on. I'm covering your six professionally. We'll handle our personal shit later. That was the deal."

"Okay," he said, but he meant *thank you* and he knew she knew it. "Update?"

Decent Folks

He'd texted her the address where Tommy was staying and surveillance shots he'd taken of the six military-aged males who'd come and gone over the past twenty-four hours.

Joey rattled off a breakdown of names, aliases, ages, and criminal records to match the photos. There was a host of misdemeanor stuff—vandalism, drunk and disorderly, traffic violations, burglary. Along with the Hildebrandt kid who went by "Red," the brothers Lucas and Burt had shaken off a number of assault-and-battery charges stemming from local fights at various public venues. Myriad reports and charges had been filed with the sheriff, Grady Joy, only to peter out.

Evan figured a good-ole-boy network was in place, "justice" handled through other means. Though the picture seemed pretty clear, the First Commandment reminded him: *Assume nothing.*

Setting his thigh against the metal frame of the bed, he nudged it along the wall, sliding it until it hit the corner. If he sat on it with his shoulders to the wall, he'd have a good view of the parking lot and the main road running in. "Any idea why Tommy's bunking in with them?"

"I ran some intersection algorithms—ya know, a binary search over sorted interval sequences, each corresponding to an inverted list and constructed by establishing a trie over the sequences of set identifiers," Joey said.

"As one does," Evan said, but she buzzed right on.

"Turns out Tommy served with Delmont Hickenlooper's old man, now deceased. I'm guessing family friend, something like that."

Evan thought about the kid he'd seen over Tommy's right shoulder hunched on the couch. He'd had a trucker getup, the mesh hat, worn jeans, scraggly hair. A solid kid. Awkward energy, unsure of himself. He'd filled out his chest and arms from weightlifting but his frame had been built to hang about 155 pounds on so he was always going to be a 155-pound kid bulked up into the wrong shape.

"I doubt Tommy rolled all the way here for a social call," Evan said. "What's he up to?"

"I have a theory."

"Say more."

"Sheriff's databases show an investigation for a recent mass killing," Joey said. "Four people dead—mom, dad, adult son, eight-year-old nephew."

Evan checked the back of the bathroom door. A hanging mirror in a cheap wood frame was tacked on with finishing nails. It slid right off. "Shooting?" he asked.

"Run over by a truck."

"Rough way to go."

"Yeah. In the middle of a big party at a park just on the Calvary side of the tracks."

"What's on the other side of the tracks?"

"*Una comunidad mexicana robusta*," she said. "Mostly immigrants and first-gen. Right across the county line in Hayesville."

He set the mirror on the floor in the threshold between rooms at a forty-five-degree angle. "That's where the victims were from?"

"Yeah. Judging from online news and the aforementioned cluster of assault charges, there looks to be some good old-fashioned racial tension between the youth of said towns."

Returning to the bed, Evan sat with his back to the wall and checked the angle of the mirror's reflection into room 132. Not quite right—it gave him a view of the neighboring wall and bed but only a third of the window. He hopped back up. "The victims' family members. Get me names. I'd like to talk with them, see if they can shed any light."

"Okay."

"Any witnesses? To the murders?"

"Some descriptions were given. Vague—it was nighttime. But reading through them, I'd put my money on Red Hildebrandt and Tommy's new charity case."

"Delmont Hickenlooper, Jr." He adjusted the mirror's tilt against the doorjamb by about an inch and a half.

"And yet Sheriff Joy just can't seem to figure out how to connect the dots. Despite the fact that—according to the lobby surveillance cameras—both of those young men visited him at the sheriff's station one hour and twenty-seven minutes after the murders at Calvary Park."

Evan said, "Right."

"And Hickenlooper's sole registered possession? A truck matching the description of the murder weapon."

Back in position on the bed, Evan gauged the adjustment he'd made to the mirror. Now it gave him a clean view through the connecting room to the window looking out the back of the building. "No license plates?"

"None on the truck on the day. No surveillance cameras at Calvary Park."

"Any ATMs along the route, store security cams?"

"No. The county isn't exactly wired."

He thought about all those misdemeanor traffic violations Joey had detailed. "How about speeding cameras on stoplights?"

A slight hesitation; she hated not thinking of everything herself. "I'll check."

"You've pulled together a lot of evidence," Evan said. "All circumstantial, but still."

"I know, I know, the First Commandment. I could find out more if I could get into Hickenlooper and Hildebrandt's laptops or phones."

"I breached the local internet at the house already," Evan said, biting off a length of duct tape. "Got in with Aircrack-ng this morning." The software had captured enough packets that it could recover the password, speeding the intrusion by implementing a standard FMS attack with optimizations. "And I copied the credentials for SSH on the router so we can get into their network whenever we want." He tapped at his RoamZone, sending her the credentials.

"Look at you, all independent." She seemed to remember they weren't supposed to be bantering and cleared her throat. "Have you dug around in their AD profiles yet?"

He taped the mirror into place against the doorframe, wedging a pillow behind it to hold the angle. "Not yet. Busy surveilling."

"I'll look, too," she said.

"Good."

"Have you—" She caught herself.

He waited.

"Have you talked to Tommy?"

"Yeah."

A longer pause.

Then: "How'd it go? I mean, can you make up?"

"We're far from that, Joey."

Back in 132, he drew the sheer privacy curtains so no one could see in. The muscles across his chest plate felt tight from the battle at Tommy's and the long drive. He needed some focused stretching to open his shoulders and release his ribs but he didn't have time for that right now. He was busy making sure he wouldn't get killed.

"Where's this heading, X? I mean, are you gonna just—"

"Did you get anything back on the guy who set his attack dogs on me at Tommy's place?"

A pause as she reset back into her lane. "Janus? Not yet. I have the bots crawling through every database I could find and finding new ones as it does it. In the meantime, I've been busy fleshing out the story in Calvary."

He moved through both rooms, checking the angles on the mirror from different perspectives. "Good."

"That it?"

He sat on his bed, 270 degrees of surveillance open to his sight line, whether direct or reflected. "Yes."

She hung up.

24

The Most Dangerous Man Alive

Hick's bathroom upstairs was buttcrack nasty, but Tommy had once sheltered for a week and change in a Rabat slum that made the Hilderanch look like the Ritz, so he shook it off. Hitting the rainlocker, he washed pits and parts, doing his best to steam his head clear after the encounter with Evan. Having Evan in the mix was like lighting up a sparkler in an armory, but what was here was here and now he'd have to deal with it like he dealt with everything else.

He'd already placed his three calls, spinning up a black-bag team to clean up the mess back at his shop. The half dozen corpses Evan had left behind meant there was a hurricane brewing, a storm no one could stop. But maybe Tommy could do a bit of good here before it made landfall.

Naked and dripping, he searched for a towel in the cupboard beneath the sink but found nothing except a toilet plunger and a crusted spray bottle of grime remover that had died a slow death of ironic neglect. After using his old shirt to dry himself off, he dressed in the bedroom, stumbling over that stack of VHS tapes.

Then he took a pull of Jim Beam from his flask to settle his stomach and ambled downstairs.

He'd told the boys to shower, too, since the house was starting to smell like a locker room inside a barn and there they were scattered around the living room, slouched on couches and chairs like invertebrates, phones lolling in their hands or resting on the cushions beside them emitting dings and chimes and video-clip blasts. It was goddamned hard enough to keep an uncontaminated mind without carnival barkers screaming out of every flat surface but that's what it was these days. The young men were arrayed in a loose horseshoe around the TV, which was tuned to the usual cable station, emitting a steady drip of outrage.

They perked up at Tommy's entrance. Red was wearing a superhero T-shirt that read I REMEMBER WHEN CAPTAIN AMERICA WAS WHITE.

"That guy who busted in," Red breathed. "Who *was* that guy?"

Tommy had refused to answer questions before showering off and he still wasn't certain how to explain the Nowhere Man to the present company.

"No one you ever want to know," Tommy said.

Trent's cheek was still red from the scrape against the floor and he rubbed the band of raw skin at his wrist where the flex-cuffs had bitten in. He was slumped over in his chair, his posture worse than ever, that bruised rib not helping matters. "Why's he here?"

"Looking for me. Your only job is keep your head down and make sure he doesn't start looking for you."

Hick now: "Why's that?"

"Because he's the most dangerous man alive."

Hick's eyes widened and Red flushed. Burt gave a creaky laugh but took note of Tommy's face and stopped abruptly.

"What makes him so dangerous?" Lucas asked.

"He knows his mind. And he knows his body."

Burt: "That it?"

"That's it," Tommy said. "You think you know either, boy?"

"Yeah, I do."

Tommy dug his ball of keys from his pocket, winged them at the wall three feet above Burt's head. They hit with a jangle, banked off, and smacked him in the back of the neck. Burt lurched forward, rubbing the spot they'd struck. "Ouch!"

Tommy walked over, held out his hand. Abashed, Burt dug for the keys and handed them back. Already red marks dappled the back of his neck.

Tommy's shoulder ached from throwing the keys; he couldn't decide if that was more aggravating or pathetic, so he decided on both. Crossing the room, he gripped the doorjamb to the kitchen and stretched his wing back, setting on fire the tight web of muscle across his chest and deltoid.

"You really got shot once?" Hick asked. "In the leg and shoulder?"

"Yup. Won the slow-mover badge for that one."

"Slow-mover badge?"

"Purple heart."

The boys grinned. They liked being in on the joke.

"I'm gonna do everything I can to keep that man away from you," Tommy said. "And you do everything you can to keep away from him."

"He kicked in *my* door." Red went to the TV, clicked on a first-person-shooter video game, and settled back into an armchair in the corner. "Like you said."

"That's right." Elijah's voice was high-pitched. He stuck a thumb through a hole in his T-shirt, tugging at it nervously. "He'd do well to stay away from *us*."

"Oh yeah?" Tommy said. "Y'all in tip-top operational shape from all your tactical late-night militia-flag spray-painting?"

Hick looked down at his thumb and forefinger, still stained with black paint, and rubbed them together.

"Sure," Red grinned. "That's what we did last night. Made flags."

Tommy let go of the doorframe, his shoulder tingling from the stretch. "What'd you do, then?" he said.

No one spoke.

"Yeah, knuckleheads. Why don't you tell the man what you did last night?" Leslie was in the kitchen behind Tommy; she must've come in through the garage. She breezed past Tommy into the room, eyed the assemblage with disdain, refastening that pony-tail. "Regular profiles in courage, these heroes."

"Shut yer hole, *Les*." Red cast a conspiratorial eye to his friends. "'Member in those old movies? When they used to slap ladies for getting all hysterical?" That grin again. "Bullshit you're not thinkin' it, too."

"Good thing no woman ever gets within slapping distance of you," Leslie said. "So you don't gotta worry your purdy head over keeping them in line."

"What do you know about being a woman, *Les*?"

"I could draw an anatomy chart for you if you'd like. Spell out the ladyparts phonetically."

Red cast his joystick aside and hopped to his feet.

Tommy stepped forward. "Hey, now."

Red's face was so flushed it looked like it was on fire. He jabbed a finger at his sister. "Don't you talk shit to me with what you get up to. It ain't natural. I don't like it."

"She probably doesn't like that yer dumb ass smells like sour-cream-and-onion potato chips," Tommy said. "You don't have to like it. Just don't like it over there in your seat."

Red glared past Tommy at Leslie and she glared right back. Red tilted back his head, sucked his teeth at her, and returned to his chair.

Only now did Leslie blink a few times and loosen her shoulders. Tommy could see her coming off high alert, the unease beneath her façade. Pointedly unrushed, she pulled a pack of cigarettes from her shirt pocket, walked to the loose front door, and moved out onto the porch. The door swung shut behind her, the dead bolt tapping impotently against the blown-open housing, a final punctuation to all the failed sentry business the boys had been playing at.

"What'd y'all get up to last night?" Tommy asked the young men again. "With the spray paint? Did you go over to Hayesville and do something else we're gonna regret?"

They looked at one another and kept mum.

"We're sick of this shit," Lucas said.

Burt: "We gotta take a stand."

"What shit?" Tommy asked. "A stand against what?"

"Everything," Red said, visibly flustered now. He had a habit of speaking with his head tilted back on his neck. His front teeth had a gap worse than Tommy's own and he huffed a bit, winded from God knew what. "Like—like everything's 'pride this' and 'pride that.' As a Christian, there's only so much celebrating pride I can take. It *is* a damn sin, after all. At least they say so when *we* show it. Plus everyone on TV now's black or brown or whatever. There's no white people in commercials no more. You can't turn on Netflix without it looking like Kwanzaa."

Tommy crossed his arms. "Why give a flying fornication about the amount of melanin in some Hollywood goat rodeo?"

Red grew redder. "It's the principle."

"Not if you have to say so."

"I don't like black people," Lucas said. "I don't like Mexicans. Jews or Muslims neither. I'm not comfortable with them. And fuck—they ain't comfortable with us either. No problem. I respect that. It's how the world works."

"Bullshit you're not thinkin' it, too," Red said.

Tommy said, "Boy, you don't know what I think."

Elijah came in again: "Ain't one of them doesn't think it, too, a dozen times a day, so why don't we just call it what it is?"

"Jungle rules, man," Red said. "How do you think it is in prison? That's the natural order. Us versus them. Them versus us. They stay with their fucking people, we stay with ours."

"Maybe you'll have a chance to find out once we deal with the goddamned disaster at the park that emerged from this grand philosophizing," Tommy said. "See if you like it better that way. In prison."

Red didn't say anything.

He didn't say anything at all.

"What'd you do last night?" Tommy asked again. "With the spray paint?"

"We don't gotta celebrate all this bullshit all the time," Elijah said, as if Tommy hadn't spoken at all.

Lucas: "'Celebrate what we tell you to or you're a racist.'"

"Celebrate what?" Tommy asked.

"The whole anti-America agenda," Burt said.

"It's *their* fault," Hick blurted. "They been pushing and pushing and at some point, it's too much."

Hick said it with an angry kind of vehemence Tommy didn't quite understand. Then he realized: The boy had to stay mad enough at the Mexicans he'd killed for whatever imagined slights they represented to justify what he'd done. If he let go of that, let go of dressing up the incident-accident as a necessary retaliation, it'd just be him alone with his conscience and four murders on his head. He was already cracking, doubt pouring through at the seams. He needed more time. And Tommy wasn't sure how much more time they had.

Red had regained his composure. "They're *forcing* us. They're forcing us to celebrate it. It's bullshit. Everywhere we look, it's like they're taking over, schools and the media, brainwashing everyone."

Tommy drew in a deep breath, let it out slow. "I know it's annoying as shit to turn on a screen and feel like you're getting preached at and condescended to and told how to live your life. But that's called annoying as shit. It ain't called being forced. Son, I spent eleven days in captivity in the Baghdad Biltmore. I can explain to you what real coercion feels like. Feels like rubber hoses and ax handles. There was a Kuwaiti prisoner in there they'd starved so long he was eating the scabs off his own body."

"You think it can't get there?" Lucas said. "Here? In the U.S.?"

"I know it can get there," Tommy said. "If we keep leading it there."

"That's what we're trying to stop," Red said.

"You doing that sitting here in yer skivvies playing video games?"

Red glowered at him.

"You doing that by running over an unarmed family in your truck and then hiding in yer daddy's house like a bunch of quiche-eating nancy boys?"

Anger was seeping in at the edges, so Tommy took a moment, his chest heaving. Exhaustion settled in his bones. These boys were twisted up a dozen different kinds of wrong and the local law wouldn't help any in the unknotting, and now Tommy had a goddamned world-class assassin poking his snout into the mix. The hurdles were stacking up fast on the runway ahead, obstacle after obstacle to prevent Tommy's steering these boys toward the light.

When he spoke again, he was much quieter. "Getting out in the world and making shit work with people you don't agree with is hard. Not having a country broken up into tribes tryin' to kill one another is hard. Stability is hard. Hard is good. All this whining? It's easy. It just fakes you into thinking it's hard. And you'd better wake your asses up. This ain't a no-child-left-behind world. And your asses? Are getting left behind."

"Yeah, we are," Lucas said. "With all the Mexicans replacing us."

The front door swung open and Tommy turned, expecting to see Leslie coming in from her smoke. But instead there stood a Latina woman in her fifties. She had a grocery bag under one arm, a giant cooking pot under the other, and a turquoise leather purse the size of a feed bag hooked over a shoulder.

A flurry of greetings met her entrance, the boys lighting up and finding their feet: "Yesenia!"

"*Hola*, boys." She strode inside and adjusted her load, freeing a hand to muss Red's wet hair. "Glad you took a shower this week."

They laughed.

"Hang on." Tommy's hand was out, fingers splayed. "Just *hang on.*"

His voice was low and gravelly and everyone stopped and looked at him.

"I know I'm old and my eyesight is for shit," Tommy said. "But I swear to Christ that that there is an honest-to-goodness Latina woman."

"She's *Salvadoran*," Red said, with great authority. "That's, like, mostly Spanish."

"Yes." Yesenia rolled her eyes for Tommy's benefit, though in clear view of the boys. "I'm practically *European*." She thunked her massive purse down on the coffee table among a scattering of handguns and cell phones, looked over at Tommy's bemused expression, and sighed. "You're not from around here, are you?"

Tommy said, "No, ma'am."

She jerked her head. "Kitchen."

As she walked past, he gathered himself and then followed her in.

She was at the sink, peeling potatoes. "You're gonna ask how can I possibly take care of these boys given all their stupid blathering."

"*Are* you taking care of them?"

"I bring them food now and then so they eat. So yes."

"No matter what they do?"

"What they do's no business of mine. I just make sure they're fed a meal once in a while. If I did it in a restaurant, you think I'd take a moral inventory of every *tonto* who sat at a table?"

"No, ma'am, I do not."

"Then stop asking your silly questions."

"But I have more."

The mound of skinned and halved potatoes grew. Already the vat was starting to simmer, the kitchen filling with the starchy reek of spuds.

"What else, then?" She spoke with a tone of strained tolerance that Tommy found winning.

"You know anything about what they might've gotten up to with spray paint last night? Something to do with Mexicans in Hayesville?"

"I do not."

Red stuck his head into the kitchen. "What do we got today?"

Yesenia said, "Potatoes."

"And what else?"

"Just potatoes."

Red groaned.

"Prices are higher than a best man at a bachelor party," Yesenia said. "You want to find a job and pitch in grocery money, you can have filet mignon. But today? Potatoes."

"Okay."

"Not 'Okay.' 'Thank you.'"

Red ducked his head sheepishly. "Thank you."

She spun around, elbowed open the freezer, shot a stern look at the contents. "You still have my casserole in here."

"It got all hard and icy," Red said. "The freezer sucks."

"Eat it faster, then. I do not bring casserole here to die of freezer burn."

"Okay. Thank you."

"Did you do your laundry?"

"No."

"Do your laundry."

"Okay. Sorry."

He withdrew.

She went back to slicing, her hands a blur. "The closest thing we have to a grocery store here is the gas-station shop. I have to get what's on sale." From the bag she removed a massive bag of carrots. They were desiccated, barely holding on to orange. "But when the harvests come in, people are generous here. Neighborly."

"Small-town folks are the finest folks."

"First sensible thing you've said."

He couldn't help but smile.

"These boys, they have it rough. Have you met Mr. Hildebrandt? Victor?"

Tommy said, "I have not."

"Wait till you do. Imagine Red growing up under that man's roof. And Delmont Junior? He never could protect his *mamá*, not from his own father. You know what that does to a boy?"

Tommy felt it deep in his chest. He said, "Yes."

"I'm not making excuses. I just find no usefulness in taking offense. I'm from Latin America. Everyone's mad at everyone else all the time. Nicaraguans and Costa Ricans. Peruvians and Ecuadorians. Venezuelans and Colombians. Puerto Ricans and Mexicans. Chileans and Argentineans—actually, all of us and Argentineans." She gestured loosely to the living room with the paring knife. "So these boys? I don't care what they *think* they think. These are good stupid boys, same as all the other good stupid boys. You think it should be any different because they all stand under the same flag?"

"Yeah," Tommy said. "Yeah, I do."

For the first time, she stopped and looked at him and he saw on her face that she also wished it to be true. Then she returned to dicing. "I love this country. And I *appreciate* it as only an immigrant can. But the politicians?" She made a noise of disgust, air rushing against clenched teeth. "If you're not interested in fixing stupid, you must aim it somewhere. So that's what they do. Aim this side at that side. Aim that side at this. If you're born here, you think it's the first time it's ever happened. If you're born somewhere else, you know the playbook. It's as old as time."

"How come it ain't aimed at you?"

"As a Salvadoran? Easy. Anytime someone brings up MS-13 we shake our fists and shout, 'Not here! Not for one damn minute!'" She smiled, showing a gleaming line of perfect teeth. "Do you know how far MS-13 types are from a town like this?"

"Things keep going the way they're going, not so far as we might think."

"Amen to that."

She dumped the carrots into a salad bowl and headed for the living room; once again Tommy found himself in her wake. "Boys! Snack!"

A scramble of excitement across couches and chairs.

She thumped the bowl down on the coffee table. The boys all groaned.

"Stop your complaining," she told them.

"Can hardly blame them." Tommy gestured at the mound of carrots. "That ain't food. That's what food *eats*."

Yesenia ignored him, shaking a finger at the boys. "Eat your vegetables or your teeth are gonna fall out."

"Is that what happens?" Tommy said.

"Something." She pointed emphatically with the paring knife and withdrew to the kitchen.

The boys simmered down, grabbed handfuls, slumped back into their chairs, and crunched and thumbed at their phones.

Tommy stared at them. They might as well have been twelve years old.

He stepped out onto the porch. The easterly breeze smelled of marsh—wet weeds and sweet rot.

Leslie was sitting on the top step staring out at nothing. The American flag snapped overhead. He eased down beside her with a groan.

She did not look over.

"Bum a smoke?"

She dug in her shirt pocket, snicked up the last stick from the pack. Tommy took it and tossed it between his lips. He thumbed at his Zippo, got nothing but sparks. Again. Again.

With faint annoyance, Leslie pulled out a cheap plastic lighter and lit his cigarette for him. He took in the fire, dragon-breathed smoke through his nose.

God, tobacco could be magical.

He drew once more, shot a stream out into the crisp afternoon. That flag whispered its silky whisper overhead and he thought about the dented bumper of that Dodge Ram in the garage, the caved-in front panel. It had to be answered for, that dented bumper, before God and the flag overhead, but he was still gathering situational awareness, getting the read of local customs. He knew to learn the ways of a place before setting to change them. Every place was different. Every place had a different entry point, a different path to walk through to what was universal. He'd learned that in dank sniper hides and Slavic forests perforated by shells. He'd learned it by taking lives with steel and lead and having men like old Delmont bleed out in his lap. He'd learned it by doing it wrong and once in a while by the grace of God getting something right.

And goddamn it, with everything cinching in on him right now like a noose, he wanted to get it right. This one thing. This one stupid-ass kid, Delmont Hickenlooper, Jr., with his stupid-ass choices, who'd taken lives for stupid-ass reasons, who just might be able to be saved, whatever the hell that meant anymore.

It would start, as with all things, by stopping.

"What'd they do?" Tommy asked. "Last night? With the spray paint."

He had to know. He had to know that part first.

Leslie squinted into the cold. She had a handsome face, pretty eyes, that unruly hair the color of natural copper. "Defaced a building."

"Which building?"

"Can't tell you."

"Why not?"

She glanced over at him. She had the least beguiling face he'd ever seen. Authentic through and through. "He might be a prick," she said, "but he's my brother. You can't figure it out yourself, you ain't earned the right to interfere."

He nodded. Took another puff.

She held out her hand.

He handed the Marlboro across. She took a long draw, closing her eyes into it, and then offered it back.

He hesitated, felt an age-old bias churn inside him, deeper than muscle memory. But he took the cigarette back.

Sitting side by side, they smoked it down together.

25

Churn of Hatred

The man took the corner booth, the same one that out-of-town charmer Tommy had sat in earlier. And like Tommy, he sat facing the door with a calm kind of focus. Average size, average build, forgettable face. Not bad-looking but not too handsome either.

Judy moved over to him. Her ankles were swollen to hell and her arches ached but that was the job.

"What'll it be, hon?"

The man did not look up. He was busy arranging his fork and knife, lining them fastidiously at the edges of the paper placemat. He used a napkin to wipe a spot of maple syrup off the table, then held it crumpled in his hand, looking mildly distressed.

"Get that for you?"

He handed it to her. "Thank you."

"That's what we're here for." She tapped her pencil on her pad. "We're still serving breakfast, too. I'd recommend the number-four scramble."

His focus was intense but not creepy like how some men looked at you when it felt like a violation. It was more like he was a computer scanner that mapped everything it encountered, committed it to memory, and right now she just happened to be standing in front of the feed. His eyes moved with a smooth alertness, neither rushed nor nervous, from her to the door to the windows to the other patrons and back to her.

"Two turkey sandwiches," he said. "Sprouts, no mayonnaise. Glass of water. Another napkin. Thank you."

Not much of a conversationalist. But at least he had manners.

The sandwiches were perfect, the toasted bread holding a bit of warmth. The smell of diner coffee in combination with the decor elicited in Evan a nostalgia for a past that, as a broke foster kid from East Baltimore, he'd never personally inhabited. Yet still he found comfort in this brand of Americana, a welcoming embrace that felt familiar even to an outsider. It was a hard-to-define sensation, the kind of thing Germans made up words for.

The jukebox had been sending out a steady stream of good mood, songs about everyday heroes and simple blessings and red-dirt roads. The flannel-intensive folks lining the counter and scattered through the four-tops kept up a hum of affable conversation. Hands chapped from real work, faces chapped from real weather, kindness showing around the eyes. A warm shelter from the bite of December.

For the past fifteen minutes, Evan had been keeping an eye on his burner laptop, where a data-scraping AI bot rifled through Hick's emails, texts, social-media posts, and search history from the last year, collating them into different clusters. Right now, a torrent of multimodal content was flashing by—animated GIFs, virulent memes, and 8chan poison. They loaded and sorted in fast-forward, a card-deck shuffle before his eyes. It was fascinating to behold the fire hose of reality-warping toxins that had blasted into a single human mind over twelve months. During his unsanctioned missions as Orphan X, Evan had swum in plenty of similar currents, learning how to identify patterns and webs of influence, how to source the tributaries feeding into a stream of persuasion until it reached critical mass to overpower sense and sensibility.

He caught one image flying by, a speck of snow in a storm, and a sting of recognition moved electrically up his spine.

He tapped to stop the churn of hatred, clicked backward through dozens and dozens of images searching for the cartoon.

There it was.

An Arab man. Long beard, dark eyes, jackboot shoved down on the back of a woman in a hijab, squashing her into the ground. INJUSTICE AGAINST WOMEN ANYWHERE IS A THREAT TO JUSTICE EVERYWHERE.

The meme Joey had disseminated.

Here in the dead middle of the country on the computer of an angry young man who'd likely run over a family of immigrants.

Well. Shit.

That didn't mean Joey was responsible. It wasn't as if her few added bytes of noxiousness had tipped Hick and Red from civil to murderous. But it certainly hadn't helped. Joey had mucked around in matters she hadn't understood and her efforts had found their way here in full color.

His heartbeat had quickened. He felt it there in his chest, fluttering the side of his neck.

Few things escaped Joey's notice. If he'd caught it, that meant she'd catch it, too. And then what?

The waitress was there at his elbow, reaching for his plate. "Keep your fork?"

He answered on autopilot. "I'd like a clean one, please."

"Having pie?"

"No."

"Then what do you need a clean fork for?"

He looked up. "Just the check please."

As the waitress withdrew, he felt the hum of his RoamZone in his pocket.

Joey on caller ID.

He took a breath, braced for impact, and answered. "Go."

"I got it."

He waited, stared at the frozen meme on his computer. "Say more."

"The family of the people who were run over. Most of the relatives are in Chiapas. But the eight-year-old boy who was killed? Gabriel Martinez?" She rolled the first "r," lending the name appropriate musicality. "His parents are in Hayesville. Lidia and Santiago. I'll text address and pictures."

"Copy that. I'll head there now."

"I'm still searching for Janus. And I'm getting at the traffic-light cameras around the park and along the route back to the Calvary Sheriff's Station."

He stared at the meme on the screen before him. The Arab man in his *pakol* hat and *tunban* had dark beady eyes, teeth showing in an animal grimace.

She hadn't pried to get more answers about Tommy. Uncharacteristic. He wondered if she was just still mad or if she'd anticipated he'd seen the meme.

"Is that it?" he said.

Her voice, shot through with suspicion: "What else would there be?"

He caught himself. "Nothing," he said, and cut the line.

26

Unconventional Cravings and Poor Impulse Control

There were four of them, slender and strong.

They wore leather dusters, balaclava masks, and wraparound shades to hide their eyes.

One of them stood out on the balcony holding a man upside down off the railing. She was the Female One.

It was hard to hold a man over a balcony. Men were heavy. This one wore a suit, his tie flickering horizontally like a skinny flag. Wind mussed his hair. He wore argyle socks and expensive leather boots, shiny black with pointed elf toes. He'd wet himself, a dark splotch on his gray linen slacks. One eye had been put out. It resided temporarily in the Female One's pocket until it could be mailed out to their employer in a package labeled PERISHABLE.

She bear-hugged his ankles, keeping his calves pressed tight to the railing. The One Who Was Her Half Brother and the One Who Was Her Nephew stood on either side of her.

They were five stories up. The corner of Olive Way and Eighth Avenue was bustling, commercial. Below, people scurried obliviously in forest-green fleeces and beige overcoats, umbrellas swinging at their sides. Though it was not currently raining, the wind carried the scent of coffee and rain. The smell of Seattle.

The man was very still, swaying gently, a meditative bat.

Fear could paralyze men. She had seen it many a time.

His eye was closed.

The One Who Was Her Second Cousin stood inside beyond the sliding glass door, checking the stamp beneath a cardinal-red vase with a narrow neck. He tapped it twice against its museum-like white pedestal, testing its durability. He liked unusual weapons. His face was often sweaty and it gleamed now with eager anticipation.

She did not like to sleep in the same room as the One Who Was Her Second Cousin. He had unconventional cravings and poor impulse control.

Other museum pedestals and art lay toppled on the floorboards inside, a wash of broken shards and pieces, the wake of the hunt. One had been a glass visage of a homely woman. One had been a porcelain platter with a ripple pattern. A gorilla constructed of scrap metal had fared best, lying intact on its side.

Despite all their travels, the Four Horsemen still found the world ceaselessly exotic. A chunk of the Female One's early life had been spent squatting in various unfinished mansions that dotted the Albanian cliffs overlooking the Ionian Sea. The cold concrete husks were remnants of the pyramid schemes that had proliferated in the mid-1990s' transition to a so-called capitalist market. Along with her siblings and cousins, she'd roamed the hard surrounding terrain with rebar, shivs, and shitty knockoffs of Chinese assault rifles. Food was scarce, expectations plentiful, supervision minimal. They'd learned what they needed to in order to progress within the family. Or they had not, their bodies consigned to the choppy gray sea.

She turned her focus back to the man swinging beneath her, looking past him to the sidewalk below. Foot traffic was clearing up. She tightened her grip, grimacing against the knots in her biceps and the ache in her hands. As the Female One, she was unwilling to concede physical weakness.

"Why we wait?" said the One Who Was Her Nephew.

"So we don't hit anyone below," she said.

"Why?" asked the One Who Was Her Half Brother. "We evade and escape easier the bigger the d-d-d—"

"Diversion."

The dangling man opened his remaining eye, looked around, gave a little groan.

She grunted, adjusting her arms around his ankles. "We don't need unnecessary—"

Her grip slipped. She grabbed him by the feet but then his boots popped off and she stumbled back with them in hand.

Regaining her footing, she dropped the empty boots and peered over the edge, the One Who Was Her Nephew and the One Who Was Her Half Brother at her sides.

Even as the man in the suit fell, he remained silent, pinwheeling his arms and legs as if running somewhere.

He clanged off a parking meter, dented the side of a Prius, and landed half on the curb, half in the gutter. This rearranged his anatomy significantly.

A woman on the sidewalk dropped an armload of Whole Foods grocery bags and screamed.

The Female One and the One Who Was Her Nephew and the One Who Was Her Half Brother looked at one another. The One Who Was Her Second Cousin stepped out onto the balcony, swinging the vase by its neck.

Standing beside them, he peered down.

The Four Horsemen.

The woman below kept screaming. Green apples rolled at her feet into the gutter, where sludge was spreading beneath the man in the suit.

The One Who Was Her Second Cousin held the vase out over the railing and squinted down, taking careful aim.

He released it.

It dropped, a streak of cardinal red.

It glanced off the side of the woman's head, shattering pyrotechnically.

She crumpled.

The screaming stopped.

The One Who Was Her Second Cousin looked at his fellow Horsemen.

And he grinned.

27

Transcendent Beauty

The instant Tommy stepped into the diner, the corner booth demanded his focus.

Empty.

But the bottles had been lined up in a perfect row on the table, three inches back from the edge. Ketchup, mustard, Tabasco. The maple-syrup caddy was on the other side, a matching three inches off the wall, perfectly parallel.

The packets inside the sugar caddy were ordered by color—white, fake pink shit, and turbinado cane that any self-respecting human used. The caddy itself was set at the precise middle of the surface as if someone had measured to center. The surface was spotless, nothing to clean, though the table hadn't been reset.

Tommy felt heat along the band of his trucker cap, a sudden uptick in body temperature.

Judy ambled over to him. "Hiya, sweet pea, getcha yer booth?"

Tommy was surprised at the density he felt inside his chest, how hard it was for him to refocus. "Actually came for you."

"Gonna sweep me away from all this, somewhere with a spa-blue beach and them umbrella drinks?"

"I should be so lucky," he said, and she smiled a true smile at that and looked for a moment like a bashful thing. "I need some ground truth."

"I love when you GIs talk dirty to me."

"Salty dog," he said. "But I figured you'd swoon at the lingo."

She tittered. "Consider me swooned."

"I heard someone vandalized a building over in Hayesville," he said. "Spray paint and whatnot. I figure you hear just about everything goes down in these four corners."

"Hayesville?" Judy shook her head. "Not so much."

He bit his lower lip, felt the mustache poke into the skin. There were plenty of others in the diner but none he could ask without raising a clamor. Especially with Sheriff Joy circling the matter with his sniffer uncorked.

"You want to ask around more, I'm happy to point you to some other folks who most *other* folks around here talk to. *And* listen to." She shot him a practiced wink. "You know, us ordinary folks who actually handle everything."

"Sounds positively democratic."

"Alarming, ain't it?"

"I'll take you up on it if I can't get to the bottom of this vandalism business."

"There ain't nothing around here one of us don't know something about." She jotted on her order pad, tore off the sheet, and handed it to him. "This here's my phone number. Now don't go gettin' any ideas. I'm just being neighborly."

"I shall be the picture of chivalry. I'll even mail you the key to my chastity belt before I dial."

Big Booty Judy gave her best version of a wicked grin and it wasn't half bad. "Now you might not want to give me that much control, sailor. 'Specially once I'm into my holiday eggnog."

"I can't believe it's Christmas already Wednesday." Tommy shook his head. "That just can't be possible."

"Dates whip by, don't they?"

"Feel like I'm eating breakfast every five minutes these days."

He heeled back a step, cast one more glance at that corner booth. He could practically sense Evan's presence still hovering over it like an OCD ghost.

"Hey." Judy paused, half turned away. "It's probably not what you're askin' about. But the mosque here in town got marked up last night."

Tommy stopped with a shoulder to the glass door, the chimes dinging overhead to match the epiphany. He exhaled but it didn't release the heaviness in his chest. "And where might that be?"

The mosque was a plain rectangle of a building, likely once an unimaginative house. No minaret, no gold-plated dome. Tommy stood in the parking lot with his hands on his hips, taking it in.

Black paint on the white stucco read *PROPHIT OF BUTCHERS*.

Across one of the windows: *TERORIZE YOUR OWN COUNTRY*.

Vertically on the honey-brown front door: *GO HOME!*

The spray-painted letters dripped down like blood.

Tommy chewed his lip.

He'd arrived smack between Dhuhr and Asr prayers, so the grounds were quiet, the parking lot empty aside from his rig. The midday sun was bright through the cold, cold air, making him squint despite his Oakley wraparounds. Atop a well-tended patch of garden perched a wooden sign with carved letters: *ISLAMIC COMMUNITY CENTER*.

He strode up. The door was locked and he figured he knew why. He rapped a straight rat-a-tat-tat, figuring "shave and a haircut" would be too jaunty an introduction given the circumstances.

No answer, no sound aside from wind drawing itself across the side of the building with a faint moan.

He knocked once more, louder, and stepped back a good ten feet, giving respectful distance. No one with those words on their holy house would appreciate feeling crowded.

This time he heard the faint shushing of feet across carpet within.

The door opened.

The imam wore a *thobe*, crisply ironed and spotlessly white. The ankle-length long-sleeved robe fluttered gently with the breeze.

His *ghutra*, also impeccably white, was expertly folded and tucked at the base of his skull, showing off impressive layering. A black tasseled *aqel* cinched it into place. He was a broad man, portly but not fat, and he wore Geppetto readers that caught the light in rectangular glints. His well-proportioned beard was feathered gray around the jawline and tip of the chin. He looked meticulous and gentle and stubborn as hell.

Tommy nodded at the spray paint. "I think some of mine did this."

The imam nodded thoughtfully. Near the door, he pushed his feet into leather sandals cracked with use. Then he shuffled out to Tommy and stood beside him, surveying the defacement scrawled across his building. He took in the dripping words dispassionately. Tommy took them in again through the imam's eyes. It was hard to do but he did it. The door had closed in the man's wake, showing off the childish lettering once more: *GO HOME!*

They stood for a time, shoulder to shoulder. Tommy noticed they'd both crossed their arms, inadvertently mirroring each other.

"I *am*," the imam said, in reply to the words on the door. "Home."

An Arabic accent, faint and fancy, maybe Lebanese.

"I know," Tommy said.

The imam looked over at him. Wary, but not distrustful. He extended a sleeved arm toward the door in invitation and Tommy marveled once more at how he managed to keep the *thobe* pristine in all this grit and dirt.

Removing his combat boots took some stooping and grunting but Tommy wrangled them off and stuffed them into a wooden cubby by the door. The imam waited patiently.

The prayer room was the size of a living room and a dining room put together, which Tommy imagined was precisely what it was. Well-padded carpet yielded pleasantly underfoot. There was no dome, not in a mosque this humble, but geometric shapes had been painted on the ceiling, trying for a sense of depth and grandeur. The Arabic word for pulpit escaped him but there it was, a freestanding unit that didn't match the surroundings, five wooden steps leading to a covered square pedestal. The only object of transcendent beauty was the mihrab, the niche pointing the way to Mecca. It was adorned with mosaic tiles of royal blues and whites, embellished with elaborate patterns interwoven with Arabic text. It brought Tommy back to the smell of smoked chickpeas in the souks, the taste of fresh-crushed pomegranate, the multisplendored palette of tubs brimming with lavender and frankincense, saffron and chamomile. He'd headhunted plenty through that world, had put more Hamas and al-Qaeda in the dirt than he could count, and on every last mission his ass had been reliant on *al-mukhābarāt* allies, tribal militia partners, or peerless Arab hospitality.

The imam led him down a brief hall into the kitchen. Aside from a few utilitarian concessions, it looked untouched since the original build. The cupboard doors had been taken off for easier access, and industrial-size bins of nuts and fruit and loose tea lined the counters.

The imam gestured at a seat at a round table near the window, and Tommy sat. His hips ached plenty and he felt the pull of habit to cross his legs and rest ankle on knee but he didn't want to show the sole of his foot. A framed picture on the wall captured the imam, his bright-eyed wife wearing a hijab, and a college-aged man, handsome and fit. It was a candid shot, the son's arm around his mother as they laughed together, the imam looking at them tenderly from the side.

The imam busied himself at the refrigerator and stove, gathering items. In short order, a tray of figs and marinated olives was laid before Tommy and he was being poured tea from a modern Arabian teapot of stainless steel.

"*Shukran*," Tommy said.

They sat. And they sipped.

The olives were small and black-brown, fat and bright green, garlic and rosemary, and goddamned delicious.

Tommy took another, careful to reach with his right hand. He chewed, spat the seeds politely into his palm. He said, "Mmm."

The imam nodded. "I know, yes?"

He took off his little rectangular eyeglasses and polished them on a microfiber cloth that magically appeared from somewhere in his *thobe*. Then he set the glasses down on the table between them. They were exceedingly delicate and gentlemanly, the rims plated gold.

"Nice readers," Tommy said, just to have something to say.

The slightest hesitation. "Have them," the imam said. "Please."

"No, no," Tommy said. "Just remarking."

"I insist," the imam said.

Tommy showed his palm. "Really."

The imam picked up the readers and proffered them to Tommy. His hand unwavering.

Tommy recalled the ritual he'd stumbled into. They could go back and forth a hundred and one times and he'd still lose. He took the readers. "Thank you."

He put them on, felt his aching eyes relax, the world abruptly clearer. "These are great," he said. "Damn."

The imam almost smiled.

Tommy patted his shirt, then checked his pants pockets. Nothing. He held up a finger.

The imam nodded and took some more tea.

Outside, Tommy shoved his boots half on, shuffled to the truck, and dug through the glove box, freeing a cascade of Skoal tins, mostly empty. Found what he was looking for in the center console.

Headed back.

The imam had allowed the front door to remain unlocked.

Progress.

Entering the kitchen, Tommy showed his drugstore readers, only now noting how down-market they were. Nicotine-yellow plastic rims, one lens chipped from a shell ejected from a misbehaving Beretta. He set them on the table. "So you can read your prescription bottles."

The imam picked them up and regarded them, amused.

Next Tommy gave him his Oakley razors.

The imam tried them on. The mirrored lenses had a purple tint. Against his timeless face they looked discordant, anachronistic.

"You look like a tough guy," Tommy said.

"I am a tough guy."

"I don't doubt it."

Tommy adjusted the delicate readers on his face. The imam surveyed the room in the Oakleys.

They smirked at each other a little.

They took the glasses back off, Tommy slipping the readers into his breast pocket.

There came a long silence but not an awkward one.

"These boys," the imam said, "they're not your sons."

Tommy said, "No."

"Your tribe."

"I wish it weren't so. But yeah, I suppose I gotta claim them."

The imam nodded. And then nodded again. "I understand this responsibility. Of having to claim those who do not speak for you."

"I apologize for the disrespect. We will make amends."

The imam's chair pushed back with a screech. He exited down a back hall.

Tommy sat, hand tented over his teacup, steam moistening his palm. He thought about those words sprayed across the mosque. He thought about the rat nest of the Hilderanch and the boys slumped around with their poisonous plans and dime-store sophistry. He thought about a family getting dressed up and going to the park to celebrate a fifteenth-birthday party, not knowing they'd be met with blind hatred and the bumper of an '89 Dodge Ram.

Footsteps padded back and the imam stood over Tommy. In his hand, a well-loved paperback *Scribner-Bantam English Dictionary.* "They can start with this."

"Fair," Tommy said. "Even imbeciles should have the self-respect to spell their slurs right."

"Maybe that is the first step," the imam agreed.

Tommy took the book.

The imam remained standing.

Tommy rose. They walked back out.

Like a good host, the imam waited in the doorway while Tommy wrestled his boots back on. Tommy turned to face him across the threshold.

The imam had something else in his hand now, something dark, low at his side.

Tommy tensed.

"And this," the imam said, and lifted it to the space between them.

A tiny pocket book with edge gilding, no bigger than a deck of playing cards. Stamped on the black cover: UNITED STATES CONSTITUTION.

Somehow, Tommy knew.

He took the book, turned it over. Embossed on the back was a gold-star foil seal set against a royal purple background, the emblem honoring family members of fallen soldiers.

Tommy pictured that handsome young man in the photo, arm around his mother. He pinched his eyes a moment, caught his breath. Then he removed his trucker's cap.

He had to clear his throat twice before speaking. *"Allah yerhamo."*

The imam said nothing. He just looked at Tommy with sad, wise eyes, and Tommy looked back with whatever he had in his.

Tommy offered his hand.

They shook.

28

Shitty Outcomes of a Different Flavor

The low billowing clouds looked like inverted sand dunes. They dampened the sun and crowded the sky, made it feel close and claustrophobic. The road Evan drove dipped and banked with the topography, a natural route that rode the land instead of asserting itself against it.

Scraggly elms with old-man bark folded overhead, branches holding hands. Now and then a leafy bough scraped along the side of the truck. There weren't potholes so much as craters where the elements had had their way with the asphalt. Puddles proliferated.

He barreled along, grateful for the Ford F-150. American roads needed American trucks, and in places like Wayne, Michigan, and Kansas City, Missouri, plant workers knew how to build them.

When he turned east for Hayesville, the truck spat out onto a red-dirt road worthy of that diner jukebox. His tires thrummed past ranches and tumbledown houses.

A rare traffic light held him up at the outskirts of Hayesville. He checked it for a speed camera. Sure enough there was a lens atop a skinny pole thrust up from the signal and a pole-mounted controller box nearby. He wondered if Joey had hacked into this one yet and what she might dig up.

Across the intersection on a torn-up field, a football team ran practice. Evan watched the high-school boys dropping and rolling, hammering tackle dummies, plowing into sleds. The equipment was cracked and sun-faded, their scrimmage pinnies tattered, the school in the background washed dull with poverty. Lockers spotted with rust, water fountain broken right off a wall, patch repairs and blocks of mismatched paint slopped over damage. But the kids kept at their drills as if they were on the finest facility in the land, as if the glory of the coming Friday night was the focal point of the universe, as if they were the first young men ever to sweat and strive. The world hadn't promised them much but here they were, battling toward the mythic in their tiny corner of the nation.

Team sports fascinated Evan. He'd never had the luxury of risking injury on a field, not once Jack had started his Program training at the age of twelve. Orphans were raised in separate silos, no joint tutelage, no team ops. They remained perfect outsiders who would not be missed should the probable fate befall them.

These athletes were good kids. Evan could tell by how they nodded earnestly at the coaches barking orders and how they offered a hand to the fallen, hoisting one another back up onto their feet. He thought about what it would have been like to be on a team. Lacing up cleats together, riding buses, inside jokes and easy banter.

Community.

The eternal mirage.

A twitch of a missing limb, an ache, a tug of envy he could scarcely acknowledge within himself.

But if he'd been born under a different star, if he'd had that camaraderie, had what these kids had, he'd have been consigned to the same fate as most of them. They faced the same shitty outcomes as his foster brothers from the East Baltimore home. Shitty outcomes of a different flavor.

The odds of a Jack Johns walking into a town like this were about the same as those of him walking into Pride House and plucking Evan unripe from the vine. About one in 350 million.

Shitty Outcomes of a Different Flavor

The blare of an air horn caught him off guard.

A poultry-transport truck behind him, stacked container-ship high with crates crammed with chickens. A perpetual cloud of feathers plumed around the truck, which was offset enough for Evan to make out one wall of the pale and hopeless stock. A few motionless claws stuck out through the mesh wire.

The driver extended his arm and uncurled his middle finger.

The light had changed to green.

Evan turned right and entered Hayesville.

29

Justice of an Acceptable Flavor

The imam's dictionary and pocket Constitution rode shotgun. Tommy liked driving the roads out here. You could expand your chest when you took a breath.

A motorcyclist on a Harley with fat cruising tires zipped up on him, big in the rearview, hands high on the ape hangers. The guy had a mustache like Tommy's, the wind whipping his hair. No helmet.

Tommy liked that.

This had been glorious, sacred land once. Settlers had cleared these hills and valleys, dales and fields; they'd braved slings and arrows and hanged horse thieves. And even a modern-day tender-skin should have the right to ride free and bash in his own damn head if he wanted to. That's what turned Tommy's engine over for America, the leave-me-the-hell-alone freedoms.

Nevada was grand but lately it had a bit of the wrong coast eating into it. He *comprendo*'ed some of the regulations—why you couldn't let Big Pharma charge steak-dinner prices for a shot of insulin, why you didn't want the food lobbyists injecting growth hormones into your Froot Loops, why it made sense to buckle yer baby into a car seat so it wouldn't go full projectile through a windshield. But still, hell. Interfere sparingly. And don't be so fucking condescending about it.

The biker kept a respectful distance off the rear bumper but even so Tommy could tell he was holding him back. He eased over until the tires rattled across the rumble strips, giving him a wide berth to pass. The biker did, flaring a gloved hand from the throttle in thanks.

Roaring its magnificent roar, the Harley turned the rider into a shrinking dot. Then it was just Tommy alone with the open road and the passel of hazards he was negotiating.

For a moment, the mess that Hick had ensconced him in felt overwhelming. Too many tentacles to lop off. Innocent folks had been run over and the law didn't care. The reckless stupidity of the boys who were his inadvertent charges seemed to know no bounds and yet Tommy had to forge some way through to justice of an acceptable flavor. The dead he'd had cleaned out of his lair back in Las Vegas wouldn't stay dead; they'd be back soon enough in a stronger iteration, hellbent on succeeding where those before them had failed. And he was due to meet Evan shortly, a confrontation that threatened to go full Chernobyl if one of them sneezed wrong.

Tommy didn't like despairing; he'd never worn it well. So he breathed it away and reset himself. He'd wade back in at the Hilde-ranch and give it his navy best. But first he had to contend with Evan. That was the most dangerous piece. He could afford no more complications, not with sundown coming.

He didn't notice the sheriff's deputy car at first. Not until it coasted up, tailgating his bumper, and set its lights flashing.

He eased off onto the muddy shoulder, clicked on the dome light so no one could claim he was reaching for anything, kept his hands at the ten and two.

The deputies got out. Jug Ears and that bull cop, the one who looked like a regular on the MMA circuit. The big fella lingered back by the cruiser, probably to sneak in some extra squats and snort creatine powder.

Jug Ears came up on the driver's side. Tommy rolled down the window, not wanting to deal with the knuckle-tap ritual.

The kid's name tag read RONNY RATLIFF. His badge had a five-tipped crown at the top, a golden wreath, and a CHIEF DEPUTY band across the base that matched the patch on his shoulder. Number two to Sheriff Grady Joy.

"Know why we pulled you over?"

"The bullshit reason or the real reason?" Tommy said, handing over license and reg.

Ronny's eyes danced a bit with amusement. "Both."

The bull cop had wedged himself back into the cruiser. Now he was glaring at Tommy through the windshield. Eyes glinting, neck like a Goodyear tire. The bull was straight-up deputy muscle, which meant that Ronny held his leash.

Tommy kept filling in the picture. He needed to understand the hierarchy of the law in Calvary and who could be trusted when it came time for the boys to answer for what they'd done.

He cleared his throat. "The bullshit reason is that I was going, dunno, ten miles over. I doubt fifty in a forty is much of a panty-knotter around these here parts"—he put some twang on the last three words—"but if it is and I'm outta step with the unspoken local traditions, I'll take the ticket without bitching and rein in the lead foot."

"And the real reason?"

"The sheriff doesn't know what to make of me and he wants me to know he's keeping an eye out. Which I already knew, so we can save this bit of clever gum-flapping and get on with our evenings."

Ronny tapped Tommy's license against his palm. He hadn't bothered to look at it. "It's true," he said. "Sheriff ain't sure about you."

"Son, *I* ain't sure about me half the damn time."

Ronny smirked, his face softening a touch. "Seems another new fellow showed up here, too."

"That's the scuttlebutt?"

"That's the scuttlebutt," Ronny said. "Anything you got to say about him?"

"Stay away," Tommy said.

"He a threat?"

"Not unless you make him one."

"Then he is?"

"Then you're dead."

Ronny pursed his lips, made a pronounced nod. "Well, then. I'm sure you can understand Sheriff Joy's concern. He don't like people coming in here with their outside notions and messing up the balance."

"The balance of what?"

"Law and order."

"Law," Tommy said, thoughtfully. "And order."

Ronny shifted uncomfortably. He was lanky but deceptively powerful and he had a strong jaw. Tommy liked strong jaws. They spoke to character. Except when they didn't.

Tommy said, "It's good you're focused on that, what with all the craziness going down around here. I heard a whole damn family got run over by a truck at the public park. In the middle of a party, no less." He shook his head. "And no one can seem to crack the case."

Ronny's face reddened and he looked out and away, as if the horizon held sudden great interest. Uneasy. Maybe even a little mad at the position in which he'd found himself.

Interesting.

"We got community here," Ronny said. "We got boys we have to protect."

So it was out on the table, then. Progress.

"What do you think about all that?" Tommy said, quietly. "You personally, Deputy Ratliff?"

Ronny pinched his lip between his teeth until the skin whitened. "Only way my pop protected me was holding me to account so I could learn."

"Huh," Tommy said. "Is that a minority position here?"

"Not in town."

"But at the station?"

Ronny handed Tommy back his license and registration, gave a big smile. "You stay safe now, Mr. Stojack."

30

Every Curse Has a Blessing

In the driveway sat a Honda Civic with tinted windows and a headlight bra. Plastic candy canes lined the front walk, which was made of wide granite stepping stones separated by strips of dead grass. Through the front window Evan made out a Christmas tree draped with tinsel.

He rang the doorbell.

Santiago Martinez answered. The dead boy's father.

A dapper man, five foot eight, worker's build without an ounce of fat. He wore a mustard-yellow Carhartt shirt tucked into dark-blue jeans fastened by a brown leather belt with a silver oval buckle. He was mid-thirties but his eyes had gone ancient with sorrow.

On the plastic-slipcovered couches in the family room were a venerable woman Evan assumed was the grandmother and a couple he guessed were friends and not family. The young mother had a removable car seat at her foot, which she rocked like a cradle. The front mesh shield was drawn down, hiding the baby.

The mood was somber, pained with worry and hurt.

Every Curse Has a Blessing

Under the tree, presents of various sizes rose like a cityscape from a snowfall made of taffied cotton balls. Most of the wrapping was decorated with baseball bats and race cars. Evan imagined that some gifts had been set out early with the decorations but the Santa stash waited hidden in a closet somewhere. When Santiago and Lidia had wrapped those gifts, their boy had still been alive. Nine days and a lifetime ago. What would they do with the gifts now? Unwrap and return them? Give them away? Store them untouched in the attic?

Atop the mantel, a resin Virgin Mary was on prominent display, arms spread, head tilted to the right, face mournful. She wore a loose-fitting blue robe trimmed with white, a cowl covering her tresses. The pedestal upon which she stood was one hemisphere of the globe. A snake twisted from the hem of her gown just outside her left foot. Grace and sin balancing the world.

Four stockings nailed beneath her perch matched the red felt tree skirt. Names spelled out in glitter-speckled glue: *Santiago, Lidia, Gabriel,* and *Lita,* which Evan took to be short for *Abuelita*.

A movement from the hall drew his focus, Lidia edging into view. She wore a housecoat over a nightgown, her hair greasy and unkempt, her face swollen through the upper cheeks and bridge of her nose, her eyes puffy. The wreckage of grief.

Nailed to the wall and framed cheaply in gold, a school portrait peered out over her shoulder. Gabriel wore a navy sweater and navy slacks—school uniform. He had apple cheeks and an impish smile, his head tilted back as if he was on the verge of laughing.

Evan looked from Lidia's ravaged face to her eight-year-old son, frozen in joy just behind her, hovering like a ghost.

Everyone stared at him with blank faces.

His mouth was uncharacteristically dry.

Santiago said, "*Sí?*"

"*Siento mucho su pérdido.*" The Spanish felt clunky in his mouth. There were no good words for this in any language.

"*Quién es usted?*"

Who are you? Santiago had matched Evan's formal form of address.

Evan said, "English or Spanish?"

215

"English," Santiago said. His accent was heavy but probably no heavier than Evan's on the other side.

"I want to find out who killed your boy." Evan shifted his attention to Lidia. "And your sister, her husband, your nephew."

Lidia swayed on her bare feet, set a palm on the wall to steady herself. The others looked at him from the couches, unblinking. He couldn't tell whether they didn't understand English or were simply deferring to Santiago.

"*Por qué?*" In his surprise, Santiago had reset to Spanish.

"To make them answer for what they have done."

"It doesn't matter." Lidia spoke in perfect English. "Nothing matters."

She was looking at Evan but not looking at him at all.

Santiago's mouth firmed, his head retracting, shoulders drawing back. "You are not police."

"No."

"Why do you do this?"

"Because it's right."

"Why should we trust you?" Santiago's eyes tightened. "Why should we believe you?"

Evan didn't have a ready answer. He resisted chewing the inside of his cheek and looked at the Christmas tree. Those presents. The invisible baby fussed and the mother on the couch rocked the makeshift bassinet with her foot. The grandmother watched the proceedings with the patience of stone. She was used to things taking forever and going nowhere.

Evan said "May I?" as he reached for his pocket.

Out came the RoamZone. He dialed.

She answered on the first ring.

"I'm here," he said. "At the Martinez house. They've expressed reasonable doubts about my intentions."

Joey said, "Hand the phone over."

Evan offered it across the welcome mat.

Santiago looked at the device as if it might be explosive. Lidia lingered at the mouth of the hall, an apparition.

Santiago took the RoamZone, pressed it to his cheek. "*Sí?*"

Evan could make out the melodic cadence of Joey's Spanish, the effortless fluidity of her native tongue. He couldn't tell what she was saying but her words rolled like a river and there was passion and kindness in them.

Santiago said, "Uh-huh."

And then, "Uh-huh."

And then, "Uh-huh."

He hung up the phone. Handed it back to Evan. Then said, "Okay."

He stepped aside. Evan entered. Lidia floated forward two steps and stood unsurely on bare feet.

Evan looked at the couple and Abuelita on the couches. "Were any of you there the night of the murders?"

"Thank you," Lidia said, with intense appreciation. "For not saying 'accident.' Or 'incident.' *Murder.* It was *murder.*"

The mother with the baby and her husband raised their hands in the affirmative as if they were in class.

On his phone, Evan thumbed up the photo he'd taken of the Hickenlooper boy and displayed it. "Was this man there?"

"Yes!" The mother pointed with equal parts agitation and excitement. "There. Him."

Her husband nodded his accord.

Evan swiped to the next shot: Red on the porch in the morning, scratching his lower back. "And him?"

"Yes. Also. In the truck."

"Anyone else?"

Husband and wife shook their heads rapidly in concert.

"Just them," she said. "They are the ones who did this. They are the ones who took Gabriel."

"How come you found them?" Lidia said. "And the police could not?"

Evan said, "Because the police don't want to find them."

Her eyes shimmered wetly. "You speak truth," she said. "Truth is the only thing we have left. The only thing that matters anymore."

Evan said, "I understand."

She stumbled as she withdrew. Weak from lack of sleep, lack of calories, lack of will to go on breathing.

Santiago caught the eye of the woman on the couch and together they moved back to check on Lidia.

The young husband looked intensely uncomfortable. He got up, smiling apologetically, and stepped outside to have a smoke.

Evan waited there on his feet until the *abuela* gestured for him to sit. The plastic slipcover crinkled beneath him. The house smelled of pine and the *veladoras* flickering on a side table. The air, humid with the last cooked meal.

"*Gabriel was a miracle,*" she said. "*He was her miracle. My daughter-in-law.*" An indigenous dialect, maybe Nahuatl or Mixtec, flavored her Spanish, and Evan had to listen intently to understand. "*The day he was born was the happiest day of her life. And then the next day. And then every day after for eight and a half years.*"

He listened. He just listened.

Abuelita composed herself. "*Lidia had complications before. And complications with the birth.*"

Complicaciones. The word rolled around in Evan's head.

He didn't get it.

And then he did.

The miracle.

"She can't have children again," he said.

Abuelita nodded sagely. "*That boy, he was our everything. Our joy and our future.*"

Animal keening issued from deep in the house. Then came hushing sounds and it faded away.

Abuelita struggled to rise from the recesses of the couch. Evan got up, offered his hand. She took it. Hers was light as a bird claw; the bones felt hollow. Her skin, dry and warm, rasped against his. She made use of his grip, trusted him with her weight. She was used to receiving help.

She walked back slowly, her knobby hands gripping couch backs and side tables to steady her on her path.

Evan was alone before the tree.

A hiccupping noise broke the stillness, and then a high-pitched cry issued from the covered car seat.

He froze dumbly.

Murmuring came from the rear of the house, sporadic sobs and a steady hum of consolation.

The baby worked up into a full cry.

Evan looked out through the front window. The father was on the sidewalk, smoking and talking on his phone.

Just Evan and a crying baby in a strange house.

The thought came to him unbidden: *What would Aragón do?*

His only friend, a man of family, of strength and warmth and wisdom.

Evan crouched over the car seat, rocked it a few times gently as the mother had. The cries escalated and grew irritated, digging beneath his skin. He couldn't see clearly through the dark mesh but sensed movement.

Gently, he peeled back the front hood.

The baby screamed. He didn't know ages. She looked older than a newborn but still new. Eyes scrunched shut, tiny fists clenched, mouth ajar. Her curled tongue wavered with her cries. Tiny feet shoved out, arching her back.

An agony of feeling.

He unclipped the plastic buckle across her chest, lifted her out. Her flower-dotted onesie was warm, moist with sweat in the back.

He held her before him like a wet cat.

She screamed.

He was used to tuning babies out. But he let himself listen.

Hers was a bottomless grief. Hungry? Lonely? Scared? In pain?

He pulled her in as he'd seen people do, cradled her in his arm tilted upward, her face pointed at his.

She looked terrified.

If he actually took in her emotion, it was unbearable.

He wondered if this was what other people heard all the time when babies cried.

He swayed a little back and forth.

Her eyes blinked open. Rich brown.

Her breath stuttered in and then released in a sigh.

He looked down at her. She looked up at him, her mouth popping open and shut.

He noticed something odd. His body was aching. It was as though someone had turned up the volume on his nerves. His spine throbbed arthritically. A needle memory beneath the ribs from the tension pneumothorax he'd self-punctured in a mechanic shop outside Ankara. Pain haunted his ankles and knees, reminders of that ill-fated HALO landing back in the summer Jack went Airborne on him. The back of his head and left elbow were tender from the death-grappling he'd engaged in at Tommy's armory and his ribs spoke out about a brawl he'd once had with the Wolf's driver in a downtown squat house. His head hurt and his neck hurt and he hurt within, sinew and muscle, fascia and blood.

The sensations had been there, he realized, all along. It was his awareness that had intensified.

But still he held that baby's gaze and she held his and he felt.

He felt.

All at once the mother was there before him, her expression grateful. She held out her arms. The strangest thing happened. Evan didn't want to relinquish the baby.

She looked up at him adoringly and mushed her mouth some more.

One of her tiny pink hands had curled around his shirt, a vestigial monkey grip. He pried her off his chest, kept her neck and head supported with the bough of his arm. Tenderly he handed her over.

The mother sidled close to receive her in kind, and he could smell a trace of perfume, the tang of her deodorant. They completed the handoff.

And just like that, the pains that had crept forward from the recesses of his body receded, each one turning off like a switch.

Every curse has a blessing.

"Thank you." The mother smiled a shy smile, her teeth charmingly crooked.

He remembered growing up that kind of broke, where braces were as out-of-reach as a Ferrari. He'd been blessed with decent genetics in that regard. His shame had lived elsewhere—in his diminutive twelve-year-old size, in his sneakers with the heels scraped through to sock, in the way he'd eyed other kids' lunches.

Clucking at the baby, the mother picked up the car seat and walked out to join her husband.

Evan was unsure what to do. He'd gotten the positive ID on Hick and Red he'd come for. Yet it seemed improper to leave.

He stood with the Christmas tree and the wrapped presents and Mother Mary and the four stockings hung on the mantel with care.

He was relieved to hear movement in the hall, and then Santiago reappeared. He paused at the mantel and crossed himself before Mary, kissing his thumb.

Then he looked at Evan, his arms loose at his sides. They didn't really have anything else to say to each other. And yet Santiago's face seemed to be fighting with itself. He looked lost.

He studied some point on Evan's chest. *"This is all there is. For me. Forever. This is the beginning and the end. This house. This . . . family."* He'd reset to Spanish again. *"The loss of him, it is all there is. And no one cares."*

Evan had nothing to say. He just took in what Santiago said and held it as best he could.

"What I am feeling, it is intolerable. And yet my wife, she is feeling it even more. It doesn't seem possible but she is." He wet his lips. *"I don't know how she is going to ever not be broken by this. I don't know what our life will be."*

That pain crept up in Evan's joints again, though now it was just a low hum.

He looked at Santiago with neither contempt nor pity. "That sounds terrifying."

Santiago lifted his eyes to him. "Yes," he said in English, with something like relief or even appreciation. "That is what it is. It is terrifying."

He nodded a good-bye and withdrew once more.

Evan stepped outside. He'd forgotten what fresh air tasted like.

Afternoon was fading, the air taking on the gritty texture of dusk. The countdown to the meeting with Tommy had begun.

He got in his truck and made for the ghost town. He'd arrive early and recon, in keeping with the Third Commandment: *Master your surroundings.*

He turned back onto the red-dirt road, felt the tread take proper hold of the earth. Thought about Lidia's face, hollowed out with grief. And her husband, giving voice to the untenable, the unimaginable. The courage of that kind of honesty.

And the wrapping paper, baseball bats and race cars.

That feeling came up again, the one he'd felt when he'd held the baby. Sensation, too, heavy in his rib cage, threatening to climb up his throat and choke him.

He pulled the truck over, left it running.

He got out, tasted the air.

A split-rail fence ran forever along the road.

He crouched, taking weight off his back. Touched his hand to a patch of grass between his boots to steady himself.

The wrapped presents.

God, the presents.

He stared through the fence.

And he breathed.

31

Holy Mess

The Hilderanch looked to be empty.

But when Tommy stepped inside, a scraping sound issued from the kitchen. Sure enough, Hick was eating not-quite-defrosted casserole off a paper plate over the sink, crunching audibly. His cell phone lolled in front of his face in his hand as he chewed. The thrown light reflected in his eyes, turned them into dimes.

At Tommy's entrance, Hick turned, the phone now dangling in hand at his side. On the out-facing screen, a newsgirl vamped for her viewers. A sexed-up thing in her twenties, the eternal cheerleader with razor-straight blond bangs and evocative lips, riling up the boys to charge out there and do this or that about this or that.

Tommy said, "Where're the others?"

Hick gave a one-shoulder shrug. "Went to rustle up some booze for tonight."

Tommy walked over, took Hick's arm at the wrist, twisted the hand to show the black paint on his fingers. Hick winced a little and dropped the plate in the sink, where it landed with a clink.

"What?"

"'Terrorize your own country'?"

Hick jerked his hand free. "Well, they should."

"I'm out here trying to unfuck the holy mess you got yourself into," Tommy said. "Your ass-backward stupidity that got four people killed. And *after* I'm here, under this roof, you go out and defile a house of God? Didn't you learn a goddamned thing? *Can you learn a goddamned thing?*"

"What?" Hick repeated again, dumbly. "You know what they're planning."

"Who?"

"Muslims. You know what they think. And we're just supposed to allow it all? We're just supposed to allow everything?"

Tommy felt overcome. It was too daunting to crack, this towering wall of idiocy, and for a moment he wondered why the hell he'd bothered to come out here at all. The boy was benighted, doomed. Maybe they all were.

He mustered up the words because there was no other way to go: "I went and saw the imam."

"A what?"

"Muslim priest, sorta."

Hick whitened. Then puffed himself up again into something else, some other person—maybe Red, maybe a version of himself he thought his daddy had always wanted to see. He produced a smirk that didn't fit his face. "He sending a suicide bomber after us?"

Tommy took out the dictionary and shook it in Hick's face. "*This. This* is what he sent after y'all's dumb asses *misspelled the slurs* you sprayed on his wall. And?" Now he wagged the tiny book with edge gilding. "The Constitution. So you could pull yourself out of what you're wallowing in."

Hick took the books roughly, tossed them to the counter. The Gold Star family Constitution slid across and fell into the sink. "That dune coon thinks he can talk shit to us—"

Tommy lost his temper.

He couldn't remember the last time when.

He slammed Hick down into the rickety kitchen chair and then with a gathering of rage kicked out the legs because the chair wasn't low enough for him. The boy collapsed another foot and change, landed jarringly in the pile of kindling, and stared up at him, eyes popping. The cell phone lay in the wreckage, screen cracked, that lady still jawing and jawing.

"Why did you call me?" Tommy roared down at him.

"'Cause I had a problem! I was in deep shit!"

"No. You had it all locked up. All you had to do was listen to Red and the sheriff and all them assholes covering up for you. No one would've ever made you answer for what you did. Why did you call me?"

Hick had scuttled back a few feet but he didn't dare rise. His lips were trembling.

"Why did you call me?"

"Because! Because . . . I needed help, okay? I didn't know what to do. I don't know what to do. I need your help."

Tommy stood over him, shoulders heaving.

Hick was breathing just as hard there on the floor. He looked like maybe he'd start crying. His face had gone pale with spots of color at the cheekbones.

"Okay, then," Tommy said, in a quiet rasp. "You ready to take it?"

Hick nodded, nostrils flaring.

"Get up."

Hick crab-walked back another few feet so he could rise safely out of Tommy's reach.

"Only a world-class idiot would insult ten billion people in a single breath," Tommy said. "And I don't waste my time with world-class idiots."

Another jerky nod.

"You get that Constitution outta the sink."

Keeping his eyes on Tommy, Hick eased along the counter and retrieved the small book.

"Know what they nicknamed it?" Tommy said.

It took Hick a moment to understand what he meant, and then he looked down at the tiny book in his hands. He shook his head.

"The 'bundle of compromises,'" Tommy said. "No one gets everything they want. Understand?"

Hick nodded.

"You read it. Every last word. You hear me? You don't understand something, use the dictionary."

"Yes, sir."

The shadows were starting to stretch across the floor.

"Everything will be different now." Tommy's voice was deep in his throat with emotion or dread or a combination of both. "*Everything*. From this moment hence. We clear?"

"Yes, sir."

Hick crouched and picked up his phone. "You cracked my screen."

Tommy left the boy there among the splinters of the kitchen chair.

Stepping out onto the porch, he noted the low gold light at the horizon.

Sundown.

It was time to go and meet his former friend.

It was time to confront Orphan X.

32

Equal-Opportunity Executioner

The ghost town called itself Dawnfall with a straight face. There was a billboard at the end of the one-street cow town, the name rendered in old-timey script, buckshot dimpling the wood by design. A placard nailed outside the faux funeral home laid out Dawnfall's undistinguished provenance—erected in the 1980s for some Western movie Evan had never heard of, turned into a tourist attraction back when anyone had any money to spend. Along with the factories and mines and manufacturing plants, it had shut down during the recession. But there was nothing to ship overseas, so here it sat year after year, gathering dust and cobwebs, slowly falling apart.

Some of the storefronts had been built out; others remained mere façades with rear scaffolding that had once accommodated camera crews and stunt men. There was a bank and a sheriff's office with a jail, a mercantile and a feed and supply, a chapel and the saloon in which Evan now sat alone at the bar, facing the artfully speckled mirror backdrop.

In the thickening dusk, he'd scouted the town along with a trio of wild burros who nibbled at shrubs and urinated prodigiously. He'd half expected to see tumbleweeds rattle by or a tragic saloon girl in need of rescuing but it was just him and the wind blowing grit and desolation, urging him inside.

Weather had eaten through a patch of roof, freeing a column of light to descend on the seat next to him, the seat reserved for Tommy. It wasn't bright exactly, just less dim than the rest of the saloon, which yielded by the second to the crepuscular gloom. There were shingles on the tables and a coat of grime across the rustic hickory bar top; there were vintage stools and empty shelves holding fallen bottles faded to sea glass.

Evan had wiped down two stools and the apron of surface before them so he could rest his elbows on the bar without feeling dirt against his sleeves.

He kept his back to the entrance, a show of strength.

He waited, watching those swinging saloon doors in the faded mirror.

Soon enough over the wind, he heard the cough and crackle of Tommy's engine.

Then the rig stilled.

A truck door creaked open.

A full ten seconds later it slammed shut.

Tommy took his time. His joints demanded it these days, sure, but he'd always been an unrushed man.

Boots appeared beneath the saloon doors. A shadow fell across the slats.

Then he swept in, the doors screaming on ailing hinges, wobbling back and forth, back and forth, until they quieted at his back.

Tommy met Evan's stare in the mirror.

His steps tick-tocked across the planks.

His barstool squeaked as he pulled it out. He hefted himself up with an old-man groan and they sat side by side, hands in sight on the hickory wood, staring dead ahead at the toppled bottles and their own smoky reflections.

After a time, Tommy dug into an inside pocket of his duck-canvas coat and came out with a battered silver flask. He unscrewed the lid, took a swig, offered it across to Evan.

"What is it?" Evan asked.

"Beam."

Evan fanned his hand low across the bar top, palm down, a blackjack "stay."

Tommy took another swig, made the flask disappear.

Evan said, "We gonna talk about it?"

"What's that?"

"This Wild West motif we've found ourselves in the middle of?"

Tommy said, "Nah."

They sat for a time longer.

Evan said, "What then?"

"Don't you dare come back to that house," Tommy said. "There's innocents there. A sister. A lady comes by to cook."

Evan said, "I know how to refrain from no-shoots."

"This ain't your business. No one needs you around, busting inta things, waving guns and flexing your nipples."

"Then tell me why you supplied hardware to the Wolf," Evan said. "Why you helped her kill people."

Tommy took off his cap, wiped his forehead, shook his head. "You got no right to ask me that. Now or ever."

"Not a right," Evan said.

Tommy's tongue readjusted the tobacco bulging out his lower lip.

"Those bikers at your shop," Evan said. "Janus and his crew. They weren't there for me, were they?"

Tommy looked around for somewhere to spit, decided against it, and gutted the swallow. "No," he said, softly. "They weren't."

Evan had been working toward that confirmation for a while now and having it cleared should have brought relief but instead it just dumped him back where he'd started, with Tommy's supplying arms to a cold-blooded killer. And now he had Lidia and Santiago's grief pressing in at him on top of that, the mission sprawling out in ways he did not—could not—grasp and contain. At least not right now in front of Tommy.

"They were there for you? Busted deal?"

"You could say that. But it's my business. You hear? *My business.* I ain't dealing with any of that with you or anyone else." Tommy's voice, rusty at the edges, took on an aggressive undercurrent. His biker's mustache was untrimmed, hoary. He looked grizzled as hell but the half-light came down and laid itself across his shoulders and made him look like something to be venerated. "I gotta deal with what's in front of me."

"What's in front of you? Is just another layer of fuckup."

"A seven-layer dip of fuckup. But what do you know about it? What do you know about anything here? This ain't one a yer fancy missions, off hunting billionaires or heads of state, slurping your avocado-based vodka and diddling with hacker tech doodads. These are hard folks made from hard times. You're not welcome here."

"Not welcome. Like those people from Hayesville? The ones your boys killed?"

Tommy stiffened on his barstool. Awareness settled across his face. It looked like dread. His mouth pulsed a few times beneath that ragged mustache. His dry knuckles rasped against the lapel of his coat, and then he brought the flask to his lips again and took a long pull.

"*Or,*" Tommy said, "they were drunk and stupid, crashed through a fence to scare some Mexicans and lost control of the truck."

"'To scare some Mexicans,'" Evan said. "Aragón Urrea would feed you your own balls for that."

"Oh, you get one Mexican buddy and now you got the keys to the moral universe? From a cartel motherfucker who rained about a billion kilos of fentanyl down on these very neighborhoods? That's yer exemplar?"

"I was a throwaway kid in a city, Tommy," Evan said quietly. "Who do you think my brothers were?"

Tommy drew in a breath through his nose, reset. "I got plenty of Mexican brothers-in-arms, too. Hell, you don't get anywhere worth being in this country without coming across a mess of them busting their asses and making shit better. But even they'll tell you. They got their bad players. You've killed plenty yourself."

"I'm an equal-opportunity executioner," Evan said. "I doubt the same can be said for those men you're protecting back at the militia den."

"Not men," Tommy said. *"Boys."*

"Military-aged."

"These kids are *my* dumbasses and fuckups. Same as yours runnin' around cities with do-rags and nickel-plated .22s. And they need help."

"Funny how everyone develops patience and mercy," Evan said, "when it's their own kind."

Tommy rubbed his eyes hard, the skin shifting around beneath his thumbs and fingers. "'Member the marital bed in the *Odyssey*?"

"Carved from the stump of a living olive tree."

"That's right. That's the center of the bedroom. Center of the house, too. It's the foundation. Of faith and family. Of the world." Tommy paused, moistened his lips. "There's no bed for those boys back at the house. No foundation, no nothing."

"Everyone's equal under the law," Evan said. "Doesn't matter if you've got the best sob story on the block or you're the president of the United States."

"Fair enough, sloganeer," Tommy said. "But you ain't the law."

Evan absorbed the blow. He'd walked right into it, felt the steel teeth sink into his ankle.

"I'm figuring out what to do," Tommy said. "Let me sort it. Don't go after them. Stay out of what these boys did. Clean up the shit in your backyard, I'll clean up the shit in mine."

"That's not good enough."

"Who're you? Who're you to judge? Me, them, everyone?"

"A family, Tommy. They killed a family at that park. A mother, father. A son serving in the United States Marines. Eight-year-old boy, too."

"Well, this is a fucking family, too, right here. What's left of one. And Hick, Hick wasn't even driving. What do you want me to do? I made a pledge. I swore an oath to his father."

"I didn't."

Tommy made a fist, pressed it against the ledge of the bar. His knuckles were white, his teeth clenched. "Stubborn," he said. "You are so goddamned stubborn."

It wasn't stubbornness. Evan knew that. He was simply what he was.

A hunter of humans. The monster sent to kill monsters.

"A family, Tommy. An eight-year-old boy. They didn't know them. They put them in the ground. Because of what?"

Tommy rubbed his face with both hands, palms covering his eyes, cheeks shoved out. He gave a groan that sounded like a growl. "I know," he said. "I know."

Evan pictured the woman on the Martinezes' couch, the way her eyes flared with recognition when Evan had showed her the photos of Hick and Red: *They are the ones who did this. They are the ones who took Gabriel.*

"They're rabid," Evan said. "Preying on folks who can't protect themselves."

"Maybe they can be saved."

"Saved." Evan shook his head. "Who's the soft one now, Tommy?"

"Maybe they can be saved," Tommy said again, more to himself than to Evan.

Evan thought about that little boy in the navy sweater and navy slacks, the wrapped presents beneath the Christmas tree, Lidia hovering ghostlike in the hall, wrung pale with grief. *I don't know how she is going to ever not be broken by this. I don't know what our life will be.*

"It's too late," Evan said. "They have to answer. No matter how bad you want to play hero."

"Hero." Tommy sneered. "Heroes gotta be dead and half forgotten so they can be rewritten by men with weaker chins. There are no heroes. Not me." His watery blue eyes looked cloudy in the dimness. They gazed unseeingly at Evan. "And not you."

Evan swung one leg off the barstool.

"I'm coming," he said. "I will kill those who did this. Tell them."

"I will," Tommy said. "But you won't."

"Why not?"

"Because I'll be on *their* side this time. Not yours."

Evan was standing now, wide stance, joints loose, checking strike targets. Back of the jaw. Hammer fist to locked elbow. Fragile bone of the orbital socket.

But that was ridiculous. They were not going to fight. Not now.

Tommy stayed a quarter turn away, hands ledging the hickory. He was very, very still. Evan knew his peripheral was for shit.

"You're on the side of the racist militia who killed four people just for being Mexican," Evan said, blading his shoulders toward the door, telegraphing his exit. "Think about what you just said."

Tommy turned his head real slow, his eyes still milky in the gloaming, which had crept inside to fill the saloon. "And you," he said, "think about what you *are*."

33

Adulting

Joey and Dog the dog were having an argument over grapes.

They were sitting on the couch together, Dog curled into her with his giant head floating over the bowl while she typed away on her laptop, reviewing Delmont Hickenlooper's online life.

She understood Dog's issue. Grapes were perfect dog-size snacks like any other she shared with him so he didn't get why he couldn't eat them. She'd explained to him that they were toxic to dogs but he didn't care and every time she ate one, he rammed his wet nose into her elbow and looked at her like she was the Most Selfish Human Ever.

Anyways. That's what'd been going on with them all evening.

Served her right for eating proper fruit instead of going with grape-flavored Sour Patch Kids, but she was seventeen and that meant adulting now and then.

Even if she hated adulting.

Across the room in her work pod, her Parallella computer cluster was crawling, scraping, and automatically tagging data. Evan had texted her updates: that he'd gotten a positive eyewitness ID on

Hick and Red from the Martinez house; that Tommy had claimed that Hick hadn't been driving the truck at the time of the murders. Evan needed more puzzle pieces to satisfy the First Commandment, so that's what she was trying to generate. In order to reconstruct Red and Hick's movements on the night of the murder, she was using Fog Reveal, a law-enforcement cell-phone-location tracking tool effective enough to make the Fourth Amendment blush. She'd geofenced the whole damn county and was still trying to identify traffic cams along their route, which required finding intersections between disparate datasets. It took a lot of horsepower and more time than she had patience for.

Dog pinned her with his yellow-glazed brown eyes and made a low whine. Grape-lustful, he pawed her bare forearm impatiently. His nails were long, curved, designed for gripping rock and packed dirt in pursuit of the lions he was bred to hunt. They raised four streaks on her skin.

"Ow!"

With a curled knuckle, she gave him a firm tap on the snout. It made a hollow sound. He winced and retracted his head, blinked twice hard.

She felt guilty. His nose was dog-sensitive.

But still.

Those claw marks. They'd swell and turn red like they always did and then she'd have to walk around for days looking like she had some kind of weird sex fetish.

She went back to reading sullenly and he rested his great big head on the union of his giant paws just as sullenly.

They took their space, nursing their respective hurts.

A few minutes later at the same time they leaned in toward each other.

He lifted his face to hers.

They touched noses and then went back to their business.

She finished the bowl and set it down on the floor and Dog leapt down and sniff-slobbered the bunch stems and she felt bad but then he jumped back on the couch, circled twice, and settled down with a harumph. His wide dog ass landed on her right thigh, manhole-cover-heavy, knocking the laptop askew.

His perked ears were right there, soft like velvet, demanding a good scritching. Aside from Dr Pepper and Red Vines, there was nothing in the world she loved more than ridgeback ears. On occasion she fantasized about making a Cruella de Vil pillowcase from ridgeback ears but the image of earless shivering ridgebacks undid her. Dog's eyes were sleepy, those ears pinned back. Overcome with cuteness aggression, she wanted to chew his whole face off.

She contented herself instead with rubbing her thumb gently on the top seam of one ear, and he sighed a sigh of deep satisfaction. But then all of a sudden a blackness welled up inside her and she felt it choking her, closing off her throat.

She remembered what X had taught her—four-count in, hold for four, four-count exhalation, hold empty for four.

But it was a lot and she was petting Dog's ear and everything felt swimmy.

She dialed.

He answered. "Go."

Mr. One-Syllable.

"I need a time-out from our deal." Even to her own ears, her voice sounded tight. She knew he'd notice. He noticed everything.

He said, "Okay."

"I'm still mad at you, okay? And we're still only having professional comms for the mission. But . . . but . . ."

He said nothing.

"What if I'm too close to Dog?"

"Say more."

He was driving; she could hear the road rolling beneath his pickup.

"I'm, like, *really* close to him," she whispered, and she felt it releasing from her chest. Just being able to shape the fears into words, to talk about them, made it worse and somehow better.

"I know," he said.

"What if that's weird?" Her vision was blurry now and Dog looked up at her and his soft yellow eyes and furrowed ridgeback brow held concern and he was so attuned to her and made her feel so much less alone. "What if that's . . . not healthy."

"It's not weird. It's not unhealthy. He is your dog. And you are his person."

"But he's gonna die, X. Before me."

"Yes."

"I already know I'll never have another dog like Dog. I'll never love another dog this way."

"You don't know what will happen."

"Yes. I do. He's a person in a dog suit. He's like a dog from a movie. There will never be another dog who understands me like Dog."

"Beginner's mind, Joey. See everything as if for the first time."

"Don't come at me with more of Jack's Zen bullshit."

"It's not Zen bullshit. It's strategy. Whether your dead bolt is two millimeters offset from where you left it. Which cars are driving around you every time you're on the road. Every threat, every conversation, every interaction, every pain, every opportunity."

"What's that have to do with Dog?"

"Maybe someday there will be another puppy. And you will see that puppy as who he is—"

"Or *she*."

"—and not through the prism of your expectations."

She buried her nose in the super soft velvety spot behind Dog's ear. It smelled like cinnamon and sunshine. Grief clamped down on her like a vise. "Dogs are always who they are. Why can't people just be dogs?"

Evan didn't speak for a moment. "Because we're not good enough."

Her heart ached for a loss that didn't yet exist. "I mean, I know he's young. But still. That's what's gonna happen. What if I'm too, dunno, reliant on him? Like, emotionally? What if I can't handle it when he . . . ?" She couldn't say it again.

"Then you'll learn to handle it."

"That sounds awful."

"Yes," he said. "And no."

"Why *no*? How could it be *no*?"

"Because it will make you stronger."

Dots of moisture landed on Dog's head and he didn't even pull away or do his shaky-shake or anything.

"It's too late now." She felt dumb now, mourning a living, healthy dog who was curled up half on her lap, warm and comforting. "I'm trapped."

"We're all trapped," he said. "If you want to feel, you have to feel."

That sounded terrible. So terrible.

On the laptop, she saw it whir past, embedded in a flurry of memes. Her breath caught in her throat. She clicked to stop the carousel, fingers moving fast, and reversed and reversed some more.

INJUSTICE AGAINST WOMEN ANYWHERE IS A THREAT TO JUSTICE EVERYWHERE.

She goosenecked a wrist, used it to wipe her cheeks. Her mouth was dry. She shook her hands out.

If she saw it there on Hick's computer that meant Evan probably had, too. But he hadn't told her. He wasn't a told-you-so guy. But still. Fuck. There it was.

"It's not my fault." The words escaped her before she could think about them. "They killed that family. Red and Hick. *They* did. It doesn't matter what I . . ."

There was a long pause. Somehow she knew that X had made the conversational U-turn with her. That he knew what she was talking about, what she had seen, what she was grappling with. Because he just knew stuff like that. The way he knew was comforting, infuriating.

"*They* made the choice to go to that park. It's their fault." She was confused and scared and angry. "They can go suck a bag of dicks for eternity."

"That is," Evan said, "Dantesque."

Her phone dinged with a text. It was Cassidy Ann, Pretty White Pasadena Girl, President of WEG, the Women's Empowerment Group.

Adulting

meet me at ackerman food court asap weve got a sitch.

A situation.
Shit. *Shit shit shit.*
This was the last thing Joey needed.
Every time she had contact with Other Living Organisms all it brought was stress, anxiety, fear. The stupid meme she'd blasted out had wound up in front of a murderer, and Tommy and Evan were gonna kill each other, and Dog was gonna die one day, and now there was a problem with Cassie Ann and this whole group of potential girlfriends, and her life was falling apart around her.
If you want to feel, you have to feel.
Right now it felt *so* not worth it.
She heard Evan rack the truck into park and climb out, and then she made out the clank of a gas nozzle lifting from its holster. "We done?" he asked.
X and his single-digit EQ.
"Yeah. We're done."
Hanging up, she shot Cassie Ann the brown thumbs-up emoji, tucked her laptop under her arm, and reluctantly extracted herself from Dog's heft.

34

Riding the Waves of a Communal Sea

Gas was expensive here, as it was everywhere else. Filling his rig would cost around seven hours of minimum-wage work, and Evan wondered how the hell anyone afforded anything anymore. He had pulled over at a small town on the way back from Dawnfall, and he chewed his lip in the sudden hard coldness of night, his thoughts interrupted by the thrumming of a bass guitar from a freestanding bar next door.

The sign fluttering against the brick wall declaimed: MAKE MONDAY NITE RITE! LINE DANCING 18+!

The vibration coming through the building seemed different from the dive bar at Calvary; it felt bouncy, joyful. A trio of young cowboys smoked out front by a hitching post with nothing hitched to it, and a few girls walked past arm in arm wearing flare jeans and frilly blouses, and the cowboys touched the brims of their Stetsons and dipped their chins in greeting.

As the gas-pump meter whirred up and up, Evan found himself drifting away from his truck and across the curb, boots crunching over the glittering remains of a Michelob bottle. He eased over to the one high-set window, which was tinted but not so tinted that he could not see inside.

For a moment he couldn't register what he was looking at. Forty or so bodies spread evenly across a dance floor twisting, hip-cocking, boot-tapping, moving in concert. A handsome young man, square-jawed beneath a cowboy hat and yet so, so light on his feet, spun his partner in time, their dance stitching into the movement of the others around them. He anticipated her, hand ready for hers off the twirl, eyes locking each time she swung around, the leg-length fringes lifting off her suede jeans, and he dipped and swung her, showcasing her in all her feminine glory. And they were shiny and grand and sensuous, every move a risked fall or stumble and yet every last time he snapped her back into place and they kept on harmonizing along the cliff edge. Evan would have thought that no boy that manly could move so elegantly on a dance floor, but he'd seen it before, seen it when Jamal and Tyrell got jiggy to the foster-home radio, seen it when Danny and skinny-ass Ramón had their aggressive-as-fuck boom-box dance-off on the cracked handball court, seen it in the hips of the pimps and players the times he and Andre had snuck into house parties at the apartment of Jalilah's nana before she burned down the building smoking a blunt in bed.

Folks sipped brown and clear around tables on the carpet and tapped their feet and pointed at the mounted TVs cycling nostalgic trivia questions about nineties sitcoms and the band on the hay-strewn dais sipped their watery whiskeys and the female lead singer had cleavage for days and the drummer's beard glittered with sweat under the lights and they all clapped and hollered until a few more of the line dancers switched into partnered two-steps, couples breaking apart and joining in new combinations, and all of them were striving for excellence not just of moves or looks or peacock swagger but excellence in the resonance with all of it, of everything—the crisp tapping of the snare drum, the glittering yokes on the sweated-through Western shirts, the two-fingered lift of a longneck bottle, the perfect lipstick arc on the rim of a four-dollar cosmo, the wild-eyed freedom of moving in a shared trance, of rhythm and release, of being alive and together breathing shared nighttime air.

And the younger girls wore crop tops that were likely too cropped for their parents but not shrunken into lasciviousness, and the boys wore charcoal T-shirts bearing tattered American flags and one girl glowered with live, sensuous eyes above a waifish nose, her black lipstick pierced by a half dozen silver rings. And another gal was a little too old for her dress and one guy a little too butch in his swagger and there was a woman with a mullet and a bouncy Filipina in her mid-thirties glowing with grace and pink lipstick beneath a rust-colored straw cowboy hat and a pale kid with dandruff-flaked shoulders who consistently snapped on the downbeat and two, maybe three Mexicans and a white kid in a proper sky-blue La Celeste *fútbol* jersey and a chunky girl loose in the wrists, elbows, and hips having more fun than anyone else, and a single black guy in ironed true-blue jeans, and an older gentleman with a gently encouraging permanent smile and a diabetes monitor stuck on the back of his arm, and every last person knew their place within the whole and they nodded and smiled and deferred and admired one another and they were gentlemen and ladies.

And standing there, a shadow with its face to the tinted glass, Evan felt an age-old stab of envy. For him dancing was too improvisational, too free, a language unknown to his muscle and joints. He didn't know how to lose himself in something like that, in the pulsing bloodstream of a shared experience. And he stood before the window, staring as if into a TV at this clean, well-lighted place, staring at the unmitigated beauty inside, a beauty of joined movement and known roles, a beauty that so many feared because to join it one had to learn to shine while ceding at the same time, and he knew that fear because he had it, it was a fear inside him, a fear of shining, of being known. And he thought about what might have happened if Andre walked in there or Ramón in his stolen acid-washed Cavariccis or anyone else who came from broken nothingness, and he saw that any of them could fare just fine if they showed enough grace to read the river, to learn the currents and ripples, he saw that a place could be made for anyone to join the ebb and flow.

For anyone *else*.

And it struck him that Red and Hick and the other shitstains

Riding the Waves of a Communal Sea

Tommy had bedded down with were the fringiest fringe of the fringe who would have no place here. Just like Evan.

And the next song started, a true line dance, everyone falling into rhythm together, stomping and smacking their heels. And an autistic Asian teenager in white orthopedic Velcro sneakers and a stretched-out T-shirt with its hem low across her thighs got up and stood outside the seething, rhythmic mass, watching the footwork, calculating the cogs and wheels within the beautiful machine, and her lips were moving as she counted and she was hopping stiffly as she watched from the fringe a half dozen feet off the dance floor and her stiff hopping evolved into something else until she bounced with plucked-string perfection, her movement elegant and singular and hypnotic and she had the footwork down now and she turned around to face the same way as everyone else and held the movement still and she slid slowly backward toward the dance floor, now at the edge of the parquet, now three feet off-set from the mass, and everyone else was equidistant, machine-dropped into their slots on the dance floor, uniform and unique all at once, and then she stepped backward again and again and then she was there with everyone else, folded into the heaving organism of the whole, riding the waves of a communal sea, and folks smiled and clapped for her and she was bouncing, her lips shaped with mirth, cheeks flushed with happiness, and they all glided together in shimmering synchronization, a school of fish in glittering motion.

And it was there. It was right there.

The center.

The center was holding.

And a darkness roiled up in Evan sudden and unannounced that he was not a part of this, that he never could be, that his own cowardice had consigned him to the shadows beyond the wondrous balance making itself known in the tapping of boots against parquet, in the chorus-line flare of legs, the rhyming movement to a shared melody.

Tommy's parting words came to him. *And you,* he'd said, *think about what you* are.

He was the answer for Gabriel Martinez.

And for Lidia. For Santiago.

And he loathed himself. He loathed himself for being necessary.

He could not tear his eyes away. Standing there in a whiff of secondhand smoke, he was transfixed.

Someone jostled him.

He snapped into himself, sliding one foot to set his base, dropping his center of gravity.

"Sorry, man," a guy mumbled, and strode around him with his friends, keeping on toward the parking lot.

Evan hadn't noted the trio's approach. He hadn't assessed bulges in jackets, read body language, gauged angles of retreat and identified makeshift weapons around him.

For the first time he could remember, he'd slid straight out of his operational awareness, straight out of time, straight out of himself.

In a semi-daze he drifted back to his truck. The gas pump had clicked off already.

He didn't know how long he'd stood at that window, lost.

Lost.

And yet found.

35

¯_(ツ)_/¯

Empty.

That's how Joey felt.

She sat in the food court alone.

Cassie Ann had arrived with a cohort from WEG and they'd laid out the "situation" for Joey with a breathlessness that betrayed enjoyment of the very drama they claimed to be suffering through. From WEG's social-media profiles, the memes Joey had propagated had gone viral. Of course they had. She knew how to pull levers online better than any living human except maybe Kevin Poulsen and who even knew what he was up to these days. There were tens of thousands of shares and a bunch of blowback and now they were being accused of Islamophobia and privilege (ha!) and Cassie Ann just. Couldn't. Right. Now.

None of the girls said it outright but there'd been unspoken blame aimed in Joey's direction, and Kasey, Cassie Ann's right-hand girl, had twice mused that if Joey hadn't been so, like, professional-level good at her job then no one would have noticed and they could still just be a small college group doing good and helping women instead of it becoming A Whole Thing. And that since they'd outsourced meme creation to a contract graphic designer, the only member of WEG who *technically* had her hands dirty was Joey. And that an apology likely needed to be issued and WEG had to decide who should make that apology for the good of the whole organization.

So that meant Joey was gonna be the one thrown under the bus when under-the-bus-throwing time got here. After the impromptu meeting, Cassie Ann and the girls stood up together, their chairs chirping against the tile in unison. They'd offered Joey support and told her they were all in it together.

Then they'd left her.

And now here she was at the stupid table in the stupid food court with this thing she'd unleashed crawling across the internet and her stomach growling.

There was a slice place and a Panda Express and a Carl's Jr. and a Veggie Grill (but blech, who tf ate at Veggie Grill?). Joey wanted pepperoni slices and kung pao chicken and a Double Western Bacon Cheeseburger.

She knew in advance how it would feel when it hit her stomach, warm and filling, and then she'd get sluggish and relaxed, satiated, and then it would feel like she might be okay, that the world still had comfort to offer.

Ding!

A text from X.

You good?

Okay, then. Maybe his EQ wasn't single-digit. Maybe it was low double digits.

She gave him the kaomoji shrug: ¯_(ツ)_/¯.

X never knew what to do with emojis.

And she was still mad at him, even if he'd been right about her stupid club and the stupid memes and her stupid screwups. Plus he was a hypocrite! He'd made a bunch of assumptions about Tommy in full breach of the First Commandment then charged off

¯_(ツ)_/¯

to some other state without learning the ground truth. So he could lecture all he wanted but still: pot, meet kettle.

She decided on slices and got up to order, leaving her jacket at the table to hold her seat. She brought her laptop with her because she never left it unattended, not ever. Using it as a tray, she balanced the two paper plates atop it and made her way back to her table.

As she chewed she popped the screen back open.

An alert had come in from the scraper she'd left running on her system at home. It had accessed another crime-scene report from the Calvary Sheriff's Department, and she blinked at the screen a few times, trying to make sense of it.

Gabriel Martinez's body hadn't been recovered at the impact site.

It had been dumped three miles away by the side of the road.

They had taken him. They'd kidnapped the boy.

And then dumped his body.

There was a photo.

Gabriel's skin was so smooth. His face was intact, or at least the side shown in the picture. He had long eyelashes. There was a lack of visible gore but a clear crumpling of form beneath his clothes, the bones' position not making sense, and his shirt and pants held splotches like oil stains. He looked like a broken doll.

She stared at the picture for a long, long time, the bite of pizza growing cold in her mouth. Her hands were greasy, so she wiped them on her jeans. Then she texted X the crime report. And the photo.

A pause.

Then the three bubbles appeared.

Then they disappeared.

Why the hell would Hick and Red have taken the boy? To torture him? Hold him for ransom? To terrorize the Hayesville community?

She wolfed down the rest of the first slice. The table next to her was filled with college boys with matching swoopy hair and those leather strappy bracelets and AXE body spray and they were sneaking looks at her and laughing and they all had perfect teeth.

247

Her fingertips were still greasy and she'd forgotten napkins because who could remember napkins when you had two hot slices of pepperoni so she used the heels of her hands to carry the laptop over and get napkins and when she got back to her seat, her other piece of pizza and the plate were missing.

She stared at the spot where the plate had been, the small fog spot still evanescing, and she smelled AXE body spray even stronger and she looked across at the boys and they had their mouths ducked behind hands and forearms and they were giggling and she saw the piece of pizza hidden badly on the floor between two of their chairs and they saw she saw and there was a moment of tense silence.

The boy nearest to her—the cutest one—said, "Hiya, tough girl. We like your squint."

Something gave way in her.

It just gave way.

And then the kid was flying up out of his chair and her fists were wrapped up in the lapels of his hoodie and she was the one making him fly and his eyes were bulging and she flung him to the floor and he landed hard on his hip and skidded on his side and his wallet and phone flew out of his pocket and Joey said, "Don't fuck with my food," and her voice contained a lot of fucking anger to cover everything else that had welled up inside her.

He was scared. He had his arm up protectively and he said, "Jesus, okay, sorry. I just . . . I just thought you were cute."

The rest of the guys at the table hushed and everything felt different. She'd escalated too hard too fast and everyone in the food court was staring at her and she saw Mateo from her Optimal Parameter Estimation and Experiment Design course who had an awkward crush on her and even he looked dismayed. Other girls looked at her with their heads drawn back on swan necks and their eyes blinking with contempt and someone whispered, "Psycho bitch," and then she grabbed her jacket and stormed out, her face burning.

And her stomach roiled with acid and shame, and a memory flew in at her from the snake pit of a foster home she'd grown up in. A bike chain and padlock securing the handles of the harvest-

¯_(ツ)_/¯

yellow refrigerator, a measure put in place by one of Nemma's many male visitors to preserve whatever scarce food he'd put in there for himself.

And she felt all the blackness inside her but it didn't fill up the emptiness. It was like an abyss proving that everything was wrong with her, that she was different, broken, that she'd never learn how to control the tap on what she felt so it could come out slow enough that she might stand it.

Her face was hot but she would not cry. She would not.

Rushing through the union, darting through the UCLA store with all the rah-rah teddy Bruins and sweatshirts, she felt the electricity of all that terrible human focus at her back, and then she was shoving out through the doors into Bruin Plaza and running smack into a pack of women, some of them wearing headscarves and others Star of David pendants, and she drew up short, nearly dropping her laptop.

The one in front said, "Cassidy Ann Perkins told us we'd find you here."

The woman next to her said, "And that you are responsible."

36

Young Man

The young men were spread across the living room like paste, slumped on cushions and chairs, staring slack-jawed at their cell phones, looking zombified. Except for Hick, who had the tiny book open in one hand and the dictionary set face down on his thigh.

Tommy came in with a bundle under his arm. Driving back from Dawnfall, he'd picked up a few things for Elijah at the Walmart, little-man clothes with no damn holes in them.

Hick stood up from the couch but the others hardly stirred.

Tommy walked over, dropped the bundle in Elijah's lap. Elijah looked up. His pupils were dilated, his face leached of affect. "What's this?"

"What's it look like?"

Elijah set down his phone, unfolded the top shirt. It was a flannel, yellow and black. Beneath, a pair of Dickies jeans. He looked confused.

"Who's it for?"

"Who ya think it's for?"

Young Man

His face had life in it now. Redness at the flanges of his nostrils. "I didn't ask for this."

"I didn't say you did."

Elijah looked down again at the flannel. Ran his thumb across it. There were stickers on the clothes saying what size everything was and tags. Everything looked bright and brand-new against the ragged-ass clothes he was wearing.

Lucas scratched his lower belly just above the belt line. "He's a regular social worker now."

He and Burt laughed. They had the same laugh and it sounded creepy in stereo.

Tommy flicked a finger at Hick. "Let's go."

Hick started toward him.

"Where you going?" Burt said.

"The mosque."

That got everyone's attention.

Trent's cheek had scabbed up some from when Evan had slid him across the planks like a curling stone. He scratched at it, raising beads of blood. "I ain't going."

"No one invited your ignorant ass. I'm going with Hick. And Red."

"No way," Red said. "I'm not going inside a sleeper cell to listen to some terrorist try'n refudiate what we all know."

Refudiate.

"Boy," Tommy said, "it's a wonder you remember to keep breathing."

"Why should I go with you?"

"The man who came here? The one who Skee-Balled Trent across the floor and put a round a quarter inch off Lucas's nose? He wants to kill you. And Hick."

Red swallowed hard, his head doing a little Pez-dispenser nod. "*Us?* What? What for?"

"For taking that truck to run over them folks."

Red stood up now, too, wiped his palms on his pants. They left sweat marks by the pockets.

Burt: "I'd like to see him try."

Tommy held focus on Red. "You're gonna stay with me."

Red screwed up his face. "Till when?"

A damn fine question. The whole drive back from Dawnfall, Tommy had worked the phone, calling hooks in various law-enforcement offices, putting out feelers at the state level, and drumming up some leads on defense lawyers. He was trying to figure out what options there might be for Hick and Red if the Calvary Sheriff's Department proved corrupt beyond remedy. Given the necessary vagueness of his queries and the peculiarities of regional constabularies, he hadn't drummed up a lot of answers. But he'd keep working the cud around, sending it down to one stomach or another and then back up until this goddamned mess got processed properly. He needed to deliver the boys to some kind of justice. He needed to keep them out of Evan's sights. He needed a slug of Beam and a carton of Camel Wides.

"Till you're not dead and not about to get dead," Tommy said.

"You need this old man to protect you?" Lucas said.

Red looked at his shoes.

Hick said, "Yes."

Lucas laughed. "You're more pathetic than I thought."

Tommy and Hick started out.

Head still down, Red followed.

Driving in the dark, Hick in the passenger seat, Red in the back. The road gave good rattle, the shocks taking the bumps and dips with rough animal grace. Tommy had confiscated Red's big-dick revolver and locked it in the glove box, which only added to the shades of moping emanating from the back of the cab.

Red's voice floated up: "I'm not getting out. I'm not doing shit."

Tommy ignored him.

Hick's hands rested on his knees, knuckles tightening as he squeezed, a nervous tic.

Tommy turned onto paved road now, the yellow dotted line stretching out to the headlights' horizon, ever renewing. Felt like riding on a treadmill, going hard and getting nowhere at all.

Hick said, "What are we gonna do?"

"This," Tommy said. "We're gonna get this right. And then we're gonna get the next thing right. And then the thing after that."

Tommy rapped on the door of the mosque, then withdrew a good fifteen feet, where Hick had stopped. There was no wind, just the crickets holding their own against the deathly quiet night. They stared at all those words slathered across the mosque's white stuccoed walls.

"I don't know about this," Hick said.

Tommy said, "I know."

"I want to go."

"I know."

Hick was holding the pocket Constitution formally in both hands like a Book of Psalms or a business card in China. He shot a nervous glance behind him. Tommy had left Red in the truck parked in the lot facing the mosque so he'd have a good view. His face floated there in the darkness of the backseat, barely visible.

"Can't I just wait in the—"

"No."

The door opened.

The imam with his wife at his side. She was covered up with a beautiful hijab, lavender with gold flowers, and she wore Levi's and a black sweatshirt three sizes too big with USMC block-lettered in red and rimmed with yellow and it looked old and worn and very, very well-loved.

The imam noted them there, leaned toward his wife without taking his eyes off Tommy and Hick, and said something softly to her in Arabic. She nodded and withdrew.

The imam walked out to them.

On the building: *PROPHIT OF BUTCHERS.*

TERORIZE YOUR OWN COUNTRY.

GO HOME!

At Tommy's side, Hick's respiration quickened, his breath stale. Tommy could feel the heat of his sweat. The pocket Constitution trembled in his hands.

The imam stood before him, his gaze steady.

Hick would not meet his eyes. He stared at the man's chest.

The imam hugged him.

Hick froze, shoulders bunched at his ears. He didn't move. He held the little book still, his arms trapped before him.

The imam released him, walked back toward the building. He keyed in a code at the side of the garage and the big door lifted open creakily.

The imam entered.

It was dark in the garage.

The imam emerged with two old-fashioned web-mesh lawn chairs. He unfolded them next to Tommy, facing the mosque.

He walked back into the garage. Sounds of clanking, of cabinets opening.

He emerged once more carrying a big white plastic pail in one hand and a paint roller in the other. He walked back over, set them down by the tips of Hick's boots.

He stood before Hick.

Hick had not dared to lift his gaze.

The imam set a hand on Hick's cheek. And looked directly at him. It was a kind look.

It took a moment but Hick lifted his gaze.

Hick cleared his throat. Cleared it again.

"Sorry," he said. "I'm sorry."

The imam nodded once, and then sat in the lawn chair, gesturing for Tommy to join him.

Tommy did.

Hick picked up the paint bucket and roller and got to work.

They watched him make slow but steady progress.

"I appreciate this," Tommy said. "Letting him work it off."

"Work it off," the imam said. "And *learn* it off." He produced Tommy's Oakley razors from a pocket and donned them even at night, the purple tint lending a comedic flourish to his dignified mien. "A few of ours defiled a synagogue over in Eastbrooke last year. When I found out and brought them to the rabbi as you brought yours to me, he showed my young men this same firmness and grace."

Tommy made a noise deep in his throat. "How it should be.

Americans know how to solve our own problems when the whole damn world ain't dragged into it."

"Indeed. And now I have the chance to pay it forward as it was paid forward to me."

"Almost like beneath all the bullshit, we're the same."

"*No*," the imam said. And then, a sly smile. "Rabbi Cohen is a Yankees fan."

Tommy couldn't help a grin from busting out.

A moment later the imam's wife emerged holding a tray with a tea service. She set it down before the men.

There were three glass mugs.

"Thank you," she said to Tommy, with a slight Southern accent.

"Thank you," Tommy said to her.

She walked back toward the house. Hick paused, paint roller in hand, dripping white into the bucket.

"Young man," she said, by way of acknowledgment.

Hick's chin wobbled. His eyes glinted. He nodded but the nod said everything it needed to say.

She went back inside.

Tommy and the imam sipped tea and watched Hick work.

Tommy glanced over his shoulder. From the depths of the cab behind them, he could barely see Red's eyes glinting. But he was watching.

He watched the whole time.

37

Without Permission

Joey was home.

She was freaking out.

It was bad.

So bad she'd built a pillow fort, sitting against the headboard and pressing pillows into either side of her and across her shins. Less a fort, more like a sculling boat. But still.

She was confused. Like: really confused.

Everything was a mess.

She didn't even want to lose herself in gaming or coding or hacking into the Russian Foreign Intelligence Service.

She felt profoundly foolish.

And scared.

And alone.

Dog sat at the end of the bed, looking at her, whining gently, his distress matching hers.

She didn't know what to do.

She picked up her phone, hesitated, chewed the edge of

her thumb. Then she dialed a number she'd never called before.

Not without permission.

38

Wait in the Truck

They are the ones who did this. They are the ones who took Gabriel.

Evan had not understood. He'd thought "took" meant "killed."

Not that Hick and Red had actually taken the eight-year-old and driven off with him.

The First Commandment: *Assume nothing.*

He had to drill down further.

He had to bolt the facts to the ground. Find proof undeniable to his own eyes. That's what he required for what he was to bring.

Gabriel, the messenger angel. His broken body discarded in a roadside ditch five kilometers away from the park. Evan had come here for Tommy but would not—could not—ignore what had been done to that child.

The sheriff's station was easy enough to find, since most everything in Calvary was lined neatly on one road. It was at the west edge of the row of commerce, past the diner and a shuttered bowling alley and the sole bar, innovatively named the Watering Hole.

Lights off, decent surveillance-camera setup. Front and back doors sported Medeco locks—key-in-knobs augmented by Maxum dead bolts with hardened steel inserts and rotating pins that presented some resistance to picks and drills. The front door was made of glass, which made the entire lock enterprise irrelevant to anyone with a hammer or a decent-size rock. But at least it had nice stenciled letters reading CALVARY SHERIFF'S STATION in a strong sans-serif typeface that matched the dated website.

Evan sat in his F-150 across the street, out of the purview of the security lens.

A Ford Interceptor SUV was parked a half block up in front of the bar. Navy-blue paint, a giant SHERIFF decal stretched across the side doors to differentiate Grady Joy's cruiser from those of his mere deputies. On the facing sidewalk sat an old-fashioned wooden bench, which Evan walked to now.

He'd already driven by Sheriff Joy's house, conveniently listed in the old-world phone book in the Emerald Bay Motel lobby. The lights had been off at the house, too. Evan hoped to put himself in the path of local law enforcement to elicit some mild harassment, but it was proving trickier than he'd hoped.

He sat on the bench, let the cold eat at the edges of his clothes and seep in around the cuffs. Muffled noise emanated from the bar—country music, laughter, the occasional roar of inebriated conversation. At one point, a robust gentleman stumbled out the front door, retched fruitfully into the gutter, and stood a moment doubled over, swaying on his feet. He wiped his mouth, straightened up, noticed Evan.

"Evenin'," he said.

"Good evening," Evan said.

The guy staggered back inside.

Across the street, a plastic tarp billowed where the bowling alley's front window had been. When it fluttered high enough, moonlight leaked inside, showing the gutted interior. Stained floors and protruding rebar and wooden posts, a stack of crumbling Sheetrock, rusting construction tools, all crusted with a film of sawdust and concrete powder. So much of the town felt half-built or half-destroyed, as if someone had pressed a PAUSE button years ago and the survivors were making do with whatever wreckage remained.

Evan waited and then waited some more.

Finally the door swung open and Sheriff Grady Joy emerged, wife on his arm. They looked pristine, glossy, a power couple out on the town.

Evan watched Grady closely.

He looked as smooth as his website photo.

It took him less than a second to key to Evan there on the bench, within spitting distance of his shiny SUV.

He started over, wife clutching his elbow and minding the high-heel wobbles. She was an antelope-faced model type, long-legged and toned of arm. Enough workout time to lend a tinge of testosterone to her aggressive femininity. Pronounced jawline, not quite enough fat to balance the sinewy muscle. She shivered and Grady slipped off his sport coat and eased it across her bare shoulders. The wool-blend quarters flapped at her thighs, lower than the hem of her dress, which looked oh-so-adorable. Grady wore a piece unabashedly in a hip holster.

They approached.

They stopped about five feet from Evan and stared at him.

"Elise," Grady said, "wait in the truck."

Her eyes were contact-enhanced to an improbable turquoise. She flashed them at Evan, then rose onto tiptoes, kissed her husband on the cheek in a manner suggesting he was someone to be adored and deferred to, and folded herself into the passenger seat.

Grady crossed his arms, making his biceps flex. He was solidly built but Evan knew he could render him inert with a *bil jee* finger strike to the larynx or those tough gray eyes.

"What do you think you're doing?" Grady said.

"Settin' a spell," Evan said, enjoying the phrasing. Sometimes you had to make your own fun.

In the truck across from them, Elise busied herself fixing her face in the visor mirror, popping her mouth to get the lipstick right. Then she fussed with her bangs, a studied jitter of her forked fingers to get them to lie just so. The vigilance required to remain perennially photogenic seemed exhausting to Evan, but it was clearly a prime life focus for Elise.

Grady set his hands on his hips and looked out at the darkness as if waiting for someone to come shoot his portrait for a Men in Uniform calendar. He had that glow of prosperity, of sureness in his station of life.

"You don't belong here."

"I don't belong anywhere," Evan said.

"Yeah, well, you especially don't belong here."

"You might be right," Evan said.

"So why don't you skedaddle? The Emerald Bay Motel can't be that strong a draw."

"I'm looking forward to skedaddling," Evan said. "But there's this thorn in my side."

"What thorn is that?"

"A kidnapping."

"Kidnapping? We haven't had a kidnapping around here in . . . well, forever."

"So what do you call it," Evan asked, watching Grady closely, "when someone snatches a boy in front of witnesses and dumps his body three miles away?"

Grady's forehead, eyebrows, and upper eyelids elevated suddenly, dramatically. An adrenaline surge manifesting in upper facial contraction, revving him up for the lie to come.

"I don't know about any of that," he said. "But eyewitnesses can be a powerful source of evidence. Especially when they're law-abiding members of the community with nothing to hide." That handsome grin again. "All their papers in order, stuff like that."

In the SUV, Elise continued to ignore them, tapping at her phone with manicured nails painted a creamy ivory.

Grady took a step closer, pulled himself higher on his heels. He smelled powerfully of mints and aftershave, but beneath it the bar's cigarette smoke wafted from his clothes, as subtle as hidden rot. "What do you think this town was like before I came in as sheriff?"

"Oh," Evan said. "You're *that* guy."

Grady had a grin like a quarterback's. "What guy?"

"The guy who's the hero of every story he tells."

The grin wavered, but just barely. "All of a sudden folks from who knows where are blowing through here like tumbleweeds, poking their snouts into things. I don't like it."

"An upsetting influx," Evan said, "of snouted tumbleweeds."

Grady blinked at him. Hoisted his belt. "You might think it's funny. But I promise you this, friend, it's gonna get unfunny real fast."

He made a casual sweep of his hand, taking care to place it on the side of his tailored shirt just above the gleaming grip of his holstered piece. Then he eased forward again, crowding Evan's space.

For the particularly grueling summer of Evan's fifteenth year, Jack had placed him in the care of a petite Japanese master who'd mopped the dojo mat with him. For part of his training, she'd made him do push-ups on his thumbs to strengthen them. Right now Evan had an eye on the top of Grady's chest, just above the clavicle where the phrenic nerve travels through the neck into the thorax, providing motor function to the diaphragm. A well-placed thumb jab could momentarily paralyze the lungs and—with a bit of luck—strike the vagus nerve, drop blood pressure, and disrupt consciousness. The power of the thumb jab determines whether the target merely experiences excruciating discomfort or suffocates inside his own locked-up body.

Evan had kept up with his thumb push-ups. Fifty a day. And Grady was grating on him.

"Listen," Evan said. "I know you think you're important in this town with your designer wife and your burly SUV with your job title painted across the side in case you forget it. I'm sure you think you know how to fight, how to use the SIG P226 jammed into that fancy high-ride holster that's canted ten degrees too far forward. But I want you to look at me. Look at me closely. And ask yourself: Do I look scared?"

Grady's shoulders loosened some and he took a step back and then another. "Well," he said, "you *should* be."

He circled the vehicle and climbed in. As if by rote, Elise leaned over and they kissed fully, Grady's eyes flashing past her cheek to find Evan even with their lips locked. But he didn't bother to glance at Evan again when he pulled out.

Evan sat a spell longer with the wind and the cold.

He looked at the bar, gauged the odds of its having any vodka worth sipping. The witch-brewed turpentine back in Las Vegas had put him off booze, but it had been a long day and he felt a need to cleanse himself with something strong and bracing.

A stream of warm air gusted across him as he entered. The place was in full swing—dartboards and ashtrays and high-top tables blanketed with empty pint glasses gilded with lipstick crescents. There was a slight stir, his entrance noted and then pointedly ignored.

One empty stool, dead center at the bar.

Evan took it.

On either side of him were men who smelled powerfully unwashed. Odors were hardest on his OCD. He always thought of the particles he was breathing in, pictured them roosting in the billowy walls of his lungs. When he was operating, he could turn it off. When he was X or the Nowhere Man he became a battle surgeon or an abattoir meat cutter, a specialist on task and on mission, the other parts of himself muted into irrelevance.

At the end of the bar a *Dukes of Hazzard* pinball machine dinged and flashed. Folks were having work-night fun, blowing off steam. Dancing and laughing and flirting. The women were done up— sundresses and tan boots, long feathered hair, jean shorts with white stars and white fringe and legs forever. But some of the other socializing seemed washed out from repetition, same jokes, same folks perched on proprietary stools, same drunks slurring the same words, same end-of-night choices. Evan was an unapologetic drinker but he'd never liked drink-more culture. He saw plenty of that here in red-rimmed eyes, on veined noses, in the way abdominal fat bulged low over belt buckles. There was genuine merrymaking and then there was holding off despair, and each seemed to propel the other, a feedback loop.

The array of libations was minimal. No floating shelves, just a three-tiered wooden step display showing off the usual suspects. Triple sec and Baileys, Gordon's and Smirnoff, Bacardi and Cuervo Gold, Beam and Red Label. But peeking out from behind a crusted Midori lurked a familiar vodka. Nicely shaped bottle with an indented band two-thirds up for ease of handling. A slight bulge plumped the slender neck, which was ridged top and bottom for a firm grip on the pour. Designed for bartenders right down to the simple twist cap and the vertically etched scale to measure volume.

The bottle looked empty.

The bartender came over and looked at Evan, evident dislike in his pale eyes. Evan had heard him called Dougie. Scraggly facial hair sprouted in random bursts along his cheeks and jawline. Dougie might have been twenty-five or forty-five.

"The Aylesbury Duck," Evan said. "Any left?"

"Why would we keep an empty bottle on the shelf?"

"To remind you to reorder it."

Dougie plucked the bottle up with a toss and grab, tilted it. It was about a fourth full. On the label, two anthropomorphized ducks sparred. The back of the label, visible through glass and booze, was decorated with old steamship routes, and the bottom of the bottle was embossed with a logo. Everything held together, form following function, a precise, thought-through sum of fine parts.

Dougie sloshed around the vodka, which left a pleasingly even coat on the bottle. "This is the last of it."

The sole drinkable bottle in the sole bar in town. That meant Evan would have to ration.

He gave a nod.

"How'd you want it?"

Evan didn't trust Dougie to shake a martini properly. He wanted it on a globe or a block cube that wouldn't melt too fast and leave it watered down.

"What kind of ice do you have?"

"The kind made from water." Dougie mopped at the bar surface, more for effect than anything else. "I eat my Thanksgiving turkey with ketchup. We don't put on airs about ice cubes around here."

Evan said, "Fair. I'll have it with three ice cubes, please."

Dougie shoveled a scoop of ice cubes into a lowball glass, shook some out, then slopped a few fingers in, leaving about two pours left in the bottle. He plunked the glass down in front of Evan.

Seven. There were seven ice cubes in the vodka.

Despite that travesty, it looked silvery and delicious. Slowly fermented from white winter wheat, it was distilled but not carbon-filtered, so the character held up. It would go well in a Bloody Mary, though he was not in the mood for a salad.

He sipped.

Oily, heavy-bodied, cereal grain and root vegetables. A fresh-bread note came on mid-palate, and it finished with a touch of spice.

He could get three more sips out of it, maybe four, before all that surface area from the seven ice cubes melted it into tap water and ethanol.

He let the mood seep into him through his pores. There was a twitch in the air here, a current of latent resentment, as if everyone had already resigned themselves to some impending battle and they were just biding their time.

The men at his sides leaned away and then he sensed a presence at his back. He took another sip of the Aylesbury Duck to get it in while he could and then he felt the poke at his shoulder. Two wide fingers, maybe three, pressing him forward roughly.

He turned.

A large man, rancher-strong, ruddy of face and full of beard. He had a decade and fifty pounds on Evan and big rough hands.

One of those big rough hands snatched up Evan's glass. The man stuck a callused finger into the drink, swirled it around a few times, and then sucked it. Evan registered a pang of dismay to see the last potable vodka in town diminished by 33 percent.

"Mmm." The big guy smacked his lips. "Fancy."

The men had vacated the stools at Evan's side and the bar hadn't fallen quiet but much of the motion had stilled, the emergent scene drawing attention.

"Duke, c'mon, pal," Dougie said. "At least take it outside this time."

But Duke kept his gaze fixed on Evan. He was up tight on him, leaving him little room to swivel or rise. The rest of the barstools had cleared off as well, everyone leaving decent standoff room for whatever was coming.

"Heard you been harassing Vic's boy," Duke said.

"I don't know who Vic is."

"Lucky for you. He'd put a hole in your head with his knuckles, Vic would."

"I'm grateful," Evan said, "to have been spared."

"Vic's boy is Red," Duke said. "Red Hildebrandt. And Vic's a close friend of mine. In fact, you could almost call us family. So whatever you do to a Hildebrandt, you do to me."

He extended Evan's glass over the bar and poured it out. It tapped down on the lacquered wood, pooled, and waterfalled off the edge next to Evan's thigh.

Evan swiveled back to Dougie, who'd drawn back from the bar. Reaching slowly, Evan removed his money clip. He counted off two tens from the stack, laid them on the bar. "For the vodka. And . . ." He peeled a few hundreds from the inside of the fold. "For the broken pinball machine."

Dougie said, "It's not broken."

Evan shot up and jabbed Duke in the gut with a bladed hand. Duke's mouth gaped and he curled forward breathlessly. Evan spun him around with a kick to the Achilles tendon, took hold of his collar and the back of his belt, frog-marched him three strides down the bar, and smashed his face down through the pinball glass.

He was careful to lead with the top curve of the forehead to spare Duke's eyesight.

Duke reared up with a cry, clutching at his bloody face. He fell to his knees, rose unevenly, and staggered to hammer out through the back door.

The bar had fallen silent and all Evan could see anywhere was eyes.

He walked calmly back to his barstool. It had toppled over when he'd exploded up out of it. He righted it, set it back in place, nicely tucked in. Dougie was as far back from the bar as he could get, his shoulders to the bottles and his head retracted posteriorly as if a long jab could reach him.

Evan said, "It is now," and walked out.

39

Your Basic Assassin Friends

The water-streaked blue-lit front window of Mastro's Steakhouse projected signage onto the sidewalk in front. Everything about it was quintessential Beverly Hills—speakeasy-dim lighting, dry-ice mist rising from seafood platters, bubbling mixology concoctions that would've made X gag.

For the meeting, Joey had donned a pair of black jeans and her nicest hoodie, the one with a rhinestone skull on the sleeve. But still she felt like a child. Standing in the crowded foyer and scanning the restaurant, she didn't see her dinner companion.

But she could read the energy of the room and knew it would point the way.

A magnetic current. Joey traced it from the hunched groups of men whispering, from girlfriends tight-lipped with envy, to the rubbernecking waiter bearing a tray of martinis who nearly walked into a potted plant.

She stepped farther into the restaurant proper, bringing the distant side into view.

There she sat.

At the edge of a corner booth, wrapped in a canary-yellow sequined dress, one sleek leg nudged through a dangerous-looking slit, knee swayed ever so slightly open. Hair twisted up, staked through with a silver chopstick, one tendril curled vine-like in a half-inch float off her left cheek. A cascade of blond tresses across her shoulders. The dress was high-backed, sleeved to the wrists, and it was so form-fitted that she looked more naked than if she were naked. Bright eyes behind giant round librarian eyeglasses, a nerdy-chic twist that electrified her entire appearance, making her glow from some hidden pheromonal dimension that defied space and time.

Joey's breath snagged in her throat.

She threaded through the tables on her dumb little-girl legs, the sleeves of her hoodie pulled over her hands, feeling like an asexual Girl Scout.

Then she scooted into the booth across from Candy McClure.

Orphan V, the most dangerous living product of the Program aside from X. She and Evan had a crazy-weird charged relationship, like Catwoman and Batman if Catwoman was part Brigitte Bardot and part, like, lioness and if Batman was infuriating all the time and freaked out over Cool Ranch Dorito crumbs on his countertops. Candy had tried to kill Evan a bunch, and one time, like way long ago, he'd knocked her into the supply of concentrated hydrofluoric acid she'd brought in hopes of dissolving his body. Her back, hidden by the dress, was a mess of swirling scar tissue, the only flaw in her otherwise transcendental appearance. At some point Candy had realized the Orphan Program was as effed up as Evan said and she'd gone off the radar also and they kinda-sorta partnered on missions and when they were together you needed a blowtorch to cut through the sexual tension between them.

So: your basic assassin friends.

A sugary smell laced the air, no doubt from the glaze enhancing Candy's plump lips. There was a trace of citrus, too—but a naughty citrus, like grapefruit—and somehow Joey knew it emanated from the diamond-shaped gap in the dress that revealed V's décolletage. And her eyebrows—they were fucking perfect. Bold but not too bold, shaped perfectly but also natural. Whoever would have thought eyebrows could be that sexy?

Joey set her hands on the table, noted her chewed fingernails, slid them back into her lap. She reminded herself not to hunch.

"You wanted to see me," Candy said.

"Yeah, uh, I—"

"Madam, the gentleman at the table in the corner sent this over for you." A waiter lowered a lemon drop in a frosted glass in front of Candy.

Joey jerked her head around to see a silver-haired dude in a light blue blazer sitting at a table across the restaurant eagerly awaiting eye contact. He had a waiting smile and a glass in his hand ready to lift in a toast.

But Candy didn't look over.

Instead she sipped the cocktail. It left a trace of sugar on her bottom lip. She ran her finger across it, sucked the grains off her fingertip, then set the drink aside.

Only now did Joey note that there were three other cocktails by Candy's elbow, all of them full minus one sip.

Joey looked back at the guy who'd sent the drink over. Still sitting like an idiot with his drink half hoisted.

His and Joey's gaze met awkwardly and his smile dimmed. Clearly displeased with the consolation eye contact, he bobbed the glass at Joey and busied himself over his filet mignon.

Joey felt exasperated. "Did you have to come here all, you know?"

"You asked to meet. That means going out." Candy whisked a bright red cherry from atop one of the other rejected drinks, an orangey something in a hurricane glass, popped it into her mouth, and tugged the stem free. One of the men at the four-top next to them dropped his bread knife with a clatter. "This is how I go out."

That was V.

"Couldn't we have just met at, like, In-N-Out?"

"You think this wouldn't happen at In-N-Out?"

"I'm just saying, maybe we could have a second of—"

"Hello, ladies. You two are sisters, right?"

A different guy looming over them. He wore a fitted cashmere sweater, sleeves shoved up over muscular forearms. He looked like a professional tennis player or an actor who'd play a fireman.

Candy didn't look up.

Joey didn't understand how she could not look up. The pull of social pressure to acknowledge someone addressing you from two feet away was overwhelming, a law of basic physics. But Candy was immune to physics as she was immune to most things. So once again, there was Joey gawking at a prospective suitor like some orthodontured prepubescent social reject while Candy smoldered with high-octane inscrutability.

"I'm in town for a few days," he told the side of Candy's face. "From London."

Joey blinked. She realized that the grin she'd approximated for his benefit—or hers?—had frozen on her face like a grimace.

"And if you're not attached, perhaps I could buy you a drink."

Still not favoring him with a glance, Candy fanned her hand to the quartet of drinks lined beside the bread basket. The movement brought the faintest ripple to the top swell of her breasts peeking through the ace-of-spades gap in the yellow sequins, and Joey heard the tennis-player-actor-fireman's breath quicken.

He shifted on his feet, thumb fussing nervously at the fourth finger of his left hand where a pale band of skin betrayed the missing ring. "I'll just leave you my card."

He held one end and thumbed it down so it snapped audibly on the table to show off the thick stock. "I'm at JPMorgan," he said. "Vice president."

Nothing happened.

It was excruciating.

Joey had to stop herself from pulling her hood up and trying to melt through the cushioned bench. She stared imploringly at Candy.

Candy looked back at her, calm as could be. It wasn't merely like the man did not exist; it was as though he had no right to exist.

He didn't so much retreat as fade away.

"Okay," Joey hissed at Candy. "Can you just *stop*?"

"What?"

Joey waved her hand around, indicating all the Candyness. "Turn it off. All this."

"Oh," Candy said, with pity. "Child. *This?* Can't just be turned off."

"Well, I can't talk to you with every dude in, like, nine square miles trying to hump your leg."

Candy's lips were pursed. Still glossy. They looked deliciously sticky, spun from caramel. "Very well."

She swung her other leg over to meet the one peeking from the slit and then gravitated elegantly to her feet. She wore high, high heels, each with a tiny anklet bow and a strap down the top of the foot, leaving the sides exposed. If feet could wear lingerie, that's how they'd do it.

She walked out.

Every head turned. The waitstaff and patrons parted as if for Moses. Candy's hips rolled with each step, but her carriage remained erect, her torso gliding forward with its abundant endowments. She dipped her head to give a busboy a through-the-lashes glimpse of her eyes and he blanched, backed to a wall with his water pitcher, and lowered his eyes with reverence.

Then she was gone.

And everything turned ordinary again.

Joey reached across the table, grabbed the orangey cocktail, and took a few slurps to steady herself.

Five minutes passed and then another five and Joey wondered if Candy had ditched her.

A woman entered the restaurant and walked toward her.

Joey did an actual double take.

Shoulders rolled forward and down, a brief mannish stride, hurried energy. Shapeless sweater, baggy jeans, no makeup, hair shoved messily beneath a black Lululemon baseball cap.

Candy slumped down into the booth heavily.

Aside from Joey, no one had taken notice. The restaurant hummed with conversation, silverware clinked against plates, the world once again spinning on its same boring axis.

Candy said, "Better?"

Joey took a moment to catch her breath. "How do you even *do* that?"

"I don't *do* anything," Candy said. "I just let myself."

"Let yourself what?"

"Whatever I want," Candy said.

Joey picked up the hurricane cocktail and sucked it dry.

"Men cannot contend with our, hmm, fullness. If they see a woman who is . . . *embodied,* they must have her. They are desperate for you to mother them, or fuck them, or denigrate them to prove their theory of the world. Or to latch you up in a shiny box so they can take you out when no one else is around and make you play with them and only them. And most women comply. But. If you are unapologetically the whole entire thing, they can do little but stand trembling before you in awe. They scarcely know what to do with themselves. You are everything they want and everything that can judge them as unfit at the same time. It paralyzes them with want, with need, with shame at the sudden illumination of their inadequacies. You can make their heads explode with a look or render them suicidally obsessed with the faintest touch of the side of your neck."

She demonstrated, tracing two fingertips up the outer edge of her throat, and Joey felt something twist confusedly in her stomach.

"If you don't comply with letting the world limit you," Candy said, "then that is the power you hold. And that's the power they fear even as they lust after you for possessing it."

Joey remembered to breathe. "All men?"

Candy considered. "Not every last one."

"Why are you in Los Angeles?" Joey asked. "I mean, for a while now. You could be anywhere."

Candy looked away, the first chip in the flawless façade. There was nothing for her here in L.A. Except Evan.

Candy shrugged. Then lit up a cigarette.

"What are you doing?" Joey said. "You can't smoke in here."

"I'm pretty sure I am."

The maître d' appeared, rubbing his hands. "Madam, I'm terribly sorry, but we don't allow smoking here. It's a state ordinance."

When Candy looked up from beneath the brim of her cap, she had on her other self. "But I like it." Her voice rolled out low, confessional. She gave him an up-from-under look, head demurely tipped down, gaze filtered once again through those long, long lashes.

The maître d' looked lost within himself. He'd drifted back a few steps, seeming to have forgotten where he was. He nodded twice with a slightly canted head and then withdrew, mumbling something to the air.

Candy French-inhaled, releasing a ghostly sheet of smoke from her mouth and pulling it through her nostrils, a closed circuit of enchantment. "What did you want to talk to me about?"

"I'm in trouble."

"Tell me," Candy said.

So Joey laid it all out. From the Women's Empowerment Group to the dinner at Cassidy Ann's house to the memes Joey helped propagate to the passive-aggressive confrontation at the food court.

And then to the collision with the group of women afterward that had knocked her right off her stilts.

"So I don't know what to do," Joey said, in conclusion. "Anything I do is gonna, like, infuriate one side or the other, and whatever social cred I had is totally gone, and this whole thing is threatening to blow up and become something huger and I don't know how to stop it."

Candy drew once on the cigarette and shot a neat stream across the bread basket. A lady a few tables over coughed performatively and waved her hand in front of her face.

"I don't even know why I bothered you," Joey said. "It's not like you can help me figure out what to do."

"Why *did* you call me?"

Joey didn't know. And then she did. "I wanted to talk to you because . . . I don't know what to do, sure. But also . . . ?"

She felt her throat starting to constrict and thought: Fuck that. No way. She was *not* gonna get all teary here, not in front of Orphan V.

Candy's cigarette bore the faintest dimple from her lips. "Also what?"

"I don't know who to *be*," Joey said.

Some words were so goddamned hard to say. Speaking the fear out loud, even that quietly, was admitting the truth of it on some deeper level, was making it real, and she felt her throat tighten more and her eyes burn and she blinked hard and looked down but refused to lift her hand to her face.

She heard Candy shift in her seat. And then a cool hand rested on her sleeve, the pressure firm, not precisely maternal but somehow nourishing.

"Be your fullest self." Candy's voice came low, honeyed without the sweetness. "Unapologetically."

"How about other people?"

"Let their broken pieces fall where they may."

The hand withdrew from her arm. When Candy took a sip of water, Joey wiped her cheeks as quickly as she could. She felt her throat start to loosen, thought maybe she'd be able to breathe again.

"As for what you should *do*," Candy said, "who can help with that?"

"X."

A painful admission.

Candy's smile was impossible to look away from. "Not me?"

"No." Joey found a tight little smile. "You're *way* too much."

"I know, sweetie." Candy stubbed out her cigarette on the JP-Morgan business card, dropped the butt in the lemon drop. "Believe me, it's *exhausting*."

40

Dead Meat

There were four of them, slender and strong.

They wore leather dusters, balaclava masks, and wraparound shades to hide their eyes.

They were in the industrial kitchen of a premium meat market in Mountlake Terrace.

It was after hours, lights off, but the stainless-steel machinery gleamed in the ambient glow of a streetlight in the empty back parking lot.

There were meat grinders and standing bone saws and a meat slicer.

A skinny young man stood in front of the meat slicer, blindfolded, hands bound at the small of his back. He had a well-groomed lumberjack beard and long hair, easy for the Female One to grip.

This one, the second-to-last target, lived in a cottage-style home across the street.

He worked in IT.

He had plenty of access, which had meant plenty of temptation.

They were tasked with delivering a slice of his face in a sealed

Styrofoam box on a nest of dry ice. Perhaps there would be DNA testing to confirm. But more likely it was mere theatrics.

Getting through the nose first would be necessary.

The Female One wanted to kill the target before for ease of handling.

But the One Who Was Her Second Cousin insisted that was not in keeping with the contract.

She didn't know how anyone could tell whether the slice had been taken off live meat or dead meat, but when in doubt they had to default to strictest contractual definitions.

As always, the One Who Was Her Nephew was lookout, keeping an eye on that desolate back parking lot. Rain pattered across the dark asphalt.

The One Who Was Her Half Brother examined the meat slicer, focusing on knobs and switches. The thickness-control dial scaled from 1 to 20.

The Female One thought a medium slice would be the best cut.

The One Who Was Her Second Cousin stood over the open Styrofoam box, dry ice leaking upward, forming an upward cascade through which his eager eyes and impatient smile shone.

He stepped behind the meat slicer, displacing the One Who Was Her Half Brother, and thumbed the ON switch. The serrated round blade spun to life, the sound unmistakable.

Behind his blindfold, the target began to scream.

Looking down at his phone, the One Who Was Her Half Brother raised his hand to halt.

The One Who Was Her Second Cousin punched the OFF switch.

The round blade wound down.

It took awhile for the whir and rasp to silence.

The target was hyperventilating and making animal grunting noises.

The Female One released his hair. "We need quiet," she told him gently.

He kept shuddering, jerking in breaths.

"We need quiet," she said again, "*now.*"

He rolled his lower lip inward and bit down. His nostrils quivered. A thread of blood leaked from the corner of his mouth where an incisor had punched through skin.

The One Who Was Her Half Brother gestured with the phone. "We have Janus texting. We have imp-imp-imp—"

"Impatience," she said.

"Yes. To get to Calvary."

"We finish here," the One Who Was Her Second Cousin said. "We finish this job. And the last name on the list. And then we go."

Mucus streamed from the target's nose. His cheeks trembled. A panic stink wafted from him.

The Female One did not always agree with the One Who Was Her Second Cousin but he was correct now.

"We honor our word," she said. "We honor the code."

The One Who Was Her Half Brother said, "W-w-w-what do we tell Janus?"

"Tomorrow we finish the last name. We complete this job. And then we go. We tell Janus that."

The One Who Was Her Nephew turned away from the window and the raindrops tap-dancing against the parking lot, making buttercup splashes. The night custodians, a Hispanic husband-wife team, lay on the floor at his feet, their throats slit. "We go to Calvary."

Clenching the target's head from the back again, the Female One nodded at the One Who Was Her Second Cousin.

He clicked on the meat slicer and the screaming resumed once more.

41

No One Can

Tommy sat at the round kitchen table in one of the three remaining chairs.

Red and Hick were in the other two.

It was dark.

They'd been sitting here awhile and no one had bothered to turn on the lights. Or talk.

A lot had yet to sink in from the visit to the mosque, all sorts of round pegs and square pegs sorting themselves, trying to find matching holes.

Red and Hick were on their phones, heads bent, faces blank, thumb-thumb-thumbing.

Tommy sipped from his flask. His eyes were bloodshot. He didn't want to admit it but he sensed the shadow over him that Janus had released, a scavenger bird trailing his moves until a kill team caught up once again. He felt the weight of that shadow more and more, a tangible darkness. He just had to keep out from under it long enough to resolve whatever he could here.

The damage around his rotator cuff throbbed, but he didn't have the mettle to dig at the knotted muscle with a thumb just now.

The house was still. Trent was out front, having resumed his sporadic sentry duty. When Tommy had gone upstairs to take a leak, he'd spotted Elijah through a cracked bedroom door. He'd been wearing his new clothes and striking subtle poses in the mirror tacked to the closet door.

Lucas and Burt hadn't come out of their room and Tommy didn't miss their company, not one bit.

But here they came now, wearing black, low-rent ninjas dressed for trouble. The Glock was rammed into the front of Lucas's jeans, and Burt held a shotgun slung like a shovel over his shoulder.

They had war-paint streaks darkening their foreheads and eye black underlining their lower lids and thick squiggly marks on their right cheeks. They were amped up and not just from adrenaline.

Tommy said, "What the hell's that on your cheeks?"

Burt said, "The don't-tread-on-me snake."

"Looks like a giant dick."

"Well it ain't," Lucas said. "It's the don't-tread-on-me snake."

"Yeah, you said."

Hick and Red managed to tear their eyes from their phones to watch the proceedings. Red's mouth was slightly ajar. For once he wasn't rattling on.

"You going where I think you're going?" Tommy said.

"Damn straight," Burt said. "We can't let a man waltz into our HQ, threaten us, and just do nothing."

"You said yourself he's planning to kill these two." Lucas gave a pointed glare at Hick and Red in their chairs. "So we're not gonna sit here and hide like pussies."

Tommy took another swig, closed his eyes into the burn, felt the whiskey breath roll up and through his nostrils dragon-hot. "Boys," he said gently, "if you go out there, you're going to come back dead. I'm not telling you that to rile you up. I'm not tellin' you that to dare you. I'm telling you that 'cuz that's what's going to happen."

"Everyone tells us what we *can't* do," Lucas said. "All the time."

"That's no reason to do something."

"We got plenty of others. And no one's gonna tell us we can't. Not this time."

"You can't do this," Tommy said. "No one can."

Lucas took this in, his eyes shiny, excited.

"Well, watch us." Burt's fingers were jittering, thrumming against the shotgun stock.

Lucas fixed that glare once more on Hick and Red. He couldn't keep his teeth from grinding. "You coming?"

"No," Tommy said. "They ain't."

Red opened his mouth and then shut it.

Lucas and Burt shifted on their feet, cracked their necks. They didn't look ready, not anymore. They looked scared. With masturbatory talk and chemical enhancement, they'd wound themselves up in anticipation and now here they were.

"This ain't a video game." Tommy kept his gaze on his hands gripping the flask on the scarred table top. "You don't have to go through with it. You can go upstairs and sleep it off. No one'll think less of you for it."

"We gotta act," Lucas said. "We have to do something."

"'If you wait by the river long enough,'" Tommy said, "'the bodies of your enemies will float by.'"

"What's that?"

"Sun Tzu."

Lucas gave a stutter laugh. "Like we're gonna listen to some chink."

"Catch you on the flip side," Burt said. "Red, Hick, enjoy yer little knitting circle."

Tommy heard their footsteps move out of the kitchen and across the floor planks, and then the front door opened to a howl of wind and then closed and then there was silence once more.

Red and Hick set down their phones and looked at Tommy.

Tommy took another sip from the flask, leaned back, folded his arms across his chest, closed his eyes, and waited.

There was nothing else to do.

42

Broken Down and Remade

"Go."

"X."

"J."

"I got into the county's traffic-light-camera database."

"And?"

"There aren't many. Traffic-light cams. But there's a few along the route Hick and Red drove to Calvary Park."

"You saw photographs? Them in the truck?"

"A couple times, yeah, heading there."

Evan was sitting on his bed in the Kinkade Suite with the lights off, his shoulders to the wall, a folded pillow providing lumbar support. He had a clear view out the window and across the parking lot to that sole road leading in. His pickup was the only vehicle in the lot; Dot had departed the front office long ago. In the threshold between rooms the mirror remained on a tilt, granting an unobstructed angle out the window of 132 to the rear of the motel.

He'd pressed the RoamZone to the wall at his side, the nano-suction backing adhering it next to his cheek. Joey's words danced above the polyether-thiourea screen, rendered as holographic sound waves.

"The cameras," she continued, "they only take pictures if you're running a red light or speeding. And they were speeding—not a ton, not enough to get sent a ticket. Just, like, five to ten over the limit. But that's enough for the sensors to alert and record."

"'Heading there,' you said. But not leaving."

"Funny you should ask," Joey said. "There are precisely three traffic-light cameras between Calvary Park and the spot where they dumped Gabriel's body. One shows nothing inside the truck 'cuz the angle on the windows is wrong and there's too much reflection. The other captured only the hood and the place a front plate shoulda been."

Her voice flickered beside his head, orange like a flame. The holograph fooled the eye, conveying a sense of depth, but the images were twenty-five nanometers thin, about one-thousandth the breadth of a strand of hair.

"And the third?"

"The third," Joey said, "is missing. A conveniently timed glitch in the system."

"Can you recover it?"

"Nope. A full wipe was performed late on the night of the killings."

He didn't say anything. He let her keep driving to her point. There was a cadence to these calls with Joey, a particular order to how she turned over her cards. Even in this formal new iteration of their comms, he had to honor that.

"Guess who has sole control over the county traffic-light-camera database?" Joey said.

"The Calvary Sheriff's Station."

"More coincidences than a Victorian novel."

She waited for a prompt.

He complied: "But the good news is . . . ?"

"The ~/.zsh_history file shows that someone made a physical copy right before the secure deletion. Ye olde ass-covering insurance policy."

"Sheriff Grady Joy."

"Or Miss Scarlett in the billiard room with the lead pipe."

"What?"

"Never mind. Yes, Grady Joy. I breached the surveillance cams at the station and he was the only one there when that copy was made at two thirty-seven in the morning."

"And then you hacked into the GPS in his cruiser to see where he went afterwards."

"Indeed I did. He went straight home."

A pair of headlights flared shadows up along the trees lining the road. Evan watched. A brown Durango passed into view, kept driving.

"So that's where the USB drive is," he said. "At Grady's house."

"Zip drive, thumb drive, flash, whatever. But yeah, that's my guess."

"So I need to break into the sheriff's house to find it."

"I'm pretty sure I know where it is."

"How?"

"Digital camera set up in the bedroom for sex tapes. They're a fine-looking couple but still: *Gross.* Trust me. No one needs to see that."

"And you figured out how to turn the camera on even when it's not on."

"And there's a gun safe in the closet and the angle was right for me to catch a reflection in the door mirror of the good sheriff punching in the combination."

"Which is?"

"One two three four."

"You're joking."

"Would that I were."

In the brief absence of holographic sound waves, the room was dark. The parking lot and road beyond were quiet. The treetops dipped and rustled in the wind. The ground shimmered wetly.

"Got it," Evan said, and moved to hang up.

"*Wait.*"

He waited.

"Okay, *fine.*"

He waited some more.

"I need to pause our deal again. A quick time-out."

"Okay."

"Just for, like, a sec."

"Okay."

"And talk to you about, dunno, some personal shit."

"Okay."

"And you can't say told-you-so."

"Josephine. Talk."

Another science-fiction shift in the light against the trees heralded the next set of headlights and sure enough a poultry-transport truck blasted into view, crammed with miserable denizens, there and gone.

The night quieted once more.

"I need help, X. It blew up on me. The stupid meme-propagation thing."

A wave of irritation and impatience came on. Evan had entered the mission phase where he'd flattened himself out. Off turf and off high ground, surrounded by enemies, narrowed to a single focus. It was hard for him to concede the luxury of deeper thought and feeling. It was hard for him to operate in this world and care about the other. It was hard for him to give a shit about Joey's memes and the drama they had predictably produced.

Four-count breath. Four-count hold. Four-count exhale. Hold.

Then he said, "Blew up where?"

"On the group's Twitter account."

Evan laughed.

"What are you laughing at?"

"Nothing."

Joey took a few seconds to fume silently and then told him about the whole shitshow in the food court with Cassidy Ann and the Women's Empowerment Group.

And then walking outside and jump-scaring straight into, like, the *entire* Levant Culture Club, who'd calmly and surgically dismantled WEG's glomming on to the meme wars to elevate its own profile.

She was done now.

Evan breathed and stared at that sole painting on the wall.

Broken Down and Remade

Ducks on a pond and stone-walled cottages and a red barn, all of it suffused with a cozy glow. He'd never known anything like it. Not in the foster home in East Baltimore, a row house wedged peg-like into a crowded sprawl of concrete and housing projects. Not on Third World cargo planes or in five-star hotels. Not when crawling through sewers or scuttling across rooftops en route to complete a mission by sniper round or Strider knife.

And yet.

Jack's farmhouse, the home of his delayed childhood. He'd been there from twelve years of age to nineteen. He'd been broken down and remade there. Broken down and remade enough times that he'd learned that was precisely what life was. That the only thing he'd ever control was the way his own body and mind could respond to change that was endless, wild, ungovernable.

He pictured the fireplace that glowed amber through Jack's book-filled study that smelled of leather and peat. There were corded pillows on the couch, an ancient scent of pipe tobacco in the rug, a rug woven halfway around the world and brought there because it epitomized excellence and beauty. Outside were forever oaks, a carpet of leaves that rose to the shins and flurried wake-like when he plowed through autumn.

It had been a home, too. Not just a brutal training ground.

By contrast, Evan's penthouse in Castle Heights seemed juvenile. And Joey did, too.

Here she was, engaged in idiotic warfare through the only means kids not engaged in actual warfare could access. Tearing one another apart reputationally. Slashing their way up through paper-thin social hierarchies based on neither treasure, nor power, nor expertise. Forging into the world when there wasn't a god-damn battle that needed them and then making one anyway just to wring some meaning out of their disconnected lives.

She was so strong—unbreakable and blindingly brilliant. But also so young. And he couldn't push her too far too fast because she had to find her own blundering way just like he had.

Just like he did.

Just as he would. And would. And would.

"Well?" she said.

"What'd you say? To the Levant group?"

"Not much. I didn't defend myself. I just listened. It was hard as hell. But, the Fifth Commandment."

Evan's least favorite but in this instance the most apt: *If you don't know what to do, do nothing.*

"So what now?" she said. "Should I just apologize?"

"Where?"

"Aren't you listening? On the WEG Twitter feed."

"You're gonna issue an apology to a half a billion people? On a platform brimming with psyops and foreign interference?"

"Well, that's the only way to get it to die down."

"Social media is a terrorist trying to extort you for money. That is all it is. It has algorithms and billionaires and teams of addiction specialists driving it. And you don't."

"I think I know a little bit about how to handle myself online."

"If you go online with this, Joey, then you're known. If you're known, your power is diminished. And other people will have set the terms of your introduction."

"Introduction to what?"

"Public perception."

"Orphan X," she said angrily. "Haven't *you* met public perception?"

"No. It's met me. On my terms."

A frustrated pause. "So how am I supposed to apologize?"

"Who are you apologizing to?"

A hesitation. "Everyone screaming about it on social media. It's a lot, X."

"You can't apologize to a mob," Evan said. "It makes you a coward."

"Jack teach you that?"

"No, Mark Twain."

"I was just trying to help! I was trying to advocate for Muslim women! I was trying to be an ally!"

"Did anyone *ask you* to be an ally?"

Silence.

"Even if they did want help, you think they'd want it from a bunch of rich college kids in California who are going to fuck up the conversation so it can't be negotiated properly?"

"How did we fuck it up?"

"You gathered no intel. You acquired no ground truth. You neither red-teamed the permission structures nor did any coalition building."

More silence.

"It wasn't your business, Joey. You made it your business so you could fit in and feel important and you cloaked yourself in false virtue. That put you on the wrong foot tactically and strategically. You've studied military history. What happens when leaders double down from a weak position?"

"I'm not a leader."

"Clearly."

He heard her breath leave. It had landed like a gut punch. That was okay. She deserved it.

"So what do you want me to do, X? *Not* fit in? Just *never* fit in like y—"

She caught herself.

He could hear her breathing.

"Sorry," she said, in a very small voice.

"Don't apologize. If that's your fear, face it. And face it now."

"Face it how? I'm only *seventeen*, X."

"'It is easier to build strong children than to repair broken men.'"

"Another Jackism?"

"Frederick Douglass," Evan said.

"You quote a lot of dead guys."

"Those were the only friends I had," Evan said. "And they were all smarter than me."

A few more cars drove by without stopping. Behind the motel, branches wagged in the breeze.

"I didn't even design the stupid memes," she said.

"Who did?"

"Some tech firm in India. I guess it was cheaper."

Evan laughed again.

"*What?*"

"Perfect," Evan said.

"What does *that* mean?"

He was having a hard time controlling his aggravation. "Josephine. That's like if you ran a political club at an elite Chinese university and decided to contract a Romanian to create anti-misogyny propaganda featuring cartoons of Orthodox Jews beating their wives."

A sharp intake of air. "Oh God," Joey said. "Fuck." And then: "*Fuck fuck fuck.*" And then: "That's really bad."

"We done?"

"No! I mean, what am I supposed to do now? Issue a public apology to the Levant Culture Club?"

"Is that what they want?"

"I don't know what they want! They didn't say."

"Yes. They did."

"How?"

"What did they *not* do?"

"I don't get what you're saying. What are you saying?"

He did not want to be doing this right now. It didn't interest him. It was scarcely possible for him to care less.

He drew in another deep breath, held for the four count, exhaled. "They didn't run an asymmetrical escalation on you through social media. They didn't ambush you. They didn't issue demands for how you should talk and what you should think. They aren't making a play for power. They are engaging in the real world, not playing games in the fake one. They didn't go to the media. They went to *you.*"

"For what? What do they want?"

"Get your head out of the internet, Josephine. They aren't thinking about this like you are."

A long silence. Evan kept a vigilant focus on both windows. He thought he heard an engine somewhere, but no headlights were in evidence along the road.

"To talk," she said. "To understand."

Evan came out of his lean against the wall, placed both booted feet on the floor, peeled the RoamZone off the wall and dimmed the screen. "Yes."

"It's so weird that it could all just be a misunderstanding," Joey said. "I'm used to there being an asshole in the equation."

Evan said, "Right."

A half-second pause and then Joey said, "*Hey!*"

Evan rose, crept silently across the face of the front window, studied the foliage along the road. The branches at the edge of the parking lot bobbed sporadically and then less sporadically.

"You're the worst, X."

"You're the worst, too."

Through a gap in the leaves he saw flashes of movement. Two men wearing dark clothes. One had a shotgun, the other a handgun. They disappeared once more and then he spotted another flicker of motion near the dumpster at the side of the parking lot.

He said, quietly, "I'm going now."

"Why?" Joey said.

"Because people are here to kill me."

Joey only had time to say, "Oh," before he hung up.

43

Trespassers Will Be Shot

A gloved hand starfished against the windowpane and slid it painstakingly ajar.

A Glock led the way into Evan's motel room.

A trio of shots liberated puffs of feathers from the bed. Burt and Lucas logjammed in the window, tumbling through, exposing vast swaths of critical mass. They regrouped inside, stage-whispering.

"The fuck is he? Is this the right room?"

"It's the right fucking room."

At the threshold of the connecting doorway, a dark form stood still, gazing at them intently.

The shotgun rose and boomed twice, spiderwebbing the form, which fell to the floor in shards. The jamb shrapneled.

"—fucking mirror—"

"—next room—"

More firecracker pops, more flashes, the Glock's bullet count diminishing.

"Go! Go!"

Voices wrenched high with panic, trembling with adrenaline.

Trespassers Will Be Shot

The gloved hand poked around the jamb, a flurry of shots tearing haphazardly through room 132. Drywall powdering, nightstand splintering, porcelain lamp gone mosaic. Body odor thick in the air now, laced with a chemical tinge, shoved through pores by the panic-pumping of drug-laced blood. More shots.

The Glock's fifteen rounds—sixteen in the unlikely event Lucas had been collected enough to slot one in the chamber—had already diminished by two-thirds.

The brothers wheeled into the connecting room, caught a gust of damp wind in their faces.

The window was open. A patch of pines wobbled beyond, trunks like jail bars splitting darkness.

Was that the form there again, standing a few feet back from the tree line?

Burt lunged to the window, discharging the shotgun twice. When the gunpowder mist cleared, there was nothing but clean evergreen air and that corrugated darkness between trees.

"He's gone," Lucas said. "Goddamn it, he split."

"Should we go after him?"

"Out *there*? Hell, no. Let's go, let's go."

They tripped over themselves in retreat. The shotgun stock struck the floor, discharging a load past Burt's cheek into the ceiling. Scrambling back up, they launched through the window.

There that dark form was again, impossibly standing in the wide-open plain of the parking lot.

Thirty feet away, arms at rest by his sides.

He started toward them.

Lucas and Burt held their weapons loosely, barrels waving. They were not serious gunmen and their target acquisition was for shit, so Evan was unworried.

Burt yelped. Lifted the shotgun and got an empty click. His hands jiggled along the stock, desperately trying to reload.

Evan kept on, unrushed.

Lucas fired blindly, running down his count—five, four, three, two, one, and sure enough, no chambered sixteenth round.

Evan drew.

He stitched shots up one target diagonally—ankle, knee, hip, shoulder—and down the next—shoulder, hip, knee, ankle. They were vertical still, their bodies not yet registering the damage. Sweeping the high-profile Straight Eight sights, he caught Lucas's gun hand on the way back because why tempt fate.

Red mist, torn flesh and fabric, joints bent wrong.

They fell in a scarecrow collapse, limbs gnarled, grunting into the dew-wet asphalt.

Drifting forward, Evan released the magazine to reload.

It hitched, not dropping cleanly. Second time this goddamned week.

Again the thought sailed in before he could stop it—*Have to have Tommy fix that*—and it broke him out of instinct and reaction, even as he tugged the compromised magazine free and jammed a fresh one in.

As he eased forward to loom above the fallen targets, the hesitation slowed him from locking straight onto critical mass. Instead he regarded the young men.

Lucas hiccupped and gasped into the dew-sparkling asphalt. Burt had curled into a ball on his side, mouth locked ajar tight enough to strain the skin across his cheeks. A low, pained sound issued from his wavering lips, more a vibration than anything else.

"Why do you have piles of shit painted on your cheeks?" Evan said.

Lucas bucked and gulped. "*. . . don't tread . . . snake . . .*"

"Effective," Evan said.

The ARES aimed straight down at Burt's forehead.

Burt's eyes leaked big round tears. They stood out on his cheeks, distinct, surface tension intact.

They were children.

"Did Tommy warn you?"

Burt's cheek scraped the ground. He still couldn't find his breath.

Lucas grunted something that sounded mostly like "yes."

"That's the only reason you're still alive." Evan heard the words as he spoke them; they had come from somewhere else.

He picked up the Glock and the shotgun, walked back to his

truck, tossed them in the back of the cab. He drove at the boys fast, their terrified faces white in the headlights, and screeched over just before striking their heads. Then he got out and dropped the tailgate.

"You never came here," Evan said. "You never saw me."

"Yes . . . sir," Burt managed.

That was good. Burt had caught his breath.

Evan's stare pinned Lucas wriggling to the ground.

". . . es, suh," Lucas said.

Evan holstered the ARES and leaned down to grab the injured young man, readying to sling him into the bed of his rig.

It would be painful.

So he made sure to lift using his legs.

Evan screeched off the roadway onto the brief pocket of road before Red Hildebrandt's gate and parked beside the TRESPASSERS WILL BE SHOT sign adhered to the chain-link. He'd edged in at a slant through a broad swath of blind spot by the trash cans, dodging the idiotically arrayed surveillance cameras.

He hopped out.

Trent stood on the other side of the gate holding an old Mossberg shotgun, his mouth trembling. He was all low gut and weak chin, his eroded posture befitting a man twice his age. At least he held the shotgun properly in a two-handed ready carry.

He made no move to bring the shotgun to bear.

Evan faced him through the gate. "I have a package for delivery. Help me unload it."

Trent blinked twice and then twice more. "Sure." The word stuck in his throat, came out as a rasp.

Evan stared at him.

Trent shifted on his feet. Sweat streaked down from his sideburns, making the stubble glisten on his cheeks. His pupils, blown wide with fear.

On the roadway ten yards back, an eighteen-wheeler blew past their private standoff. Evan stared at Trent some more.

"Oh," Trent said. "Okay."

He scrambled to set down the Mossberg and unlock the gate.

Evan dropped the tailgate, grabbed Lucas by his uninjured arm and leg, and slung him through the gate. A puff of dirt kicked up when he landed and a keening noise escaped him. Trent blanched and took a step back.

Evan nodded at the bed of the pickup.

Slowed by terror, Trent crept forward and peered in. His eyes welled. "Burt," he said. "Buddy, you okay?"

Burt groaned.

Evan said, "Get him out of my truck."

Trent managed a more gentle version of what Evan had done with Lucas, hooking Burt's arm over his shoulder and dragging his dead weight. When they passed through the gate, Burt collapsed.

Both he and Trent were crying.

Evan slammed the tailgate shut. He climbed back in his Ford F-150, gave Trent a nod, and drove unrushed away from the compound.

44

Nancy Boys

Tommy felt like he was a hundred and ten years old.

He sat on the couch in the living room of the Hilderanch, sunk into the beat-down cushions so far that he knew it'd take some planning when it came time to rise. He was catching his wind and resisting the temptation to water the stack of RE-ELECT GRADY JOY FOR SHERIFF signs in the corner with a stream of tobacco spit.

The ambulance had just departed, taking Lucas and Burt to a hospital in the city forty-five minutes away, the Buckley boys in excruciating pain but luckier than they'd ever know.

Yesenia had been Tommy's first call and she was sitting as well, aching feet up on a pulled-over chair. She'd been working her phone nonstop, figuring out getting everyone where they needed to be.

Hick, Red, Elijah, and Leslie were arrayed in various chairs in a semicircle around the couch, eyes glazed with shock and exhaustion. Trent stood by the door, wan face tilted down at the floor. He'd been silent for the past hour, burning with shame.

Yesenia's phone dinged. She looked up from the screen at Red. "That's Duke. He says your father's coming home tomorrow after his shift."

Red's spine jerked straight as if he'd been hit with a cattle prod. "What? How'd he find out?"

"*Hijo*, we live in Calvary. Every last person in town knows what happened by now."

Red sprang up and started clearing cans and bottles off the surfaces. "Don't just sit there," he said to the other boys. "Help me clean this shit up."

Yesenia rose, took Red by the shoulders. "I'm going home." A nod at Tommy. "Listen to what this man says." She started out, paused at the door, swept her gaze across the others. "Don't do anything else stupid."

And she was gone.

It took some struggling and grunting but Tommy extricated himself from the couch. "We need to rack out. We'll regroup in the morning."

"What if he comes back tonight?" Elijah's words came quick with fear.

"He delivered us his message for tonight," Tommy said. "He ain't coming back."

Trent remained slumped against the wall like a rise of Jell-O. Tommy poked him. "Stand up straight. You look like a sack of shit."

"I didn't do anything to stop him," Trent said. "I just let him."

Tommy clapped a hand on the ledge of his shoulder, waited for the boy to lift his gaze. "If you'd done anything else," Tommy said, "you wouldn't be here talking to me right now."

Trent snuffled, wiped his nose. "I'm gonna go stand sentry through the night," he said softly. He picked up the Mossberg from its lean in the corner and vanished through the door into the cold night.

Tommy glowered at the remaining three young men. "No one sets foot outside this compound tonight, understand me?"

Hick said, "Yes, sir."

Nancy Boys

Elijah rocked back on his heels, trying for a bit of extra height, and jerked a quick nod.

Red said, "I should go edify that motherfucker at the point of a shotgun."

He pronounced it *eed-i-fy* but there were bigger problems afoot than elocution.

"No," Tommy said. "You're gonna wake up intact in the morning. Unlike those nancy boys getting themselves stitched back together right now. You hear?"

Red's face and neck were splotched to all damnation. He gave an affirmative tip of his head and slunk into the kitchen, Elijah and Hick following.

Tommy caught Hick by the arm as he passed. "If you listen to me, I can get you through this. You don't, I cannot."

Hick's eyes were full. He spoke in a cracked whisper. "What if I'm past being helped?"

Tommy dug deep. "No one's past being helped. We just don't know what help looks like for you yet."

Hick moved into the kitchen and then it was just Leslie and Tommy.

"Never a dull moment," she said. "Not when you live in a houseful of imbeciles."

Tommy nodded.

"*Nancy boys,*" Leslie said.

"What about it?"

"That's the kind of talk that got 'em into this mess. They got enough words like that. Why give 'em a new one?"

A bright point of anger lanced through Tommy's exhaustion. "Don't you chirp at me about how I can or can't talk. I put a brother-in-arms in the ground who was a faggot. Sobbed like a fucking baby, too. We all knew and didn't like it but we loved that motherfucker and covered for his ass in Bangkok a time or three. Literally."

"It's not funny."

"Then don't laugh. Look, sugarbritches, I had a butch commander who put the fear of God in the base of my spine whenever

I screwed up the ammo load. And I shot side by side with a big ole dyke sniper outta Jackson who I'd go to war with six days a week and twice on the holy day. So don't you collar me with any of that nonsense right now. Last thing I need to worry about is my phrasing."

Leslie didn't move from her armchair. She didn't look upset. She looked curious. "Wonder why it gets you so worked up."

"I don't gotta accede to your wondering," Tommy said.

She shoved herself out of the armchair, gathered the crazy spray of her hair even tighter in the ponytail. Then she walked over to him and stood looking into his face. "No," she said, "but it sure would be gentlemanly of you to consider it." She gave him an open-handed pat on the chest, right above his heart. "Thanks for saving my brother's life."

She clomped up the stairs in her low-heeled Ropers.

45

What Hick and Red Did

Tommy lay in bed, his joints aching to high heaven. Them stuffed animals peered at him from the foot of the bed. Monkeys, pigs, and bears, oh my.

He couldn't sleep for shit.

He wrenched himself up out of horizontal and trudged to that ancient tube TV. Pulled the button to turn it on, twisted the venerable dial. Static, static, and more static. Pure enough that there was no point in fussing with the rabbit ears.

He toed the VHS cassettes, squinting through the imam's spectacles to read the handwriting on the labels.

The Bridge on the River Kwai. Now that was a proper movie, another tick in the right column for Calvary culture.

He crouched over the VCR, his lumbar screaming at him, and slotted the tape in. It was received with a hum and a clank. A warbly image came up, a badly shot view of a classroom. The shitty video quality and room decorations put it about two decades old.

A student stood up front, no older than eight, held a sheet of paper nervously, almost as skinny as the music stand in front of her. She spoke in a high, reedy voice devoid of charisma. "Home is a house on Hummingbird Lane. Home is sprinkle cupcakes and ribbons for my hair. Home is 'Please' and 'Thank you.' Home is 'All that matters is you try your best.' Home is Dizzy the rabbit and my baby brother waking me up by tugging my eyelids open." The class laughed and the girl stopped and at last let a shy smile light her face.

Tommy wanted to reach down to kick the cassette out but his lower back told him to wait a beat. He set his hands on his hips and leaned back, staring at the ceiling as he stretched.

"My name's Delmont Hickenlooper, Jr." This high-pitched eight-year-old voice was barely recognizable. "Home is 'Don't order that, it's too expensive.' Home is 'Can I have a baby sister so I have someone to play with?' Home is 'Pick up your toys or I'll take that shit away.'"

Tommy pulled himself back to look.

There was little Hick before the music stand, looking not much bigger than the girl who'd preceded him.

"Home is 'You're just like her, you know.' Home is 'You call that a bruise?'"

Tommy watched, rapt. He barely noticed movement at the door.

Hick edged into the room, a ratty blanket under his arm.

Tommy used his big toe to poke the button on the VCR and the tape ejected with a pre-industrial sounding clank.

"Sorry, son," Tommy said. "Didn't mean to come upon that. Was just fixing to watch a movie."

Hick's head bobbed a few times. "Can't sleep?"

"Not a wink."

"Me neither." Hick took another tentative step into his bedroom. He nodded at the VCR, gave a mirthless chuckle. "That didn't go over so hot."

"Your old man found out?"

"Teacher called him."

"Oh boy."

"*Oh boy*'s right."

"What'd he say?"

The grin on Hick's face looked as lifeless as a visor on a knight's helmet. He raised a curled hand, coughed into it once. "He said, 'Wanna know what home is for me? Home is getting stuck with a lifetime of responsibility 'cuz the bitch I was fucking lied about being on the pill.'"

Tommy felt a shift in the blood beneath his face.

Hick gave another automated chuckle. "Ole Delmont said, 'So how 'bout no more boo-hoo shit from the either of us. Don't you waste my time making me have to go deal with some uppity teacher again.'" He grinned, tugged at that smear of scarred flesh at his earlobe. "Dad knew how to make his points."

Tommy thought about smirking along with Hick in the diner when Hick told him about his old man burning his ear and felt a twist of dirtiness for being the asshole who'd join a child laughing at something like that.

"Yeah," Tommy said. "He sure did."

Hick pawed at the back of his neck. "Any way I could . . . Could I sleep in here tonight? Just on the floor?"

"It's your room," Tommy said. "Don't see why not."

Hick kicked some crap out of the way on the floor, clearing space. "Borrow a pillow?"

Tommy tossed him one.

As Hick made a nest on the floor, Tommy eased back into bed. They lay there a spell, staring at the ceiling. Sleeping in the same room with someone was intimate as hell but it was a kind of intimacy Tommy was accustomed to. The service had taught him that.

Moonlight slotted through the window, straw-pale and moody.

Tommy was just drifting off when the kid spoke: "You said you were with my old man when he got the call that my mom was pregnant with me."

A pained pause in which Tommy could sense Hick mustering the courage.

He thought: *Please don't ask.*

Hick cleared his throat, which sounded thick with snot and emotion. "What'd he say?"

Tommy could barely make out Hick in the semidarkness, just

a lump there against the far wall. Tommy rolled his head back to center on the too-soft pillow, squeezed his eyes shut, exhaled silently through clenched teeth.

"I can't remember," he lied.

Hick was drowsy. He remembered being seven years old sitting halfway down the stairs in the old house, positioned high enough not to be caught spying. Richie and Dale were off sleeping at girlfriends' houses or somewhere, anywhere else.

His old man was on the phone in the kitchen with his mother, his voice knocking around off the hard surfaces. He didn't really know how to talk in a hushed tone, Delmont Senior, but this was his best attempt at it.

He heard his old man say, "What am I supposed to tell him?"

He heard him say, "Haven't you fucking done enough?"

He heard him say, "You're his goddamned mother. What am I supposed to tell him if he wants to see you again?"

Feeling like a ghost, Hick withdrew to his room and buried himself under the covers with his stuffed animals—pig, monkeys, teddy bear with a missing ear.

The next morning his father was up and waiting for him at the breakfast table. Delmont Senior poured a bowl of Lucky Charms for Hick. Hick didn't know what was happening. He usually scrounged up his own breakfast before walking to school.

He sat down.

Old Delmont got the milk from the fridge and poured it into Hick's bowl. There was a folded napkin set down on the table with a spoon already on it.

Delmont mussed his hair on his way out to work.

Hick sat there staring down at the bowl, watching the cereal soften.

That was his last flicker of conscious thought before he fell asleep.

Red pounds the gas pedal of the '89 Ram and they're careening all over the road, tire tread packed with sod from the park. Hick's in a blind panic, his senses bleeding into one another. He scarcely understands where he is and how he got here.

Hick keeps the boy propped up next to him with his arm around those skinny eight-year-old shoulders and he's holding the kid's head upright but his neck keeps lolling and there's blood spattered up Hick's shirt—it clings damp and cold to him—and none of the blood is his own. There's blood on the fender and a child-size dent in the passenger-door panel and Red's screaming at him and barking orders but Hick can't make sense of the words, not over the roar of emotion in his ears.

They took the kid.

An eight-year-old boy.

First they broke his body with a two-ton truck and then they took him in his dying moments away from anyone he'd ever known.

That's what Hick and Red did.

46

Trouble in Town

The two deputies showed up at the Emerald Bay Motel to knock on the door of the Kinkade Suite at 6:23 A.M., twenty-three minutes later than Evan expected them. He knew Sheriff Grady Joy would send emissaries first rather than lower himself to talk to him directly.

Evan stood in the doorway, not blocking it but not not blocking it either.

Ronny Ratliff, so named on his chest, did the introductions while his thickset elder Clay Clemmons lingered behind him with cold venomous energy and a barrel chest. Clemmons had a cauliflower ear, an oft-broken nose, and seams of scar tissue at the edges of his eyes like horse blinders.

He didn't bother to look at Evan, a weird dominance play that Evan found less effective than piercing eye contact, but not everyone could manage piercing eye contact.

Ronny had a lean muscular build and ears that protruded enough to look whimsical but not so far as to be laughable. He had a strong open face and seemed sure of himself, but it was easy to feel sure of yourself with a brute like Clemmons lingering off your left flank.

"There's been some trouble in town," Ronny said.

Evan ran through a half dozen retorts about horse thieves or the Widower Johnson shooting at the moon in his long johns but settled on: "Is that so."

"Anything you'd like to tell us?"

"No, sir. I'm just a tourist enjoying my stay."

"We'd like to search your room."

"Fourth Amendment doesn't hold much water in Calvary," Evan said.

"Not in motel rooms."

"An occasional right," Evan said, stepping back. "Got it."

The deputies entered and moved through the room, toeing at the furniture, checking the bathroom, eyeing the damage to the walls and ceiling. In anticipation of the visit, Evan had cleaned up the broken lamp, mirror, and perforated sheets, thrown them into a dumpster at the edge of town, and then removed all his personal items to the vaults of his pickup, which he parked off premises. He'd picked the lock of the housekeeping closet, made up the bed to cover the shot-to-shit mattress, and used a brush and dustpan to tidy up wood splinters and drywall dust.

Clemmons stuck his finger into one of the bullet holes in the wall. "What's all this?"

Evan shrugged. "Ambience? It's my first stay here. I'm still learning the local culture."

Ronny eased through the connecting door and stood before the bare nightstand, the honey wood surface sun-bleached around a perfect circle where the lamp had been. He traced a finger around the ring. "Looks like some stuff's missing."

"Yeah," Evan said. "I was thinking of commenting in a Yelp review."

"Maybe it's got something to do with you."

"Good thing I laid down a hefty security deposit," Evan said. "I'm guessing Dot'll have no trouble squaring it away with me. She doesn't seem to want for assertiveness."

On heavy boots, Clemmons clomped up close to Evan and stood

facing ninety degrees away, the boulder of his shoulder a few inches off Evan's sternum. "You think you can come here and fuck around," he said in a low grumble, "but you got no idea the kind of hell you're gonna catch if you keep pushing."

"Must be a lot of work," Evan said.

Clemmons swung his pit bull head around, giving Evan a glimpse of blue-gray eyes. "What's that?"

"Remembering to talk all growly like that to scare the citizenry."

"You're not a citizen here." Clemmons poked a thick finger into Evan's chest a tad too hard. "Don't you forget that."

"Yes, sir, Deputy Clemmons."

Clemmons walked out.

Ronny headed to the door, hesitated next to Evan. "We don't need more pain and bloodshed in this community," he said. "If that's what you're planning to bring, I'm gonna do everything I can to stop you."

"I respect that." Evan held out his hand.

Ronny stared at it a moment and then walked out without shaking.

47

Talk the Devil Down

When Tommy woke up, Hick was still in a deep slumber on the floor, curled up hugging a pillow with his mouth ajar.

Tommy squeezed out a piss, brushed his teeth, and lumbered downstairs, where he stood unnoticed at the foot of the stairs.

Red was directing traffic, getting the house tidied up. Elijah and Trent scurried around like elves with clanking bags of trash on their backs. A scarred wooden dining table had appeared from nowhere, taking up a swath of the living room by the door to the kitchen. It was already set, forks and steak knives, a roll of paper towels in the center. The dumb-ass CALVARY LIBERTY GUARD sign hung limply on the wall; it felt like a relic of some distant past.

Red's face was redder than usual, beads of sweat stitched across his hairline. His pasty ugly mug had grown on Tommy—the wide-set domino teeth, the pigged nose, the vulnerable eyes trying so hard not to be.

Red was riding herd on the other two as they hauled trash to the front door. "Get 'em packed down in the cans," he said. "Lids screwed on tight."

Trent let the big Santa Claus bag slide off his slumped shoulder. "Trash cans're overflowing already."

"How come?"

"We forgot to wheel them to the gate last Tuesday."

"Well, whose job was that?"

Trent said, "Elijah's."

"No," Elijah said. "Not this week."

"Whose then?"

Elijah pinned his shoulders back, chest pushed out, straining for those extra inches. "Prob'ly Lucas or Burt."

"Ain't that fucking convenient," Red said.

"Well, they're out at the curb now. They're just stuffed from two weeks of shit."

"Get it packed down already. No one needs Vic Hildebrandt rolling in here and seeing heaps of trash by the gate. And see if Duke'll give us some elk steaks for dinner."

"*Steaks?*"

"You heard me. Duke took down a royal twelve-point in September, promised he'd set aside some meat for when my pop was in town."

"How many?"

"Us, Les, Hick, and Tommy. Two for Dad. That's eight."

"Six," Tommy said.

They all paused, finally taking note of him.

"What do you mean 'six'?" Red said.

"Six steaks," Tommy said. "That's all we'll need. Come dinner, Elijah and Trent won't be around no more."

"What do you mean?" Trent said. "Why not?"

"You weren't in the truck that killed that family," Tommy said. "We're gonna get you long gone. He won't come after you. Getting outta his way's the only guarantee you can keep on breathing."

Trent tried to draw himself upright, got about a third of the way there. "Can we go *after* dinner?"

The kid wanted a steak.

"Boy, act like you got some sense in you. We're not putting your life on the line for a goddamned steak."

"I wasn't saying that," Trent said, though of course he was.

"Fuck that," Red said. "I ain't leaving town."

"Son, you don't have a choice," Tommy said. "You, he'll hunt down."

Red's mouth parted and he made a noise he didn't mean to make. "Well, I ain't no pussy."

"We're still figuring out what you are," Tommy said. "In the meantime we're getting our men safe one at a time." Elijah and Trent were motionless by the front door. Tommy flicked his chin at them. "Go on now."

Shouldering a few bags each, they headed out onto the porch. Red scratched the back of his neck. "You got a button-up shirt I could borrow?"

"Why?"

"Just 'cuz. I'll give it back."

Tommy studied Red. "Sure."

Red rubbed his buzz cut, face lined with worry. "My pop don't like people who get pushed around. And who don't push back."

"People?"

"You heard me." Red was breathing hard. "Everyone's talking."

"I'm sure they are."

"All kinds of stories."

"I'm sure of that, too."

"He hurt my friends. I've got a hankering to make him answer." Red was trying to put steel beneath his words. "I'm not afraid," he added, through a face that said otherwise.

"You should be."

"No. I'm not afraid. I'm not afraid anym—"

"Don't be goddamned simple, boy."

Red's eyes flared—genuine hurt—then his face clamped down, a wounded burst of rage. He came at Tommy, shoved him into the wall. "I ain't simple, okay? I ain't simple."

His voice was wrenched high, little-boy pain lining the fury. Tommy could hear it plain as day and he kept his arms low and his reactions in check.

"Okay, son."

But Red slammed him into the wall again. Tommy's shoulder blades hit hard, rattling his ribs, but he kept the back of his head from striking, too. Red was a big strong bull of a kid and stopping him by force would mean hurting him bad. The best angle Tommy had was to the windpipe but if he let loose he risked crushing it and that was an unacceptable escalation given whatever the fuck his role was here.

Red lunged at Tommy again, a hard boxer's feint with his head, screaming in his face: "I ain't simple!"

"Okay, son," Tommy said. "Jesus."

Red's nostrils flared, bull-like. He drew back against the table and gripped it hard with both hands. A few inches off from the tips of his fingers, a steak knife gleamed.

Tommy noted the eight-inch serrated blade and he knew the kid wasn't there, not yet, but he saw down that road and the seeing jarred him fully back into his responsibility here.

Red's chest was still heaving. "*Don't* call me simple."

Tommy came up off the wall, reset himself in his boots. His right shoulder blade hurt and his neck throbbed something fierce but that could all be dealt with later.

"Things got moving real fast just now," Tommy said, quietly. "Let's slow it down some."

Red breathed.

"Okay?" Tommy said, just as quiet.

Red gave a faint nod. "Okay."

"There's a lot stirred up in you."

"I know. I know there is. It's too sensational."

"Sensational?"

"All kinds of senses mixed in."

"I understand," Tommy said.

"I want to kill him. I just want to kill him."

"Who?" Tommy asked.

Red hesitated, looked at the head of the table, no doubt where his father sat. Then he looked back at Tommy. "That guy who shot up Lucas and Burt. For humiliating me. I'm so tired of being humiliated. I just want to fucking kill them."

Them.

"That's the devil talking, son," Tommy said. "I've seen the devil. I've seen it in men's eyes."

Talk the Devil Down

"So what am I supposed to do? If I got the devil in me?"

"We all do, son. We all gotta talk the devil down."

"Will you . . . ?"

"What?"

"Nothing."

"What?"

Red eased himself into a chair. His face started to tremble. He ledged the L of his thumb and forefinger across his eyes and wept silently, not letting out a single squeak or sob. He just sat there with the pain shuddering through him, holding it inside like a man who didn't know what would happen if he let it out.

Tommy stayed there near the wall, an ache reverberating up and down his spine, and let the boy do what he needed to do.

Red finally got control of himself enough to force the words out. They came thin and reedy. "Will you help me?"

Tommy said, "Son, why do you think I'm here?"

48

Ready for the Next

There were four of them, slender and strong.

They wore leather dusters, balaclava masks, and wraparound shades to hide their eyes.

The Female One had flecks of blood across her chest and mask. It crusted on the exposed band of flesh at her eyes, tightening the skin of her lids and adding a sensation of weight to the bridge of her nose. In the struggle, her shades had come loose, exposing flesh. It was challenging to control a grown male body in order to exact a pound of flesh.

They were in a discreet-armored black SUV with tinted windows. The One Who Was Her Nephew sat beside her in the back, nestling an oblong body part into an insulated foil liner. The postage on the box had been prepaid and it sported a KEEP FROZEN stamp on the side.

The One Who Was Her Second Cousin was in the passenger seat. He liked to drive, but sometimes when they were on desolate roads or deserted streets he'd swerve to clip the occasional jaywalker, hobo, or hooker. He tried not to but it was a compulsion he could not control and right now the Female One had DNA all over her person and they had fresh meat product in their possession and they could not risk the slightest break in surreptitiousness for extracurriculars.

The Female One tugged off her balaclava mask and shook her hair free. She used a baby wipe to clean her face.

The One Who Was Her Nephew finished packing and sealed up the box, adjusting the rear AC vent to clear the smell.

They'd finished the job as they always did.

They were finally ready for the next.

They were ready to do Janus's bidding.

He was their best employer, the most powerful they had ever known. She pictured the cherub and devil he'd inked on his face, soft fingers and claws gripping the ear from above and below, whispering sweet and bitter nothings.

She wondered at the insanity that roared inside his head. And wondered how much the roar in their collective heads was a match for what Janus heard.

The One Who Was Her Half Brother gripped the steering wheel. He'd identified a FedEx drop point on the way out of the state. He had navigation up on the console display, a clean blue line tracing the path from their current location to Calvary.

They'd get there by morning.

49

Pay Attention to What You Pay Attention To

Tommy and the boys found a crappy diner near the Greyhound station in the city.

The waitress was black, mid-forties, wedding ring. "Happy Christmas Eve," she said, catching all five of them flat-footed. They'd managed to forget day and month but of course that's what it was and they felt a collective shame for the manner in which they'd arrived at the holiday.

She took their orders, repeating them back carefully with her heavy Southern accent and pretending not to notice the chill coming off Red. Elijah and Trent were too shell-shocked at their impending departure to react to anything one way or another.

When the food came they ate in silence, slurping coffee and scarfing down grilled cheese sandwiches and browning refrigerator-cold iceberg lettuce tossed with too-sweet Italian dressing in plastic bowls. When the waitress set down the cream refill, Hick thanked her, drawing a rebuke of a glare from Red.

Tommy watched the boys simmering in the booth, lost to their different fears and grievances. Hell, he felt lost to a host of them his own self.

When the waitress circled back, Red lifted his half-eaten salad bowl to put it on display. "You call this lettuce?"

"I'm sorry, sir?"

"Can't you hear English?" he said. "This lettuce is all brown and shit."

"I'm sorry, sir. I'll take it off the bill."

"Yes, you will," Red said, shoving the bowl her way.

She took the bowl and retreated to the kitchen.

Red dusted his hands, hooked his elbows on the cushion ledge behind him.

When the bill arrived, Tommy set down a few twenties.

"Thank you, sir," Hick said.

Elijah, Trent, and Red rushed in with thanks of their own.

Tommy pinned Red with a stare. "You're paying the tip for your share."

"What?"

"Tip the lady for your share."

"I don't got no money."

"You have enough."

"I barely got ten bucks."

"I didn't eat the meal she served you. Tip the working man. That's a foundational American principle, same as everything you misquote when you spout off. Do it. With your own money. And you thank her when we leave."

Red's lips were parted and he wore an expression of disdainful amusement.

Tommy said, "You wipe that look off your face right now and you set down your money."

Red's mouth closed. He lowered his arms from their mock-confident sprawl. He took out a ragged Velcro wallet. He had a five, two ones, and some change in the purse.

He scrunched up his face to do the math, counted out the right amount for his share. It was a painstaking process.

Tommy laid down another twenty to cover the rest.

315

They slid around the worn red vinyl and got up.

They started out. The waitress was nowhere to be seen.

Red headed through the door but Tommy caught him at the elbow and held him back.

They waited.

A moment later the waitress emerged with three plates lined up one arm. She delivered them to another table and passed by them on her way to the register.

"Ma'am," Tommy said.

She halted. She had a soft curly updo held in place by pins. A few gray strands had escaped and she had what looked like old coffee stains across her starched white waitress shirt.

Tommy looked at Red. Red looked at his shoes.

"Thank you," Red said.

The waitress looked at Red. Then at Tommy. Then back at Red.

"You're welcome," she said.

Tommy drove the two blocks back to the station where he'd already bought tickets for Elijah and Trent. Elijah had an uncle in South Carolina, and Trent knew a buddy with a couch in San Diego.

Red sat alpha shotgun, the other three fanned across the backseat of the cab.

Tommy parked and then adjusted the rearview so it framed Elijah and Trent. He had their attention. For a brief spell, everyone just breathed and waited.

Tommy tugged at his biker mustache. He thought about the global conglomerates who monetized broken boys from broken towns like this, the Big Pharma drug dealers and the fundraising politicians and the media flamethrowers who primed the soil of their degradation, basted them in the juice of their own curdled victimhood.

As a broken-down old warhorse, did he have anything to offer besides threadbare platitudes about fifty stars and thirteen stripes? Was it even real anymore, that gallantly streaming promise? Or was it already too far gone? How could he align these lost boys with a higher purpose once more, to America in all her cruelty and promise? It felt daunting to the point of impossible.

Pay Attention to What You Pay Attention To

But he had to. He had to leave them with something.

He cleared his throat. "As a young man, I put my back to the light. Beelined straight into darkness. Know why?"

Elijah and Trent gave faint shakes of their heads.

"I was *scared*. Too scared to hide."

The boys were rapt, Trent's mouth agape.

"I was scared enough to go into that darkness to know what was there, to see what kind of monsters could come for me someday. Banging around down there, I toughened up. And it was good. That was good."

Red was nodding and the others, too.

"But you can go too far. You can get places so dark you can't find your way out. Where you can't see it anymore—the light. I found places, believe me. . . ." Tommy drew in a breath. "Places I barely wobbled back out of. And I'll tell you this: Y'all best start groping your way out. 'Cause the light, it just gets further and further away. And then afore you know it you're in the ground or jail or some alley somewhere with a needle in your arm. You only got so long to say *no*. *No* to blaming your uselessness on other kinds of folks instead of getting your own shit in order. *No* to teaching everyone lessons when you haven't learned a damn thing yourselves. *No* to letting loose resentment and calling it justice."

Red said, "I got an objection to—"

"You had plenty of say in the months leading up to this moment, boy." Tommy skewered Red with a glare. "*I'm* talking now. Understood?"

A breath whistled through Red's gapped teeth. "Understood."

Tommy returned focus to Elijah's and Trent's faces in that rearview. He cleared his throat, which needed clearing from the coffee and cigarettes and the acidic bite of long-cut wintergreen tobacco. "Pay attention to what you pay attention to. What you pay attention to is where you're headed. That's it. That's everything. And looking there?" He stabbed a blunted finger at the ceiling of his rig and the sky above. "That's your only shot at ever getting to anything that looks like good in your lives. Or. Choose to keep going like you're going. And you can ask Lucas and Burt where that leads."

They blinked at him.

"Now get outta my truck."

The boys climbed out of Tommy's rig, a few empty Skoal tins tumbling out with their shoes and rolling up the gutter at the urging of the wind. Tommy slung an elbow out the window and gave them their space.

They stood backlit in a dirty gray light with the bus depot behind them. The lobby windows were opaque from want of washing, and trash blew around the platforms. A sewage leak festered in the breeze, enough to wrinkle the nose.

Hick and Red on one side of the curb, Elijah and Trent on the other. They faced one another, no one knowing what to say. Sadness hung in the air, thick as paste.

Red lifted his hand to Elijah for a thumb-clamp handshake, leaned down for a half embrace and a back thump. Hick followed suit. They did the same with Trent.

"Y'all are my brothers." Red's voice shook a bit.

Hick said, "Go on and get safe now."

Elijah wiped at one eye. He was biting the inside of his cheek. "See ya on the other side."

Hick nodded. "The other side. Whatever it looks like."

Trent said, "Make sure one of you stands sentry, would ya? Guard that gate. Can't have dickheads blowing into the Hilderanch whenever they get a hankering."

"We can't do worse than your sorry ass," Red said, and they all chuckled a bit.

Red and Hick tore themselves away and climbed back into Tommy's cab.

Trent and Elijah stood there looking a touch lost around the eyes. Tommy gave them a stern nod, just down.

Holding Tommy's eyes, Trent pulled himself upright out of that slouch. It was a deliberate process, stage by stage, but goddamn if he didn't get to a half-decent posture. Elijah wore a fresh undershirt with no holes at the collar and one of the clean new flannels from Walmart tucked in behind a brown leather belt. He was in his old jeans, too, torn to shit, but you couldn't expect the boy to get to Cary Grant overnight.

Pay Attention to What You Pay Attention To

Tommy let off the brake, and the transmission caught and rolled him on out and away. The boys stood there at the curb, looking at the truck as he drove off.

He watched them diminish in the rearview until they were gone.

50

A Dark Shadow of a Dark Shadow

A dark charisma preceded Vic Hildebrandt's arrival. A man like him always left a smear of himself in his wake—fingerprints on the wreckage, a brand scorched into white matter. His ghostly aura lodged in the shell of the house, on the nervous system of his boy Red, and on anything that trickled out from there. Red had been tracking his pop's ETA by way of secondhand updates from Duke and Yesenia. The closer that man got, the more force his toxic specter seemed to gather, revivified by proximity.

Tommy knew that kind of energy. He'd seen it up close in dictators and warlords, narcissists drunk on the sweet poison of their own grievances. He saw it in the way Red amped up in anticipation of his father's visit, nervously checking the rooms, barking at Hick, straightening couch cushions, wiping at stains. Between tasks Red darted into the kitchen, where he kept a terrified vigil over the steaks on the pan, poking and prodding at them to make sure they came out just so. A half dozen times Leslie told her brother to chill out because him being spazzy only ever made things worse, but she finally gave up and went to her room.

A Dark Shadow of a Dark Shadow

Tommy had never seen the kid work so hard. It was exhausting to behold. Finally Tommy checked out and settled into the worn armchair to observe the bustle and stress. It was like a goddamned Restoration comedy had gone off the rails and slammed into Eugene O'Neill.

Hick finally took hold of Red by the shoulders and said, "Listen, man. The house is fine. He'll be here any minute. Let's go on up and get ready."

Red nodded a few times rapidly and then did it again. "The steaks," he said. "Pop hates them done in the middle."

"They're ready," Tommy said. "Pull 'em off and leave 'em sit on the counter to rest."

"Right," Red said. "Right."

Off to the kitchen once more, some clanking and sizzling, and then he came out sweaty of face and bulging of eyes.

Hick set a hand on Red's arm gently and Tommy loved him for it. "Okay now, pal," Hick said. "Time to get dressed."

The boys went upstairs and Tommy breathed his first quiet breath in what seemed like a month of Sundays.

He closed his eyes. It was a marvel how good it felt lately just to shut off and rest.

It wasn't long before the sound of a truck engine cut the night. The third porch step creaked and then the planks groaned and then the door hinged inward and there Vic stood framed in the threshold just as Evan had been yesterday. A dark shadow of a dark shadow.

Vic was a rugged man, hefty through the chest and shoulders, strong taper to his lats. His torso seemed to burst up from his narrow waist like a cobra hood, and his flannel sleeves were cuffed back to show off powerful forearms. Tough as chewed leather, mean and handsome, eyes flat and small.

He stared at Tommy sitting there and Tommy stared right back. Waves of menace came off the man, as palpable as the scent of meat in the air.

"You're in my chair," Vic said.

Tommy just looked at him.

"You're in my chair."

"So you said," Tommy replied. "Would you like to sit here?"

"No," Vic said, at last unsticking himself from the pose and entering. "Just so long as you know it."

Leslie bounded down the stairs in her Calvary Tack & Feed getup and Vic softened and caught her in a hug. "Hiya, baby. Brought you this." From the pocket of his Carhartt he withdrew a big chocolate bar, a chunky one with a fancy wrapper. "Dark like you like."

"The best!" Leslie pressed it to her nose, inhaled deeply, rolled back her eyes in delight. "Glad you made it home."

He noted her name tag. "Aren't you staying?"

"Tuesday night inventory."

"Even on Christmas Eve?"

"*'Specially* on Christmas Eve."

"That's my girl. You always knew how to work."

"See you when I'm back?"

"Nah, I gotta red-ass it back to Bowie tonight. The boys at work are doing a holiday thing for tomorrow. But I'll come back a stretch before the New Year and maybe we'll go camping."

Leslie fixed her father with a look. "Don't be hard on Red."

"That boy never gets anything he don't have coming."

Leslie looked at Tommy.

Vic's smile grew a touch stale. "Why're you looking at him?"

Leslie pocketed the chocolate bar. "Bye, Daddy."

And she was gone.

Vic strode across the living room and sat at the other head of the table. He stared straight ahead, ignoring Tommy.

Not two minutes later Red and Hick came downstairs.

Red's ginger hair, wet from the shower, was combed back so tight you could see the teeth lines. His entrance carried a whiff of aftershave. He wore a pair of trousers and Tommy's button-up shirt, a beige Woolrich poplin with magnetic buttons. No sign of the *Dirty Harry* S&W, probably didn't want to be called out by his pop for playing tough guy. He stood at the far end of the table, facing his father down the length of it, shuffling from foot to foot and wiping his sweaty palms on his thighs.

"Hi, Pop."

"What's with the fancy getup?"

"Oh, this?" Red plucked at the front of the shirt. "I'm gonna wear it to a work meeting I got tomorrow."

"A work meeting."

"That new auto shop behind the bowling alley. I been asking around and the manager said he might need someone for the holiday jam. He said I could come in and interview tomorrow."

Vic's lips pressed thin, his mouth set in a straight mean line angled down at either side like his son's. Deep in his throat, he made a noise of dark amusement.

Red flushed all the more. "What?"

"You think you got that interview yourself?" Vic said. "Dukey's cousin owns the fucking place. I told him to tell his Mexican to look out for you, see if he could find you anything even you couldn't screw up."

Red's face was frozen. He wiped his palms on his trousers again.

The silence hung in the air, spun glass waiting to shatter.

Hick cut in: "Why don't we get them steaks in the kitchen?" He nodded at Vic. "Hiya, Mr. Hildebrandt."

Vic said, "Beer, too."

Red said, "We don't got no beer right now."

"Ain't that perfect," Vic said. "I come home to my own house and there's nothing for me to drink."

Tommy said, "I got that case of PBR and a handle of Beam in my rig you told me to pick up, Red."

Red's face was blotched with patches of white. It took him a moment to catch Tommy's meaning and grab hold of the lifeline. "Oh, right," he said. "Thanks. Glad you remembered."

Vic's grin looked more like a smirk. "PBR and Beam," he said. "At least someone knows how to drink proper around here."

Tommy fished his keys from his pocket, tossed them to Red.

The boys split to gather up food and beverages and soon enough they all were sitting around the table, eating quietly.

Vic cut into his first steak, checked the inside. Red watched nervously. Vic made a little scowl. Took a bite. Chewed it with more emphasis than the meat required. Gave another glare at the steak interior.

"I kept the middle rare like you like, Pop," Red said. "Made up the bed, too, in case you wanna stay here the night."

Vic took a long, slow pull of Pabst Blue Ribbon. "I ain't staying here the night. I got responsibilities to get back to."

"Okay, well, it's there if you want to. Cleaned the room up, too."

"Laundry and housekeeping. You want to be your mother? That it?"

"No, sir."

Vic chinned at a tied-off trash bag in the corner, the sole straggler the boys forgot to take out. "Why's there garbage in my living room?"

Red blinked hard, his eyes squeezed shut in self-reproach. "Sorry, sir. We'll get it out straightaway."

Vic made a clicking noise of disapproval. Tommy studied the man. The drywall was shedding and the floorboards were uneven but that trash bag really chapped his ass. Vic Hildebrandt, King of the Shitheap.

"Elk's overcooked," Vic observed.

Red looked down at his plate. Hick did, too. Tommy watched them, watched their faces.

Vic speared one of his steaks, lifted the whole thing up on his fork. "You get a beautiful cut of meat, this is what you do to it?"

"Sorry, Pop." Red's voice shook a bit. "Maybe you could cook it yourself next time."

Vic dropped the steak. It hit his plate with a thunk, the fork sticking up like a flag. "And maybe you could pay the fucking mortgage."

Red swallowed his bite dryly; Tommy could hear it from across the table. Red and Hick had stopped eating. They just sat there, afraid to lift their eyes.

And then Hick glanced nervously at Tommy, cleared his throat, stared at a point on the table just in front of Vic. "He spent lots of time on the steak, sir. Getting it right for you."

"Hick the hick." Vic folded his arms, forearms flexing. "Did I ask you, boy?"

Hick blanched, bowed his head once more. "No, sir."

Vic stared at the top of Hick's head, then sawed at his steak dramatically, lifted another forkful, and chewed.

Tommy used a paper napkin to wipe his mustache. "Hey, Hick."

"Yeah?"

"*I* got a question."

Hick wet his lips nervously. But his eyes shone with excitement. "Yes, sir?"

"How much time did Red spend cooking these here steaks for us?"

Hick kept his gaze on Tommy and that gaze held more gratitude than Tommy had seen since he reached town. "A lot, sir. He really wanted to get it right."

"Huh." Tommy gave Red a nod. "Thank you, young man."

Vic dead-eyed Tommy, chewed and chewed some more.

They ate in silence for a few moments.

Then Vic said, "I heard ole Dukey got his ears pinned back by some outta-town pussy at the bar."

The boys didn't move.

"And I heard the same pussy put a buncha holes in the Buckley boys." Vic polished off his bottle, set it down. "Someone shot up *my* buddies and dumped 'em in *my* lap, he wouldn't be walking around above ground, I'll tell you that."

"He ain't just someone," Red said, quietly.

"Not just *someone*, huh?" Vic pulled a face, fluttered his fingers, wagged his head. "Some kinda supervillain, then?"

"Yes," Tommy said.

Vic's eyes cut to Tommy but he kept his words focused on those he knew he could bend. "Guess there's not much you boys can do then, huh? But sit around like useless fucks and play video games." Vic grabbed a fresh bottle of beer off the table, rammed the top into the meat of his forearm, and twisted it against the flesh so the cap popped free with a hiss. His eyes, intense and bloodshot, bored into Tommy. "They don't get it like we do."

Tommy took a measured sip of whiskey. "Like we do?"

"Men like us."

Tommy sat on that a spell. Then he said, "I'm not a man like you." His voice was soft but his gaze steady. Once the words were out he realized he wasn't just talking to Vic, he was talking to Delmont Senior, too, the way he wished he could if he was still vertical and ventilating.

"Careful," Vic said. "You're sitting at my table. Show some respect."

"Okay," Tommy said. "What do you want me to respect you for?"

The boys' heads swiveled back and forth between the ends of the table like they were watching a Ping-Pong match.

Vic said, "What?"

"You asked for respect. From *respectus*. To regard, consider. To re-spectate. To see again. So I'm sitting here. I'm looking again. Tell me what I'm supposed to respect."

"How 'bout I beat your ass," Vic said. "Maybe you'll respect that."

"I might be old," Tommy said quietly, "but if you come over here I will beat you within an inch of your life. Understand me, honcho?"

The skin around Vic's eyes gathered, pulling his face into a new kind of alignment. A mask of menace, sure, but there was a hint of concern beneath it.

Tommy cuffed up his left sleeve. Then he took another bite of steak off his fork. "Mmm," he said. "Ain't that cooked just right." He let the fork roll across his knuckles like a fixed-blade knife and caught it in a reverse grip.

"I used to have a buddy, didn't look like much, but anyone with any sense knew not to start something with him. Even had a little speech, telling them to look at him closely to see if he looked scared. Wasn't about the speech, though. If you're paying attention, it was a snake rattle. Rattlesnake's just being polite, saying, 'Don't make me kill you.' And most people have an instinct for survival and walk away." Tommy drank. "That's why bullies pick fights with folks they know'll back down. That may show all kinds a weak character, but it ain't stupid. Man starts a fight with someone not knowing the outcome, that takes a special kind of stupid."

"The fuck are you blathering on about?" Vic said.

Tommy looked down the length of the table at him. Set the tines of the fork against his bare forearm. And pressed. The skin dimpled at three points. He pressed harder. The surface tension popped. Blood welled up around the tines.

"This is my rattle, Vic."

Tommy didn't look down. He kept his stare straight across the table, locked on Vic as the blood streamed down his arm. Expressionless.

"Okay, enough," Vic said. "Jesus."

Tommy removed the fork from his forearm. Wiped it back and forth on the cuff of his sleeve.

He stabbed the steak, cut his next bite, and chewed.

The boys watched, their jaws about on the damn table.

After a spell, Vic got up, grabbed another bottle for the road, and strode out.

A few minutes after that, the boys cleared their plates.

Tommy sat alone and finished his steak.

51

What the Hell Is Happening?

Evan was sick to hell of waiting.

Patience was the first quality of an operator, as Jack had pounded into his skull, but this mission's shattering of the Fourth Commandment had put cracks in his usual forbearance.

Through Steiner tactical binoculars, Evan had been surveilling Sheriff Grady Joy's house all day, holding out for a shot at the bedroom gun safe containing the sole remaining traffic-light photograph of Hick and Red fleeing the murder scene. Though it was Tuesday, Grady didn't seem to have occasion to work. He was enjoying Christmas Eve at home with Elise, who swanned around in a pair of torn white jeans and one of her husband's oversize button-up shirts, which she wore untucked with the sleeves cuffed. She paused at every mirror she passed to make minute adjustments to her hair and makeup. She was a fine-looking woman, but the amount of focus she put into her veneer detracted from it, her appearance like a conversation she was having only with herself.

At intervals guests swung through bearing trays of baked goods or wrapped gifts. They were greeted with hot cider and then implanted into a capacious shabby-chic couch by the trimmed tree, where everyone gabbed with small-town vigor. To keep his patience from wearing out entirely, Evan practiced lipreading and body-language analysis.

It didn't help.

Both deputies had popped by in the afternoon for a brief, serious private discussion with Grady in his downstairs home office, no doubt a sitrep on Hick, Red, Tommy, and what they knew of Evan.

Evan's setup gave him a near-perfect vantage. He'd posted up in the attic of the house across the street, peering out through a dormer window. Second thing this morning he'd driven his truck over and parked it hidden among a stand of fresh Douglas firs before navigating through forest and side yards toward Grady's place. The owners of this house seemed to be away for the holidays, so Evan had squirmed through an unlocked bathroom window and made his way up from there.

If anyone came home, he could simply slip out the dormer window, scuttle to the low eave in the rear, jump-roll onto the strip of crabgrass below, and vanish into the tree line.

He'd watched and waited as twilight spilled into day and then night poured itself through twilight, and now he continued to watch and wait under cover of darkness. There was no guarantee Grady and Elise would leave the house tonight or tomorrow on Christmas proper, and Evan wasn't willing to live up here among cardboard storage boxes, dusty suitcases, and ghostly garment racks. And besides, he wanted to see what was in the safe. The image would likely condemn Red and Hick. Then he could finish the mission for Lidia and Santiago Martinez, avenge their son's murder, and figure out the next round in his death match with Tommy.

Across the street an older couple rasped up in front of the Joys' house in an old Caddy and got out. The wife wore a loose ponytail of steel hair, her husband a ripstop-nylon vest over a camo hunting crewneck. He retrieved a pie in a tin from the rear seat.

Elise received them at the door, giving air kisses on either side of their faces. When the couple returned to their car to resume their neighborhood rounds, Evan decided it was time to move.

If the Joys wouldn't leave their house, he'd have to break in with them inside.

Tired of subtlety, Evan Magic Markered *PIG* across a smooth landscape rock and threw it through the Joys' front window. The plate glass came down in jagged sheets, the living room exhaling a breath of pine and cinnamon into the chill night air. Standing on the porch, Evan caught a whiff before circling to the backyard.

After the pie drop-off, Elise and Grady had gone upstairs. She'd ducked into the bathroom for a shower and the good sheriff was working out on a BowFlex in the guest room next to the master suite.

Evan couldn't see them from down here, but he didn't need to. He'd wound up the watchwork and now the cogs and gears would rotate predictably.

By the time Grady thundered downstairs, gun in hand, Evan had already picked the back lock and was standing in the kitchen, watching the foyer through an open doorway. As Grady spun around the newel-post and launched out onto the porch, Evan walked calmly into the space the sheriff had just vacated and mounted the stairs. Though he'd smeared a thin layer of superglue across his prints, he touched as little as possible, the operational-hygiene habit hardwired into his system.

As he stepped onto the thick carpet of the second floor, he glanced out a side window in time to see Grady flashing by, safing the property.

Into the master suite. The door to the bathroom was slightly ajar, leaking a wobbly sheet of steam from the shower.

"Grady! What's going on out there? What's happening?"

The closet door was peeled back, the gun safe still hanging open from when Grady had retrieved his service weapon.

Evan didn't even need the code.

Inside were two passports, a banded stack of hundreds, and a thumb drive.

Sometimes it all just worked out.

He pocketed the thumb drive and started out.

What the Hell Is Happening?

"Grady! *What the hell is happening?* I got shampoo in my eyes! Hand me the towel, would you?"

Evan paused halfway to the door. The carpet was plush underfoot, the room scented of sandalwood from a pillar candle on the nightstand.

He walked to the bathroom.

Eased the door further open.

In the shower, Elise's eyes were scrunched shut and she was pawing at her face with one hand, the other poking out of the shower, groping at air. He unhooked a fluffy yellow towel from a hook on the back of the door and pressed it into her palm.

"Thank you. *Finally.* What *was* that? Did the Christmas tree fall over?"

He withdrew.

She was calling Grady's name as he descended the stairs.

He reached the bottom. In one corner of the foyer, giant ostrich feathers bloomed from a glass vase the size of a howitzer shell. The front door remained wide open, Grady standing at the curb by the mailbox glaring up the street, shiny SIG P226 on display.

Evan tipped over the giant vase. As it fell, he eased behind the open door, cramming into the narrow V of space against the wall.

The vase shattered against the porcelain tile.

Through the gap in the hinges, Evan watched Grady whip around. Panic rippled across his face at the sight of his unsecured house. He took one tentative step up the walk. Another. Then shock broke and he was sprinting.

From upstairs, Elise's screams echoed: *"Grady! Grady!"*

He flew inside, breathing in grunts.

Evan felt a waft of air brush over him, smelled aftershave and sweat, heard the sheriff's boots pounding up the stairs.

"Elise! I'm coming!"

Slipping out from behind the front door, Evan strolled outside, headed toward the side yard, and vanished into the forest's edge.

Sitting in his driver's seat, Evan stared at the image on his laptop screen.

Hick's Dodge Ram had been captured with its nose in the intersection. Navy-blue walls and powder-blue trim.

No front plate, big dent in the bumper and driver's-side front panel, the left headlight a shattered maw.

The damage to the truck was the least of it.

Red was driving, Hick beside him, their faces turned to animal snarls. Gabriel Martinez sat propped between them, his skin ashen, one cheek caved in, dark red blood dousing his shirt collar. His head was lolled back on his slender neck, mouth parted, spaced upper teeth and roof of his mouth on display, his eight-year-old frame contorted as if from cerebral palsy.

Red was screaming across at him, upper lip lifted, menace lighting his eyes. Hick had seized Gabriel, his teeth gritted, his gaze on fire with a kind of unleashed wildness.

Trapped between them, Gabriel looked terrified.

The time stamp showed the photograph to have been taken in the window between the murders at the park and when Gabriel's body had been discarded like trash in a ditch by the side of the road.

Overhead the pines rustled and bobbed, casting dendrite shadows across the windshield.

Heat started to seep into Evan's chest and gut but he turned the dial off fast before it flooded in.

There could be no emotion.

No three-dimensionality of feeling and empathy.

It had been a long time now without sleep. He needed at least one REM cycle to reset the neurotransmitters that affect concentration, reflexes, and emotional regulation. The next step of the mission demanded that he remain hammered flat, a fearsome implement of justice.

He had two men to kill.

52

Click, Whir, Snap

The button-up shirt Tommy had loaned to Red was on the mattress, flung down.

Hick was sitting on the floor with his back to the wall, feet planted, arms hanging between his knees, holding that tiny book with edge gilding. "The hell's 'redress of grievances' mean?"

"That's what the dictionary's for." Tommy crossed to the bed and stood gazing down at the discarded shirt through the imam's eyeglasses. "Where's Red?"

Hick's voice was hoarse with exhaustion: "Dunno."

Tommy picked up the shirt, walked down the hall to Red's room. Red was sitting on the bed wedged in the corner, his eyes dark and flat. He released the cylinder of the .44 Magnum, gave it a spin, and snapped it shut. *Click, whir, snap.*

Tommy waited but the boy didn't look up.

Red did his little movie trick once more with the Smith & Wesson.

The move would put dents and mars in the cylinder, torque the crane, and pull the cylinder out of alignment with the forcing cone.

But Tommy held his tongue on that.

Instead he asked, "You don't need the shirt no more?"

"Nah," Red said. "I don't need to work for shitty minimum wage." *Click, whir, snap.* "No point in it anyways. No point in anything. Bullshit you're not thinkin' it, too."

"I'm not," Tommy said. "I am not thinking that."

Red finally let his glare lift to find Tommy. "You think you can come here. You think you can change anything. But you can't."

"Listen, son—"

"Leave me alone, old man. Just leave me alone."

Red's focus went back to his revolver.

Click, whir, snap.

Click, whir, snap.

Click, whir, snap.

Tommy couldn't stand watching Red disrespect himself and the weapon any more so he walked downstairs.

Leslie had gotten home from work. She sat at the dining-room table in the spot where her father had been, hands flat against the scarred surface. Her copper-colored hair was loose, coning wide to meet the edges of her wide shoulders, her shirt smudged with dirt and flecked with bits of hay. She smelled of honest work, sweat, soap, and the brewery scent of pelleted horse feed.

Tommy took up his old seat at the far end, sinking down with a groan. It gave him a good view of the stairs. He wanted to make sure Red didn't leave the house, not when he was lost to that dark mood he was in.

Leslie chewed her lip. "Dinner went sideways, huh?"

Tommy nodded.

"Dad went after him?"

Tommy nodded.

"Red do anything to deserve it?"

Tommy shook his head.

Leslie welled up, blinked hard, fought the tears back into their ducts. "He can be a piece of work, our pop."

"Seems plenty fond of you."

"Oh, he'd love me no matter what. I could roll in here any which way and he'd only see his baby girl covered in unicorn sparkles. Mom, on the other hand . . ."

"Tough road?"

Leslie shrugged. "Fathers and sons. Mothers and daughters." She shrugged again. "Know what her favorite thing was to tell me? 'That's not very *ladylike,* Leslie.' It was her favorite sentence in the whole wide world."

Tommy listened for the creak of floorboards upstairs, watched the stairs.

"We shoulda chiseled it on her tombstone. All it ever did was hurt me. That's the point, really, of all of it."

Tommy's head pounded. He was three steps past tired. He tugged his flask from his back pocket, took a mouthful of Beam, swallowed the blessed burn. "*What's* the point of all of it?"

"To hurt folks in a place they can't change. To turn that part of them they can't change into pain. Make it feel dirty. That's all they wanna do. Inflict suffering 'cuz they think they were built right. It's everywhere—the news, social media, politicians, preachers, all them whatever-chan sites that've cast a spell over half of everyone. I wish we could push a button, make it all disappear."

"Everyone's got a dirty part," Tommy said. "We don't all go running around asking the rest of the world to change on account of it."

"That's not what I'm doing."

"What are you doing?"

Leslie pulled a lock of hair around, fisted up a bouquet of split ends, and plucked at them. Her face looked fuller than usual and Tommy was worried she was going to start crying.

"I loved my momma. And she loved me. All the way deep. Where it mattered. But she couldn't get past this one part. Even for me. And I'm so fucking angry at her dead self about that."

Tommy took off the rectangular spectacles, rubbed his eyes, and then sipped more whiskey because he didn't know what the hell else he was supposed to do.

"And now I'm stuck here watching my daddy tear my brother to pieces in some other way for some other reason and I don't know what to do. I don't know what to do. It's like watching a movie where you know the ending already."

Here came the groan of footfall on the second-story hall and Tommy put the flask away and steeled himself to take on Red and block him from leaving if it came to that.

Shoes came visible on the stairs and then legs. But it wasn't Red who appeared.

It was Hick.

"Hey y'all," he said. "Where'd Red go?"

Tommy bolted up. "He ain't in his room?"

"Nah." Hick halted a few steps from the bottom and blanched. "Window was open, though."

Electricity shot up Tommy's back, burned in his joints.

"Oh God," he said. "Oh God."

53

The Part That Is Orphan

A shake to the shoulder jerks Evan awake.

Jack stands over his bed, fully dressed, waxed-canvas jacket zipped up. That means it's time to train.

Evan grinds a fist into his eye, feels the bite of sleep crust against the lid. "What time is it?"

"Time to train," *Jack says.*

Evan regrets asking something he already knew the answer to. He's still half asleep but that's the point. Another Jackism: When they come to kill you, you don't get to tell them you aren't ready.

Evan is fifteen years old and feels like he can't grow up fast enough to keep pace with the challenges thrown at him day and any hour of night. Jack pushes him with a calm relentless constancy that allows for neither complaint nor failure. Evan's hormones have been freight-training their way through his insides of late. They've made him irritable, moody, prone to flashes of temper. And though he's putting on some muscle, he doesn't yet have the benefit of a man's build.

"Ten minutes downstairs. Light sweats, full flexibility." *Jack smells of coffee and leather.* "Don't make me wait."

And that's it.

Jack withdraws.

Strider stretches half on and half off the circular rug, back arching, tongue curling. His ribs show when he stretches, the strip of reversed fur on his spine bristling. He makes an audible cartoon-worthy yawn, lies down once more, and lets his head clunk heavily back onto the floorboards.

Evan gets up and makes his bed, pulling the sheets taut, making sure the edges are smoothed straight even on the underside of the mattress.

His dormer bedroom is in perfect order. Aside from a few stray ridgeback hairs, the floor is spotless. The window bears no streaks. No dust alights on the furniture. The rolling chair sits centered at the wooden desk. Spotless blotter. The floating shelf holds a row of books arranged in decreasing order by height: the definitive edition of Churchill's War Speeches, *Narrative of the Life of Frederick Douglass, a book on Colonel John Boyd's* OODA loop, Three Years in Mississippi, *and Herodotus'* The Persian Wars.

Evan's head is foggy from getting yanked out of REM. He stumbles around as he dresses, stumbling as he pulls on socks. He uses a wet tissue to get Strider's shed hairs up off the floor, then brushes his teeth and splashes water in his face.

He is downstairs in nine minutes and twenty-seven seconds.

Through the sidelights bookending the front door he makes out the bleary brake lights of Jack's truck.

When he steps outside, the night air seeps through his clothes, tightens his skin.

Evan gets into the truck, rubs his hands to warm them. He can see his breath. "Where we going?"

Jack says, "To train."

They drive in silence, the wipers sluicing dew from the windshield. It is 2:27 in the morning.

Rattling over dirt roads, a stretch of highway humming beneath the tires, then Jack veers off at the third exit. Evan's stomach tightens in anticipation.

Sure enough, the dojo draws into sight.

Evan thinks: Fuck.

The dojo is in a strip mall nestled between a coin-collector shop and a used bookstore. The lights are off. Everything is dark, the lot empty, the streets deserted.

Jack gets out and approaches the dojo, not waiting for Evan.

By the time Evan catches up, Jack has unlocked the front door. Evan has trained here many times after hours, one-on-one with a sensei. He did not know Jack had a key to the facility, but it makes sense. Jack has keys to everywhere.

In the threshold, Jack pauses a moment, hand up on the jamb, looking down at the floor and at nothing at all. He is gathering himself for something, for whatever is to come, which only serves to quicken Evan's dread.

Then Jack moves through the dark lobby, clicks on the lights in the training hall. When Evan steps through, he blinks against the sudden daylight.

Jack sloughs his jacket. He's wearing those fucking old-fashioned sweatpants with the bunchy waist pulled up slightly too far, a formfitting T-shirt tucked in tight. Drawn high into himself, chest bared, he looks part Russian gymnast, part starting catcher for the Orioles. He loosens his arms, hug-slapping his shoulders like a swimmer on the blocks. Then he stretches his groin on either side. His posture is perfect, even elegant.

"Get on the mat," he says.

Evan kicks off his shoes, peels off his socks, jogs in place at the edge of the center ring, loosening up.

Jack shuffle-steps in. Evan raises his guard—not fast enough—and Jack cuffs him. The Indonesian pencak silat open-hand slap to the ear rings Evan's bell, and he dances back, shakes his head.

He starts to reset but Jack is on him again, another hard slap to the left jaw, snapping Evan's head to the side.

And then another.

Evan is awake now but not functional. He's gone from sleepy to disoriented to dizzy with pain. He tries for a jab to open up space but Jack knocks it aside, cuffs him again, hard.

Evan shoves Jack but Jack is bulkier by sixty pounds and so the shove moves Evan, not Jack.

"What the hell?" Evan regains his composure, sets his base, lifts his guard. "Gimme a—"

Slap.

"Knock it off! Quit—"

Slap.

Slap.

Slap.

Evan's temper flares and this time he can't catch it. Teeth gritting, charging, swinging wildly. Jack redirects Evan's fist, slides a hand to catch the wrist, twists to an arm bar, and rides him down. Slams him on the mat, knee in his back. Evan's ribs groan as they compress. The air leaves his mouth, spilling out with a spray of saliva.

Stars.

Taste of blood.

Jack keeps the arm, presses a hand over Evan's face, mashing it to the mat.

Jack says, "What's running you right now?"

Dead-calm voice.

Evan bucks and kicks but gets nowhere. It just hurts him more. "Get the fuck off me!"

"What's running you right now? What's running you?"

Evan struggles but he is pinned there. He is dominated.

"Your adrenal glands just dumped a bunch of catecholamines," *Jack says evenly. The pressure on Evan's face is unrelenting.* "Adrenaline, noradrenaline. Heart rate north of a hundred. Blood pressure's spiked, too— probably up to two hundred over one twenty. Your blunt pain response is compromised. You've got tunnel vision. Your breathing's shallow. Your perception's shot, your endurance is shot, your fighting efficacy shot."

Evan stops fighting. He goes limp.

"What's running you?" *Jack says again.* "Anything useful? Anything you want to give control of yourself over to?"

"No." *The word comes out muffled against the vinyl.*

Jack shoves up off Evan hard to ensure a clean getaway. But Evan's incapable of lashing out. His face burns. His chest aches. There's a hole at the pit of his stomach, in the pit of his throat—it's all the same seized-up blackness. He lies in the fetal position, letting breaths shudder through him.

Jack is standing impassively at the center ring.

It is a full two minutes before Evan finds a knee. He dry-heaves twice, wipes the thick cord of drool from his chin before it can reach the mat.

He rises, unsteady. His vision wobbles, snaps back into focus.

The Part That Is Orphan

He pitches forward one step but his equilibrium returns in time for him not to topple.

Jack waits patiently in the center ring, hands laced at the small of his back. Not a glisten of sweat touches his forehead. He's just standing there.

Evan walks to the spot opposite him.

Jack says, "We did this in here for a reason. Do you understand?"

Evan waits a minute, thinks he does, then actually gets it. He nods.

"Do you understand?"

"Yes, sir."

Jack bows to him.

Evan bows to Jack.

Jack nods at the mop in the corner. Evan uses it to wipe his sweat, saliva, and blood off the mat. Jack turns off the lights, and Evan follows him out through darkness, waits outside in the cold while Jack locks the door behind them.

They climb back into the truck.

Instead of turning over the engine, Jack sits staring out at the darkness for a time, hand cuffed over the top of the wheel. His mouth works for a second, goes still.

His voice comes gruff and low when he finally does speak: "Next time," he says.

Back home, Evan heads straight up to his room. Strider lifts his head with vague interest and then goes back to sleep.

Evan runs the shower but does not undress, zoning out as steam fogs the mirror.

He turns it off.

Goes back downstairs.

Jack is sitting in the study with the mallard-green walls and the cedar logs burning, a finger of pale yellow scotch swirling in a cut-glass tumbler. Spinning on the phonograph: Brahms's Symphony no. 3 in F Major—the Klemperer, not the surprisingly uptight Toscanini. Besides learning to use peroxide-soaked Q-tips to clear crusted blood from his nostrils and doing field sutures on his own thigh when he fucks up with the karambit knife, this is the shit Evan has to know.

He stands in the doorway, breathing hard.

Jack nods for him to enter.

Evan moves to the couch. He is still angry. And wounded in confusing ways that thrum through him with each pulse of his headache.

"Have you come to complain?" Jack asks.

Of course Evan has. And of course he won't.

He shakes his head. "Tell me why it's worth it."

"It's not," Jack says. "Unless you decide it is."

This is what Evan deals with. All the time.

"You're training me to become a killer. But you want me to remain human. That's impossible."

"Not impossible," Jack says. "Complicated. Everything is complicated. You'll learn that soon enough. You have the Commandments to guide you. To make clear what must be clear."

"Which is?"

"As an Orphan you will be tasked with protecting a country that is flawed and imperfect but the best version of any country there has ever been. The targets assigned to you represent existential threats to this nation. You will render those targets unable to inflict damage on this nation and the people of this nation and you will ensure that they cannot retaliate at any point in the future. You will achieve that result by ending them. That's what you must do if you are to be what we require you to be. Is that an arrangement you can tolerate?"

Every few months, Jack asks Evan if he consents to this devil's deal, this becoming of whatever he is becoming. It is as if he wants to keep it on the surface of Evan's consciousness every step of the way. As if this shadowy path he is leading Evan down is too lethal to be consigned to shadow in Evan's mind.

He lifts his head. He feels so small, so weak. "Yes," he says.

"Becoming an Orphan is sacred. In that sacred role there is no place for emotion. For loss of control. Ever."

The symphony is into the clarinet-led andante, the violins gathering steam. Evan remembers Jack telling him that this piece was Brahms's ode to his mentor Schumann's inner landscape, all ecstatic heights and moody lows. He thinks about how every person has two sides that fight each other and if it takes a Schumann or a Brahms to bring them into harmony, how the fuck is he supposed to figure it out as a dumb-shit foster kid from East Baltimore?

Jack is still waiting for him to respond.

"In the world," Evan says, "I can keep trying. But in my head? My body? All my emotions?"

"How you do anything is how you do everything."

"No." Fire seeps up beneath Evan's skin. "No. Not when I want to punch you in the face. Not when I'm wondering what the hell I'm doing all this for. Not when I wish I was back in that shitty foster home where at least I'd be normal."

His voice ticks up but Jack doesn't get mad.

Instead, he looks amused. He's not smiling, not directly, but his mouth is tensed, his eyes alive with excitement. A flush tinges Jack's cheeks. When he is one and two-thirds drinks in, Jack is his fullest self, vulnerable to offering rare bits of illicit knowledge from beyond the steel parameters that bind the handler-Orphan relationship. Evan senses that now, senses a tiny fissure in the armor protecting them both, senses that Jack is right on the verge of giving him something he needs to know.

"That's just the circus roaring its insanity at the periphery."

"It's not *insanity. It's real."*

"What is? Your fear? Resentment? Grief? Insecurity?" Finally the left side of Jack's mouth curls up a millimeter or two. "Your rage.*"*

"Yes. Sure. All of that."

"Of course they're real. However. When they're roaring? They are insane. They are discordant. They are running you instead of your running them."

"So what am I supposed to do?"

"Invite them in, one at a time. Have each one pull up a stool. Listen to what it has to say. Whether it's shrilling or plucking or thundering away. Learn its timbre, its pitch, its intensity. Then assign it its place in the pit below you. Each one. Grief, fear, rage. Set the orchestra in order a section at a time." Jack knifed his hand like a shark fin and used it to slot everything into place—the strings and woodwinds, brass and percussion, keyboard and harp. "You stay above the pit. You become the conductor."

"You think I have any part of me knows how to conduct an orchestra?"

Jack lifts his head. Tilts it down. A nod.

Evan strains to hide the exasperation from his voice: "What part?"

"The part that is still. The part that stands undaunted before the others. The part that sets them in harmony." Jack knocks back the rest of his

scotch in a single belt, a rare break in his perennial gentleman's demeanor. "The part that is Orphan," he says. "The part that is X."

Evan finds it impossible to express how impossible this sounds. Before he can catch it, the apprehension takes roost in his posture.

Jack's eyes read him. "I told you before why I chose you. Do you remember why?"

"Because I know what it's like to be powerless."

Jack pours another splash of scotch from the bottle on the silver tray, dips his head in a faint nod. "Soon enough you won't be. Soon enough you will have more power than should ever be bestowed upon a human being."

The words dawn across Evan like a sunrise.

But then Jack adds, "And God help any of us if you forget."

"Forget what?"

"What it feels like to be powerless."

Evan knuckles his left nostril again, and again the wrinkles come back lined with scarlet. "So that's why you grinded my face in the mat? So I'll remember what it feels like?"

"No. I did it because if you lose your temper—one day, one time?" Jack raises his hand slowly and then snaps his fingers, the noise sharp off the walls of the study. "People will die. The wrong people. At your hand. And then everything we have trained for, everything we are fighting for, will be undone."

Evan feels his head shaking before he knows he is doing it. "Maybe we shouldn't do this. Any of this. Maybe this isn't good."

Jack takes a moment, leaning back in his chair and letting his palm rasp across his stubble. His pupils are large and dark right now, the cedar fire finding no purchase in them. When the words finally come, he is looking at Evan but not looking at him at all.

He says, "Never let the good be the enemy of the great."

54

Horror Freshly Dawning

Red drove up boldly on the Emerald Bay Motel with the head-lights turned off, veering into the parking lot haphazardly so the tires banged against the curb. At the lot's periphery he cut the engine, drifted past the sole parked truck, and coasted toward the building in neutral with his foot stomped down on the clutch.

He stopped hidden behind the dumpsters, well out of sight of room 117. When he hopped out, he left the driver's door open for a quick getaway, the dome light clicked off.

His fist was tight and sweaty around the walnut grip of his revolver.

He thumbed the cylinder release and gave the wheel a Russian-roulette spin though all six chambers were loaded—*Click, whir, snap*—and his heart was pounding and his thoughts thundering—*We're not gonna sit here and hide like pussies*—and he crept up on the window so he could see inside, the lump of sleeping body beneath the sheets, the covers pulled up high, and he lifted the revolver and hesitated with his hand quivering—*Someone shot up my buddies and dumped 'em on my porch, he wouldn't be walking around above ground*—and he could scarcely find oxygen and his vision dotted with static and he could feel the individual pulses of his heart throbbing with pain and a need to be something, anything bigger than he was and he steadied his hand and lifted that big bad barrel to the glass and the gun bucked twice powerfully in his hand and the pane blew in and the bedsheets jumped with impact and slid aside.

There was no one in the bed. Just three pillows laid end-to-end under the sheets.

And he wasn't crying, not really, but tears leaked from the corners of his eyes and the thumping of his heart pounded in his ears and he felt the beat-by-beat shove of blood through every last inch of his veins and there came over him a blast of gratitude so pure it made him believe in God just to have someone to direct it at. Maybe that's what it was, faith revealing itself, subtle as a winking eye.

And through the dream haze of his perception he looked again to make sure but there was no one in the bed and he could walk away from this place not a cold-blooded murderer and the wash of moonlight across the run-down motel and potholed asphalt looked as holy as any light he'd ever known.

He turned.

Across the parking lot a man—*the* man—stood in the bed of the parked truck. The tarp had been flung aside.

Red felt his breath catch. His mouth guppied but no oxygen could get in.

The man had been hiding out there beneath the tarp in anticipation of the ambush.

He stared across the asphalt stretch at Red, his face nothing more than an oval of shadow. He was motionless, cast in iron.

A strobe-light blink later, his hands were raised, giving off a glint of metal at their union.

But then a deputy car spilled into the parking lot, siren blipping, spotlight capturing the man in its beam.

Through the glare Red could make out the shape of Ronny Ratliff behind the wheel and Clay Clemmons filling out the passenger seat. Their focus was on the man, not on Red, and he jerked backward between the dumpsters before the spotlight could swing over and find him, too.

Peering through the gap, he watched the man holster his gun and raise his hands, pointing toward the shattered window of room 117.

Red stumbled toward his truck, leapt in, and accelerated unseen around the back of the motel. Bouncing violently over the rear curb, he veered onto a logging trail cut through the trees.

He drove hard for home, branches thrashing against the windows, rapping the side panels like outstretched arms of skeletons. He'd sweated through his shirt; it hung wet and heavy on his frame.

A quarter mile away his throat finally unseized and he drew in breath after screeching breath, trying to respire away the fear. A few seconds later, he broke from tree cover, careening onto solid road, righting the truck, and aiming for home.

That overwhelming sense of gratitude poured through him again and he laughed through the sweat and tears washing his face, thumped the steering wheel with the heel of his hand, and released a hoot of something like triumph.

He wasn't a cold-blooded murderer.

And he was still alive.

Tommy's stomach was roiling and indigestion kept crawling up his throat. He knew his voice'd be even hoarser come morning but he didn't care so long as morning got here without Red coming home dead.

Sitting on the porch with his shotgun across his knees, he washed down the acid with coffee, which he knew was a dumb middle-to-long-term strategy but he had no fucks to give about anything but getting through the short term.

He needed to be awake for whatever news drove through that gate.

He'd logged a buncha follow-up calls to his contacts at the state level, two defense lawyers who seemed not too bad, and a prosecutor from two districts over, piecing together a few half-baked notions about how to proceed if Red and Hick lived long enough to have a chance to. Possibilities and pitfalls kept churning—jurisdictions, realpolitik, interagency rivalries, graft, sandbagging, red tape. Land mines were plentiful. There was no clear path ahead, but then again there rarely was.

Here came headlights.

And then—Was it? Yes!—Red's truck rattling up on the Hilde-ranch looking much worse for wear. It eased to a stop next to Tommy's rig there by the flagpole and then the door hinged open and Red stepped out.

He was a hot mess, hair twisted in hornlike clumps this way and that, his face splotchier than Jupiter. But he wore a bright shining smile that looked devoid of malice.

It took a moment for Tommy to catch up to his relief. He rose. "You didn't do anything stupid, did you?"

"Yeah." Red's chest was heaving. "But fate intervened. It was . . . It was like a miracle."

Tommy felt dead on his feet. His voice came as a grumble: "Get inside. We'll talk more in the morning."

"Yes, sir," Red said.

The "sir" caught Tommy off guard and he paused on his way through the front door with his head down-tilted. He knocked once on the jamb and went back upstairs. Pausing at the landing, he waited until Red was inside with the door shut behind him before continuing to his room.

Hick was in the same position he'd been in all night, sitting on the floor, thumbing the little bound book, stuck in whatever whirl of thoughts were rotating through his skull.

At the sight of Tommy, he shoved himself upright. "Red's back?"

"Yeah."

"He okay?"

"We'll deal with him and the rest of the world in the A.M. Now let's rack out and grab some shut-eye while we can."

Hick moved to his mound of blanket and bedded down.

Tommy climbed back into bed, kept the shotgun lying there at his side, safety on, barrel pointed down parallel to his legs. He doubted Evan would storm the house, but if he did, Tommy would be ready for him.

Going horizontal didn't help his acid reflux any. There it came climbing up his throat, a boil of coffee and bourbon, cigarettes and hot sauce. He smacked his pillows into shape and eased higher on them, putting his digestive tract on a downhill.

He closed his eyes. It felt divine.

He was just drifting off when the door creaked open.

Red stood in the gap, holding a blanket scrunched up at his side like Linus from *Peanuts*. For the moment, he didn't look much older.

He said, "Can I bunk in here tonight?"

Hick was up on his elbows. His head swung to Tommy.

"Sure," Tommy said.

Hick pulled his bedding over toward the wall. "C'mon, pal," he said, with a boyish kindness that about broke Tommy's heart. "Here's some space for you."

Red huffed around, setting himself up. Once he was down, the three of them lay there in the darkness.

The wind sucked at the windowpane. The old house creaked and groaned under the weight of age. Tommy could relate. There were aches inside him right now he couldn't have dreamed of as a young man, spreading their reach, joining up until his whole damn body felt like one throbbing mess.

Red cracked the silence: "I thought even if the truck slipped out, it'd just clip someone, like when them bulls throw a clown in the air. Like that."

It took a moment for Tommy to slot the puzzle piece into place. Calvary Park. Hick's truck. The folks Red had run over at the *quinceañera*.

"It wasn't a rodeo, son," Tommy said.

"No." Red's voice was shaking. "It wasn't."

Outside the tree tops swayed in the wind, slicing the moonlight.

"I shouldn't've drove that truck down there. To scare them Mexicans." Red's voice was shot through with emotion, horror freshly dawning. "Bullshit you're not thinkin' it, too."

"I am." Tommy's words were hard like arrows. "I most certainly am."

There was silence and more silence.

Then the soft rasp of the boy crying himself to sleep.

"There's nothing I can do now," Red said, quietly. "It's too late."

Tommy felt for the comforting solidity of the shotgun at his side. By habit, his thumb double-checked the safety. He could make out Red's wan face there in the darkness. Anguish emanated off the kid, a low vibration.

He was in it now, deep.

In the hurt.

Tommy cleared his throat, which took some clearing. "There's *always* something you can do to make things better. Or at least slightly less terrible."

It took some doing, but Red choked out the question: "What?"

"We'll find it in the daylight," Tommy said.

55

Endless Supply of Tatted-up Reprobates

Joey was pacing on the curb outside the building. It was only a few blocks from her apartment, a big concrete box, the construction sturdy, utilitarian. The front door was tall, painted a dull green. Spots of rust flecked the metal placard above the call box. Through the drawn curtains of the brightly lit first floor she could see movement. Music and laughter carried out onto the empty sidewalk where Joey stood.

She was gathering her nerve.

She wore a hoodie pulled up over her head 'cuz that felt soothing and protective even through X always told her it compromised her peripheral vision. She wore a tiny emerald in her left nostril to turn up the color of her eyes, a bracelet with a clasp formed of magnetic skulls, and the diamond solitaire necklace Evan had given her for her birthday. As always in social settings, she wanted to be overlooked and noticed at the same time.

She was about to approach the staircase leading to that olive door when her phone dinged.

Another alert thrown off by NIST's Tatt-E biometric project

database. She'd kept the algorithms nibbling away at the endless supply of tatted-up reprobates, waiting for a match of the crazy angel-devil tattoo Evan had described on the ear and cheek of Janus. She'd gotten all sorts of near and far misses—a *Where's Waldo* Waldo poking out from behind a lobe, a six-headed Scylla with a Charybdis vortex swirling around the ear canal, the spider-limbed girl from *The Exorcist* pulling herself from brain onto cheek.

But this one hit the cherries.

In the coldness of night, she stared at her illuminated screen. The mug shot showed a man with intense dark eyes, his head pulled back haughtily on his neck in a simulation of perfect posture, his top lip curled with disdain. Jarrett Nugent Sanderson. A baby-faced cherub whispered down into his left ear and a pointy-clawed devil murmured from below.

His head wasn't shaved as Evan had said. Dirty blond curls curtained his face and he'd been made to hold back the hair on the left side so the tattoo could be memorialized by the forensic photographer. Joey cursed herself for setting the search parameters to *hair: none,* which had thrown a stream of red-herring skinheads her way. Obviously any dipshit could use a razor.

Sanderson had served a few brief stints in prison. He'd been convicted twice for assault and battery, once for statutory rape, three times for possession of an illegal weapon. A dismissed manslaughter charge. Pending or dead-ended investigations for human trafficking, illegal storage of explosives, distribution of controlled substances, interstate transportation of firearms. His known-associates list was lengthy and ripe with noxious characters.

She scrolled down the profile to *Aliases.*

None.

She chewed her lip. Between the hair and no known aliases, she was unsure. Even peculiar tattoos weren't necessarily unique. People caught wind of crazy designs online. Maybe Sanderson had seen the cherub-demon design inked onto someone in the pen or displayed on the sample wall of a tattoo parlor.

She scrolled back up, looked at the face.

Jarrett Nugent Sanderson.

*J*Arrett *NU*gent *S*anderson.

Janus.

Got you, motherfucker! She gave a little whoop, punched the air, fired off a text to Evan.

Then she toggled off her phone. Pulling herself upright, she skinned off the hood, took a deep breath, and mounted the steps to that dull green door.

She reached for the button on the call box. Hesitated.

The placard read LEVANT CULTURE CLUB.

She rang.

56

Wreckage

Evan parked his Ford F-150 across the roadway from the target location, way back on the shoulder where it tilted away from the raised strip of tarmac into head-high weeds. Not a streetlamp in sight. In fact there was no artificial light of any kind, just the darkness of the natural world and a few pinpricks of other worlds high in the firmament. The breeze came slow and steady. It smelled of bark and wildflowers and carried a distant tinge of woodsmoke and manure or rotting logs or both.

In the inky darkness Evan leaned against the closed driver's door of his truck, arms crossed.

At this late hour Red Hildebrandt's gate on the far side, set ten yards back from the asphalt, was little more than an intimation of something man-made amid the dark jagged wildness of the forest all around.

Evan pictured that freeze-frame captured by the traffic light.

Red and Hick in that venerable Dodge Ram, the terrified eight-year-old between them, contorted with pain. Hick clenching the boy from the side. Red's tugged-up lip, the menace in his glare, mouth peeled open in a shout. All that blood on Gabriel's collar forging downward, a crimson bib. The terror in the boy's eyes as the light leaked out of him.

Evan thought about those wrapped presents beneath the tree and wondered what would come of them tomorrow, on Christmas morning. He thought about Gabriel's parents waking up and having a brief moment of reprieve before remembrance and devastation flooded in. How many mornings began with that cruel trick of the half-awake mind? Was that how every day would greet Santiago and Lidia for the rest of their lives?

A semitruck announced itself at the horizon, two pale yellow eyes boring through the darkness. The noise and light came on stronger and stronger and then swept past. Tucked back into the weeds, Evan and the dark pickup went unnoticed.

His RoamZone alerted.

He checked Joey's text, Janus's face jumping out at him.

Those dead eyes.

He scrolled through the profile, specific charges standing out. Possession of an illegal weapon, illegal storage of explosives, interstate transportation of firearms.

Tommy's contributions spelled out in black-and-white.

He texted Joey back: Get me address or last known.

As Evan went to turn off his phone, Janus glared up from the screen.

He hadn't come for Evan. He'd come for Tommy. In that old saloon bar in Dawnfall, Evan had asked Tommy outright if Janus had hunted him down over a busted deal.

Tommy's reply? *You could say that.*

First he'd dealt weapons to the Lone Wolf. Then to this piece-of-shit rapist and human trafficker.

Anger stirred inside Evan, a dust devil getting up momentum. He let it flurry. He watched it closely, watched it rage and billow.

Eventually it died down.

He set it in its proper place: brass and percussion, right between those wrapped Christmas presents and the image of a young boy's cheek staved in from a truck that outweighed a rhinoceros.

Back at the motel earlier, the deputies had arrived just in time to hear Red's truck speeding off. Rather than pursue, they'd stuck with Evan, Ronny Ratliff poking the tip of a pen at the shattered motel window and Clemmons glowering at Evan like he planned to chew him to pieces and use his shattered bones as toothpicks. Disappointed that they couldn't hold Evan for being shot at, Ronny had jotted down one of his many backstopped identities, promising to be in touch when the formal investigation began.

After summoning Dot, the deputies had shut down the motel until forensics could get there from the city. That was fine. Evan no longer required a bed. Before the sound of Red's truck had awakened him, he'd grabbed ninety-three minutes of sleep beneath the tarp. Now he'd reached the point in the mission where he'd probably not sleep until it was done.

Evan debated whether he wanted to breach the house to eliminate Red and Hick. That likely would mean drawing fire from Tommy, which meant he'd have to put his onetime friend down as well.

Between Tommy's dealings with the Lone Wolf and Janus and his continued protection of two racist murderers, he was 99 percent there.

But the First Commandment—*Assume nothing*—demanded he get to one hundred.

The ache in Evan's chest had intensified, knitted up further from his sleeping in the bed of his F-150. It could be rectified with twenty focused minutes and a private space but right now he had neither.

In the east, the first premonition of morning glowed. The sun wasn't in sight, not even the top point of the blazing globe, but a sheet of dirty gray light had begun to permeate the air. The world felt thin and fragile, the air like gossamer, easily torn.

First he heard a crunching of footsteps. And then he sensed movement beyond the chain-link.

Sure enough, the padlock clinked, the chain rattled through the fence, and the gate creaked open.

Red Hildebrandt stood there, holding a stuffed-to-the-brim trash bag, eyes bleary from sleep. That big bad .44 Magnum was shoved stupidly into the front of his jeans, the walnut grip flared over the appendix. The same revolver Red had fired, just hours ago, into what he thought was Evan's face.

Evan stood as still as a deer, observing.

Red opened the trash-can lid and shoved the bag in. It took some doing, since the can was already overpacked, but he cuffed up his sleeves and put his back into it. When he was done he used the lid to shove the contents down further. Once it was mostly shut, he paused, winded, and dusted his hands.

The sun inched up farther, not yet cresting the foothills, intensifying the gleam of Christmas morning. Red aimed his face to the light, closed his eyes. For a while he breathed. In the tall weeds, Evan breathed with him, coming into increasing plain sight with dawn.

The low hum of an eighteen-wheeler announced a truck at the horizon, descending toward them as if emerging out of the sun itself.

Red kept his head tilted back, his eyes shut. Evan wondered if whatever was rattling through his mind included thoughts of the family he'd left in wreckage. The truck was closer now, close enough that Evan could make out wire-mesh cages stacked high and the shedding feathers in its wake.

When Red opened his eyes and swung to walk back inside, he spotted Evan.

His mouth gaped.

They were slightly more than thirty meters apart—the shoulder of the road, the road itself, the length of turnoff before the gate.

Evan saw Red with crystal clarity. Saw his lips twitch and his right hand stiffen in anticipation of the draw.

Evan spoke just loud enough to be heard across the road and the hum of the diesel engine closing in. "If you draw on me, I'm gonna put a bullet through your nose."

The poultry-transport truck bore down on them.

He watched Red's eyes tighten up. He watched him think about it. He watched his hand dive for that walnut grip.

Evan had already breached his shirt, parting the magnetic buttons, freeing the ARES from the Kydex holster. The truck blasted past them, plowing before it the stink of excrement, rank as ammonia. The chickens were crammed together a dozen to a cage, thousands of them tucked into themselves half conscious or clucking with terrified agitation. The wall of squirming life wiped Red from Evan's view and when it passed Evan had already re-seated his gun and Red was standing just as he'd been, his stiff right hand frozen a half inch into the draw and the hole of his left nostril enlarged by two millimeters.

His eyes held comprehension even as his legs gave out, even as his knees jarred the ground, buckling his head. He slumped onto his side.

Evan got back in his truck and drove away.

57

The Tug of the Old Ways

Tommy was halfway down the stairs rubbing sleep from his eyes when Hick burst into the house, his face blanched, awash in panic. He was stammering something, words bleeding together into an unbroken run of gibberish.

A door slammed upstairs then Leslie shot out and joined Tommy in the living room. She wore a stretched T-shirt, and her bare feet poked out from men's pajama bottoms.

Hick set an arm against the wall by the front door to brace himself. The sounds had stopped. Now his mouth wobbled every which way but no noise came out.

Tommy lumbered down the stairs to him. "What? *What?* God-damn it, what is it? Spit it out."

Hick scrunched his eyes shut. He shook his head violently, like a little kid.

"Hick." Leslie's voice came soft with dread, as quiet as Tommy had ever heard it. "Tell us what happened."

Hick raised a trembling arm and pointed out the open door.

* * *

It was early afternoon by the time Sheriff Grady Joy, his deputies, various townsfolk, and the coroner (an off-duty notary public) cleaned up Red and the mess left behind in front of the Hilde-ranch. Yesenia showed up briefly, weeping into the shoulder of her husband, and Big Booty Judy from the diner swung by to offer condolences and a cardboard box of coffee-to-go for the work-ers. Tommy held position at the gate like a failed member of the Queen's Guard. He watched the commotion unfurl like a picnic, all blinking lights and crime-scene cones and photo markers, until it all got packed up again and carted off.

After the deputies had finished interviewing Hick, Tommy had stashed him in the storm cellar with a shotgun and that's where he planned to keep him until he and Evan finished what they needed to finish. Leslie was in her room packing; between the hubbub and the questioning, she'd made arrangements to stay at a friend's house for a spell.

The trash cans to Tommy's side were bursting with garbage, the air thick with the sickly-sweet fumes of spilled beer and rotting food. Moving slowly, Judy collected discarded paper cups from the ground, groaning as she crouched. Then she found her way over to Tommy. "Cryin' shame," she said.

Tommy watched a few cars spin around on the roadway and take off. He nodded.

"I wish I could say it was rare." Her eyes misted ever so slightly but there was no break in her voice. "Our young men dying."

Tommy nodded again. He was having trouble taking in infor-mation in real time. His brain felt vacant, Judy's words echoing around the cavern of his skull.

"How's Delmont Junior holding up?" she asked.

"Barely," Tommy said.

"He ain't safe neither, is he? From whatever kicked off?"

Very slowly, Tommy shook his head.

She cursed softly under her breath, the dirty cups rustling in the grocery bag at her side. Across the road, Sheriff Joy paused from fill-ing out paperwork on a clipboard, observing Tommy coldly.

"Time's come," Tommy said quietly. "To talk to some of them

folks you say everyone else in town listens to. The ones who decide everything."

"What for?"

"I'm still figuring that."

"When?"

"Soon as possible."

"It's Christmas."

The hearse pulled away from the long patch of dirt in front of the gate, low on its shocks with the weight of Red's corpse. Its tires threw up dust as they found purchase and veered onto the roadway. Judy followed Tommy's focus, watched the taillights driving away.

"Right," Judy said. "Soon as possible it is."

"I appreciate that."

She rose on tiptoes to hug Tommy. Despite the December chill, her blouse was damp with sweat across the small of her back. She smelled like green apples from some kind of drugstore perfume, and in the tightness of her squeeze Tommy could feel her oft-broken heart. "Watch over Hick," she said. "He's a good boy deep down."

"I know he is," Tommy said.

Judy's ankles and hip must've been acting up, because she headed to her little Honda with a waddle that Tommy had employed a time or two when his own joints were on tilt. She pulled out along with another few cars, and the dust rose and settled once more.

The sheriff was last to leave.

After tossing the clipboard into the back of his spotless SUV, he halted, turned on his heel, and walked over to where Tommy was leaning against the fence.

Grady said, "We'll see what forensics turns up."

"Ain't nuthin' gonna turn up."

Grady ran his tongue across his top row of shiny teeth. "Now how would you know a thing like that?"

Tommy thought: *Because I machined the gun from a solid block of aluminum, coated the bullets with a nanoceramic, and loaded them into cases with no headstamp.*

He said, "Guess I don't."

"If you hadn't brought trouble here, that boy'd still be alive."

Tommy thought about knocking those pretty teeth down the sheriff's throat, caving in his windpipe, curb-stomping his smug fucking skull. Tommy was angry. He was angry because Grady was right. He felt it rise in him, the tug of the old ways, the siren call to deploy fists, steel, and lead to obliterate someone else's sliver of rightness in the face of all their sins.

Over his heart, Grady wore the six-pointed sheriff's badge.

Tommy set the stub of his forefinger against Grady's badge and pushed. Hard.

"Know what them six points stand for?" Tommy said. "Integrity, courage, professionalism, service, commitment, and respect." With each virtue, he shoved the nailless tip of his knuckle against the metal. "The star's to remind you that you're the guardian of the community. The *whole* community. That you protect citizens— citizens like Gabriel Martinez and his family."

He'd not spoken the name aloud yet and in doing so he felt something well up behind his face. He clenched his jaw, willed it down. "Know what *else* that star stands for? That you'll uphold the law. Not apply it as you see fit. *Uphold* it." He leaned close enough to see the capillaries of Grady's eyes, the touch of red at the flanges of his flared nostrils. "If you'd done *that,* if you'd done the job you took an oath to do, that boy wouldn't be laid out in the back of a hearse, he'd be in the legal system getting sorted out properly."

Grady's lips trembled, his anger barely restrained. "Let me remind you that breaking and entering is a felony—"

Tommy said, "What the hell are you on about now?"

"—and that evidence obtained illegally cannot be used in a court of law."

"Evidence? What evidence?"

"I assume you wouldn't be so reckless as to make claims of corruption against a law-enforcement officer without evidence." Grady's teeth were clenched, his jaw flexed, the words hissing out. "If you step foot inside my house again, I will fucking finish you."

The puzzle piece dropped.

Evan must have broken into Grady's house and stolen some

kind of evidence that showed what Hick and Red had done. That had sealed Red's fate. Hick was certainly next. And Sheriff Joy was too far in to change the story without incriminating himself, so he planned to ride it out no matter how many more bodies hit the deck.

Before Tommy could find any words, the sheriff was ambling back to his SUV, his boots crunching across the compacted dirt.

Weakness washed through Tommy. Easing inside the gate, he locked it and then clutched at his chest, angina tightening its electric grip around his heart.

He had to get to Evan. He had to stop this any way he could.

He raised his phone to text. It was shaking violently but it wasn't the phone, it was his hands, so he paused, grabbing for the gate, and breathed slow and steady, puffing out his cheeks. He'd seized the fence roughly, hand clenching the links at face level, his goddamned rotator cuff lit up with a ring of fire. When he lowered the arm, the joint snap-crackle-popped.

He managed to get the text off: Bar. One hour.

When he looked up, Leslie was standing there, the house rising way down the drive behind her. She looked a mess. Her hair had come half undone from the ponytail, lumped to one side, and she still wore her sleep shirt and PJ bottoms, though her feet were now shoved into sneakers. Her face was puffy but she hadn't cried yet, not once, not during the endless questions from the deputies and the sheriff and everyone else.

Her mouth opened. Closed. She swayed on her feet, blinked a few times as if she'd forgotten where she was. Awareness came back into her eyes. "Pop called back."

"What'd he say?"

She had on a screen-saver face, no emotion at all. She stared straight through Tommy. "He said, 'Figures.'"

Her eyes darted past Tommy's shoulders and he turned to see what he already knew she'd locked on to, that wet blotch in the dirt just beyond the gate.

"Stupid," she said. "Stupid, stupid white-trash idiot." Then she kicked at the fence with grown-man strength, yelling from some place deep inside her, out of control, eyes rolling and wild. She tore a trespassing sign straight off its wire twists and hurled it and then she hammered the bottom of her fist against a tree trunk and kicked it, too, for good measure and stumbled away in a dazed circle. Her cheeks were blotched red and the air huffed out of her in agitated chunks, her chest heaving powerfully. She looked like an overgrown child.

"I know, I know." She spat the words bitterly and angrily toward Tommy but not quite at him. "Not very ladylike."

The heel of her hand was scuffed, her pajama bottoms were torn, and she'd lost a sneaker in the blowup.

Tommy said, "You be whatever you need to be right now."

Her mouth tugged downward and quavered.

Tommy squared his shoulders and faced her, moving neither toward her nor away. At last she broke.

She was an ugly, ugly crier. Lips smeared to one side, lashes clumped. She stumbled toward Tommy and fell into him and he held her as she sobbed.

58

Critical Mass

The first thing Evan clocked when he entered the Watering Hole was Tommy's position and body language. His former friend sat at one of the few lowboy cocktail tables across from a single empty chair—presumably Evan's. Tommy faced three-quarters away from the door, a show of confidence, and he did not acknowledge Evan's entrance. His legs were crossed in a wide figure-four lock, left ankle resting on right kneecap, a position broadcasting dominance, fortitude, truculence. It also put anything in a left ankle holster within reach of his shooting hand.

The rest of the tables were empty, the other patrons gathered several deep at the bar, Christmas drunks filling up before heading home for turkey and wine. Electricity circled the place, the drinkers on edge, speaking in low voices, the collective focus moving between Evan and Tommy. From the few phrases Evan caught, it seemed everyone was abuzz with news of Red's death.

Dougie manned the bar, a knit cap screwed over unkempt hair, scraggly wisps of beard tufting out from his chin and jawline. His arms were set wide on the lacquered bar, elbows locked.

As Evan moved to him, the cluster of folks parted and silenced. He nodded at the ridged bottle. "Aylesbury Duck. Rocks."

Dougie grabbed up a fistful of ice cubes, dropped them in a lowball glass, and poured in half of the scant remaining liquid.

Perched a few stools down, Dot swished something creamy— Baileys or Carolans—in a water-stained snifter. Her embroidered green sweater read EMERALD BAY MOTEL: YOUR DREAM HOME AWAY FROM HOME. He had to respect her marketing acumen.

She studied Evan through translucent maroon readers. "Your security deposit was insufficient to cover the damage."

"Apologies," he said. "It was a challenge trying to protect the furnishings from all that incoming gunfire."

One of the men at the periphery said, "Heard there was outgoing, too."

Evan scanned the loose group, but no one took up the cause. Duke was at the end of the bar near the pinball table his face had shattered. A seam of fresh sutures slanted like an accent mark over his left eyebrow, the skin beneath shiny with ointment. When Evan looked over, Duke became studiously interested in his pint glass.

Evan took his drink across the wood-laminate dance floor. Tommy didn't stir as Evan set down his glass and settled into the opposing chair.

Cupped in Tommy's palm was a Pabst Blue Ribbon, a considered choice since he preferred whiskey. Between the PBR, his untucked flannel, and a trucker's hat with the Ruger emblem, he was flashing all the gang signs, pushing out an even tougher rural exterior than usual. He wore the brim of his cap low, his eyes shadowed, and he smelled of Speed Stick and unfiltered cigarettes.

That cramping around Evan's rib cage throbbed, the muscle still tightened up. He pushed through it with a deep inhalation.

Tommy's voice came like a growl: "That boy you killed, he had a sister."

"You want me to care that a target has relatives? Who might be upset?"

Waves came off Tommy, palpable like heat—fury, contempt, and something softer and more human that Evan couldn't quite read. His perception wobbled for an instant, the space around him blending with that other bar where he'd watched the folks sway-ing and twirling in graceful synchronization. For an instant he saw himself as a bullet punching a hole straight through the heart of the community, but then his perception restored itself and he was back in the same watering hole with the same faces scattered around in haphazard clusters and Gabriel was still dead and not fully avenged.

Tommy took a slug off the bottle, set it back down a bit too hard so the beer foamed up. "I didn't have enough time. I just . . ." His voice cracked. "I didn't have enough goddamned time."

"For what?"

"Can't you see?" Tommy said. "Can't you see a goddamned thing?"

The vodka warmed Evan's mouth. He felt it slide down his throat, coat the sides of his stomach, purifying and strong. He placed the glass down precisely in the condensation ring it had left on the cheap wood laminate.

"He ran over four people in cold blood," Evan said. "I can see that."

The shadow across Tommy's eyes betrayed nothing.

"And you're an illegal arms dealer to killers and traffickers," Evan said. "So let's not get operatic in our sanctimony."

Tommy's lips bunched, mustache bristling. "I asked you here to warn you. A final time. Leave town. I will clean up this mess."

"You gonna clean up the mess for Gabriel Martinez's parents, too?"

Tommy winced. "I will make Hick answer."

"You gonna do that despite his hiding out and a dirty sheriff hellbent on his *not* answering?"

"I'll find a way. You and I can finish up what we need to finish up after. We'll spill blood between us then."

"I've been told to stick around by local law enforcement. Seems I'm a key witness in a motel window shooting from when your innocent boy—the dead one—tried to put two rounds through my head."

"I'm not fucking around. You leave Delmont, Jr. alone. He's like . . . I don't know. He's like Joey to me."

The claim landed wrong on Evan. "You've known him what, four days? He's not Joey to you. And last I checked, Joey hasn't killed anyone."

Tommy banged the table hard enough to make the bottle jump. Evan snatched up his glass to save the vodka from splashing out. There were only a few ounces of Aylesbury Duck left in the zip code.

"And if she did? What would you do, Evan? *What would you do?*" Tommy leaned forward, bringing his eyes visible beneath the brim, his words simmering with rage. "Would you shoot her in the face?"

"If she ran over an eight-year-old boy because she didn't like the color of his skin? You'd better believe I'd consider it."

Tommy thundered up onto his feet, hurling the table aside. His chair tumbled back and broke apart; the bottle of PBR flew end over end and bounced unbroken across the dance floor, spraying foam. "Don't you lay a fucking hand on that boy! Not *one hand,* you hear me? *Hear me?*"

Evan had never seen Tommy this out of control, looming over him, face purpled, eyes bulging. The other customers were frozen against the backdrop of the bar, bas-reliefs in a marble frieze. No jukebox, no tinkle of glasses, not a cough or whisper.

Exposed in the sole remaining chair in reach, Evan sat calmly. His face was level with Tommy's not insubstantial gut. He took another sip. Set down the glass on the floor beside his chair.

Slowly he reached in his pocket, extracted the RoamZone, thumbed up the traffic-light photograph of Gabriel in the truck. That ashen face, the caved-in cheek, the head rolled back, mouth parted in agony, his frame contorted and broken. And those two animals on either side of him, wild-eyed.

He held it up to Tommy. "They took him. He was still alive. And they took him. Look at his face." He shook the phone emphatically. "Look at his face, Tommy. Look how terrified that child is. And tell me again not to lay a hand on the man with his arm wrapped around that boy's broken neck."

The sight staggered Tommy for a split second—his left knee buckled a quarter inch and his shoulders dropped and his sad hound-dog eyes came recognizable again. But it was a mere flicker before he tensed once more, a coil of muscle and girth.

It happened too quickly for Evan to get ahead of it.

Tommy's right hand was already diving—*Wait*—and Evan realized what he was doing—*Please*—and the tips of his fingers had already passed his floating rib—*No*—en route to the holster sitting atop the iliac crest. Evan's hand flew along the same route but faster, catching up as he always did, and they both cleared leather at the same time and the barrels came around, came around to full, and Evan saw Tommy's trigger finger tightening as his own slid through the guard and curled around the marine-grade stainless-steel sliver that separated potential from kinetic and they were aiming directly into each other's critical mass from extreme close quarters, Tommy pointing down into Evan's chest and Evan aiming up to pierce the upper abdomen at a forty-five-degree rise angled right to shred the left ventricle, left atrium, pulmonary artery, and aorta. There was only a quarter pound of pressure left for Evan before the round would fly and he was gauging from Tommy's creased knuckle where his finger was in the press and then a phone rang right on top of them, so loud it might've been inside their collective skulls.

An old-fashioned ring but Evan knew it to be Tommy's cell phone, turned high to account for his detonation-battered eardrums.

They caught themselves at the edge of the cliff, Tommy's mouth ajar, spreading the horseshoe fringe of mustache, his eyes watery and stunned by what had just nearly lit off.

Evan's heartbeat pulsed in the side of his neck, steady as a conductor's wand, keeping time above the churn of emotions down in the pit.

Tommy's breath jerked in. He swallowed roughly, his throat clutching beneath the stubble. Then he took an unsteady step back and they both lowered their handguns in concert.

It was as though no one else was there, as if they were alone spotlit in darkness.

The phone shrilled again, resonant off the hard surfaces.

And once more.

With a shaking hand, Tommy reholstered. He answered, his voice gruff. "Yeah?"

He listened, a vein throbbing in his forehead.

"Come again?"

And then: "Who?"

And then: "When?"

He palmed his forehead, knocking his cap back on his head, let out a whistling breath. "Copy that," he said, and hung up.

His gaze was loose, eyes bulging. He wet his chapped lips and then wet them again. "The Four Horsemen," he said. "Know of them?"

Evan was still sitting. Though his ARES was back in the holster, his hand remained on the butt. His arm was tensed, sending a nerve dagger through his cramped chest. His voice sounded foreign to his own ears. "Course," he said.

"They're on their way here. To me." Tommy stared at the dead phone in his palm transmitting IMEI signals, the same ones Evan had used himself to track Tommy down. Tommy fumbled now to turn his phone off. "I got a black-hat cyber guy covering my hide. He just caught up to Janus's comms."

"How far out are they?"

"Forty-five minutes. Hour, tops."

Evan rose. He took the phone from Tommy, turned it back on. "We have to get them away from these people. I'm two blocks east."

"My rig's in the back."

"I know. Pull out behind me and we'll convoy."

Tommy nodded sharply, nodded again. He rubbed his fingers against his palms, calluses rasping. "Where we going?"

Evan smiled.

59

Tough, Well-Trained, Psychotic

The half-broken-down movie set of the chapel was an ideal place to stash two trucks. The pews had been shoved to the sides, leaving a nice wide apron before the altar. Evan's pickup bounced readily up the three broad steps in front and eased through the wide double doors he'd laid open seconds before. Tommy followed.

They parked at a deferential slant before the pulpit.

Getting out, they busied themselves at their respective vaults, armoring up.

Evan said, "My backup mag hitches on the drop."

Tommy was elbows-deep in a Hardigg case, assembling a battle rifle that at a glance looked to be an FN SCAR Heavy chambered in 7.62×51 mm NATO. Without glancing over, he tossed Evan a fresh loaded .45 ACP magazine.

Evan slotted it into his ARES, thumbed the release. It slid out. He tested it again and then a third time for good measure.

Tommy cocked his head to gauge the sound of Evan's mag dropping. "Smooth as a Ken doll."

Making a noise of assent, Evan seated the 1911 in his appendix carry.

Tommy held out the battle rifle for Evan. "Much as I'd prefer to shoot you now and save time, for what's coming I'm gonna need you with a rifle, not a peashooter."

Evan stared at the long gun hanging in the air between them. He thought about the weaponry Tommy had supplied to Lone Wolf and Janus, bit back an edged remark, took the offering. Staring through the scope, he adjusted the focus.

A second Hardigg case rattled out of Tommy's truck vault onto the bed, where Tommy snapped together another FN SCAR with brisk, concise movements. His proficiency around hardware was as ever something to behold. Barrel and gas tube, lower receiver pins, stock, bolt group—they flew into place with an efficiency that seemed machine-automated. He slid the scope onto the base, secured it with QD levers, focused it with a practiced twist of his fingers.

Pocketing extra mags of military black-tip ammo, he hoisted the rifle over a shoulder and got busy with flat black 100 mph tape, wrapping the sling swivels so the metal loops wouldn't clink and give away position. "Wish I'd brought some Barrett M107s but I didn't figure I was going to war."

Up against the fabled Four Horsemen, the Barrett would've been good. It could knock a helicopter out of the sky, ignite a bulk fuel tank, and aerate body armor at a thousand meters. But if modest 7.62×51 mm NATOs were what Tommy had, that's what they'd use.

Tommy threw two backup mags for the rifle at Evan hard enough to strike Evan's chest, and Evan made them disappear into his cargo pockets. Tommy hesitated at his tailgate before grabbing a backup tin of Skoal and adding a mag of tracers to his loadout.

Exiting the chapel, they swung the large wooden doors shut behind them, making their vehicles vanish. The sun, a charred cigar-cherry orange, had begun its downward tug to the mountains in the west. It pulled Evan's and Tommy's shadows long when they stepped onto the dirt stretch of Dawnfall's Main Street.

The ersatz buildings on the east side of the road were interspersed with vacant lots and livery stables. The west sported an unbroken run of façades—bank, sheriff's office, mercantile, feed and supply, hotel, blacksmith, funeral home, and saloon connected by a raised wooden boardwalk. The bank, funeral home, and saloon had been built out, but the others remained mere frontages hiding ladders, stairs, and perches designed to service film crews and actors. The sign stenciled on the funeral home read UNDERTAKER AND FURNITURE MAKER, a few dusty caskets still propped up in the front window.

Tommy spit a brown stream of tobacco into the dust, squinted at the ghost town. "You thinkin' what I'm thinkin'?"

"Set up on the west, gives us a clear vantage on the sole approach route and movement from building to building all the way up and down the strip."

"Since I ain't as ambulatory as you, I'll take the far end and shoot down the length of Main Street. I didn't bring copper sabot 12-gauges or AP .50 BMG so I can't crack the engine block but I'll put rounds through their tires and get after the gas tank to stop 'em here for you." Tommy pointed to the faux bank building end-stopping the entrance to Main Street. "Sound fair?"

"Fair enough. I'll set up on top of the bank, ambush them at close range when they spill out of the vehicle. If I have to move, I'll move."

"And I'll keep crosshairs on 'em the whole damn time, cover yer six."

"Do we know anything about these Four Horsemen? These in particular?"

"Two got blown up in some business in Croatia a few years back, long replaced. I heard one's a lady right now. Don't matter. They're interchangeable—tough, well-trained, psychotic."

"They're professionals. It'll be a proper firefight."

"Yeah, well, who wants to live forever." Ambling off, Tommy tossed Evan an earpiece, a match for his own.

Entering the bank, Evan screwed it into place. "Got me?"

Tommy came back: "Lima Charlie." *Loud and clear.*

Several spots of the two-story ceiling sagged from weather, drywall udders leaking drip-drip-drips. The stairs were old, soft with rot and rain, so he took the flight up slowly. A three-foot-tall parapet capped with pretty latticework rimmed the wide bare roof. It made for perfect shooting—film or rifles. Though there was no gap between the bank and the sheriff's station, the latter's roof was a good five feet lower and it was less a roof than a narrow plywood catwalk hidden behind a chipped yellow frontage.

Setting down the rifle, Evan walked the perimeter in full. At a spot toward the middle, the largest puddle of water bowed the roof downward. He considered it a moment before driving the heel of his Original S.W.A.T. through the edge. Plaster and broken slats spiraled into the void and water drooled through the hole, pattering on the floorboards thirty feet below. He jabbed his boot at the wound a few more times, expanding the hole to the size of a Frisbee.

That was all he'd need.

Walking back to the edge, Evan considered the parapet. The concrete trellis-design topping looked like a mash-up of Frank Lloyd Wright hollyhocks and geometric snowflakes. Plenty of makeshift ports to keep him shielded and let him fire hidden from most sight lines below.

He leaned past the parapet to gaze up Main Street. Tommy was walking down the center of the strip, his elongated shadow strolling alongside him, rippling across the packed dirt, man and living silhouette connected boots-to-boots. He hadn't gotten very far.

Dropping to a knee, Evan disassembled Tommy's battle rifle, piece by piece, checked everything for sabotage. He removed each cartridge from the mag and by touch made sure there were no high-seated rounds or high or low primers, and that the crimp on each projectile felt the same. Tommy wanted him dead, and impairing Evan's weaponry would be the easiest way to get him there.

Everything looked squared away.

But the itch of discomfort wouldn't depart. The glare guard on the scope, Tommy's preferred killFlash ARD honeycomb mesh, looked up to standard. Nonetheless, Evan clicked on the LED flashlight from his RoamZone and examined the guard under directed light to see if the metal had been tampered with to throw a glint. That was the second-fastest way to locate an emplaced rifleman. The fastest way was muzzle flash. Evan removed the quick-detach titanium suppressor. It felt about the right weight. Peering down the bore, he saw the concentric spiraling vent holes, designed to work with the twist rate of the rifle's barrel. Everything looked centered, so he reattached it over the dedicated flash hider and snugged it firmly into place. A loose suppressor at the end of a battle rifle could ruin your day in more ways than one.

As near as he could tell, nothing Tommy had handed him had been tampered with.

He knew he was being paranoid. He didn't think Tommy would eliminate him in backhanded fashion, but he didn't really know him anymore, did he? He didn't recognize the Tommy who'd dealt with the Lone Wolf and Janus. Nor the Tommy who protected members of a racist militia.

Evan checked Tommy's progress up Main Street.

The old bastard was still strolling along, canted to one side to favor that bad hip. Watching his pained gait, Evan was caught off guard by a stab of affection.

Shaking it off, he posted up behind the parapet to gauge the best firing ports.

A few minutes later he glanced up the strip once more. Tommy had finally reached the saloon at the far end, where he and Evan had had their fateful meeting. He paused before the wooden stairs to the swinging saloon doors, shifting the rifle on its sling, and then started up.

He disappeared inside.

Set up in his perch, Evan waited. Dusk thickened the air and thickened it some more.

His earpiece crackled, Tommy's two-pack-a-day voice grumbling through. "In position."

"Copy that. Me, too."

As if on cue, a pair of headlights appeared on the sole road to the south, banking toward them.

"Incoming," Evan said.

"Okay," Tommy breathed. "Let's disaggregate these mother-fuckers."

The vehicle drew closer, descending in Evan's reticle.

"Black SUV," Evan said. "Tinted windows."

"No shit." The rasp of Tommy's breath, the click of the safety lever. "I got eyes."

The road formed the sole slash through dead, flat landscape. There was nowhere to hide. The SUV beetle-crawled closer and closer yet.

Evan sighted at the tinted window where the driver would be. The SUV looked armored up, the bumper reinforced, low on the shocks, extra air intakes on the front near the hood. He fought a brief temptation to pick off the driver but knew the first round wouldn't make it through the bullet-resistant windshield. It would just alert the Horsemen and lead to an extended siege.

So he waited.

As the SUV slowly crested a rise in the rutted dirt road, Evan watched it at 6× magnification. It slowed to a crawl. Fifty meters out. Now forty.

Evan found his breath. The safety was off, his finger inside the trigger guard.

Twenty yards out.

It nosed forward, barely creeping, all black metal and opaque glass. Thick Yagi antennae on either side articulated as if sniffing the air.

Now Evan could hear the hum of the engine.

Now he could hear the soft crackle of tires across road grit.

That reinforced front bumper drew level with him, the SUV stopping right there at the verge of Main Street.

The obsidian driver's window mirrored back the falling sun.

The SUV didn't move. Evan didn't move. He barely breathed. The wind whipped up a carpet of undulating dust that settled again into stillness.

The front tire deflated at the same instant Evan heard the crack of Tommy's projectile. Evan hadn't thought Tommy could find the angle for it, but he could bring shock and awe with the best of them.

Then the other front tire.

Wondrous how quickly Tommy could reset for a second shot.

Evan held steady. He waited for the SUV to reverse or skid forward into a turn. But it just sat there.

What the hell were the Horsemen doing in there? What were they preparing?

In rapid succession, two more shots hammered the area behind the back wheel, throwing up spalls and sparks.

A thin trickle of gasoline cut through the dust of the rear panel. Pressure valves in the tank would already be venting to the outside, ensuring the SUV wouldn't go up in a Hollywood explosion.

Evan remembered the tracer rounds Tommy had grabbed before leaving the chapel. They'd light up the gasoline, make the vehicle uninhabitable.

That's what the Horsemen were doing. Waiting for the shooter to change magazines and cartridges, which would give them just enough time to—

Evan heard the hissing but did not initially register what his eyes were telling him. Down below the front tires expanded in concert. They were self-reinflating. He had to rewind his mental tape deck to recall what he'd just seen on the nearest tire, a second rubber skin inflating itself beneath the puncture.

Now the sunroof blew skyward with a *whomp whomp* of explosive bolts.

Jack-in-the-box movement lurched up out of the SUV. Evan sighted on the balaclava mask and put a round straight through the eyehole. Too late he realized the mask had been stretched over a torn-free armrest, padding and leather blowing out the rear. And that he'd given away his position for nothing.

Now two forms exploded up through the sunroof, leading with massive barrels.

M60s with soft canvas 50-round teaser belts fastened to the left side. And at least 100-round belts crisscrossed around the torso of each gunner like they'd popped out of an old Pancho Villa movie.

Fed by disintegrating belts of M13 links, 150 rounds apiece times two meant 300 rounds, plus whatever hardware the other Horsemen were wielding.

One aimed in the general direction of Tommy's hide.

The other trained directly on Evan.

60

I'll Be Waiting

Rounds obliterated the parapet, the report of the M60 grunting like a barnyard hog.

Under cover of the big guns, an armed form flew from the SUV's rear door, bolting for the bank entrance below Evan.

Evan pulled back from the roof perimeter, but the 7.62×51 mm NATOs aerated the thinly built façade and ceiling, penetrating the roof even at depth. He rolled to a stop on his belly near the hole he'd kicked through the roof, his rifle tumbling away.

Rounds kept coming, erupting all around him at a slant.

He looked down through the gash in time to spot movement in the lobby below.

One shooter, slender and strong.

He wore a leather duster, a balaclava mask, and wraparound shades to hide his eyes.

In the dimness of the bank, he skinned off his glasses, the mask coming with it. A shockingly handsome young man of unclear mixed heritage. Filipino, Polynesian, Hispanic—it was impossible to tell.

I'll Be Waiting

He crept through the lobby, cheek pressed to the buttstock of an AR-15, face and barrel swiveling expertly to cover corners and hiding places. Systematic, professional, dead-cold calm.

But he didn't look up.

They rarely did.

Evan rolled away to free his ARES from the holster, rolled back to face through the gash, steadied his grip.

Down on the road the Hog thundered on, rounds chewing up the bank façade and lifting chunks of roof, covering the noise of Evan's movements. A length of parapet tumbled inward, pieces spilling across the rooftop like a billiards break.

Below, the man darted swiftly through the lobby, moving in and out of view.

With the sights, Evan tracked him around the teller box, waiting for him to emerge at the base of the stairs. Around Evan the air throbbed with lead and steel, the building trembling from the onslaught.

The man stepped from cover below, rushing up the stairs.

Evan fired.

In the commotion he missed the head, but the round struck the man's shoulder, knocking him over. He skidded stiffly down several steps, rotating so his head was low, boots up. He stopped in the puddle of light afforded by the hole in the roof. Evan's shadow cut a perfect silhouette from the golden circle—dark form, faceless head, gun aimed.

The man's arm was a mess. The bullet had traveled through the ball of the shoulder and bored through the length of the humerus. He was shuddering, lips blue. The AR-15 scuttled down the steps out of reach.

Upside-down on the stairs, he gazed up at Evan, blinking. "G-g-g-got us."

Around Evan the roof surged and bucked, shrapnel fountaining.

Evan sighted on the man's forehead.

The man shook more violently now, going into shock. But his eyes stayed trained on Evan.

He gave a faint nod.

The ARES bucked in Evan's grip and the man jerked, his lifeless form bumping down a few more steps.

"One down," Evan said.

Before he could hear Tommy's reply, a spate of rounds sawed horizontally through the bank interior, cutting the meager staircase in half. A clump of steps fell away, caving in and bringing down an avalanche of wood, railing, and balusters with it. The section of roof behind Evan followed, the surface rolling away into nothingness like a sinkhole or tank tread, the abyss yawning forward toward Evan.

Popping to his feet, he ran at a slant toward the northwest corner of the bank, the roof collapsing at his heels. He leapt for the sheriff's office. He cleared the side parapet before the skinny neighboring catwalk came into view and caught a gasp of midair relief to see he'd gauged the angle right.

He dropped five feet, tumbled across the catwalk, and bounced off into thin air. Twisting around, he grabbed a scaffolding post that bowed terrifyingly before snapping back to deliver him onto the safety of the plywood.

He glanced up through the tangle of hair sweeping across the tops of his eyes.

Down on Main Street, one M60 pounded away at Tommy's position. The other rotated toward him there on the catwalk.

Shoving himself up, he sprinted along the plank.

Rounds blazed behind him, catching up.

A haphazard jump onto the roof of the mercantile. In his peripheral vision he saw the SUV blazing forward, tracking him up Main Street. Shingles went to pieces around him, rounds cutting through rooftops and platforms, obliterating wood. He ran the length of the store and leapt onto the roof of the feed and supply, barely keeping ahead of the devastation.

A tracer round streaked down Main Street, Evan glancing over just in time to see it spark off the side of the SUV, lighting up the gasoline spill along the rear panel. As the next tracer sailed in, the three remaining Horsemen rolled out of the vehicle, sprinting for the buildings below Evan.

Another crack from the far end of the strip and one of the Horsemen yelped and went down.

The other two disappeared into the buildings below before Evan could get an angle.

The empty SUV rolled forward. A third tracer struck the tank, releasing a muffled *thoomp*. The vehicle rocked up on two tires and settled back down, engulfed in flame. Veering lazily east, it buried itself in the front porch of the casino on the far side, setting it on fire.

Evan's momentum carried him onto the platforms above the feed and supply. A network of fire-escape-like ladders and planks zigzagged down to earth. He aimed his ARES through the grid of crossbeams, but no one came into sight.

Another crack, another bright red streak of burning phosphor blazing down Main Street, another scream. Tommy was still using tracers, literally lighting the fallen Horseman up.

Evan jumped onto the roof of the neighboring hotel, risked a peek over the rooftop.

Tommy's target lay broken a few feet from the boardwalk. His hip was shattered, flesh and bone glistening through his jeans, and another round had obliterated his right buttock, the fabric singed. He'd shed his duster and his mask and was gasping into the ground, half his sweaty face powdered with dirt. Pale white skin, Nordic-blue eyes.

The next shot from Tommy took his knee.

The man recoiled, his body jumping in the dirt from impact. His leg came down bent wrong, tibia offset ninety degrees from thigh.

Another round sailed in to crush his shoulder.

Tommy trying to draw the others from cover.

No such luck.

Chin ribboned with frothy saliva, the wounded man looked up and spotted Evan. He tilted his head at Evan's position for his invisible colleagues, an admirable show of tactical prowess given his condition. And then, with his functional arm, he unholstered a sidearm and shot himself in the temple.

Tommy's voice rasped in Evan's ear: "Two down."

Before Evan could exhale, a semiauto coughed in the building below him, rounds blasting up through the roof. Another running jump sent Evan across the alley onto the scaffolding backing the façade of the blacksmith.

The plywood did not hold.

Riding an avalanche of splintering wood, he cascaded down, hitting a platform fifteen feet below. Miraculously it held.

But the scaffolding wobbled and started to tip.

Evan grabbed for a metal post and rode it down, boots ramming into an old blacksmith forge. He propelled himself off, tumbling free of the waterfall of materials smashing down behind him.

A burst of rounds followed him.

He dove for cover behind a heap of wreckage, risked a peek to pin down muzzle flash from the semiauto. A burly man, dark South Asian, sunglasses swung around backward so the arms pinched the sides of his substantial neck. His missing balaclava was probably the mask wrapped around the decoy armrest that Evan had shot at. Moving through pillars of fallen scaffolding, the man advanced, unleashing three-round bursts.

Evan squeezed off several rounds, opening space to scamper behind a massive anvil. Incoming sparked off the cast iron. Evan dropped flat, fired low, aiming for feet and ankles.

A groan announced the façade shifting overhead.

The whole building rocked vertiginously so it seemed that Evan was moving rather than the framed-out smithy around him.

He rose to a kneeling position, firing to hold his adversary at bay so the shop would cave in on him. At nine shots he dropped the magazine, snugged the new one, let fly two more rounds.

Another support beam snapped.

Evan sprinted for a side window and dove through. The stuntman-ready breakaway glass broke away and Evan landed in a heap in the alley.

The front of the blacksmith imploded but the side wall held. A billow of dust and detritus swept through the shattered window, swirling around Evan like a sandstorm. He found hands and knees, coughing and spitting, praying the big guy had been buried alive.

Not two seconds later the cheap siding gave way, the man bursting through the wall with linebacker strength, creating his own makeshift door. He collided with Evan, knocking the ARES into the dirt. His face was caked with debris, his fluttering eyes leaking tears.

He swung wildly. Evan gave him the gut, absorbing the blow to take the arm. Wrenching the limb into an arm bar, he spun the man down and around. Stepping over the shoulder for leverage, he broke the arm.

The man collapsed on his face and Evan snatched his ARES off the ground and shot him twice through the left shoulder blade and once through the head.

Tommy came over the radio channel: "Sounds like Pompeii lighting off. What's the sitrep, over?"

Evan coughed some more, his throat raw and dry. "Three down. You got eyes on four?"

"Negative."

Staggering to his feet, Evan threw an elbow through the window of the funeral home across the alley and hauled himself through. The trio of caskets standing on end in the window lent sporadic piano-key cover from the road.

"I'm next door now," Evan said, "heading for higher ground."

He limped for the stairs and hauled himself up. A musty loft stowed disassembled furniture, and a brief wooden ladder led to the roof. The big window facing Main Street was opaque from want of cleaning.

He swiped at the pane to get eyes on the fourth Horseman, saw nothing but a burro blinking at him dumbly from a vacant lot across the street, elastic lips stretching to gather in a thatch of weeds.

"Eyes up eyes up," Tommy barked in his ear. "On the porch right below y—"

The floor fountained around Evan's feet.

He jumped onto the ladder, scrambled to the roof, rungs disintegrating below his boots.

The roofs of the funeral home and saloon were level, a small blessing that made Evan's leap the easiest yet.

Until he landed and crashed straight through the saloon roof.

In a hail of drywall, he barreled down into the second-floor hallway, caught a flash of human beneath—Tommy with his rifle at the corner window. The collision knocked them along the carpet runner and onto the grand sweeping staircase to the bar.

In a tangle of limbs, they tumbled lower, pooling midway down. One of Tommy's wide-set front teeth was sitting at the wrong angle.

Tommy shoved Evan off, clutched at his shoulder with a grimace. "Nice aim, dumbass."

"Unintentional."

Tommy's rifle had been left behind toward the top of the stairs. As he scrambled up for it, Evan drew his ARES and bolted for the swinging saloon doors.

He waited at the threshold, pistol ready, listening for any sound from outside.

Three rounds punched through the wall behind him. He dropped, rolled out beneath the swinging doors, popped up in a crouch.

The last Horseman was waiting on the porch in front of the funeral home. The balaclava had been tugged back, the eye gap stretched wide, a face birthed through the gap. Flash of pretty green irises, wavy blond hair.

She fired another burst at his head before vanishing behind a pillar on the porch. Firing so she'd stay put, Evan rolled off the connecting boardwalk and fell three feet to the dirt.

A fist-size rock ground into his sternum, electrifying the knots in his chest. He snatched it up and threw it at the saloon doors. It struck the one on the right, setting it creaking on its hinges.

He dropped back out of sight, flat on his stomach.

"Tommy," he hissed beneath the screech of the swinging door. "Make noise inside."

"Copy that."

A clunk inside sounded like a rifle butt striking the stairs.

Hiding in the shadow of the boardwalk, Evan removed the

empty magazine. The slide on the ARES was forward—one cartridge left in the pistol. As silently as he could, he seated a fresh magazine and pressed it until he felt the click of the mag catch engaging.

Deep breath. Then he combat-crawled along the ground toward the funeral home as quietly as he could, shoving furrows of dirt before his forearms.

Bootfall strained the planks of the boardwalk. She'd swung around the pillar but held fire.

Behind Evan the swinging door groaned a few more times, making a dry-paint rasp against its counterpart as it slowed. Evan prayed she'd hold focus there, thinking he'd retreated inside the saloon.

Tommy made another thump inside, this one less obvious.

Evan dragged himself forward, kneecaps aching, ARES in his left hand.

He heard the faint click of a bootheel setting down just above on the boardwalk and then the tap of a toe. She was no more than five yards ahead of him, easing along toward the saloon as he tugged himself quietly forward beneath her. All she had to do was lean over the boardwalk and there he'd be, laid out like a spatchcocked chicken.

Another click of heel. Another tap.

The saloon doors were quiet now, Tommy refraining from making more racket inside.

Evan inchwormed another few feet forward, hunched to draw a knee beneath him for an explosive rise.

Click. Tap.

She was right there on the boardwalk above him. He heard the rush of her steady breathing. Then silence.

Had she heard him? Was she readying to lunge over the boardwalk? If so, his pistol was a poor match for her AR-15.

Waiting, he strained his ears.

Then he heard it. The slightest tick of a sling swivel on her rifle stock.

He kicked out perpendicular from the base of the boardwalk, sliding on his back through the dirt, pistol steady in both hands.

She wheeled but there was no time to get the big barrel around.

Evan fired upward through her pelvis in case she had on body armor, knocking her back through the window, the stenciled words—UNDERTAKER AND FURNITURE MAKER—fragmenting into Scrabble pieces.

She struck the center coffin sideways, embedded fetally into the rotted velvet lining. He popped to his feet, sights leveled on her face, but she was no longer a threat. Her mouth moved, a croak issuing forth: "We . . . we *are*."

And then she stilled. A crimson bubble formed at her lips, popped. Her head sagged to the side, eyes open, staring blankly at Evan. A beading of blood crept from the corner of her mouth.

"These fuckin' people. They keep gettin' killed."

Evan started at Tommy's voice, swiveling to aim at him.

Tommy was aiming right back.

Just where they'd left matters at the Watering Hole.

The air tasted like dirt and hay and they were both breathing hard. Neither lowered his weapon. Across the street, black smoke belched from the casino.

Tommy said, "They tore down the whole goddamned town but here we are, still standing."

"Yes," Evan said. "We are." When he swallowed, his throat felt chalky. "What now?"

Dust powdered Tommy's beard. "What now indeed?"

They watched each other's eyes and trigger fingers. Tommy's front tooth, the crooked one, looked fine already. Maybe that was a Tommy thing. When a tooth got knocked loose, he just snapped it back into place.

Tommy lowered the rifle and a moment later, Evan holstered his pistol.

"You look like shit on toast," Tommy said, and began ambling down Main Street.

Evan paused to stare back at the last Horseman.

Motionless, curled on her side, fair of hair and eye.

All four of the assassins looked wildly different and yet somehow alike, their varied features made to rhyme by the matching non-expressions sitting atop them. Cold and reptilian, they were dispassionate operators, pure killers in the mode in which Evan himself had been raised.

He stared at her a long time before trudging after Tommy.

With Tommy's hips and their respective aches, the walk to the chapel took longer than it should have. At his rig, Tommy disassembled his battle rifle, seated the components back into the Hardigg, slid the case into his truck vault.

"Gimme my rifle mags back," Tommy said.

They sat hard and dense in Evan's right thigh cargo pocket, the skin beneath bruised from all his tumbling. He ripped the Velcro flap open, handed them both to Tommy.

"And the 1911 magazine."

"Not that one," Evan said. "It was a replacement for your faulty product."

Tommy spit a stream of tobacco juice between his and Evan's boots. "Fair."

Then he drew his pistol and shot out Evan's back tire.

Evan said, "What the fuck?"

"You got a spare," Tommy said. "I need a head start back to town."

"Why do you get the head start?"

"'Cuz I loaned you the rifle."

"And I came out here to cover your ass from hit men who wanted to kill you."

"No. You did it so them assholes wouldn't go to town and turn innocent folk into collateral damage. 'Cuz you're so fucking pure." Tommy slammed the tailgate up. "So be pure. Fix your tire. I'll be waiting for you back in town."

Swinging open the driver's door, Tommy grabbed the oh-shit bar and hauled himself in with a groan. Reversing away from the altar, he rolled down the window, spit once more in Evan's direction. "Namaste, motherfucker."

61

Cracked Wide with Remorse

Tommy knocked out a tattoo against the storm cellar. "It's me, open the fuck up."

Impatient, he banged some more.

The primed steel bulkhead door yawned upward and Hick blinked up into the light. He held the shotgun horizontally at his side.

"Inside," Tommy said.

As Hick clanked up the ladder, Tommy kept an alert watch on the dirt path to the front gate. It was impossible that Evan would have gotten his truck back online and here already but old habits die hard. Hick followed him to the porch.

Once they were inside, Tommy wheeled on him. "You took that boy? You took him from the park?"

Hick sipped in a stuttering inhalation.

"You *lied* to me? Why'd you take that boy?" Tommy's restraint was shot. His shoulder was throbbing from the spill down the saloon stairs. His thoughts tumbled with images—the photograph Evan had shoved in his face, the terror in that poor boy's eyes when he was bleeding out in the truck, Hick's gritted teeth as he clenched the child in his grip. "You'd better talk, boy, right now."

Hick was starting to hyperventilate.

"God*damn it.* What the hell did you do?" Tommy tensed up, a red-hot iron of pain jabbing through his deltoid. Reflexively he jerked his other hand back to clutch the shoulder.

At first he didn't understand what was happening.

Hick flinched away violently, hands thrown up in front of his face, palms out. "I'm sorry, I'm sorry, okay?" His legs buckled and he collapsed on the floor, forearm raised in a bar across his face. The words came warped through sobs: "I'm sorry—just don't—sorry—please, just—" His left cheek was lost to a twitch, bunching again and again at the temple, and his shoulder had arched up protectively toward his ear, head ducked behind it as if to brace against a belt lash. "I'm sorry, just don't, just don't . . ."

The dime dropped and Tommy caught up to the situation, that his own arm looked to be drawn back for a blow.

He lowered it.

When he looked again at Hick on the floor, he saw right down into him, saw a boy raised in the shadow of his father's rage, saw the adolescent bellowing as a lit cigar turned his right ear into a smear of scar tissue, saw the young man who'd filled himself with poison and hate just to feel something other than empty.

Tommy sank to his haunches, his hip aching to high heaven. Hick sobbed some more, scuttling away on the floor. Tommy showed him his palms.

"It's okay," Tommy said softly. "I'm not gonna hurt you. I wasn't gonna hurt you."

"I'm going to hell. I helped kill that boy and them people. I'm going to hell." Hick was weeping fully now, cracked wide with remorse, as pure and low and heartbreaking a register of grief as Tommy had ever heard. "I deserve to die for it. I deserve it."

Tommy set a hand on Hick's shoulder and the boy didn't jerk away. Hick's sweat and body heat came up through his flannel against Tommy's palm.

"I don't wanna go to jail." Hick sobbed into the floorboards, one hand clutching the tattered skirt of the ruinous couch. "Don't let them take me. Don't leave me. Please don't leave me. I don't got no one else."

Tommy's eyes misted. He said, "I know."

"Please don't leave me. Please."

Tommy's phone shrilled that old-fashioned ringtone. He rose, knees cracking, and checked caller ID. It was Judy from the diner.

At his feet, Hick cried like a baby. There was no other phrase for it.

Tommy's callused thumb found the button. He lifted the phone to his ear, said, "Yeah?"

"I got them folks here like you asked," Judy said. "Christmas Day and all. You have my address."

Tommy said, "On our way."

62

All Kinds of Bad

The Hildebrandt house was abandoned.

Evan searched it stem to stern. Basement, attic, storm cellar, beneath the porch.

He stood in the dank garage awhile staring at that Dodge Ram trimmed in powder blue. No plates. Dented bumper. Caved-in front panel. Shattered left headlight.

A two-ton murder weapon blasted through the heart of a *quinceañera* and the body of an eight-year-old boy.

His hand tightened around the grip of his ARES 1911.

In his mind he recited the names of the dead.

Gabriel Martinez.

Incarnazión and Eberardo Escareño, the aunt and uncle.

Atanasio Escareño, the son home on leave from the marines.

Which one of their skulls had caused the depression in the bumper? Whose body had cratered the front panel? What bone had fractured the headlight?

The muscles across Evan's chest plate were tighter than ever. He dug at them with his fingertips, felt the corded fibers roll across the ribs. Pectoralis major and minor, latissimus dorsi, subscapularis, serratus anterior, coracobrachialis—a Latin mess of spasm.

He walked back to his truck. An American flag snapped and rustled atop the majestic pole. Seeing it raised above this house felt grotesque, perverse, and Evan fought an urge to pulley it down, fold it up, and carry it away from this place.

Instead he drove into town.

Tommy had turned his phone off—old dog, new tricks—so Evan prowled the brief stretch of downtown, looking for his rig. Nowhere in sight. The sheriff's station was lit up, the interior visible from the road. No cruiser or SUV in the lot, no sign of Tommy, Hick, or Sheriff Narcissus. Just Deputy Ronny Ratliff at his desk, working late, chewing the end of a pen as he clicked away at his computer, looking troubled.

Evan waited a spell to see if someone else emerged from the station bathroom, but twenty minutes said it was just Deputy Ratliff in there.

Where the hell was everyone else?

Evan cruised slowly past the diner, the boarded-up movie house, and the gas station. The dilapidated bowling alley fluttered with movement, the plastic sheets nailed to its gutted frame rattling in the wind. Cutting behind the bar, he spotted the deputy cruiser in the rear lot.

Clay Clemmons.

That's what Evan would do, then. Kick over one domino and watch the rest fall.

He parked.

This time he entered the Watering Hole from the back door.

He'd anticipated some hostility but the reaction to his entrance was cinematic in its intensity.

As the door clamped shut behind him, all faces swiveled in unison, a school of fish turning in concert. Someone pulled the plug on the jukebox, terminating Willie Nelson's highwayman days. The patrons—mostly men—bristled and tugged together, shoulder to shoulder, tightening into the security of a pack.

The *knock-knock-knock* of Evan's boots across the floor echoed off the hard surfaces.

Hands lowered, he walked toward the dead center of the pack, which gave way around him.

Clay Clemmons was bellied up to the bar, sipping a PBR.

Evan elbowed up next to him. Behind the bar, Dougie was working a toothpick around in his mouth, loose-jawed. The other men stayed back a few steps, forming a half-assed semicircle that pinned Evan in. But he wasn't scared. He didn't have to be, because he could smell that they were.

Clemmons said, "Buy you a drink?"

Evan said, "That's why I came."

Dougie snatched the bottle of Aylesbury Duck from the wooden step display, set it down in front of Evan alongside a lowball loaded with too much ice. About two ounces of clear liquid remained at the bottom of that designer bottle, the last pour of decent vodka within city limits.

Evan wanted those two ounces in his system. Two ounces and not a drop more. Alcohol was the best kind of poison for him. It muted the roar thrumming beneath the icy surface, helped cage the mess and chaos of feeling.

He was just reaching for the bottle to pour when Clemmons said, "You killed Vic's boy."

"Did I?" Evan said.

"We both know you did."

"Got evidence? Prints, footage, forensics, DNA? Lined out motive, means, opportunity?"

Clemmons rolled his lips inward, a nonverbal tell, suppressing intense emotion. "You know it. We all know it."

"And why do you think," Evan said, "I'd do a thing like that? Did Red do something bad?"

Clemmons glowered at him. Then he set his broad strong hands on the ledge of the lacquered bar and pushed his barstool out, the wooden legs giving a cry against the floor. He pulled himself up.

He wasn't tall but he wasn't short either, an ideal heavyweight fighter's build. Chest at least forty inches thick, sixteen-inch arms. He was somewhat muscle-bound, which would help, but if he landed a direct blow it would be crippling. When he knuckled his smashed nose, it gave a crackling of cartilage. The scar tissue at the edges of his eyes squared his head, gave him pit-bull intensity.

He wore a SIG P226 at his hip and a badge on that barrel chest.

"We don't gotta act no more," he said. "So what do you say we cut the pleasantries and get to it."

The gaggle of men pulled back from them several strides more, clearing room. A few women at the perimeter tittered nervously.

"Am I talking to you as a cop?" Evan said. "Because I don't fight cops."

"What do you do, then?" Clemmons asked.

"Run away, generally."

Clemmons pinched his lower lip between his teeth. "Figures, don't it." Now a half smile came on. "Lucky for you, I'm willing to accommodate."

He took off his badge, unbuckled his gun belt with his holstered pistol, and set both on the bar. He picked up his empty PBR bottle, flipped it, caught it by the neck.

"Any chance you want to talk this out instead?" Evan said.

"Not one single chance in hell."

"That's too bad," Evan said. "I was hoping I wouldn't have to hurt you."

Clemmons's face tightened. With no warning, he swung the bottle at Evan's head.

Evan got his forearm up in time to take the brunt, his face turned so the shards pattered harmlessly off the back of his skull. Already he was rising, kicking the stool out from under him to make space.

Clemmons led with a big sloppy haymaker, Evan limboing out of the way of the swooping fist. As Clemmons's momentum carried him by, Evan had a clear angle for a throat strike to collapse the windpipe. It would've been the most efficient way out, but: manners.

Instead he threw a jab to the kidney, but it barely shuddered the big man, who pivoted once more, leading with a side hammer fist. This one came closer but Evan slipped it, resisting the twitch of muscle memory impelling him to jam *bil jee* thrusting fingers through the deputy's eye into his brain. Restraining himself, he instead dislocated the right thumb with a quick raking grab-and-twist and then gave an open-hand slap to Clemmons's ear, ringing his bell.

The others were clapping and shouting now, urging the deputy on.

Clemmons roared and pivoted to bull Evan off his feet, clipping Evan's eye with the top of his head and smashing him through two barstools, their occupants flying up and off just in time. Evan bounced off the bar, keeping his feet. He'd taken Clemmons's dominant hand out of the fight but the guy was still much stronger and having to not kill him put Evan at a disadvantage.

Evan's left eye throbbed, an ache at the top of the orbit. Clemmons's thumb sagged low toward the wrist, the meaty base bulging and red. Resetting himself, he gripped the thumb with his opposing fist and snapped it back into place.

Evan snatched the vodka bottle off the bar, spun it around his left hand to wield it like a club, the label flashing by as he drew it back. Those precious last few ounces swished inside, making him loath to smash the bottle. He hesitated.

Clemmons charged, swinging wildly. Switching his grip to protect the bottle, Evan skipped back from the flurry, jabbing him with the thick glass bottom—crotch, solar plexus, sternum—between blows. That slowed the man's momentum, each step taking on more weight, his knees starting to give.

That bulged neck of the bottle and its ridges, spaced the width of a fist for easy handling, made the makeshift weapon feel not so makeshift.

Off-balance, Clemmons threw a jab. Evan countered with a forearm block and gave him a bottle knock to the forehead, sending the deputy sprawling. Clemmons bowling-balled into the legs of the onlookers. They tried to help him up, but he thrashed at them and raged up to his feet again under his own power, nostrils flaring.

Thrusting rather than swinging the bottle had kept it from shattering, preserving the vodka. Evan set the intact bottle back down, showed his palms. "Try again?"

Clemmons lunged not at Evan but for the bar. Ripping his SIG P226 from the holster, he swung it at Evan.

Evan caught the barrel, shoving it away from the patrons and north as Clemmons tugged the trigger, riddling the ceiling. The muzzle flash burned Evan's palm, a fighter's stigmata, but he held tight and wrenched the weapon free, dislocating Clemmons's thumb again. His hands blurred as he field-stripped it in seconds—mag dropping, slide levered free, spring flipped into thin air, barrel flicked loose. The parts rained down at his feet.

The bottle's stamp on Clemmons's forehead looked like a horse hoof. The deputy dabbed at the swollen ring of red with his fingertips, then readied for the next charge.

"Stop!"

The voice froze Clemmons in place.

The crowd unfolded from its half circle, revealing Ronny Ratliff. His hand resting on his holstered pistol, he slowly closed the distance from the front door.

The others yielded to him.

He looked from Clemmons to Evan to the disassembled pistol at Evan's feet.

"That your service weapon?" Ronny asked.

Clemmons said nothing.

Ronny's focus moved to the badge on the bar. "Did you take that off?" he asked. "Of your own volition?"

Clemmons's lantern jaw shifted left, right.

"I need an answer now, Deputy."

Clemmons gave a little nod.

Ronny walked to the bar, stared down at the six-point star. "You take your badge off in a situation like this, you lose the right to wear it anywhere else." He picked up Clemmons's badge, slid it into his back pocket. "Consider yourself on administrative leave, Deputy."

Clemmons started to answer but Ronny said, "Go."

Clemmons grimaced, ran his tongue beneath his lower lip. He glowered once more at Evan and then walked out.

Ronny looked at Dougie and then the others, who shuffled on their feet sheepishly.

Finally he brought his attention to Evan, his eyes flicking to the bulge of the holster beneath his shirt. Ronny drew in a nervous breath but his eyes were resolute. He removed his hand from the butt of his SIG.

"You're trying to get to the bottom of what happened at Calvary Park," he told Evan.

Evan dipped his chin. Affirmative.

"I am, too."

Evan thought about Ronny's spending Christmas evening holed up alone in the station on his computer and believed him.

The chief deputy was tall and slender but filled out his uniform with a solid build. A strong jawline offset those jug ears. He was young still and plenty affable, but he didn't seem eager to please. He seemed centered around an inner calm.

"Deputy Clemmons has been relieved of duty," Ronny said. "I'm not gonna play games and charge you with assaulting an officer when it looks plenty clear that he assaulted you right back."

Evan said, "Understood."

"Just because we don't have anything to charge you with yet doesn't mean I don't know that you're all kinds of bad." Ronny's eyes found the bulge of the pistol at Evan's waistline once more. "I know you could probably hurt me if you chose to. Or any of these people or Hick or anyone else. But I want you to know. I'll stand up to you if I have to."

Evan said, "Understood."

"I'm in charge here right now. I'm wearing my badge. Right over my heart. I'm asking you to leave the premises peacefully. I'm asking you to respect my authority. Will you do that?"

"Yes, sir," Evan said, and meant it. He glanced at the Aylesbury Duck on the bar, that last bit of vodka banding the base. "Just a sip and I'll be on my way."

Focused on the confrontation, Dougie reached for the bottle but knocked it with the back of his hand. It slid off the bar, shattering at his feet.

Dougie cursed, looked down at the broken glass, then up at Evan.

Evan looked back at him, forlorn. *"Really?"*

He was done here now.

He moved to the rear door, walking backward, keeping an eye

on the townsfolk. Clemmons's cruiser was gone from the lot. Evan climbed into his truck.

He pulled an iPhone from his cargo pocket, the one he'd lifted off Clay Clemmons in the brawl.

It was locked, password-protected.

On his RoamZone, Evan called up his gallery of master faces. The tech had come out of a computer-science school in Tel Aviv. Built using a generative adversarial network, the nine master faces embodied enough high-level semantic features to successfully impersonate 87 percent of the population.

He held one screen up to face the other, scrolled through the images with his thumb, and was inside Clemmons's device in seconds.

Going to the messaging app, he flicked through various conversations, finding Sheriff Joy close to the top. SHARE LOCATION was toggled on.

He looked at the dot holding steady in a residential section of Calvary several miles away.

He had a hunch that wherever Grady Joy was, Hick and Tommy wouldn't be far behind. Or vice versa.

Initiating GPS routing, he pulled out from the lot. It had been a long brutal mission.

It was time to end it.

63

Lying in Wait

When Judy greeted Tommy and Hick at her front door, her face looked wrong—ruddy and tense, no sign of the softer lines he'd grown accustomed to.

Wordlessly, she stepped back and let them in.

Tommy braced himself and followed, keeping Hick at his back.

A tiny crowded living room let into the kitchen, where pots bubbled on stovetops and a turkey browned inside a wall oven. Yesenia was present, that lady Dot from the motel, and the coroner-notary, a short man with a rotund belly, a troll's nose, and tufts of hair sprouting from his ears. There were a few more village elders Tommy recognized from the diner and the bar.

Lying in wait in front of the TV cabinet, uniform starched and creased, teeth gleaming in a matinee smile, was Sheriff Grady Joy. He aimed that wolfish grin at Tommy, waiting for a reaction Tommy did not give.

"Hick, why don't you go back to the bedroom," Grady said. "Let the adults talk."

Hick hesitated at Tommy's side.

"Don't look at him," Grady said. "Get."

Hick glanced tentatively from face to face but got nothing back.

Judy said, "Mawmaw's in the back, honey, watchin' the TV. Why don't you set a spell with her?"

Tommy gave Hick a slight nod and then Hick withdrew up the hall.

Though Judy's big dinner was still making, she'd set out snacks and fixings for the guests. The men ate off soggy paper plates sagging under clumps of mac and cheese mixed with canned chili. The coroner-notary hovered over a mason jar filled with pickled asparagus, eating spear after spear like pretzel sticks. On a red Christmas plate, Wheat Thins wreathed a ball of pimento cheese rolled in nuts. A fire crackled in the hearth, throwing off the aroma of cherrywood.

Sheriff Joy crossed his arms, leaned back so his gym-tempered chest puffed out. "You really thought you could call a meeting in *my* town and I wouldn't catch wind?"

"I didn't give it much thought one way or another."

"We take care of our own here," Grady said. "A concept you types just don't seem to get."

Tommy laughed.

"Something funny?"

"Yeah. Yeah it is."

"Why don't you edify us?"

"'Take care of your own,'" Tommy said. "You got two boys shot to shit, another dead, and that one there"—he jabbed his finger stub toward the hall down which Hick had just vanished—"next up in the crosshairs."

"You think I can't protect that boy?"

"No," Tommy said. "I *know* you can't protect that boy. Your track record knows it, too."

Dot looked up, lips pursed, and the coroner-notary paused his mastication mid-crunch.

"Listen close because here's the plan," Grady said. "You're gonna get in your truck and you're gonna drive outta town straightaway. And then I won't lock you up for obstruction of justice."

"Me obstructing justice," Tommy said. "That's rich, given all the shit you've shoveled to cover up what happened at Calvary Park."

"Wasn't no cover-up," Grady said.

"What happened at Calvary Park?" Yesenia asked. "Those people who got run down?"

Grady didn't answer.

Tommy said, "You won't charge Hick for what he did because that'd implicate you."

"Implicate him?" Dot said. "In what?"

Grady kept his smile steady, patting the air with his palms. "There's nothing for me to be implicated in," he told Tommy. "No matter if your friend told you otherwise."

"He's not my friend."

"That's good. Because I'm not extending the same offer to him I'm giving you. He's not free to leave. He's gonna answer for what he's done. Next time he pops his head up, we're gonna put a hole through it. It's been a rocky few weeks but I'm gonna get order restored around here. No more Mexican gangsters. No more random shootings. No more terrorizing the good working people of this town."

Tommy looked around the room. "Does he speak for you?"

Averted eye contact, shuffling of feet. Someone coughed.

"I asked a question. Does he speak for all of you?"

The coroner piped up: "Been a lotta killing. You see a better way through?"

Tommy pawed at his mustache. "Y'all got an escalating goat f—" He caught himself. "Same problems getting worse all the time. You can't just throw a thesaurus at 'em and expect anything to be different."

"What do you know about our problems?" Dot said.

"There's a time-stamped photograph," Tommy said, "showing Red and Hick in their truck with that boy from Calvary Park. The one they ran over along with three other folks. He's dying right there in their truck."

A few sharp inhalations. Dot straightened up in her armchair.

"Is that what happened?" Yesenia said. "Is that really what happened?"

"That photograph's not real," Grady said. "They can deepfake that stuff now in no time flat."

"So lemme get this straight," Tommy said. "Four people were killed in your jurisdiction—"

"Gang violence," Grady said.

"—and not only do you still have no leads and no suspects, but someone else took the trouble to gin up a fake photo incriminating Hick and Red. Why would they do that?"

"I can't answer for crazy."

"How about for incompetence?" Tommy asked. "How much time you spend over in Hayesville knocking on doors and following leads? I assume you've got all sorts of casework in the system, time logged and what-have-you."

Grady wet his lips. "Chief Deputy Ratliff investigated some."

"But not you or Deputy Clemmons. Wonder why that is. Four folks killed on my watch might make me want to kick over a few rocks."

Grady's smile faltered. "Boys do stupid shit. Retaliate and whatnot. Isn't it my job to protect our boys?" Quickly he added, "Against false claims."

Shock dawned across Yesenia's face. "You covered for those boys?"

"People were killed at the park," Judy said. "That little boy."

"And you swept it under the rug?" Yesenia's cheeks burned with indignation. "Those families?" Her voice cracked. "And you kept Red free where that—that *sicario* could get to him?"

"I kept us safe," Grady said evenly. "That's my job. To protect us all from those animals over in Hayesville. You want that shitshow coming here?"

"A shitshow's coming all right," Tommy said. "I been talking to folks at the state level, a few prosecutors, too. They're reluctant to get involved but if things don't clean up fast they will. And if they do, they're gonna turn this town inside out, tear it apart, find out what other deals Sheriff Joy struck in the name of keeping his kind of order. You think you can afford that, Sheriff? Buncha outsiders shaking you to see what else falls outta yer pockets? On the eve of an election?"

"They won't find anything but falsified evidence. And even if it *was* real, doesn't mean I knew anything about it. Your buddy wants to leak that tape, he can go right ahead."

"He ain't my buddy," Tommy said. "And he won't leak it. That's not his game."

"No? What's his game?"

"Killing folks who deserve it."

Grady's clean-shaven cheeks glistened, a thin film of perspiration. "Did Red deserve it?"

"Yeah, he did," Tommy said. "But that don't mean it shoulda happened. And guess what, cowboy? If you keep covering up the murder of four people to save your own hide, you'll deserve it, too."

Grady wasn't smiling anymore. "I'm a trained sheriff. What's your friend gonna do?"

"He's not my friend," Tommy said. "He's the Nowhere Man."

Grady's face went pallid. He crossed his arms again just to have something to do with them. He didn't look so tough in his uniform now, he looked like a kid playing dress-up. "No, sir. That's not real. He's not real."

A few of the others were in shock. The coroner leaned forward slowly and placed the mason jar back on the coffee table. Dot took off her spectacles and tipped her face into her hand. One of the women Tommy didn't recognize said, "Who's that? Who's the Nowhere Man?"

Grady took a napkin off the side table, dabbed at his forehead. "Just an urban legend. He's just a myth."

"But you know better, don't you?" Tommy said. "So listen close because here's the *real* plan. You step aside and get gone while you can. Take that symmetrical wife of yours away for a spell. Chief Deputy Ratliff takes over as acting sheriff. Is it too late to get his name on the ballot?"

Yesenia said, "Jim?"

The coroner-notary, evidently also the county election official, said, "It is not."

Tommy said, "I bring Hick in, Ratliff charges him properly. I got a lawyer coming in first thing tomorrow morning for the boy, already covered the retainer."

"What about your friend?" Grady asked.

"He ain't my friend. And. He might find himself less keen on bringing Hick to justice if he's already being brought to justice. Funny how that works. Almost like we should make laws around this stuff."

"No, I mean, will he come after *me*?" A moment too late, Grady realized the words that had escaped his mouth.

From the looks of the others, they were none too impressed hearing the top-of-mind concern of the most powerful man in town.

Tommy let him marinate in the room's reaction a bit. Then he said, "He don't like killing law enforcement. But he makes an exception for those who cross a line and stay across it."

Grady glanced around the room, gauging temperatures. Judy looked away from him. And then Yesenia. The coroner–notary–county election official followed, and then the ladies on the couch and the men standing at the periphery averted their eyes, too.

Grady ran his tongue over his teeth, gathered himself, glared haughtily around the room. "Okay. That's what you want. You want some junior deputy standing between you and the kind of chaos and crime out there waiting past town limits, be my guest."

With a stiff, angry posture, he walked out. The door slammed.

For a time the only noise was the crackle of the fire and hum of the stovetop. Yesenia pressed a handkerchief to one eye and then the other. She set her hands in her lap, stared down at her knuckles. "Hick agreed to all this?"

Tommy shook his head. "Not yet."

"You gonna go talk to him?"

"I am." Tommy hesitated. "I was hoping you would, too."

Yesenia's face broke, mouth downbent, forehead furled with grief. She pressed her fist to her mouth. She made no noise but her shoulders rose and quivered and she hunched against a few sobs.

Tommy waited patiently at the mouth of the hall, and everyone else waited right along with him.

She composed herself.

And then she rose and led Tommy back.

64

The Vaguest Premonition of Loosening

The gathering was letting out, folks streaming down the diner waitress's walkway, finding their respective vehicles. They looked beaten down, breath misting in the air as they said their farewells. The sheriff had crawled out of there first, looking worse for wear.

On the rooftop of the house across the street, Evan knelt between a brick chimney and a satellite-TV dish. While the smoke wisping from the chimney didn't warm him, it gave texture to the air.

Tommy's rig remained at the curb in front.

Evan figured he had Hick with him inside that house. Ten minutes passed and then another ten. Evan wondered what they were getting up to.

The cold inhalations cramped up his chest even more. He pulled his shoulders back to stretch out his intercostals, but the pain migrated, knitting up the spaces between his ribs. He couldn't remember the last time his muscles felt so locked up—maybe after the fight in that surgical suite in Guaridón.

Rising, he spread his arms and put the heel of one hand against the chimney and the other against the backing post of the sat dish. Drawing in a deep breath, he leaned forward into the stretch, his arms bowing back. From pectorals to biceps, the muscles across the front of his torso screamed. He found the edge, leaned into it, not forcing it too hard.

At first nothing happened except pain. Then he felt the vaguest premonition of loosening. His arms started tingling from the choked-off blood flow. He found his breath, let it guide him, allowed his focus to move inside his body. The muscles yielded millimeter by millimeter, tendons stretching, the sheath of the fascia pulling itself smooth.

Breath. Pain. Release.

That was all he was. His breath was his center and the point of dissolution.

Below him Tommy's rig and the front door of the waitress's house grew swimmy. He held the stretch, held it longer, balancing on the knife's edge between releasing muscle and tearing it. Static bubbled across his field of vision, his thoughts dissolving and re-forming hypnopompically.

He awakens in his room, a thousand stars disrupting the creamy black sky beyond the dormer window. Strider stirs on the rug beside his bed, collar clanking.

Evan rises.

Is this a memory? Or is it a dream?

Something draws him out into the upstairs hall, and then his bare feet are padding down the worn runner of the stairs. Jack's farmhouse is dark, but a golden glow from the study maps patterns across the downstairs hall. Jack never goes to bed without pokering out the embers, which means he's still in there among his towering walls of books and his memories, basking in the fireplace.

Evan's footfall is silent on the ground floor. He wears boxer shorts, and a T-shirt that his fifteen-year-old frame is only just able to fill out.

He nears the study's doorless entrance.

Light pools across the floor like water, flickers across the ceiling. On the wall across from the doorway, shadows dance like ragged puppets.

Evan keeps on silently. He nears the doorway, breathes in a welcoming waft of peat, cedar, the comforting must of oft-thumbed books. He hesitates, drawn to the room. But then he eases past unseen, Jack's dark form beckoning in his peripheral vision.

He does not turn his head.

Instead he keeps on, his legs carrying him to the front door.

On cold feet he steps onto the porch, the world yawning open, vast and perpetually indecipherable. It is no longer night, but the first pale stirring of morning. As he stands beholding the unbounded universe, the sun gives an abrupt lurch upward, its full globe clearing the jagged crest of the not-quite-mountains to the east, rays of light trumpeting down on him.

Warmed in their glow, he blinks against the pain of seeing.

There on the freezing rooftop, gripping chimney and backing post like a low-rent Samson, Evan's wings cracked open, fascia and tendon de-webbing, his intercostals yielding with a hot cherry burn.

His shoulders unyoked from their binding of spasm and scar tissue, his chest bowing forward, unbound.

He gasped.

Sweat streamed down his face, fording the edges of his lips.

He gasped again, felt the crisp air press his lungs outward, felt it expand to fill new spaces.

He released his hold, torso afire and alive.

Down below, the front door of the waitress's house opened.

Tommy led Hick down the walk to his rig. Hick kept his head lowered, shoulders slumped. He looked like a wrung rag.

Tommy opened the passenger door and Hick climbed in.

Tommy walked around, got in himself, glanced around suspiciously, and then drove away.

Evan crab-walked down the shingles, dangled from the gutter, slipped from the roof. His pickup waited hidden behind the neighboring barn.

He climbed in.

And pursued.

65

Oh, God

Tommy drove toward town. He'd raised Chief Deputy Ratliff on the phone, told him to expect them. Hick sat in the passenger seat, arms wrapped around his midsection in a low hug, face wan.

He trembled.

Tommy kept vigilant, eyes ticking from the rearview to the dark streets ahead, minding intersections, driveways, the dark haunted spaces between trees in the runs of forest.

As he neared town, a pair of headlights glowed to life too close behind him.

He stiffened.

Hick said, "What?"

He turned around.

"Oh," he said. "Oh, God."

Tommy sped up, careening onto the main drag of Calvary, speeding for the sheriff's station. His knee held the steering wheel steady as he clicked down the driver's window, his right hand groping along the bench seat in the back, searching for the Benelli shotgun.

"What do we do?" Hick said. "What are we supposed to do?"
Tommy said, "Quiet."

He found the stock, tugged the shotgun forward, rested the barrel across his forearm aimed out the open window for when Evan drew level.

It'd be a race to the sheriff's station. They flew past the old movie house, the bar, and then Evan made his move.

Too late Tommy saw he was going for a PIT maneuver. He slammed on the brakes to change the angle of impact but Evan's pickup nudged the rear right panel just behind the wheel well, sending Tommy's rig coasting sideways on the road. It rotated in an arc across the front of Evan's hood and slammed into the gutted bowling alley, knocking a maw through the plastic tarps and window framing. Rubble rained down on Tommy's roof and hood, the truck embedded in the building.

Grabbing Hick by the collar, Tommy rolled out the driver's door into the building, dragging the boy with him and flinging him toward the interior. Silt sheeted down across their shoulders. "Go," he said. "*Go.*"

Hick kicked to get his feet beneath him, sliding out on the shattered hardwood floor.

Tommy cast a look back through the windows of his truck in time to catch a shadowy form melt from the pickup. The Ford F-150 idled at the curb behind Evan, exhaust misting up across his shoulders.

He started for them.

Tommy stumbled back, checking the load on the Benelli, his hip banging into a stack of rain-soggy Sheetrock.

The plastic tarps heaved against the wind, sails at high sea. The dark form appeared here—no, there. Tommy swiveled the shotgun, holding aim.

But then at once Evan was in front of him, no longer a form but a person. Before Tommy could adjust, Evan slammed the shotgun north. It discharged into what remained of the roof. Tommy stumbled back, face twisted in anguish.

Evan kept on, steady, unremitting.

Tommy drew for the piece at his side but Evan swatted it aside and Tommy kept staggering back, trying to hold ground on what was left in his aching legs.

He heard his own voice, an old man's croak shouting hoarsely, "Go, Hick! Run, boy. *Run!*"

Evan coasted forward, his face uncreased and lifeless, a train coasting on well-greased tracks. Watching him come, Tommy felt terror—terror that what he saw before him could be contained in the same thing he thought he'd known before.

Tommy retreated another few clumsy steps, felt his groin muscle ache and ache. Demo and weather had stripped the studs bare. They rose up around them like saplings or the bars of a cell.

Tommy ripped a combat knife from the sheath at his belt but Evan's hands blurred and the blade was gone, skittering into the darkness, and Tommy could hear Hick crying out in terror behind him.

A post struck him in the back and his hip almost gave but he reset his base and swung at Evan.

Evan dodged the blow, kicked him in the chest, and he felt a rib crack, felt the floor rise up to smack his shoulder blades, knocking the air from his frame in a single clump.

Evan gave up no space, keeping right there on him. Tommy lashed out at him with a boot, felt his groin muscle go, and yelped.

He was terrified. He was roaring. *"Stop, Evan! Evan, stop!"*

The ARES was in Evan's hand, the beautiful 1911 Tommy himself had machined lovingly, had freed the graceful living shape of death from inside a block of metal, had drilled the pivot points for the fire-control group, had oiled and nestled with great care in the foam of a Pelican case. Now his own work of art was pointed down at him.

Behind him he could hear Hick weeping. The boy had given up, fallen to the floor. There was no running from the Nowhere Man. There was never any running from the Nowhere Man, and even Hick knew it.

Evan crouched over Tommy, backlit. He had no face, no eyes.

Evan's hand pulsed around the ARES and Tommy winced but then the pistol was spun around, handle lowered to Tommy, an offering.

"Go on, then." Evan's voice came low, steady. "You want to stop me, stop me. Prove your code. Prove it over mine. After what that boy did, you prove it."

Tommy tried to scuttle back, had nowhere to go. "You fucking crazy?"

"Stand up," Evan said.

Tommy jerked in a breath, fire rolling up his left side. He tried to suppress a moan but failed.

Evan said, "Stand up, old man."

"My ribs are broke."

"Stand. Up."

Tommy rolled to his side, ribs, hip, and groin groaning. But that was okay. He'd known pain of every stripe and shade and it wasn't gonna stop him now. He grabbed on to a load-bearing post and pulled himself to his feet. He was drooling blood, a ribbon dangling from his chin. Somewhere in the fracas he'd split his lower lip and swallowed his tobacco. He armed off the blood, breath catching.

Evan stood there, unmoving, the proffered ARES 1911 still hanging in the air between them.

"Do it, then," Evan said. "*Do it.*"

Tommy's eyes filled. Behind him, Hick had quieted but he could still hear the boy rustling there on the floor.

His four-and-a-half-fingered hand rose for the weapon. Hesitated, trembling.

And then rose further, past the pistol.

Tommy hooked the back of Evan's head, tugged it forward, pressed forehead to forehead. He hugged him hard, body heat moving through his flannel, the smell of sweat and blood and tobacco thick between them.

He did not take the gun.

"Please, Evan," Tommy breathed. "*Please.* He's turning himself in."

For a moment, Evan loosened.

For a moment, Tommy could recognize his eyes.

And then Evan shoved him aside.

Tommy's legs could hold no longer. He grabbed the post, slid down, taking splinters to both palms, kneecaps striking floor.

Evan stepped over his slumped body. Tommy clutched at his pant leg but Evan kicked free.

Hick was there in the next cage of studs, lying on his side. He pushed himself back across the floor and then up to sit with his back against a rotting old counter.

Evan stood over the boy. The Christmas moon came through the flapping tarps and ruptured roof to stretch his shadow long and lay it across the boy.

The ARES 1911 gleamed in the ambient light.

Evan sighted down on Hick's forehead.

66

Excruciating, Blinding Clarity

For an instant everything was still.

Evan pinned the Straight Eight sights in the dead center of Delmont Hickenlooper, Jr.'s round face. The sights were high-profile so they wouldn't block a suppressor, but Evan had no suppressor now.

He wanted to hear the bang.

To feel the recoil of justice discharging against his palm.

The wrapped Christmas presents demanded it.

Lidia Martinez demanded it, she demanded it with her grief-ravaged face and her unkempt hair and her housecoat over a nightgown, demanded it because of the school portrait of her child in navy sweater and slacks nailed to the same wall against which she had to lean to steady herself against her grief.

And Gabriel's father demanded it, too, for the world and future and family taken from him forever. *The loss of him, it is all there is. And no one cares.*

No one cared.

The Nowhere Man did.

Evan tightened pressure on the trigger.

Hick was no longer crying. His face had softened and he gazed not at Evan but at the space between his boots. He looked not scared but awash in something deeper than thought.

Evan readied to apply the last 4.5 pounds of pressure to drop the hammer.

And then Hick spoke.

"It's okay," he said.

"I understand," he said.

"I deserve it," he said.

That sliver of steel dimpled the pad of Evan's forefinger. Another millimeter was all it would take. The sights were lined at the spot between Hick's eyes. He saw the point of entry as clear as he had before he'd let the round fly at Red. All he had to do was press.

He could hear Tommy's pained breathing behind him. The exhalation leaking out of Hick's mouth. His own heartbeat, psychopathically steady in his chest.

And then something else.

The faintest whisper of the First Commandment, giving him an instant of pause.

His voice came as a scratch in his throat. "Why?" he heard himself ask. "Why do you deserve it?"

Hick stands at the gates he'd laid open with the bolt cutters to let his truck through and he's staring down at the picnic below and his brain cannot process what has happened.

The images are there, shards rammed into the white matter of his brain, but his thoughts refuse to absorb them.

His dad's truck berserking through the partygoers, knocking over tables and crushing coolers.

Folks shouting and clearing out of the way.

Red's face split with a grin, laughing with Jack Daniel's abandon.

And then.

And then the rear left tire, a big Super Swamper with that 27/32 tread depth, catches on a picnic blanket. Fabric wads up into the wheel well, the truck canting wildly.

And then the engine snarls like something living, something alive and out of control, 160 horsepower, 400 pounds of torque, 1,700 rpm.

And then Red's face is no longer laughing and his hands are fighting the steering wheel.

And then the two-ton truck swings around like a bucking bronc and slams straight through a family trying to clear out and there is a boy, a child, flying fifteen feet in the air, knocked clear out of his shoes.

And then his body lands, twisted.

And then one shoe lands.

And then the other.

And then Hick is running down the slope, slipping and rising and slipping again, wet grass between his fingers, up his sleeves, in his teeth.

And then the other families are clearing the park and Red has control of the beast once more and sits idling among the wreckage and the bodies, window down, his face on fire, lit with horror.

And then Hick is sliding to the boy, his knees plowing furrows in the turf, and the boy twitches and it's a terrible miracle-nightmare that he is still alive like the deer Hick shot wrong when he was eleven and missed the heart but pierced a lung and found it curled up on a riverbank barely blinking after three miles of his father's berating and his own mounting remorse at causing unimaginable agony to one of God's gentle creatures.

Red is shouting at him—"Leave him, leave him, we gotta go!"

Hick's nose is cold and his face is numb and his fingers are hot with the insides of the boy who blinks up at him like the deer and he hears his own shout, shot through with panic and purpose: "Ambulance won't get here in time!"

"He's done, Hick. It won't matter."

"No," Hick is sobbing. "No, no, no."

And the boy has long pretty eyelashes and part of his face is caved in and his shirt is matted with blood and he is scared, so scared, and his lips are moving but Hick cannot hear what he is saying.

And Hick is looking into his eyes and the boy is looking back at him and Hick is speaking nonsense—"It's okay, you're gonna be okay, I swear it, I promise."

415

I promise.

When he hauls the boy up the boy arches with pain and Hick staggers to the truck with the boy in his arms trying not to imagine the jagged bones shifting inside his skin and tearing fresh openings and Red is shouting, "Fuck, no. Leave him! Leave him!"

Hick fights open the passenger door and loads the boy in and Red is still screaming at him but Hick doesn't care. One of the boy's socks is pulled down halfway off his foot and his neck seems broken, his head bobbing and his eyes blinking, the light coming in and out.

And Red is driving up the slope toward the gate that Hick cut open, driving to the hospital despite everything he is saying, and what he is saying is "It's too late. He's gonna die."

Hick says, "No," *again and again dumbly, and his thoughts are racing and belief rages in him stronger than he has ever felt it because he is right now tumbling through a bottomless hell, blackened and charred and forever deep, and that means that everything opposite has to be real, too, and he will do anything, accept anything—anything—to stop falling like this and he is praying without knowing he is praying:* Please, let him live, if you let him live I will vanquish hate from my heart and only do good forever.

But humming deep beneath his consciousness, he is already striking a terrible deal within himself, another voice whispering promises: If he dies, you must bury this deep and gone where the other Bad Memories are and forget you ever knew it.

He is drenched with sweat. And he tries to hold the boy's head up on the broken stalk of his neck, and the boy is still murmuring feverishly.

"We're gonna get caught!" *Red shouts.* "We can't have him in here! You gotta throw him outta the truck."

"No," *Hick says.* "No, no, no."

Red is driving fast, banging over curbs. "He's dead," *he yells.* "We gotta dump him now."

But Hick cannot let go of the boy.

"You killed them," *Hick says, his voice hushed with horror.* "You killed all these people."

"No," *Red says, his voice cracking into a maybe sob.* "Mexicans. We just killed Mexicans."

Excruciating, Blinding Clarity

And the "we" sails through Hick, rattles around the four chambers of his heart, a ricocheting bullet.

And the boy's head rolls toward Hick and their faces are close and there is an unbounded terror in the boy's eyes and his chapped lips move with a barely-whisper and at last Hick can make out the words.

"Mamá," the boy is saying. "Mamá."

And then the gentle cries cease and he is staring dead-eyed at Hick.

The ARES was still there, an unshaking extension of Evan's arm, aimed right into Delmont Hickenlooper, Jr.'s eight-year-old-boy-killing face.

Hick looked up at him through the sights.

He did not cringe. He did not beg.

For the first time, Evan noticed the faintest speckling of freckles across the bridge of his nose.

Evan had read his file. Eight years old when his mother had killed herself in the house. Twelve when his father had died, the same age Evan had been when Jack pulled him out of the group home in East Baltimore.

The instruments inside Evan were all screeching at once, out of tune, out of harmony, a cacophonous bellow. Tommy dragged himself closer and clutched at Evan's boot and his eyes held the weight of the ages and they said *Assume nothing* and the Fourth Commandment roared in Evan's ears and the Eighth and the Tenth and they thundered through him, igniting the pain in his joints, and the instruments screamed and thundered and there came a flood of fire pouring through his veins and a breaking through of order into chaos and chaos into order and a shuddering of his mind, rent tectonically, and then everything inside him snapped together differently with excruciating, blinding clarity.

He roared, felt the cords stand up in his neck, the black hole of fury whirling in his chest, and spun to hammer his fist clenching the gun straight through the nearest stud. Pain shuddered up Evan's arm and caps of skin lifted off all four knuckles and splinters and fragments flew. His gun-tempered fist had blown right through the wooden rise.

Even out of control, he'd found control, or at least his muscle memory had—it had set his base and thrown the weight of his hips into the pivot, had lined up wrist and knuckles, had blown flesh through wood.

He sank to his haunches. He drove the barrel of the ARES into the ground, letting it support his weight, in violation of Jack's rules and Tommy's, and stayed there, locked on to the orphan he'd been about to kill.

Behind him, Tommy pulled himself to his feet, clutching the counter to hold upright, and Hick sat right where he'd been.

A faint breeze scuttled dead leaves across the floor. The tattered hem of the tarp against concrete shushed rhythmically, like boots shuffling across a parquet floor. The jagged top length of stud swung pendulously and then fell away, bringing with it a patch of roof that crumbled harmlessly across the countertop. The ceiling sagged but held. Moonlight spilled through the newly formed gash, casting a Caravaggio glow across the three of them arrayed in their dusty tableau.

Still crouched, Evan breathed hard, pistol now dangling limply at the inside of his left knee. Blood drained from his knuckles, a steady patter between his boots.

"The law," he said. "He goes to the law."

He rose.

And slipped through the rustling tarp, evanescing.

67

Lucky

The tiny Christmas tree on the counter glistened with tinsel and the sheriff's station smelled of sugar cookies and burnt coffee. Back in the bullpen, Chief Deputy Ronny Ratliff was on his feet at his desk, ready to take what was coming at him.

Tommy dragged his legs forward. Hick hovered off his right flank and slightly behind, letting Tommy clear the way through whatever real or imagined obstacles might materialize. Discordantly a Muzak version of "O Come, All Ye Faithful" buzzed over shitty speakers.

Tommy set the ledge of his forearm on the counter, gasped in a few breaths. His ribs were pissed off to high heaven.

Ratliff met them on the far side of the counter. He looked surprised but not shocked and he knew better than to talk and interrupt whatever was happening.

Tommy pivoted on his elbow as best he could and gave the boy a nod.

Hick stepped around him into clear sight. "I want to make a statement." His shoulders were pinned back and his voice didn't shake, not one bit.

"Lawyer's coming in tomorrow," Tommy said. "It'll wait till then."

Ratliff hesitated, gave a nod.

Tommy flicked his bloody chin at the old-fashioned drunk tank in the back corner of the station. "Might wanna hold him there till then," he said.

Ratliff walked behind the counter and opened the door to the lobby. Hick started toward him, stopped, looked back at Tommy.

"Thank you, sir," he said.

When Tommy found his voice, it was gruffer than usual. "I'll be with you, son," he said. "No matter which way this spins."

Docile as a lamb, Hick walked through the door, across the room, and into the pen, where he sat on the little cot. Ratliff watched him go, made no move to lock the barred gate after him.

With considerable effort, Tommy shoved himself off the counter back onto his wobbly legs. They held as he hobbled across the lobby.

"Where's the other fellow?" Ratliff said.

"You won't see him again."

"That maniac blew through town, shot up half the boys."

Tommy paused with one hand on the front door. It was cracked open a few inches, the cold seeping in across his battered face.

"We're lucky," Tommy said. "We got off light."

He pushed through and limped out into the night.

68

Tales of Anguish

Word had reached Janus.

All four Horsemen killed.

This had never happened before. They'd had one taken off the board several times, and there were rumors that two had gone to their maker in Croatia awhile back. But never three and certainly never four.

That was okay. The Four Horsemen were the Menudo of the assassin set. They'd reconstitute themselves as they always did, a quartet of fresh destroyers stepping forth to fill the leather dusters, balaclava masks, and wraparound shades.

Conquest, War, Famine, Death—they were eternal, inevitable, forever replenishing.

Janus would not wait for the sprawling, patchwork family of lore to heave forth the new foursome to do his bidding. They had failed.

The automated process he'd set in motion would comb through the dark web, twist its tentacles through various sites he had employed in the past, algorithmically select the next assassin to stop Tommy Stojack's heart from beating.

Janus made his way down to the museum he'd built in the basement of his compound. Weapons of every type mounted behind display glass. Viking combat battle-axes. Vintage nineteenth-century Irish flintlock dueling pistols. A Borchardt C-93 with its slender barrel, its iron sights, and that snail-shell bulge housing the recoil spring.

He checked his phone, but the software was still crawling through the digital underworld, prying into dark corners, deciding which killer to elevate next. Soon enough it would select Tommy Stojack's next visitor.

And if that selection failed, it would choose the next and the next after that. It would keep going forever into eternity.

Janus felt safe here within the concrete walls of the basement, surrounded by murder weapons of centuries past. He wondered how many lives these iron and bronze tools had claimed. He wondered how many lives *he* had claimed. Their disembodied voices whispered in his ear, some from above, some from below, spinning their tales of anguish.

He was eager to add one more vanquished soul to the chorus.

69

The Fight, the Contact, the Bond

Evan knocked twice on the apartment door midway down the hall of the second floor.

"Come in!" The command conveyed aggravation at the intrusion into whatever digital peregrinations she was currently lost in. He'd given her a mission-only phone update on what had happened in Calvary, but they hadn't yet seen each other face-to-face. He wasn't sure what to expect.

All three dead bolts were locked, which pleased him.

Of course he had a key.

When he entered, Dog the dog flurried up from his disk bed to greet him. A playful growl, front legs locked out in a low stretch, hindquarters up, back sloped, tail going strong enough to wag his entire rear end.

No doubt Dog had sensed the tension between Evan and Joey over the past week and had a confusion of energy to work out from places inside him he didn't care to understand. There was just the fight, the contact, the bond.

Joey was inside her circular desk, the monitors rising all around her two and three high like opera balconies. Chewing her lip, sucking on a Big Gulp, typing.

"Do you wish to gain entry to the inner sanctum?"

"I do," Evan said.

"Then earn your passage," she said, flicking the large plastic cup in Dog's direction.

Dog barked at Evan, head swinging back and forth, approximating a Cerberus-worthy span of fangs.

Evan dropped to all fours. Dog growled, smiling, tail going harder.

He pounced.

Gnawing on Evan's forearm, clawing at his shoulder, panting hot dog breath in his face. They rolled and wrestled, aggression and affection blending together. Evan and Joey had trained Dog in bite inhibition for anyone inside the pack so the chomping was mischievous, not hostile.

Dog scurried free and sat, panting. He bore marks from when he'd been a bait dog in a dogfighting ring. A horseshoe scar marked his chest, a thin stroke of healed white tissue darted up one cheek, and the fur was permanently patchy in bands at his rear ankle joints where they'd once been duct-taped. A magnificent, proud creature.

Evan rose to his knees, offered his hand—the right one, since his left was swollen and bandaged.

Dog came forward to mouth it, not chewing too hard.

Evan hugged him and scratched his neck and Dog hugged him back, snout tight to the side of Evan's neck. Finished with the ritual, Dog abruptly retreated, circled on his bed to mat down imaginary grass, and thumped into the nest of fabric.

Evan rose.

Joey was standing at the missing pie slice of her circular desk, the point of entry. With her crossed arms and wide stance, she looked like a bouncer.

Evidently she and Evan were still fighting.

"Well?" she said.

One of Joey's favorite ways to begin a conversation.

He waited.

The Fight, the Contact, the Bond

Patience was not her long suit.

"Aren't you gonna ask me what happened?"

"With your propaganda memes?"

Her scowl tightened. "I wouldn't say it like that."

"Why not?"

"I don't know. It sounds so . . . dismissive."

He waited some more.

"X!"

He intoned: "What happened with your propaganda memes?"

"Nothing. I just ignored all that and the interwebs moved on. But! I did go to see them, like you suggested. The Levant Culture Club."

"And?"

At once she animated: "Plot twist! They were supercool! I told them I was Catholic so don't get all recruity and they laughed at me and said they wouldn't if I didn't go all Jesuit missionary. And? Their co-pres, her name's Fatima, she's studying robotics engineering and, like, *seriously* knows her shit. And the other leader, Adah, she's got cool street style and great curly hair and is, like, fully in her Zendaya era. We compared versions of Taylor Swift songs and then wound up playing Cards Against Humanity and I legit ate and left no crumbs."

"Josephine. Is any of this English?"

"X!" she said. "It was *so fun.*"

"But you didn't solve worldwide injustice?"

"No. We ate kibbeh in yogurt sauce and kosher chicken schnitzel and made root beer floats."

"Huh," Evan said. "It's almost like children and students don't have all the answers for today's complex problems."

"Yo. Joan of Arc was leading armies as a teenager. Mary Shelley was, like, nineteen when she wrote *Frankenstein.* What'd *you* accomplish by that age?"

"Five dozen solo confirmed-unconfirmed kills in denied areas."

"Fair," Joey said.

"What next?"

"I'm gonna leave WEG," she said. "Cassidy Ann's group."

"Why?"

"They're a bunch of backstabbing bitches."

"But besides that?"

"X!"

"So now that all this is resolved, are you and I still in a cold war?"

"No," she said. "Time in again—for good. But! Even if you were right about some of this stuff, you didn't have to be such an asshole."

"Yes, I did. I was the necessary level of assholic."

Joey considered and then eased back a step to deflate into her chair. "You don't get it, X. Do you have any idea how impossible it is to go to college right now and learn *anything*?"

"Yes."

"How am I supposed to make a difference in the world?" Slumped in her gamer chair, she looked like a deshelled mollusk. "I mean the *real* world?"

He thought about it. "When it's not for show. When people need help—*really* need help. Maybe that's it."

"I don't know, X. It's all so weird. Nothing makes sense."

"It will again. But when it does, remember to be less sure of yourself."

"Why?"

"Because at some point nothing will make sense again and you don't want to have too much to answer for from when you thought it did."

She screwed up her face, looking delightfully youthful, and parsed the sentence a time or two. Then the dime dropped. "But everyone acts like you have to know everything about *everything*. Or at least have an opinion on it." She hesitated. "Except you."

"I was raised up outside all that. Think what my training was."

"Orphan training?"

"Alone, with Jack, or with one other person who knew more about what I was learning than nearly any other person on earth. So I'd always remember."

"What?

"Do I know as much about hacking as you, Joey?"

She snorted. "No."

"Am I as good a shot as Tommy?"

"No."

"As good a counterfeiter as Melinda?"

"Not even close."

"You think I knew as much about escrima knife fighting as the master who trained me? Or long-range precision shooting as the woman who instructed me? Or enhanced interrogation as the CIA operative who waterboarded me?"

"You were *waterboarded*? As a kid?"

"One master at one time. Beating it into me."

"What?" She hesitated. "Oh. *Humility*."

"Not as an abstract notion. But because my skills were insufficient in the face of theirs to protect me from pain and failure."

"That sounds terrible."

"No. It was a privilege. To focus on one thing and one thing only, shut off from anything else. It's the opposite."

"The opposite of what?"

"Everything now." He waved a hand at the windows and the drab rise of apartments beyond. "*Everything*."

"Why do you care, then?" Joey looked at him with those bright green eyes. "Why do you keep going out there? Doing missions?"

He shrugged. "What else can I do?"

"It's so messy and effed up," she said. "There are so many"—she searched for the word—"*consequences* to everything these days."

"Better than the alternative."

"Which is?"

"Living in a world with *no* consequences."

For once she was quiet, her face receptive. "So what am I supposed to do now?"

"That's not up to me," he said. "That's up to you."

She nodded. It was the answer she wanted but also the answer she feared.

"Well," she said, "thanks for coming, X. To check on me." She hesitated. "I assume that *is* why you came?"

"I need Janus's address."

The softness evaporated from her face, but he could tell she wasn't truly angry, not like before. She was just exasperated with him, which was one of the ways she showed affection.

"Evan Smoak," she said, "you have the emotional intelligence of a fruit fly."

"Blueprints, floor layouts, profiles of hires, surveillance cameras, sat imagery."

"You gonna storm his HQ?"

"Yes."

"By yourself?"

"Yes."

"Okay," she said. "I'll get it. And? I'm glad you and Tommy made up."

"We didn't make up."

"Yeah, but you didn't kill each other." She shrugged. "Progress."

He started out.

"Wait."

He stopped.

"You can't just *leave*."

"Am I supposed to stand here and watch you type?"

"First of all, it's not typing. It's highly skilled digital intrusion. Second of all, aren't you supposed to, like . . ."

"What?"

"Dunno. Leave me with some words of wisdom or something?"

"About what?"

"This whole episode?"

"What whole episode?"

"Aaargh!"

He waited.

"The whole thing with the memes and Cassidy Ann's group and all that. And I saw . . ." She dredged up the admission. "I saw our meme was on his computer. Hickenlooper's computer."

"It was probably on a lot of computers, Joey. That doesn't mean you're responsible for what he did."

"But still. I mean . . ."

"What?"

"I screwed up, X. All the ways you said, okay? I *screwed up*. So. What do I do now?"

He stared at the door, only a few feet away. Three and a half strides and he'd be free of the conversation. But Joey was looking at him and she had that dimple in her right cheek and her brow was furled with anguish and he could see it eating at her the way it ate at him when he missed a step, gauged an angle wrong, when he could have and should have done something better. The Second Commandment only worked when balanced with Jack's catchphrase, if one could call it that.

Next time.

The two best words in the English language. Next time just do it a little bit better.

"Let go of guilt," he said. "It's self-indulgent and makes everything about you. Look at it. Look at it clean. Move forward. Do better. Keep growing up."

"That's it? 'Grow up'?"

"That's all we can do. You helped propagate a piece of propaganda that flicked a few people's ears. Live with it. It's part of being alive."

She rolled her lips. Her eyes glistened. It was a hard lesson to live with. Perhaps the hardest.

"You've done worse," she said, quietly.

"A lot worse," Evan said.

"And you just . . . keep going."

"Yes."

"Why?"

"Because if I didn't, I'd go insane."

"So you run around fighting people and punching wall studs."

He smirked. "Finally, J," he said. "You get it."

She didn't smile. But her face did anyway.

She walked over to him, went up on tiptoes, and mussed his hair, a delicate Audrey Hepburn flourish. "One day, perhaps," she said, "you'll grow up, too."

70

Too Tough to Run

Tommy called him on New Year's Eve.

Evan was in his glass freezer room contemplating vodka when the RoamZone gave its distinctive ring. His excursion to Calvary had been—among other things—an exercise in spirits deprivation, so he luxuriated in the possibilities before him now as he enjoyed a brief break from poring over the intel Joey had assembled for him. It was only a bit past two o'clock, but it was later in Calvary, so he figured he'd play that card and have a sip early. Plus he'd been up since four, had already meditated and worked out twice, and required a touch of lubrication for when he returned to the Vault to continue dirt-diving the approach to Janus's compound.

He'd just decided on Idôl, a vastly underrated spirit made from pinot noir and chardonnay grapes from Burgundy, leisurely distilled seven times with virgin waters from the Côte d'Or and filtered five times after that so as to leave no measurable trace of impurities. The cylindrical bottle with its squared-off shoulder wasn't well-suited to double as a makeshift club like Aylesbury Duck, but its contents were equally precious. Plucking the bottle from a lineup of its distinguished colleagues on the third glass shelf, he poured several fingers into a waiting shaker loaded with five midsize ice cubes. Then he answered the phone.

He said, "Do you need my help?," which he thought was funny. But Tommy said, "Fuck off."

He heard the metallic buzz of Tommy at the welder, no doubt affixing a steel pin through the flash hider and barrel to get around AOW and SBR laws. He pictured him with his steampunk goggles, bottom lip pouched with Skoal Wintergreen, sparks flying back across his brow, and an anachronistic Bluetooth earpiece screwed into the side of his face.

If Tommy was working, he figured he could work, too, so he picked up the shaker and went at it hard, hammering cubes and ice back and forth until the stainless steel grew tacky against his palms.

Once relative silence had reasserted itself across the line, Evan said, "*You* called *me*."

He strained the vodka into a frosted metal martini glass. It poured with delicious viscosity, cloudy with ice crystals.

Stepping out of the chilled room, streamers of mist trailing off his shoulders, Evan moved past the vertical garden of the kitchen to regard the east-facing wall of glass.

"We gotta talk," Tommy said.

"So talk."

The dollhouse view of the building across revealed private lives in motion. A steel-haired woman practicing violin while her husband watched adoringly. A babysitter sprawled on a couch and tapping at her phone while one room over two kids in underwear jumped on their beds. A couple reading side by side on top of the covers, cups of steaming tea forgotten on their nightstands.

It felt good to be home, nestled here alone yet among people. Upon his return, he'd run the gauntlet of the usual suspects in the lobby. Hugh and Lorilee had cornered him by the mail slots to discuss the Very Serious Issue of his not purchasing anything at the Fabi-Tupperware party, which made him a Not Good Participant in the Community, and in a moment of severe moral weakness he'd agreed to order a jean jacket that he looked forward to burning in the fireplace as soon as it arrived.

Another quick mosquito buzz of the welder and then Tommy said, "Face-to-face."

Evan sipped.

Idôl was delightfully creamy, smooth top to bottom as the best grape-based vodkas were. It floated through a bell-curve hump on the palate, peaking with crisp sweetness in the middle. He gave the finish its due, then said, "Where?"

"You come to me."

"Why?"

"'Cuz I'm old as shit and some asshole broke two of my ribs so I ain't driving."

"Fair." Evan checked the Vertex fob watch dangling from his belt loop. He could leave now and make Las Vegas by sundown. "If I come see you are we gonna try'n kill each other again?"

"Only one way to find out," Tommy said, and hung up.

Twilight was threatening as Evan wove through the garden of rusting auto parts and knocked on the brand-new reinforced metal door. His nervous system wouldn't let go of the last time he was here. He couldn't help keeping watch on the sand dune from which he'd taken fire.

He knocked again.

A moment later a text hummed inside his pocket.

Come on through.

He hesitated. Then tried the door.

Unlocked.

He almost couldn't believe it. Hell freezing over, pigs flying, cows coming home.

He pushed the heavy door open, stepped into the lair, and looked around the dim interior, breathing oil and petroleum. He'd never been in here alone.

Another text.

Out back.

Unattended, he walked through Tommy's armory and out the rolling back door.

Tommy was sitting in one of those crooked goddamned strappy lawn chairs he refused to replace, bottle of Beam at his side.

There was another goddamned strappy lawn chair across from it with a different bottle set up and—Was it? Could it be?—an actual ice bucket sitting beside it.

In the fire pit, flames licked and flickered, near invisible until the gloaming got further along.

As Evan approached, Tommy swigged heartily from the bottle, took a puff of a Camel Wide, and shot a stream of tobacco-brown spit into the dirt at his side.

Evan sat in the designated chair.

The bottle resting to the side was as elegant and erotically curved as a Baroque model.

Kauffman Vintage. Still the world's greatest white spirit. It was the zaftig one-liter, the teardrop shape rising to a silver top. Seal unbroken. Since the war the cost had risen to mid four figures, but if Tommy was proficient at anything it was acquiring contraband.

A glass rested in the dirt next to the bottle. A *clean* glass, which Evan had never seen in the wild here at Tommy's lair.

The lid lifted off the ice bucket with a ping.

Impossibly, there were tongs.

He lifted out a single ice cube, completed the transfer, poured in a pinkie finger of liquid platinum. Though the knuckles of his left hand had healed some, they were still taped off and gave a low ache when he manipulated the digits.

He sipped.

Kauffman remained beyond description.

He looked across the fire pit at Tommy. Tommy looked back.

"Where'd you get the water for the ice cubes?" Evan said. "From the toilet tank?"

"Tank?" Tommy said. "Bowl."

The sun was still there to the west, making sluggish progress, the brightness overpowering the fire at their feet.

"You look like shit," Evan said.

"Yeah, well, I got banged up by a man half my age. What's your excuse?"

Evan smirked.

Tommy smirked back.

They sipped some more.

"I was threatened," Tommy said. "Bad."

"Janus," Evan said.

Tommy looked defensive. And then he didn't. "Rare-weapon collector," he said. "That's how we met. Then he asked for some heavier firepower. The tracks had already been greased. I figured why the fuck not. 'Right of the people to keep and bear arms.' Et cetera."

Evan sipped the vodka once more, found he'd lost his taste for it.

"But then?" Tommy took a heavier hit from the bottle, the fringe of his mustache glistening until he wiped it with his sleeve. "He asked for bulk. So I gave a little look-see into his affairs. Turns out he had an operation over on Michael Way." He spit once more, flicked his chin toward the northwest. A shitty part of town.

Evan set the twice-sipped glass back down in the dirt. Not two months ago he'd taken out a group of human traffickers there. A holding pen, too. They'd had Benelli M1 combat shotguns. Evan's favorite.

Ever since Tommy had introduced him to them.

"Let's just say I didn't fancy the operation," Tommy said.

"Nor did I."

"Yeah, I took notice when they vanished suddenly from the face of the earth."

Evan recalled the capo with sunken cheeks he'd confronted, the head of the trafficking operation. He'd been arrogant, menacing, right up until Evan shot him through the face. Before he'd been dispatched, he'd made clear that the operation stretched up a rung higher even above his head.

I only answer to one, he'd said.

God? Evan had asked.

The capo had shown his yellowed teeth. *You could say that.*

Janus.

The Roman god of war had two faces, one looking back at the past, the other forward to the future. He was also the deity of beginnings, transitions, and endings.

At the moment, Evan was most concerned with the latter.

"So I stopped supplying to him," Tommy said. "Once I knew."

"What about the hardware that wound up in the hands of the Lone Wolf?"

Tommy took a proper gulp now. It was still light enough out that Evan could see bloodshot squiggles coming up in his sclera. It was taking all he had to get the story out.

"That was the early stuff I'd supplied to him."

"Janus?"

"Yeah. Some collector business, a fancy four-thousand-dollar Manurhin MR73 Gendarmerie, like that, stuff I thought he was gonna park behind glass. And then some tough-guy shit—Phoenix-S thermal sights, a Dragunov SVD or two. I figured he was gonna use 'em to shoot cans of Red Bull in his backyard while snorting Viagra with some prison pals."

"But he didn't."

"No, he did not. Those weapons made their way into the hands of the Wolf. Who used them in the execution of her duties on behalf of his human-trafficking operation. And once I knew?" Tommy made a cutting-off motion, the stub of that finger slicing the air a foot in front of his unshaven throat.

Evan thought about the seventeen-year-old girl the Wolf had laid out on a butcher block. He held his tongue, did his best to strip his tone of self-righteousness before speaking: "You just let it go?"

"I asked myself: Am I at an age where I want to tangle with a seriously connected psychopath? His crews have crews. And they're serious pipe-hitting motherfuckers. I'm too tough to run. And too old to war."

Evan couldn't figure out what to say.

Tommy pressed on: "Weapons don't shoot themselves. I stopped once I knew. I reached a détente over it with God."

"Still. You made money off it."

"Which I wired out in phases, gave to Wounded Warriors, and called it a day."

Evan took a moment to take this in, to sort it. "And then they came for you."

Tommy dipped his chin, the faintest intimation of a nod. A scab clung to his lower lip where Evan had split it.

"Why didn't you ask me for help?"

"I didn't need your snout in my tent. Plus it was my own damn fault. I figure I have to answer for what I did." His eyes gleamed, stabbing into Evan. "We all do, eventually."

"Now what?"

"Janus is a tricky sonuvabitch. Once the kill order goes out, in the event of failure, the contract flips from assassin to assassin. Even if he's dead." That devilish grin shifted the biker's mustache on his face. "And don't think I haven't thought about making him dead." He tilted the bottle of bourbon before him, let the falling sun glow through the amber. "So it's checkmate."

Not quite, Evan thought.

"So that's it. I wanted to clear the air before someone or someone else comes through that door. And? Wanted to give ya this."

Tommy flipped something across the fire at him.

Evan caught it by his face.

The challenge coin, put back together. The weld joint was thin and precise, superb craftmanship. The halves joined for the first time since Evan and Tommy had laid eyes on them a decade and a half ago. It glinted beautifully there in the light.

NO GREATER FRIEND.

NO WORSE ENEMY.

Crisscross ridges slanted diagonally through the circle to form a wide hourglass, cupping the words top and bottom. Evan remembered the buzz of the welder when they'd spoken over the phone, Tommy wielding metal and fire like an ancient god. He ran his thumb across the raised ledge of the X.

Tommy said, "Figure you should hang on to it for us."

Evan nodded because he didn't trust his voice to speak.

Part of what constituted friendship was the ability to share a silence.

The earth rotated up to meet the sun, tugging at its bottom until it bled far and wide, drenching the desert in pinks and oranges.

Tommy hoisted his near-empty bottle. "Bourbon and a sunset. Like being in heaven before the devil knows you're dead."

They watched it and watched some more.

"That tire trick back at Dawnfall?" Evan said. "Reinflating tires? I want that."

"Already ran down the tech," Tommy said. "In a DARPA lab parked adjacent to Guantánamo Bay."

"We took those Horsemen apart."

"Took the whole damn ghost town apart," Tommy said, with a chuckle in his voice.

Evan had rediscovered his appetite for Kauffman. It coated his throat, warmed his stomach. He felt the slightest bit more loose. The goodness suffusing his chest wasn't a paper-thin sentiment but appreciation for a universe that had delivered him to the wholeness of this moment, to the brink of what he could imperfectly drink in with his five senses—clean air, pure liquid, the comfort of humans where he could find it despite all their imperfections.

And his.

A thought sent out to the ether caught him by surprise: *Don't get bored with me. There are surprising turns yet to come.*

Tommy snickered.

Evan said, "What?"

Tommy mimicked him from back at the Watering Hole: "'Let's not get operatic in our sanctimony.' What a dick."

Evan's mouth twitched. "You shot out my tire."

"I sure as shit did."

The sunset stretched wider now, infusing an unlikely shade of purple into a strata of low clouds.

"And you hitting that damn wall stud like the Incredible Hulk," Tommy said, with even more amused derision. He imitated Evan and made him look stupid.

Evan laughed. "You old asshole."

Tommy raised the bottle in a toast.

Evan lifted his glass.

They drank.

The fire was finally getting its chance to show its own colors as the volume turned down on the sunset.

Together they watched the light vanish in the west, the dying of an old day to make room for the new.

71

A Glorious Mess

Evan was tired of it.

His floating bed.

Detached from a foundation, the world, it felt like an adolescent fantasy, a remnant from another life.

He wanted an ordinary fucking bed, something to tether him to this earth, or at least to his ill-fitting, ridiculous place in it.

Climbing from the sheets, he dragged the mattress off the elevated slab and shoved it beneath so it could take its weight.

Then he moved into the Vault, retrieving an army of tools. Drills, circular saws, wrenches. And he set to work on the stupidly and arrogantly contrived contraption, unfastening the magnet mounts, severing the steel tethers, scuffing the concrete floor, and fighting the powerful neodymium rare-earth magnets so as not to send the metal slab flying up through the ceiling.

Three hours later he released the final bolt. The slab canted to one side and bucked wildly before hammering down onto the mattress below.

Panting from exertion, Evan sat in a glorious mess of his own making amid wrenches and pry bars, his body oiled with the honest sweat of toil.

And then he woke up.

The magnetic bed still intact beneath him.

The clock showed 11:59 P.M., a minute before the witching hour, when his alarm would sound, conveying him into the mission's final clash.

That was the best time to confront a god, or at least man's worst approximation of one.

It was the zero hour.

For one minute more he lay floating three feet above the floor.

Heaven above.

Hell below.

And him hovering dead center between them.

72

No One to Point for and
No One to Point At

He comes in the silver moonlight.

He comes with an ARES 1911, a Strider blade, and a pocketful of zip ties.

He is silent as the night. He has no fingerprints, no face, no identity.

The video feeds are shorted out, the alarm sensors neutralized, the compound laid bare for his fearsome entry.

Try to keep up with him if you can. But you can't. You can follow the contrails, perhaps, the wake of wreckage he leaves.

A guard in the shack at the top of the driveway chokes against the zip tie tightened across his mouth and around his head. The plastic band cuts through his lips on either side. He is bound to his chair and the chair is knocked over and he squirms with discomfort but can reach nothing.

A wreckage of guards delineate the perimeter, sobbing, weeping, in various stages of consciousness. They are injured badly but not fatally. They've been stripped of weapons and radios and can do nothing but wait for help to arrive.

No One to Point for and No One to Point At

If you lift your gaze to the roof, you might see a sniper slumped near the east-facing gutter, his scope shattered, blood sprayed behind him along with most of the flesh of his right shoulder. The limb will be lost. But he will live.

The sniper covering the rear of the property has fared no better. He is the one who once fired on the Nowhere Man from a sand dune outside Tommy's lair in Vegas. Currently he is adhered to the shingles with a nail gun that was liberated from the guard shack, hands and feet, and he shudders against the chill night. His weapon, a Stojack-supplied Savage 110 bolt-action, lies within tantalizing reach.

A third-story window has been duct-taped in an X to hold the shards and then broken quietly and flipped away to land softly on the grass of the backyard lawn.

Perhaps you spot the heel of an Original S.W.A.T. boot as it slips inside.

Another guard lies in the upstairs hall, thigh shot. The zip tie serving as a tourniquet is fastened even tighter than necessary on the proximal side of the leg. A hand sheathed in blood rises to point trembling down the hall, but there is no one to point for and no one to point at.

A snare noose designed for great cats has been dropped over the catwalk's balcony, secured to the rails, and cinched tight around the throat of the heavyset guard surveilling the floor below. He gurgles and twists on one tiptoe, his breath a soft but painfully sustainable rasp. He will make it, instant by excruciating instant, until the police arrive in twenty-seven minutes. His bulging eyes track the dark form as it descends the stairs to coast calmly past him, making him forget to draw even what small measure of breath he can. Long after the shadow vanishes, his eyes stay pegged painfully to the side, watching the darkness.

Can you sense the boots combat-gliding down the hall, barely touching the floor?

By the time you catch up, he is gone again. On the landing another guard lies twisted, broken arms flopping uselessly on the carpet like dying fish. His cheek is a spiderweb of torn flesh. It looks like someone smashed his face through the hanging mirror on the wall.

Someone did.

Another man has skidded halfway down the stairs, ankles zip-tied, arms duct-taped to his sides.

It's a good thing you didn't have to witness what went down on the ground floor at the foot of the stairs. There is wheezing and gasping and there are wrists rubbed raw from the hard plastic restraints. One of the men no longer has function in his legs, and a zip tie has been fastened so tight across his eyes that he weeps tears of blood.

The big picture window looking out onto the palatial grounds has been shattered; you might've heard the sound from just around the corner. A guard stammers in disbelief, his hand impaled on a fang of glass still jammed into the gum of the lower frame, his shattered face a match for the pane it broke.

In the kitchen, a man chokes as he sips oxygen through his constricted windpipe, backed to one of the decorative posts marking the transition to the formal dining room. The coil of blue-tinged high-carbon-steel wire around his neck has been secured behind the post, the sleek wooden handles intertwined and twisted tight like a hatch wheel. He'd managed to get a hand beneath the garrote in a vain attempt to push it away, but at considerable cost. Two of the fingers have pinged off at the second knuckle to land at his feet; a third dangles by a thread.

Still he clutches with what remains, his terrified gaze pointing the way to the next corridor.

By the time you arrive, you've only just processed the *pfft* of the suppressor. A guard lies slumped against the wall, shot through the body armor. He smiles in triumph as he plucks the flattened round from his Kevlar. His face changes. Blood drools from the hole in his side.

He will require a colostomy bag and three surgeries to save his large intestine.

The bookcase in the wall to his side has been pulled open, a secret door guarding hidden stairs to the basement.

Footsteps tap swiftly down the concrete steps.

You can peek.

But you know you'll see nothing.

73

A Tipped-over Cross, Not Yet Fallen

Janus was a creature of the night. He slept infrequently and irregularly, his bloodstream charged with narcotics and paranoia.

He required frequent doses of intense sensation, so he reclined now on his tattoo chair with some relief as Sir Rubin worked on his face some more, refreshing the red tinge of the devil's cheeks.

The needle pricks and soporific hum soothed him. A rice eye mask, cooled and scented of lavender, rested across his eyes.

Sir Rubin paused, no doubt for a needle change.

Janus heard a thump.

Before he could react, something zippered around his chest, locking his torso against the tattoo chair. An instant later, a smaller band cinched his throat. The rice bag flew aside and he opened his eyes.

He really wished he had not.

Sir Rubin was a fat-ass, which had pros and cons. The main drawback was that he required a double dose of propofol after Evan knocked him out with a sleeper hold. The benefit was his size 52 belt, big enough to wrap around the tattoo chair and Janus's torso, a complement for the zip tie around his neck.

Evan had dimmed the lights, so there was little of him to see as he stood silently over the tattoo chair. Once Janus noted the 2.2×60-millimeter collared needle in Evan's hand, he thrashed around in panic but succeeded only in choking himself more.

Evan couldn't blame him for the reaction.

The veterinary needle was designed to penetrate the thick hides of elephants, rhinos, and hippopotamuses.

Evan placed the heel of his hand on Janus's forehead, shoved his head back into the padding, and slid the needle past the murmuring cherub and whispering devil straight into his left ear canal.

Janus screamed and started to buck but Evan said, quietly, "I'd stop moving if I were you."

Janus conjured rage, hissed through bared teeth: "Do you have any idea—"

"Who you are," Evan said, quietly. "Yes. That's why I'm here. I see your big mansion with your big men with their big guns. And your giant bed wrapped with silk sheets. I see the bricks of gold in the closet and the crates of RPGs in the garage. I moved through your entire house and all of your men to get to you."

Janus squeezed his eyes shut.

"I know you think you throw a big shadow." Holding the needle steady, Evan leaned closer. "But I want you to look at me. Open your eyes. Open them. Now. Look at me closely. And ask yourself: Do I look scared?"

Tears leaked from the corners of Janus's eyes. He was quivering with terror. "Nu-no." The tears quickened to rivulets. His breathing caught jaggedly in his chest.

"I wouldn't risk shaking my head either. That sound you hear? That's the tip of a seven-gauge needle scratching against your eardrum."

Janus's eyes strained.

"Know how thick your eardrum is? Point-one of a millimeter, about as thick as a piece of paper. If you think this needle hurt scraping the sides of your ear canal on the way in, I want you to imagine the sensation when it pops through into the bones of the inner ear. Stapes, malleus, incus. Once it crunches through those, the next stop is the cochlea and cochlear nerve. By the time we get there, we'll have achieved a certain amount of irreversible damage. Hearing loss, tinnitus, vertigo, balance. It gets tricky past that, lots of dense bone to protect the brain. But I'm willing to get there with a mallet. Then we're into the carotid-artery branches and brain stem. That'll render you vegetative. So. When I shove this into you, whole parts of you are going to forget what they are and what they are supposed to do. The deeper I go, the worse your life will forever be. If you understand me, blink twice."

Janus blinked twice. Tears clung to his lashes.

"In case you're wondering," Evan added, "yes. I have done this before. Now. Shall we begin?"

"*No, no, no, no, no . . .*"

"Blink twice if you'd prefer to negotiate instead."

Janus blinked about seventeen times.

"You strong-armed Tommy Stojack. And then threatened him. And then tried to kill him. I had to pull this information out of him. He didn't squeal about it—out of respect for himself and, I suppose, in a twisted way, for you. But I don't respect his wishes and I don't respect you. If you understand, blink twice."

More blinks than Evan could count.

"Stojack's no longer your problem. *I* am your problem. You have become an obsession to me. If you *ever* make another demand on him, if you or anyone you hire *ever* threatens his life, I will come for you and I promise that if I come back I'll arrange it so that the movement of this needle through your eardrum and into your brain stem will take twenty excruciating minutes. And I will leave you just on this side of being able to be resuscitated medically so you will exist trapped in the solitary terror of your brain, unable to escape. So that it lives in you, the terror, alive only in your body and muscle memory, in the still-firing nerves themselves for however many years until your wrecked suffering carcass of a body can no longer be sustained by the tubes shoved into it. Blink twice if you want to continue existing in any recognizable form."

Two blinks. And then two blinks. And then two more.

His chest rattled up and down.

At Evan's heels, Sir Rubin murmured something and dropped back into unconsciousness.

"Three of your human-trafficking rapists are paraplegics. I reduced them to two limbs so they can live the rest of their years as a warning to anyone who lays eyes on them." Evan watched his knuckles whiten around the collared base of the needle but resisted the instinct rising through him. "The rest got off easier. The police will be here soon enough to see to your henchmen. And to you. I've ensured that evidence is plentiful and visible. In your time in court, in prison, you will take every step to dismantle your operations. You will end them. Cold. Or the same rules apply. And if you think I won't break into prison to administer your punishment, know that I have done that already, too. There is nowhere you will ever be safe again. Blink if you understand."

Janus blinked.

"One more thing."

"No." Janus's voice was weak, wobbly, little more than a moan. His shaved head glistened with sweat.

"I'm going to leave you something to remember me by."

"No."

"Something to remind you every time you look in the mirror."

"No."

The oven-size autoclave for sterilizing equipment and needles rested on the counter to Evan's side. It was finely made, German engineering, able to reach 273 degrees Fahrenheit, which it was approximating now. A pair of eighteen-inch stainless-steel medical tongs rested on the tray at Evan's side. He could reach everything while holding the needle steady in Janus's ear.

Convenient.

Popping the door, he used the tongs to retrieve the item he'd placed inside the pressurized chamber.

It emerged from a wash of steam.

NO GREATER FRIEND.

NO WORSE ENEMY.

The words would not be visible in the brand, just the crisscross of the raised ridges.

As it neared Janus's forehead, he said, "No, no, no—"

A Tipped-over Cross, Not Yet Fallen

The rest was drowned out by the hissing of flesh.

There it was on his forehead, the mark of the Orphan—a tipped-over cross, not yet fallen.

It blistered and steamed and Janus moaned and moaned some more. Sweat glistened across his face, pronounced against the tattoo curled around his left ear.

Angel above, devil below.

"Now," Evan said, "close your eyes. And keep them closed. Count to a thousand out loud. And don't think I won't sit here with this needle a millimeter from the edge of your earhole until you reach nine hundred ninety-nine just waiting for an excuse."

Janus closed his eyes.

His lids jerked. Tears matted his shirt. His shoulders shuddered as he desperately tried to lie still. His lips were chapped.

A dry whisper scraped the walls of his throat. "Who . . . Who are you?"

But there was only the monster-filled darkness.

74

His Friend

New Year's morning was threatening by the time Evan made Las Vegas.

He wanted to give Tommy the sitrep in person, to see his face when he learned he'd been liberated from Janus's reign of terror. Pale sunlight spilled across the dilapidated building as he pulled up. The old neon auto-repair sign buzzed and flickered like a bug light.

A corroded carburetor by the front walk bled orange into the sand. A trio of alternators pebbled a dead garden trough like metal boccie balls.

When Evan knocked, the reinforced door creaked inward.

Dread tingled at the base of his brain stem, shooting tendrils down his spine. He drew his ARES 1911 and entered. Silence inside, the air heavy with gun oil, sweet charcoal smoke, and sulfide.

Heel-toeing past the lathe, Evan cut between a cold saw and a drill press.

Through the rises of machinery, he spotted Tommy back by his favorite bench, though he could make out only his knees and legs against the Aeron rolling chair he piloted between workspaces like a wheelchair.

Tommy was still.

Moving swifter, not yet risking calling his friend's name, Evan cut up an aisle and popped out into the clearing, weapon raised.

Tommy sat slumped in his chair, head bowed forward, crumpled pack of Camels in his hand.

No sign of violence. The peaceful look on his face. How could he look peaceful? It was a dangerous thing, to envy the dead.

On the bench before him were some unmarked .308 Winchester-round casings he'd been filling with powder to build precision ammo and a castle of cigarette butts in that cracked porthole ashtray. The bathroom door in the background still hung crooked on its hinges, torn through with shrapnel.

Evan holstered his ARES.

He stood awhile. He wasn't sure how long.

Tentatively he walked forward. Pressed two fingers to the side of Tommy's throat to confirm what he already knew.

The leathered skin still held some warmth of life.

Evan lowered his hand. He took a step back. And then another. His shoulder blades struck a tall gun safe. He stopped there and stared at his friend.

His chest was doing something he did not recognize. So was his throat. And his face.

He sat on the floor.

And he wept.

75

A Jury of His Peers

Delmont Hickenlooper, Jr. was remanded into custody for arraignment on the first Monday of the
new year. He is charged with vandalism, being
in possession of a firearm in the commission of
a felony, four counts of assault with a deadly
weapon, four counts of manslaughter, false im-
prisonment, and concealment of accidental death.
His court date is pending.

He will be tried by a jury of his peers.

Acknowledgments

Borski for tech
Tadashi for steel
Samar for real-deal background
Hurwitz and Nelson for medical
McGarry and Eisner for words
Urrea for slang
Erbach Vance, Breimer, C. Dennis, and Cheng Caplan for muscle
Kahla and R. White for quarterbacking the best teams in the business
Blair for day-in, day-out
Zuma and Nala for naps
Corinne and Raya for everything else

About the Author

Melissa Hurwitz

Gregg Hurwitz is the *New York Times* #1 international bestselling author of many thrillers, including the Orphan X series. His novels have won numerous literary awards and have been published in thirty-three languages. He's also written feature screenplays, television, and graphic novels. Gregg currently serves as a copresident of International Thriller Writers (ITW). He lives in Los Angeles with his Rhodesian ridgebacks and a scruffy, ill-behaved mutt.